NO TIME LIKE THE PAST

Dave Goossen

zero
FRICTION
media

Also by Dave Goossen

Senior's High

The Living End

12 Cups of Coffee

Zero Friction Media

zerofrictionmedia.net

Ebook ISBN: 978-0-9878917-8-5

Print ISBN: 978-0-9878917-7-8

Hardcover ISBN: 978-0-9878917-9-2

For Shana, Kalli & Maya

Thank you for supporting me in this dream of mine.

And for putting up with the music I love.

For Mike Gobbi

Thank you for being my time travel expert, Photoshop guru,

and best beta reader ever.

A novel with its own rock band requires a mixtape.
Here are the songs in the novel performed by the original artists.

No Time Like The Past Soundtrack on SoundCloud
https://bit.ly/3IQeMTZ

Life can be understood backwards, but it must be lived forwards.

~ S. Kierkegaard

Gimme here and now,

'Cause nothing's gonna last.

The future's where life happens,

Ain't got no time for the past.

~ Damage Done

1

June 26, 1984
The Railway Club, Vancouver, BC

"Thank you and goodnight!" the lead singer screamed at us from the tiny stage.

The packed audience, their Bic's held high, screamed back, "One! More! Song!"

I hopped onto a rickety chair and focused fast. The perfect shot lined up, the four band members with their instruments held up triumphantly, light beams cutting through the thick cigarette smoke. I quickly pushed the shutter on my Minolta. Another fantastic shot. The aural amazingness of the performance that had just ended stunned me, my mind blown wide open. It was all I could do not to stand in the middle of the dance floor, slack-jawed in awe.

But I didn't. I hopped down, pushed my way up onto the stage, and scrambled behind the drummer. I fired off a couple of fast shots back out at the audience, with band members silhouetted by the stage lights, a sea of tiny flames floating in the darkness beyond them. The crowd cheered like it was a tied-with-minutes-to-go Stanley Cup Final, their willpower enough to catapult their team—their band—over the top.

"One! More! Song!"

Kelly lowered his battered guitar and stepped up to his mic, wiping sweat from his face. "We'd love to play more, but that's every song we've got! I swear!"

The crowd booed him good-naturedly and kept chanting. If I weren't taking photos, I'd be out in the thick of it, lighter burning my thumb, screaming for one more song. But the band gave a final exhausted wave and stumbled back into the tiny dressing room behind the stage. Everything they had they'd left on that tiny stage, the way rock-and-roll had to be. It's both more than any of us imagined and far, far less than any of us wanted.

Standing in your Shadow - Damage Done
Eponymous first album 1986 A&M Records

When we were married, we were so poor
The years were uncertain and only love for sure
I'm still playing in a five and dime band
but you've become a legend on the concert grand

You've seen the world, and you've really been around
But when you come home, you always put me down
I'm still trying to do my best for you
But I feel so helpless when my best doesn't do

And now I'm shaking, standing in your shadow
My heart's breaking, standing in your shadow
I feel alone, even when you're here
You're far away, even when you're near

I say I love you; you say that that's nice
You thought about me once, but you never thought twice

```
You're an artist I know I told you so
But tell me what it's worth if our love can never grow

And now I'm shaking, standing in your shadow
My heart's breaking, standing in your shadow
I feel alone, even when you're here
You're far away, even when you're near

And now I'm shaking, standing in your shadow
My heart's breaking, standing in your shadow
I feel alone, even when you're here
You're far away, even when you're near
```

•

On the dirty sidewalk at a quarter to midnight, I struggled to shove my Minolta zoom lens back into my camera bag. Was using 800 ISO film the right move? The club was always a challenge to shoot in—long, narrow, full of smoke, dark even at noon—and these photos needed to be perfect. Taking chances with not enough light could have ruined them.

"Do you think you got some good shots? They were so amazing."

Gina leaned against a mid-sized beige Plymouth sedan parked in one of the prized spots outside the doors to The Railway Club. She wore a tight, short pleather skirt with a sheer white blouse, her black bra visible through it. She looked great. If Time were to end, and I had nothing else: seeing this band on this night would be enough—except for the chance to kiss Gina once.

I blinked. "I sure hope so."

"I'm sure you did."

"It's just been a while since I took photos for a band."

Gina smiled. "You're a wonderful photographer, Colin. You only have to believe that."

Fed up with putting everything back correctly, I forced the zipper around the top of my battered camera bag, then leaned on the car beside her. She hopped up to sit on the long front hood, passed over her lit cigarette, and lit another for herself. I took a drag. It tasted like cherry Chapstick. Here I was, once more, standing in her amazing shadow.

I looked up at the Club in front of me as the post-show noise echoed in my ears and head.

The Railway Club occupied the top floor of an old two-story building on the corner of Dunsmuir and Seymour. It had been there forever. A model train track hung from the ceiling, a five-car train making its way around the perimeter of the room. Two narrow, heavy doors in the middle of the block opened to a long steep staircase which doglegged right before ending at a cramped landing with two more heavy doors. Polished hunks of actual rail for door handles. The doors stayed closed unless a bouncer was on duty. If it was locked, you'd have to use your member's key.

That's the trick with the Railway. It was set up as a members-only club, and in the arcane liquor rules of British Columbia, they could get away with more as a private club than as a public bar or pub. So, for twenty-five bucks a year, anyone could be a member if another member recommended them. And we were members. So we had membership cards in our wallets and these heavy brass keys to let us through the locked doors. At twenty-three, it was our only shot at experiencing the feeling that 'membership has its privileges.'

The front doors swung open, and another crowd of people stumbled onto the sidewalk. Gina and I smiled at the ones we knew, and for one night only, smiled at the ones we didn't. Because we all recognized, deep down in our souls, we were now part of something we'd remember and talk about forever.

Possibly this was the hubris of youth talking. Any event we were at became something more. If we were there, it was special. You knew that emotion, or at least remembered it.

But let's talk about what happened tonight.

A band made up of four ordinary guys changed their name, their sound, their future. And what they created through chance, luck, and divine intervention, we completed by adding the final essential ingredient —a witnessing audience.

Four guys, friends of ours since we all started at Vancouver Technical High School, working-class children of working-class parents in the working-class suburb of Vancouver known as East Van; those four guys took a musical evolutionary leap of monumental proportions right in front of us. Tonight was the night when four neighborhood guys became rock stars, even if they—and the world—didn't know it yet.

Neil exploded out the doors onto the sidewalk, his arms around a couple of edgy-looking girls—a pair of leather and lace Madonnas, back-combed hair, frosted tips, bubblegum pink lipstick that contrasted their heavy black eyeliner. They're not pretending; this was their look, all day, every day.

"Known them all since we were kids!" Neil bragged, his head swivelling back and forth to keep deep, intimate eye contact with both girls. Behind them, Terry sighed and struggled to slip around this embarrassing scene to join us.

But Neil wouldn't let him, swaying to one side and then the other on the step outside the doors. Behind him, the stairs filled up as more people tried to leave, only to be backed up by the ever socially oblivious Neil.

"Right, Terry? Known 'em since school, right?"

Terry leaned into the girl beside him, took in her blurry eyes, her spiked hair, overdone makeup, then said, "It's true. They beat Neil up daily for his lunch money."

The girls broke out laughing. While Neil punched Terry in the shoulder, they freed themselves of Neil in a move that would have made ninjas proud before stumbling away down Dunsmuir Street towards Granville and the Night Owl bus back to the suburbs.

Neil deflated slightly, allowing the crowd on the stairs to push him and Terry off the step.

"That was a dick move."

"Ha. Takes one to know one."

Neither was motivated to continue hassling the other; the night was too good to be fighting. It was one of those nights even a twenty-three-year-old knew was worth remembering for as long as they could form a complete thought. Memories our caregivers at the nursing home would weary of hearing repeatedly.

The four of us basked in the glow of a warm Vancouver summer night, with no actual place to be. We could have wandered over to Davie Street for late-night food at Did's Pizza, Fresgo's or Hamburger Mary's. Or try to make the last call at the Rose & Thorn.

"Did you have any clue they would be... that?" Terry asked. Since the start of elementary school, Terry and I have been in classes together, permanent fixtures in each other's lives since we were six. My parents were friends with his parents. My older siblings went through school with his older siblings. Our kindergarten class graduated high school together.

Considering Terry's question, the rest of us shook our heads.

Damage Done had started as an embarrassing Grade 9 mess of noise in the drummer's garage with a different guitarist and a different name. And, if not a different sound, then a sound that was dramatically different. The show finished to cheers and applause that meant something; we had to make the band understand how fantastic they were. The horrible alternative was them giving up and quitting music altogether, never realizing their amazingness.

"That was the best show I've ever seen. I swear, there won't be a show as amazing as that ever in my life."

"Come on, what about last night?"

Gina's joke started us all laughing. Last night was a mistake. Instead of the first of the two shows Damage Done had played to introduce their new sound, we had seen something else entirely. A mistake, enough said.

"Would you use your time travel trip to go back to see the show last night?"

We considered. It was a thing we did. I didn't remember how it came about, but then it existed, a part of our collective mythology. Anytime one of us missed out on something, screwed up something, lost a job, or even missed a bus, one of us posed this ultimate hypothetical question.

"Colin, you could go back and film the show!" Gina said.

I shrugged. The Railway Club would make videotaping a low-quality nightmare. Besides, I excelled at still photography.

"Wouldn't be a bad use," Terry said. "But probably not. We saw them tonight. Why waste my one trip on that? What if they had performance anxiety last night?"

That's precisely how we answered the question time and time again. Each of us would offer a dozen reasons why going back in time to fix something would end up being worse than leaving it be.

I guess that was the point of this silly game. Be happy with what you had, don't go worrying about what you couldn't change unless you could change it. But if you could change it…

"Ask me again in twenty years."

"Uh, you'd be ancient. You'd call it a 'racket' and hate every minute."

"No way. Something this epic stays epic no matter how many years pass."

"I agree with The Yipper. A magical confluence of events has brought them and us to this one place now. Even better since we saw them way back when on their first night as a band," Neil said, fishing a crumpled pack of smokes out of his battered leather jacket. Bright pins covered the lapels, remnants of his days as a full-on punk—'white punks on dope,' 'white dopes on punk,' 'my snow doesn't melt,' and album cover pins for the Sex Pistols, the Damned, DOA, Dayglo Abortions. He fired up his Zippo lighter with an impressive flick of his wrist—a move I've watched him practise for six years until he had it perfected. That was the kind of guy Neil was—the kind who wouldn't study for an exam but would spend hours perfecting a Zippo wrist flick.

"Come on, don't call me The Yipper," I muttered, weary of the nickname but even wearier of living my life with Yip as my last name.

"It's your name, Yipper," Neil said, blowing a smoke ring up into the night sky.

Neil and I had met in Eighth-grade automotive class. 1977. We had sat beside each other at a battered workbench while a scarred ex-army drill sergeant taught us about engines. Not anything we would ever need to do to a motor, like change the oil or clean the carburetor, but he showed us how to grind valves. Because that was what 14-year-old boys should do to their fathers' cars. We'd clicked through our collective indifference to automobiles and had been friends since then.

Neil grinned a grin to match the flick of his Zippo—both designed to reel in unsuspecting or suspecting women. Neil wasn't fussy. He would cast his net far and wide and inevitably caught someone willing, or something contagious.

Gina hopped off the car hood, adjusting her tight black leather skirt, whipped her gleaming black hair out of her eyes while flicking her cigarette butt into the gutter. An impressive combo move. We applauded.

An older Chinese couple came out the doors, standing out amidst the people our age. Weird to see someone who should have been socializing with my parents while playing mah-jong leaving an epic rock concert. The woman looked kind of familiar, but they moved down the block, no doubt sensing the suspicious, unwelcome vibe from us.

"It feels like the night where everything changes for them, you know?" I said. "They can't go back to what they were, even if they wanted."

"Well duh. Time travel isn't real," Terry said.

"I meant their sound, it's going to make them famous. You watch."

"Maybe you'll become famous because of those photos you took, Colin!" Gina said.

"Or maybe he forgot to put film in the camera."

"Screw you very much, Neil," I said. "You wait and see, I got a ton of epic shots tonight."

Gina grinned at me. "Hey, you're cute when you're confident."

I sputtered and almost inhaled my cigarette.

The old couple had disappeared around the corner into the alley to where they'd probably parked their four-door Chrysler LeBaron. The exiting crowd thinned, slowed, and dissipated; then it was only us.

"Gentlemen," Gina said. "We've known those idiots for a decade. When, and how, did they turn that crazy old noise of theirs into the brilliance they played tonight? That was goddamn amazing. We are blessed!"

I agreed. We were blessed. I watched my three best friends in front of the closed doors of the club. Gina, with her sheer blouse and miniskirt, Chrissie Hynde bangs over heavily made-up eyes. Neil with his leather jacket, Doc Martens and a head of hair that would make John Cougar proud. Terry in a bright yellow polo shirt, collar flipped up, acid-washed jeans, his fair curls thinning already. Then there was me, reflected in the Shaver Shop window beside them, the Chinese poster boy for average, neutral in a denim shirt and button-fly 501's and the vestiges of a mullet. I took out my camera, balanced it on top of the Plymouth, set the self-timer, and ran to join them.

Click. Perfect.

2

September 1, 2017
The Railway Stage and Beer Café, Vancouver, BC

"Kill Hitler."

"Kill Oswald."

"Stop Mark David Chapman."

For selfish reasons, keeping John Lennon alive had always won. Supposing we had an actual time machine.

We were sitting in the back half of the Railway Stage and Beer Café—which, in my mind will be called the Railway Club forever—far from the DJ spinning digital tracks on the stage. With a live band on that stage, we'd be right up in the front, digging the performance, conversation abandoned for the music. But with a DJ, what was there to watch? Sitting back here, at least we could talk without yelling or having to shoot him.

"But logic holds that if time machines exist, then someone would have already tried to kill Hitler, right? That someone didn't assassinate him is almost proof that they don't exist," Terry said.

"What if they exist, but for whatever reason, no one's been able to whack Adolf," Gina countered.

Then I complicated things. "Maybe instead of Lennon it's Paul McCartney who got shot in this alternate history, but someone went back and saved him."

This caused a ripple of heavy thinking. Everyone pondered my complication and drank their beers.

I glanced at the people I'd been hanging out with for over forty years: my two best friends and girlfriend. My grandmother called us four peas in a pod. Gina leaned against me, looking fantastic in LuluLemon yoga pants and a funky blouse. Neil had on his historically distressed leather jacket, despite the warm weather. It was as much a part of his image as his meticulously out-of-control hair. And Terry? He looked like an accountant who has been on his lunch break for seven minutes longer than his allotted hour.

"So are you suggesting that whole Paul's dead rumor from the Beatles was true, but then someone went back and unkilled him?" Terry asked.

"Terry, that somehow makes sense."

The building was long and narrow, so the club was split into three distinct parts. At one end, where you entered via the steep staircase and heavy doors, stood the stage and a tight packing of tables and chairs. The middle of the room had a long bar with stools along its length. A narrow walkway behind the stools led to the back. A long row of tall windows let in light from the street.

On the busy nights of our youth, getting from front to back was near impossible. Imagine a twenty-yard-long gauntlet through people packed along the bar and those crowded around the windows. In those days, if you bought a beer at the front end of the bar, you'd need another by the time you got to the back.

But it wasn't like that anymore.

Because of Vancouver's real estate insanity, the Railway Club—which first opened in the late 1800s for railway workers from the rail-yards three blocks away—had seen its rent raised to such levels that after years of being one of the premier places for seeing live music, it had closed its doors; and a generation grieved. The Railway Club joined a growing list of live venues shuttered by the real estate market.

Most became gleaming towers full of empty condos. The clubs lived on only in the building names, but that wasn't a consolation when you want a live band playing live music with proper instruments.

But, the Railway Club had received a second life, as a restaurant group in town bought the place. Most of it they left the same—walls covered in random photos and pictures, although the train suspended from the ceiling didn't make its rounds anymore. The long bar now had a staggering array of beer taps for its entire length. They offered live music a cautious few nights a week, but I felt in my heart that it had changed.

The things that had made it unique, a passion for presenting quality live music and the cachet of being a member had disappeared. I still wore my door key on a worn strip of leather around my neck, a kind of good luck charm. In a city changing as much as Vancouver, what was wrong with hanging on to a little bit of the past?

"I'm not sure I can take much more of this…" I said, taking a sip of my glass of Bomber Breweries Double Secret Probation Doppel Sticke Altbier.

"Thought you liked that beer," Terry said.

I pointed along the length of the club towards the stage and the DJ. It was our first time back since the Railway Club reopened. Everyone nodded in understanding. Not our music. That stage required live music. DJs were great at a disco or a wedding, but not here.

Passive-aggressively, we didn't leave. We sat at our table. We drank our beers. We declined fancy menus from the pretty server. We silently judged the table of 20-somethings by the bar, all engrossed in their phones instead of each other. The bartender and our server smirked at a video on his iPad behind the bar.

"Remember how disgusting the toilets were in here back in the day?" Neil said.

I hated him saying 'back in the day'—what were we, sitting on a park bench outside a seniors' home, remembering the good old times? Jesus. I was all for the fun of reminiscing about past events. Who didn't? But if that was the only reason you were friends, then you weren't exactly friends with them, were you? You were friends with their memories, and them with yours. Past tense friends, in the present. I wasn't living in Springsteen's Glory Days, nor did I want to.

But I had a better-than-average ability to remember places and events from the past. Sometimes, that counted as a bonus, other times a real drag. Tonight it was a real drag. I remembered a million moments of my life in this room. Vivid Kodachrome snapshots of bands, people, and events over thirty years. It would be nice if the choice to remember was something I could turn on and off, but it wasn't. Ah well.

There were things we couldn't control and things we could.

"Would you use your time travel trip to go back, buy the Railway and not change anything?" Terry asked.

We considered.

"Nah. Then I'd be the one losing money and going broke."

I downed the rest of my hop-forward beer.

"Let's get out of here. Gina and me need to work in the morning."

Once more, we stood on the sidewalk outside the club. No cars to lean on. The city had replaced the street parking years ago with a bright separated-from-traffic set of bike lanes. Gina tried to take a selfie of the four of us, but she couldn't motivate any of us enough to join her.

Sighing, she lit up a cigarette, took a deep inhale, then exhaled in relief. She and I smoked real cigarettes because vapes were like sucking on a pager. There had been no smoking in any restaurant or bar in Vancouver for years.

Back in the day—God, I was saying it now—the cigarette smoke was so thick you couldn't see from the back to the front of the Railway Club. Unless you lowered yourself to the floor like in a 'what to do in a fire' educational video. The windows only opened from the bottom. The smoke had no place to go but collect and concentrate on the ceiling. But damn, it sure made the lights for bands look great.

I'd taken incredible photos through that cloud. Those developed photos had evoked a wide range of different emotions and had a nuanced look compared to the overly retouched digital images nowadays. Film grain and smoke made those images come alive for me. There were honest shadows and nuance that were much harder to find now.

When I saw those old photos now, they were an accurate representation of a moment of my life. No digital Photoshop manipulation. The truth printed on 8x10 Ilford paper.

A Spandex-clad cyclist covered in pretend-sponsor logos on a five thousand dollar bike screamed at Gina to stop poisoning him with her cigarette smoke. Outside a club, at 10 o'clock at night.

Welcome to the new Vancouver.

3

We didn't play the time travel game out of any deep-seated regret for our life choices. More so from recognizing that we were constantly making choices we wouldn't comprehend until years in the future. I didn't regret any of the choices I had made in the past. In fact, our game helped us clarify we didn't have regrets by allowing us to look at them through the long lens of time.

How different would my life have been if I'd taken up the offer to go on the road for six weeks with the band that became Damage Done? Three months stuffed into an Econoline van with four guys and their equipment as roadie and photographer for their one and only cross-Canada tour? The experience would have opened my eyes in ways that working in East Vancouver while preparing for my first year at community college hadn't. But would I have changed enough to have a future different from the one I now had?

How would Terry's life have played out if he'd been in the other First grade class instead of mine? Would we have become friends, anyway? Or would he have moved to Australia and opened his dream restaurant in a life without me, Gina, and Neil in it?

I had a great life and, because of that, chose not to obsess about what hadn't happened.

Was it everything I wanted when I was young? Fame, fortune, travel to exotic locations, a new Ferrari every year, Russian lingerie models? No. It was none of that. Instead, my life was stable, and I was content. Wasn't that more important than a risky alternative? I had a fantastic partner, a roof over my head, enough food and booze, friends who had my back. A good job where I helped people get on their feet from unemployment. Who could ask for more than that?

Another picture-perfect Vancouver morning awaited when we dragged ourselves outside twelve hours later. The North Shore mountains were bright green against the blue sky, new houses continuing to encroach on their peaks like flotsam after high tide. Higher each year. It had rained earlier in the week, and our street smelled like fresh-cut grass, blooming flowers—like nature. Until an old delivery van rumbled down the road, its broken muffler throwing out a black cloud of diesel pollution. We waited for the noxious smoke to dissipate to begin our fifteen-minute walk. On days like this, why climb on a packed bus and smell your fellow passengers? Or drag the car out of the garage only to waste an hour finding a parking spot?

Everyone double-checked they had their Naloxone overdose kits— welcome to life in the Fentanyl age. We all carried kits in case we came across an overdose in progress.

The four of us were renting a house halfway between downtown and Commercial Drive, a short walk from the area where we grew up. Commercial—The Drive, as the locals called it—was where all the conveniences were, our left-wing town center.

Our house was a kept up three-story built at the turn of the century. Grass-covered front and back yards, a garage rotting at the rear of the property, enormous Horse Chestnut trees along the street out front. They gave us shade in the summer and literal tons of leaves and inedible chestnuts in the fall. We had lucked into the house in the early '90s and had been there ever since. The owners knew our parents—that was The Drive and how you found accommodation. Neil had grabbed the attic apartment, with its rickety outside staircase and a partial view of the North Shore mountains. Gina and I lived on the main floor, and Terry occupied the basement suite we had convinced the landlords to split off from our apartment for him. We didn't need as much room for the two of us, so Terry got a lovely garden-level apartment with easy access to our shared backyard and deck.

While we walked, Neil told us a long, convoluted story about his last trip to the horse track, which may or may not have had any bits of truth contained within. He was pissed off because none of the horses he had bet on had won. Somehow that surprised him. Gina looped her arm through mine. Neither Terry nor us were listening particularly hard to what Neil said. Nothing new there. Neil was a serial storyteller. Mostly fiction dressed up as autobiography.

Gina and I had been a couple for nearly thirty years, but we'd known each other since we started Eighth grade. We weren't a love-at-first-sight couple, neither have we been together since our fateful first meeting. In fact, it took me two years of vaguely knowing who she was before I even hung out with her and then another decade before I asked her out.

Gina wondered once how I would answer our time machine game if the question were: would I go back and ask her out sooner?

As much as I would have loved to say yes, I know if I did, and she had said yes to going out one, two or five years earlier, we wouldn't still be in a relationship. After graduating high school, I had grown up a lot, so had needed her then as a friend.

Like all the other times we had played this game, the answer was a definite no. I wouldn't use my one chance to go back, not even to have an extra month with her. Events happen for a reason, even if we don't know what that reason is.

The Ovaltine Cafe had been our hangout since we had enough money to skip high school. We would go over to East Hastings and Main Street, then drink coffee and shoot the shit until realizing we were late for dinner. We'd sprint home, wired on dozens of 6 oz cups of cheap coffee, our backpacks full of homework studiously ignored all afternoon. The cafe was less than a block off the epicenter of the Downtown Eastside, the poorest postal code in Canada. The original crossroads of Vancouver's downtown was now an area barely alive and barely healthy. If it weren't for a culturally sensitive Chinatown butted up against it to the south, the entire area would have been factories decades ago.

But Vancouver being what it was—a rapacious beast chewing up historical buildings and shitting out towers of yuppy hutches and micro-lofts—the developers were encroaching. They nibbled away at the edges, renovated the old buildings into apartments for the more daring of the city's wealthy or those who can't afford to buy a place anywhere further away from the destitution overflowing the sidewalks and alleyways.

Nearly forty years later, the Ovaltine was still our place. I hoped to be long dead when it finally was converted into apartments with a Baby Gap store on the main floor. But for now, it remained as it had always been, a hole-in-the-wall diner with booths and counter service, high ceilings, a glowing neon sign draped down the building outside and reasonable food inside. You could guess from the name they'd been in business for a long time—long enough for Ovaltine to be a great way to promote your diner. I sort of remembered having Ovaltine at friends' houses—Scottish and English families, first-generation immigrants—tables full of Marmite, marmalade, mushy peas, strange meat products. And hot milk with a couple of tablespoons of Ovaltine powder stirred in—a supposed treat on a cold, wet winter day. Ordinary for my friends, but exotic to a Chinese kid.

Faye waved as we entered the restaurant. She was the daughter of the owner, Celina Chow, who, at seventy-seven years old, came into work each day, sat behind the till, wrote out bills and took payments. A feisty old lady always cracking a joke or throwing a wiseass comment our way.

When we started coming to the diner, Celina had been our server, her mother holding court on the same stool she sat on now.

Faye, ten years younger than us, whipped around the restaurant, monitoring each of her tables. Her mother kept an eagle eye on her, the till, as well as all the customers.

"Nice shirt," Faye said as she turned over heavy coffee cups and started pouring before we were even settled. I said we came here a lot, didn't I?

"Thanks," I replied, proud of my latest acquisition, a replica Pointed Sticks tour shirt from the mid-'80s. The Pointed Sticks were one of the best post-punk bands to come out of Vancouver, and we saw them many times in a wide range of concert locations—from pubs to warehouses, house parties to nightclubs. I have all their albums. On original vinyl.

Celina had come over and was leaning against her daughter.

"Colin, let me see your shirt."

I rose in the booth and showed it off.

Celina nodded and smiled. "I saw them in 1979. They were a fun band."

There was a shocked silence from all of us before Faye said, "Mom? You went to a punk concert?"

"The Pointed Sticks were more new-wave than punk. They had harmonies."

"I was like eight years old," Faye said.

"Obviously, I didn't take you to the show. You stayed with our neighbour." She observed our stunned faces. "What? I was young once. Like you."

With that, Celina smiled and sauntered back to the front to seat a new arrival.

I said, "I did not see that coming."

Faye frowned. "My mother and I need to have a long talk about my childhood."

Because the diner was filling up for lunch, we ordered quickly. "Your usuals?" We nodded. Faye smiled and left us with our coffees.

"Average house prices up again," Terry said, and the rest of us groaned. "One point five million. How's that for insane? My parents bought their place for thirty-two thousand."

"I saw a studio apartment, less than five hundred square feet, right above the loading dock for a McDonald's. $499,000," Neil said, still angry from revisiting his losses at the track by telling them to us. "Half a million to smell chicken nuggets cooking, twenty-four-seven. Disgusting."

It wasn't clear if he was disgusted with the price of the condo or the smell of the McNuggets.

"Please, a different topic, all right? On a perfect day like this, let's have a good meal, enjoy each other's company and not talk about how fucked housing in this city is. Agreed?" I begged them. It's not like we haven't talked about this exact subject before. Once or twice. A week.

We were so far outside the housing market; we couldn't even see it from where we were. We had gotten a chance thirty years ago, but even then, when you're making $25,000 a year, buying a house for $125,000 was a crazy, high-risk pipe dream, especially with mortgage rates the way they were then, well north of ten percent. Besides, we thought we had lots of time to procure those settling-down trappings—house, kids, dog, station wagon, vacation property over on a Gulf Island.

But, for whatever reasons, none of us did any of that. Gina and I started going out but hadn't gotten married—much to the dismay of her Italian-Catholic family and my Chinese grandparents. My parents were more forgiving, maybe because they were born in Canada, my great-grandparents having immigrated in the 1920s well before the Second World War and the Communist Revolution. Lucky for me, because if they hadn't, I wouldn't be here. And we wouldn't even talk about our unwillingness, our outright intransigence, to not popping out a raft of Italian-Chinese grandchildren.

•

Celina joined us after clearing our meals. I hoped to be that spry when I got to her age. She sat across the aisle in a booth where a single older man in a gray twill suit nibbled his way through a BLT on white. If he considered reacting to her sitting down, he didn't. He was a regular like us. He knew Celina like us.

We chatted for a bit, avoiding any mention of the housing market, but a loud barrage of laughter from a nearby booth interrupted us. With a grumpy scowl, Neil stood up to take a better look. Five arrogant, scruffy twenty-somethings jostled each other, a girl with raccoon eyes and nine shades of purple hair filming their shoving with her iPhone.

"Hello? We're trying to talk over here," Neil called out.

The jostling barely paused as one kid, head half-shaved, remaining hair flopping down over his professionally distressed bomber jacket, turned around and said, "Turn up your hearing aid, you grumpy old fart." He slumped down to another barrage of laughter. The purple hair girl filmed us over her friends' heads.

Beside me, Neil was ready to head over to their table to teach them some manners. Celina rolled her eyes and tugged on the sleeve of his naturally distressed bomber jacket, and sat him down.

"Snot-nosed kids..." he muttered, channelling his aggression into shredding his napkin. Faye strolled over to the kids' table, said something, and they quietened down. Like her mother, Faye was a force to be reckoned with, and only the most clueless or drunk didn't sense that immediately upon meeting her.

Celina laughed, an unexpected sound in the now quiet diner.

"What's so funny?" Gina asked.

"Oh, remembering another group of kids who would come in here and make all sorts of noise, not caring about anyone else but themselves."

Neil sat up, paper napkin destroyed. "You want me to talk to them?"

Terry sighed. "She's talking about us."

"We were never like that..."

"If that's what you believe, God loves you. But I have vivid memories of the four of you," Celina said.

Then, knowing without seeing that someone had wandered up to the till to pay, she stood up and wove her way back to the counter.

"We were never like that," Neil said, this time to us.

I shrugged. I hoped we weren't, but I was pretty sure we were. Thank God no one had video cameras in their pockets when we were growing up. The last thing I would want was digital proof of the stupidity of my—our—youth.

"Come on. I need a cig." Neil pushed Terry out of the booth and stood up, tossing a twenty onto the table. With nothing better to do, I paid for Gina and me, Terry added to the pile, and we headed towards the back door.

"Oh, must be nap time," one kid called out, but, showing a restraint which comes with wisdom, but may or may not come with age, we ignored the snot-nosed brats and went out to the alley for a smoke.

•

Once, you could smoke everywhere. Like in 'Mad Men', they would have smoked while swimming if they could. Even as late as the '80s, I remembered people smoking on buses, in stores, definitely in theatres—it drifted up through the projection in a magical effect, sometimes more interesting than the feature film—and absolutely in restaurants, bars, and nightclubs.

But now, Vancouver—like most cities—was smoke-free. Not within 7 meters, or twenty-three feet, of a bus stop, building air intakes, public doorways, not in parks or on beaches. About the only safe place to smoke now was on the center lines of a six-lane road. But if you were standing out there, you'd likely die of something other than lung cancer.

So, the place for smoking at the Ovaltine was out the back, past the kitchen and into the alleyway.

Neil kicked the fire door open, rippling with frustration over the snot-nosed kids. We followed the swinging door out and, as it banged against the brick wall, a trio of meth addicts leapt up from behind the rolling garbage bin where they were cooking up their next fix.

"The fuck, man…"

The tweekers scrambled to their feet, all edges and nerves and twitches. Their heart rates must have been up in the techno-thrash BPM range.

"Hey, it's cool," Gina said soothingly. Gina had her training in social work, but unlike me, she spent a few years in the relentless trenches of the Downtown Eastside. I left it to her to make peace with these three.

"The fuck you want?" "Leave us alone!" "You fucking cops?"

I moved Neil and Terry back, putting them further away, but close enough to protect Gina if events went even more sideways.

Drugs have devastated this part of the city. In high school, we hadn't taken our life in our hands walking down these alleys. Not exactly safe, but not a war zone either. But now? Powerful, highly addictive drugs sold for cheap. Each successive municipal and provincial government had whittled away the social safety net until what remained were a few tattered scraps better used as a burial shroud than a safety net.

One guy waved around a dirty needle, jabbing it in our directions. Shit, this was the last thing we needed. Worse than being shot was getting stabbed with a junkies' favorite needle. I looked for a way out. Neil was behind me, probably looking for something to hit the guy with; Terry was petrified, stiff as something Neil could beat a junkie with.

Gina was accomplishing nothing, despite five years of schooling and a twenty-year career. This guy wasn't in the right mind to listen to reason, probably not in the right mind for anything except another hit, which we had rudely interrupted.

Then the door opened behind us. Celina stepped out slowly, a paper plate full of food in her hands.

"Michael, put the needle down."

Much to my surprise, Michael did. As Gina stepped back to join the rest of us, Celina handed the food to one of the others, who grabbed it then moved behind the bin with a politely whispered, "Thank you."

Michael backed up, his eyes skittering between the five of us, fast as two hummingbirds in aerial combat. With a nod of thanks, he disappeared behind the bin.

Silence, except for traffic in the distance.

"How'd you know?" I asked Celina. She pointed up at an opaque half-ball mounted on the wall, high above the door. "Full range of motion, night optics. I control it with an app on my phone."

Then, with a sad smile, she went back inside and left us in the alley, cigarettes forgotten.

4

Music was the perfect time machine.

A song could transport you back to a specific point in time and help you either forget everything or remember everything.

With a rare weekday afternoon off, I enjoyed a glass of red wine on our front porch, old local indie music playing on the stereo. For before the award-winning, gold record collecting, alt-rock hero band called Damage Done existed, there had been a god-awful mess of a band called Mayo. Glass in hand, I traveled back to a night almost 40 years ago.

June 1979

Free of school pressures, the four of us had wandered through our neighborhood that evening, aimless. We were smoking a joint and shooting the shit, being teenagers. But then we heard a discordant racket. Curious, we followed it to discover a garage full of Grade 9 classmates with musical instruments. Kelly and Duncan, redheaded Scottish cousins, had battered electric guitars. Paul Bains manhandled a bass, and Bucky Derner was on drums since it was his family's garage.

I couldn't believe I knew actual rock musicians.

"You've gotta play it for us! Come on!"

Kelly was looking pretty nervous. "We've never played it for anyone."

"We've never played anything for anyone," Bucky added.

"Now's your chance," Gina said with a smile. "We'll love it, promise." The rest of us nodded, and the band looked at each other, trying to overcome their nervousness.

"Please?" Gina said coyly, tipping her weight onto one hip to show off her curves.

And that did it. Kelly sighed. He grabbed a battered notebook and opened it on a rickety music stand. "This is the only song we've written."

While they tuned up, I tried to figure out the correct f-stop for the dim overhead lights. I hadn't expected to be taking any photographs that night, so a half roll of 400 ISO film in my camera was all I had. I knew I could push the film when I developed it, but only if I was willing to let the rest of the roll come out overexposed. Choices, choices. I figured I'd take what photos I could now and make a decision later. Photography under these conditions was as new to me as performing in front of an audience was to the band.

Then we stepped back and waited.

Bucky counted them in, and two chords assaulted us. E and A. After eight bars of intro, Kelly stopped thrashing at his guitar and sang. More accurately, he yelled into the mic. A verbal onslaught, words thrown at us across the alley, phrases piled up on top of each other, beating us into submission. Raw as fuck, edgy as a rusty knife, and absolutely glorious.

I slipped in closer and snapped photos. Ever since dad gave me his old Minolta camera two years prior, I'd loved taking pictures. That camera came with me everywhere, and allowed me to judiciously snap photographs of scenes that caught my eye. Judicious because either I used up my allowance having them developed at the local drug store or ran the risk of developing them myself in the school darkroom. I had ruined at least as many as successfully developed since I was still learning the processes.

But that night, I let go of being judicious. I slipped around the space, catching the passionate magic of art in its moment of creation. The guys in the band built upon my actions, too. I might have not been creating the music, but my taking photographs was a part of its inception. Sure, I didn't know what I was doing, having only taken photographs around our school for the yearbook, but I felt like I was on fire. I felt like a real photographer. I'd find out when I got into the darkroom if I was legit or a sad fake.

Three minutes and thirty-three seconds later, the song ended with a final reverberating crash of sound.

My camera dropped to my chest on its strap, forgotten. I rejoined my friends in the alley, where we stood in awe.

The band fussed about, refusing to make eye contact, embarrassed at their raw outpouring of emotion.

"So?" Kelly finally said.

"You wrote that?" Terry asked.

Kelly nodded. "For English."

"What were Mrs. Rayburn's thoughts?" I asked. We were in the same class, ruled by a bitter, grumpy old teacher who should have retired a couple of decades ago. She was at least fifty.

"She fucking hated it. Said I didn't understand irony at all."

We laughed. The tension eased.

"So?" Kelly asked again.

"We fucking love it!" Gina said. We enthusiastically agreed, and the band grinned at us.

"Play it again!"

Young and Over-Equipped - Mayo
Self-produced cass-single 1980

I want to complain, I want to make a fuss
But I'm just like the rest of us
I've got it made, I'm doing OK
I make a lot of noise, but I've got nothing to say

I'm young and over-equipped
I'm young and over-equipped

We're middle-class punks, we all formed a band
But we don't make any real stand
Mommy bought the amps, Daddy bought the drums
All in all, they spent enormous sums

We're young and over-equipped
We're young and over-equipped
If you must…

I got an open mind, the space between my ears
I've been this way for years and years
I'll never grow up, I'll only grow old
But I can retire when the equipment's sold

We're young and over-equipped
We're young and over-equipped

But we all understood the irony. We'd never have our parents supporting our art, buying us the tools to create something new. If we wanted something, we would need to get a part-time job, save our minuscule pay checks, and pay our own way. Like I did with my photography supplies. Like the band did with their cheap-as instruments.

I asked them once, why did they start a band?

Kelly told me it was because no one was playing the music they heard in their heads. Because being shit at something was better than being shit at nothing.

Rock n roll was about taking chances. They weren't good enough to play covers, so they wrote and performed their own songs with us to cheer them on. We supported them when they could barely walk as a band. Nurturing them like a parent with a child. Those idiots took all the chances, maybe out of stupidity or from cunning. They threw themselves at the face of Time and said, "I won't go quietly into the night! I'm gonna make some noise and break some hearts and crack open some souls before I go."

The words of that song became the motto for a select and very cynical portion of our graduating class and were meticulously enshrined in our yearbook to the school's dismay. There were moments when I felt I still resonated with the energy of that song and emotion of those words, despite being nearly forty years past anyone calling me young.

•

One of the issues I have with the relentless march of technological progress was that old, perfectly good tech became obsolete. But only if you bought into this march of progress so loved by major electronic corporations the world over. But what if you didn't? I had never rid myself of my LPs, nor my cassettes and CDs. Instead, I had carefully compiled the best stereo ever—better than I ever imagined. As a teenager, I would stand on Richards Street, staring in the window of the exclusive high-end stereo stores, feigning indifference to Worfdale speakers, Nakamichi components, Bang & Olufsen turntables. Stores I would never have entered for fear of accidentally breaking something, thus forcing my parents to get a second mortgage. Prices were not visible. If you needed to ask, you couldn't afford it.

Now, many years after a Nakamichi pre-amp cost the same as a new car, I had collected all the components of an epic stereo for a fraction of the price. I got my mint condition Worfdale speaker towers, buttressing an original Sony CD single disc player, dual cassette decks, 32 band EQ, tuner, amp, pre-amp. And last summer, I had scored big time and had picked up a Bang & Olufsen tangential tracking wall-mounted turntable. I installed it in an ornate frame Gina had found at a garage sale. Because I'd buried the audio and power cables within the wall, our guest's first impressions were of an expensive piece of modern art.

"Oh. My. God... Is that an original Douglas Coupland?" they'd say while staring at the turntable surrounded by an ornate gold leaf picture frame.

"I saw his exhibit at the Vancouver Art Gallery, stunning."

Should Doug ever show up at one of our parties, I planned to ply him with cheap wine until he was drunk, then make him sign the wall for the hell of it, below the turntable but inside the frame.

I was on the porch, off in my memories, when Gina came home with a letter from our boss, Charlie. She went inside to change and get herself a wine glass. After she left, I tore open the envelope. Inside were two smaller envelopes, one addressed to each of us.

I opened mine. I had been laid off. Fired. Just like that. The letter explained a loss of funding, necessary cuts to staffing, a promise to recall me as soon as he found new funding sources. All that and a $50 gift card to Starbucks.

When Gina returned, I passed her my letter in silence and filled up our wine glasses. We were going to need another bottle.

"How can they do that, especially to you! You've been there forever. What about the whole idea of the last hired, first fired?"

"I know! I mean, what the hell! Shit like this doesn't happen to me. I've been there forever! Bastard..."

Then I remember her letter and pass it to her.

She took a big gulp of wine and opened it.

I watched while she read. "Well?"

The record ended, forgotten.

"Son of a bitch," she said in disgust.

"You're kidding."

She tossed me her letter. A $100 gift card to Lululemon fell to the porch. Three months notice to assist in the closure of our former workplace. It was obvious to everyone she was the more valuable employee of the two of us. She loved her job, I didn't. She cared about her clients and had always gone out of her way to help them. I was good at my job but, for me, it was just a job, not a career.

"What the hell are we going to do? If they're shutting down the entire office, that means fifteen skilled and qualified people are going to be out there looking for what remaining jobs exist!"

"I don't know, Gina. To be honest, I'm glad to be out of there. That office is depressing as all hell."

"I know it's depressing, but what will we do? Night shift at a homeless shelter down at Pigeon Park? Break up fights between junkies and lock yourself in your office when they think you're their psycho father returning to kill them?"

"I don't know what I'm going to do."

"How much time you figure?" she asked, pouring us more of the cheap red wine her father and uncles make in huge batches twice a year. Thousands of bottles of low-quality plonk were stored in crawlspaces around The Drive. Vintage generic U-brew wine, aging until it became vintage generic U-brew vinegar. Gina's brother Augusto dropped off a couple of cases monthly as they forced their father to cut down on his wine consumption. But he then ordered more from his pals, which ended up with Gina's brother dropping off more wine for us. The perfect symbiotic relationship, only if you could stomach cheap red wine.

I rechecked the letter. "Eight weeks severance. I'll get the humiliating process started and go sign up for Unemployment Insurance in the morning."

By pretending to have a plan, I had calmed her down a bit. I went back inside from the porch to choose another album to play.

Opening the lid of the turntable, I considered replaying the first Pointed Sticks album I had been enjoying. Big, bright, crazy sound for a perfect day. But with all the shitty news, we needed something more aggressive. Something like young angry power-pop from Mayo. I pushed the button to start play on a mix tape of their early indie recordings. The frantic power pop of 'Here We Go Again' assaulted my ears—in a good way. I soaked in the first verse before heading outside.

I was surprised to find a couple on the porch with Gina. They were in their forties, obviously related, clearly Greek. The children of our landlords.

"Hey guys, what are you doing here? Want wine? I'll go get more glasses. Gina's dad makes the wine himself, it's not great but it does the trick."

"No, we're good, Colin," Barb said, standing close to her brother, Bill.

"Ok…"

I sat down as Mayo moved on to singing about being young and over-equipped. Except I was no longer young, and I don't think I had ever been over-equipped at anything. Except maybe photography, but that had been a long time ago.

Bill asked, "How's your mom and dad?"

Gina, never one for social niceties and in possession of one of the most finely tuned bullshit detectors known to man, sighed and said, "What's up? Just tell us, please?"

Bill and Barb glanced at each other, clearly tossing a mental coin for who had to tell us whatever they were here to say to us.

"Our parents are selling the house. It goes on the market in two months," Bill said, having won, or lost, the coin toss.

"We wanted to tell you in person," Barb continued. "It's because they're getting old. Dad had his hip replaced, mom's arthritis is horrible, and you won't believe the cost of assisted living around here."

The four of us stood there, two of us digesting this news as the other two looked guilty.

"It's not that you're not good tenants, you're the best, but this city…"

Gina smiled semi-convincingly. I was sure Bill and Barb bought her smile, but I saw the worry behind it.

"Guys, we understand. Our parents are aging, too. You're right, this house is their retirement savings plan, and now you need to cash it in."

The looks of relief on their faces were palpable. I didn't know what they expected, that we'd come at them with broken bottles or barricade ourselves inside with months' worth of freeze-dried food and bottled water? I took Gina's hand and smiled with her.

"Thanks for being so understanding. You'll tell Neil and Terry?" Barb asked.

"For sure. As soon as they get home."

Bill pulled out a thick, legal-sized envelope and handed it over.

"Gotta jump through all the legal hoops these days," he said, embarrassed. "Don't want to end up in trouble with the Rental Board."

"No, you wouldn't want that," I said as they climbed down the steps and left us with our cheap wine and our eviction notice.

We watched in silence as they drove away.

"My God, who did we piss off in a past life to get a day like this?" I asked Gina.

She didn't answer. Instead, she hugged me. I think that scared me more than getting the news. Gina was my rock, the one who always had a plan, especially when I didn't. Decisions impacting us had been made elsewhere—at our work and at our landlords. I'm not a fan of making choices, but the shit had hit the fan of our lives and we needed to do something. Fast.

I didn't love my job, but I didn't want to find another one. I would have liked a newer place to live with better sound insulation, so we didn't have to hear Neil and his concubines. But I didn't want to go looking for a new one either. I had been content with what I had. Was there a point when someone stopped looking forward to change? That they got so old or so fixed in their ways that they stopped being happy with change? When did that happen? Why?

Our recovery from the double punch to the face—no job and no home —was interrupted by Neil bounding up onto the porch, lugging a portable cooler we had never seen before.

"Why so glum? I bring beer!" He dropped the cooler with a muffled load of glass clinking and ice water sloshing. He opened the lid to display five or six different local beers neck-deep in icy water.

"Where did you find those?"

"In exchange for some work," Neil said, grabbing a Howe Sound Double Hopped IPA. Neil and work had a strained and sometimes acrimonious relationship. If he had held an officially recognized job in the past twenty-five years—one where he paid taxes on earnings—we didn't know about it. He paid his rent, chipped in for food, beer, dope and smokes, but he was intentionally vague as to what exactly he did to make money. Our assumption was a combination of gambling, dealing, and shady projects for the neighborhood guys we had grown up with.

Knowing Neil had given us as much of an answer as he would, Gina and I chose beers—a Swans Brewery Oktoberfest Flammenbeer for me and a Ravens Corvus Lingonberry Lime Gose for Gina—and took long drinks. Then we filled him in on our news.

"Well. Shit."

Really nothing more to say than that.

5

Gina phoned in sick the following day, and after sleeping in, we settled back on our porch, me with the daily Vancouver Sun newspaper and Gina with her laptop. I had made a huge Bodum of French Roast, and we had a whole banana bread, sliced and ready to be consumed.

I started through the rental section of the paper, while Gina did the same with the online versions. I wasn't sure why people paid for print ads for a rental, but I hoped those people were old and conservative. Those were the people Gina and I—with our considerable charm quotient pumped up to the max—could convince to rent to us. Gina and I had charmed the pants off Mr. and Mrs. Sefanopolous in the late '80s, and we had lived here ever since.

But this house was no longer ours, most likely to be demolished within the year, and a shiny new strata unit knocked up in its place. Strata units that grateful dual-income families would then purchase thrilled to live this close to downtown, although less excited about the homeless encampment at the end of the street and the late-night trains coming from the docks. But they would have a foot in the door of the precarious house of cards called the Vancouver housing market. Sleeping easy, safe knowing that outside a downturn in the world economy—which

Vancouver had no say in—their bank would own most of their little slice of heaven until they collapsed of nervous breakdowns from punishing 80-hour workweeks to afford 650 square feet of strata housing.

Two hours later, the news was official. We were well and truly screwed.

With a one-bedroom apartment—an awful, stinking, illegal one-bedroom apartment—going for over $2,000 a month, the cost of renting an entire house was a number shocking to even the wealthiest man.

But there weren't any houses in our neighborhood for rent. Nor in adjacent communities. The best we located was a house at least three busses and a twenty-minute hike away from where we were now. And they wanted $8,000. Each and every month! For a shitty '70s Vancouver Special with an illegal two-bedroom 'suite' knocked into the basement by a mentally deficient handyman. Meaning Neil and Terry would have to share the cellar while Gina and I endure the main floor.

I mean, had the world gone mad? Or just Vancouver? How were the people who had actual jobs doing the grunt work keeping the city moving supposed to live? Where did the baristas and hair stylists, servers and retail clerks, janitors and window washers sleep at night?

Gina slammed her laptop shut. "What a load of shit."

I closed my paper in agreement. "It's so bad out there. I had no idea."

"I know. Clients lament how finding a place to live is so hard, and my assumption was they're lazy and not looking hard enough."

"Gina, we'll find a place," I said, with way more confidence than I had.

"Where? Agassiz? The Interior? How far will you move to continue to be in this city? Because this city sure isn't doing us any favors."

I knew what she meant. Two of our co-workers bailed a couple of years ago. They had moved east across the Rockies to Regina, where they had a lovely house in an up-and-coming neighborhood, an excellent school for their daughter, potlucks on weekends, an easy commute to their jobs, all while making much more. But Claire had grown up in

Saskatchewan. She had family there, and Marcel was now a couple of hours on a plane closer to his family in Montreal. Gina and me? Neil and Terry? We had all been born at Grace Hospital, a twenty-minute drive away. But having that on your birth certificate didn't give you an advantage in the housing market. In fact, it was now the opposite.

"I don't know. I've only lived here. Christ, I've only moved a whole thirteen blocks since being born. Maybe people would consider me stuck, but I was happy with putting down roots and not moving around until we got hit with the news."

"So, do we leave Vancouver if we can't find a place? We hunt down new jobs somewhere new?"

Gina didn't look happy about the idea, but I appreciated her question. I had spent all morning with similar thoughts but hadn't wanted to express them. The thought of starting over in a new city, where we didn't know anyone, was daunting. If Vancouver hadn't been so great growing up, I would have headed back east. Why not try out life in a different city? Hop a bus to Toronto or maybe even all the way to Halifax. But when I was young, I didn't want to leave this fantastic city and everything it offered. I had chosen by choosing not to choose to leave. So here I was with my friends from childhood. Making friends during school was hard enough, which was why I still hung around with Terry and Neil. Who was the last friend I made? Some guys I worked with, but I doubt I'd be seeing them much since getting fired.

"I'm pretty old to start again."

"Yeah…"

Depressed in the downward direction my life was sliding, I retreated to our bedroom to sort through my meager belongings. I wouldn't need as much stuff when living under a bridge down by the Fraser River, whiling away my remaining days reminiscing about indie punk bands of the '70s with the rest of the dispossessed.

I dragged out the first of a dozen old wine boxes from the back of our closet and peeled back the packing tape. On top, a Cuban cigar box that used to hold my concert tickets. I put it to the side. My old Minolta camera, five yearbooks, a battered elementary school photo album, elastic-banded NHL hockey cards, old single-digit birthday cards, and a loose collection of handwritten letters and postcards. I flicked through the postcards—images of Italy, China, Scotland sent by school friends on family visits. A battered pair of Mickey Mouse ears brought back for me from SoCal. Letters half-heartedly written by pen-pals, my half-hearted replies to them most likely trashed long ago. Nothing that needed to be kept for the Colin Yip Memorial Museum and Concert Hall. I stuffed them into a recycling bag and grabbed another handful—more letters addressed in childish scrawls. Into the recycling bag for them, as well.

Bored with my early childhood already, I grabbed the cigar box and opened it up. Cards from my fiftieth birthday. Goofy ones from friends, cousins and siblings, a sentimental one from Gina announcing her surprise present—an unforgettable trip to Maui, serious cards from my parents, my grandparents and Gina's parents. But one stood out in the stack. An expensive cream envelope the Queen would have deemed acceptable. My name written in calligraphy so perfect it would make Marie Antoinette swoon. A lump of red wax on the back sealed it closed. I had no recollection of receiving this letter.

I broke the seal with care and pulled the letter itself out of the envelope, bits of old red wax breaking off and dropping into the box.

I skimmed the single page once, then twice, then read it slowly for the third time.

Forgetting the half-unpacked box but clutching the strangest note I'd ever read, I moved to the end of our bed and stared at our cluttered dresser, my mind a whirl of impossible possibilities.

•

"I love this city," Terry said with a sigh, like a high school boy crushing on Taylor Swift. Or, in Terry's case, Taylor Lautner from the

Twilight movies. No matter how much you love them, they didn't love you back because they would never know you exist.

We lounged on our porch, a couple of empty bottles of wine on the coffee table, NoMeansNo's edgy pop on the stereo. The note burning a hole in my pocket distracted me. Distracted by what it could mean for me —for us all—and when to bring it up.

"What if we had a time machine?" I said into the ensuing silence, taking a chance that the right time had come.

Everyone groaned, and Terry said, "Oh stop it, Colin."

"I'm serious. What if you could use it and be sure you couldn't do any harm?"

"But you can't. That's the whole raison d'être of the question. It's the Kobayashi Maru of questions," he said.

"No, it isn't. There has to be a right answer. If you're smart enough, you could go back in time and make one minuscule change without messing up anyone else, affecting your future life for the better."

"Well, I disagree. As soon as you land in the past, you're gonna cause ripples to flow out. Those ripples will cause more ripples, and then everyone is dead in a massive nuclear war," Terry says, putting down his wine glass to light a cigarette.

Gina leaned forward, thoughts sparking behind her eyes. "What if you traveled back, changed nothing in the past, but left something to pick up once you returned?"

Terry looked at her, considering. "That might work if you keep your contact with the past world to an absolute minimum. Don't change the past; hide something to change the future instead."

Gina smiled, happy to add a new twist to our age-old conversation.

"Neil, any thoughts you'd like to add?"

Neil swallowed his mouthful of red wine with a shudder, then said, "Gina, if you went back and got knocked up by someone famous, then you could go after them for child support."

Gina laughed. "That would have been a good plan a couple of decades ago."

"Then maybe I should go back and knock up some famous hottie."

Terry joined in, "Me, too!"

"Oh, you're going to have Elton John's baby?"

They burst out laughing. I joined in the laughter then made a decision.

"No one go anywhere. You're going to love this." I went inside to our bedroom, leaving the three still snickering over Terry having a baby with Elton John.

From the top of our bedroom dresser, I grabbed an unpretentious black lacquer box with delicate red curved lines painted onto the corners. Despite its hard-cover novel size—8 by 12 inches and 2 inches thick—it packed a heft as if constructed long ago from cast iron. I wiped the top with my T-shirt to clear away the dust buildup and took it outside.

Gina, Terry and Neil watched as I shut the front door behind me and sat down, the box on my lap.

"Voila," I said.

"Voila, what?" Terry said.

I pointed at the box on my lap.

"Jesus, Colin, let the time machine joke go."

"I'm not joking. I think this box is an actual time machine."

I gave the top of the box a gentle pat.

"Not that I'm going along with you, but where did this supposed 'time machine' come from? A Salvation Army thrift store?" Neil said in resigned disbelief.

"From my grandmother. Our family has had it for about three hundred years."

"And she said, 'Here Colin, have our family's time machine.'?"

"Well, yeah, pretty much." They didn't believe me. Of course, they didn't believe me. I wouldn't believe me.

I tried to explain. "My grandmother May gave it to me with a note on my fiftieth birthday. She dragged me away from my birthday party, remember, it was at my parents house? She took me down into the dark cellar where she opened an ancient trunk, handed me this black box and a fancy card."

Terry said, "That's the best origin story you could think up, Colin?"

Gina looked at me, curious. "And you never mentioned this until now? Even to me?"

"The sealed note she gave me was in a box of old stuff I went through two hours ago."

"You forgot about being given a time machine." Gina looked incredulous. I took the note out of my pocket and waved it around.

"You got me a trip to Maui, so I didn't read the note! Terry, help me out here!"

Terry said, "Gina, Maui versus a note from your grandmother?"

"What does the note say?" Gina asked.

I handed her the note and said, "As the second born of the second generation, the box is my sacred destiny, my heritage and my power. A time machine only I can use. It's a secret I've kept—because I never opened my grandmother's note to learn it."

Terry said, "The best way to have a secret is not to know you have one."

"Exactly," I replied.

"Lemme see it then," Neil said, and grabbed the box from my lap.

"Careful!"

He waved me back, so I stopped rising from my chair. With Terry looking over his shoulder, Neil undid the tiny brass clasp and opened the lid. They peered inside, then up at me.

"This is a time machine, but you use it to store concert ticket stubs?" Terry said in disbelief. Neil held up a dusty old roach. "Can I spark this up?"

I shrugged, so he did. Exhaling a cloud of ancient dope smoke, Neil said, "You know, just because your grandmother told you this was a time machine doesn't mean it is a time machine. Maybe your grandmother has the same terrible sense of humor you do."

"And maybe you're nothing more than a cynical asshole," I shot back.

"I may be. But I'm not trying to convince you I'm not."

Terry had removed forty years' worth of ticket stubs and looked into the empty box. "How does it work if it is a time machine?"

"I guess turn the knob in the center."

"This one?" Neil leaned over and gave the polished black obsidian knob a turn. Nothing happened.

"Yeah, that one."

Terry and Neil looked at each other for a moment. Terry put the ticket stubs back into the box while Neil finished the roach.

"It only works for me," I said, realizing how lame I sounded.

"Of course, Colin," Terry said. "Of course it only works for you."

"What happens when you turn the knob?"

"I go back in time."

They stared at me.

"For how long?"

"Well… I don't know."

Terry shook his head, exasperated. "Even if I was to believe you, who in their right mind would turn that knob, not knowing anything about the process? You could end up trapped a million years in the past."

"Maybe, but that's kind of extreme. And sort of pointless. Why make a time machine that only goes back a million years?"

"Dinosaurs!" Neil said with a grin.

"No one 'made' a time machine! It's a pretty jewelry box!"

"But what about the knob?" I countered.

"Time machines—if you could build one, which you can't—would need to either travel faster than the speed of light or do something involving quantum physics!"

Terry held up the box.

"Does this look like it can go faster than light?"

"But what if I'm right, Terry? What if it is a time machine, despite all logical arguments to the contrary?"

He huffed and took a drink. He opened the box and gave the knob a cautious turn.

Nothing happened.

"How far back in time do you go?"

"Uh, I don't know."

Neil piped up, "Can you go forward in time?"

I sighed. "I don't know."

Terry was right. Without an instruction manual, my time machine was a useless lacquered box.

Gina patted me on the arm in sympathy, then took the box from Terry.

"Guys, I've been waiting for this night for years. How about we don't let Colin's budding insanity ruin it. Let's forget about the 'time machine' for now, and we can get going. It's time to party!"

6

'Damage Done, unplugged and personal! One night only at the River Rock Casino Showroom!'

Why they were advertising on the backs of buses, I didn't know. A two-shot of Kelly MacLeod and Norm Parfitt, the remaining two members. Norm had joined the band in early '84. Kelly's cousin, Duncan, had given up on a likely subsistence career in rock n roll and moved to Alberta to apprentice as a pipe-fitter. Last we heard, he had six kids, a hobby ranch and had ridden the tar-sands boom into a multi-million dollar business, which he had sold just before oil prices crashed.

We had bought our tickets the moment they went on sale, grabbing the best seats available. But after the bots and scalpers did their work, that meant four on the aisle fifteen rows up from the stage.

Despite the looming disasters in our collective lives, we would have a great time, damnit.

Hopping off the SkyTrain at the casino, we joined a group of staff on their way to work. Together, we hiked under the parkade in a concrete corridor with flickering fluorescents towards the grand entrance of the River Rock Casino, Hotel and Showroom. A bright red Lamborghini blocked the crosswalk in front of us. A young Asian kid hopped out of the gull-wing door as the valet rushed forward to take the keys from him. Our crowd surrounded the car before leaving it, unaffected, in our wake. I glanced back as a leggy blonde model rose out of the passenger side, somehow pivoting herself out of the low seat onto five-inch heels, flashing nothing to the world. An essential skill they must now teach in modelling school. I glanced from them to us; Gina in a comfortable flowing dress, Neil in his historically significant leather jacket, Terry in an off-the-rack grey suit and me in my one white dress shirt, clean 501's and one of my dad's sixties thin lapel suit jackets. We might have put on nice clothes for our night out, but we looked like bums beside these kids.

The workers pivoted to the left through an unmarked door, leaving the four of us in the middle of the grand foyer. High arches of polished log beams rose three stories into the air. It smelled like foreign money. The check-in for the hotel was directly ahead; casino to the left; and, to the right, the entrance to the showroom.

"Look, merch!" Neil said. He split off to a row of tables covered with t-shirts, books, signed LPs, and re-issued CDs. They were even selling a artificially distressed faux-leather jacket with the Damage Done logo—the classic entwined capital 'D's—embroidered on the back. List price: $350.00. What a racket. Even basic t-shirts with the logo started at $45. Worse, all they had done was take the generic logo T and screen printed 'Unplugged and Personal tour 2017' below. Ripoff.

"Let's grab a drink while we can," Terry said. He pushed his way up to the door, ticket ready. Gina and I joined him in the well-dressed crowd, leaving Neil to chat up the twenty-something merchandise table girl. Gina rolled her eyes and said, "Yes. Let's leave the Slut to his depravity."

The Slut. Gina's nickname for him. But Neil was Neil, and Neil didn't give a shit what Gina or anyone thought. Since school, he had been practicing his lines on any woman available, including our tenth-grade French teacher, Mme LeCroix. Neil claimed to have met up with her to have sex in the back of her Honda Civic. We had doubts about the integrity of his story. Who wouldn't? But Neil pointed to his knowledge of a secret rose tattoo on her pelvis—a tattoo none of us could prove, or disprove, the existence of.

We shuffled to our seats, smarting from shelling out sixty dollars for four drinks. The theatre was a beautifully appointed room with comfortable seating, excellent sight-lines, fantastic sound and lighting system. Everything to make a concert viewing experience as pleasant and comfortable as possible. But because of that, the theatre lacked what a concert needed. The electric pulse of the crowd, the grinding throb of the dance floor, the explosive energy of a packed club. Like watching a show on a big screen TV with a Dolby 5 surround system. Gone were the crowded dance pits of our youth, replaced by new hips and comfortable reclining seats with cup holders. But no matter what, seeing Vancouver's homegrown heroes back on stage for the first time in almost a decade would be worth it.

•

Despite their inauspicious start as Mayo in that garage in '79, Damage Done's re-invention five years later with Norm on lead guitar marked a dramatic shift in their songwriting. An overnight evolution from machine-gun anarchic power punk-pop to lyric and melodic, FM-friendly power punk-pop. And their arrival on the scene and the brilliance of their debut album counterbalanced the bright, happy top ten pop on the radio that year. Damage Done was the perfect antidote to 'Karma Chameleon' and 'Girls Just Wanna Have Fun.' Their cynical views on television and radio and soul-searching songs about 'Getting Lost' or 'Television Control' were tailor made for the time. Then they continued through the '90s and early 2000s with a string of successful albums loved by critics and fans alike. Luck and good timing got them onto the first Lollapalooza tour in '91 and they continued every year until '97 when the tour took a hiatus. Being inducted into the Rock and Roll Hall of Fame in 2004 along with George Harrison, Prince and ZZ Top solidified their status in the pantheon of rock. All that lead up to this current unplugged tour.

We sat in our plush seats for a half-hour, watching the mature crowd around us poke away on their mobile phones or exchange business cards in the aisles. Then the lights dimmed, and a soothing voice requested we not take any photos or videos for a myriad of legal reasons. Kelly and Norm strolled out from the wings into an intimate circle of soft white light in the center of the stage to a round of polite applause and a few rebellious whistles. Two bar stools in front of two microphones. At each side of the stage, a row of guitars expensive enough to give Eddie Van Halen cold sweats.

"I guess no mosh pit tonight," Neil said, receiving a glare from the balding forty-year-old in front of him. Neil flicked him the finger as the crowd continued their polite applause for the boys.

"Yo, Vancouver!" Kelly called out, just as he always had. The crowd called back, "Yo yo, Kelly!" as we always had.

Norm laughed while choosing his first guitar. He picked a custom-made Ovation acoustic and plugged it in.

He had perfected the Robert Plant aging rocker look. Luxurious grey curls and a white dress shirt over jeans and polished Doc Martens. Having succumbed to his father's receding hairline in his late twenties, Kelly had done the opposite with his head and has kept it completely shaved ever since. For a time, he would let groupies draw over his skull with colored Sharpies before a show, but those days are long over. He wore his ubiquitous cargo pants and a vertical stripe black and white sleeveless t-shirt.

They looked good. Youthful complexions, fit and trim. Happy with life, and not a thing to be angry about. In their hometown for the first sold-out show of a North American tour. Life was sweet. For them.

I reached over and grabbed Gina's hand. I needed a great show to forget my lack of job and our lack of housing. She grinned and squeezed me back as the first chords of 'High Fashion' fill the room.

But it wasn't the same. Not the same at all.

Sure, their musicianship was fantastic. Forty years of playing guitar had made them better and better. But all those countless hours of practice had drained the life out of their early songs. Edgy had become nuanced. The angry songs of our youth, with their hungry clawing chords and raw and ragged solos, weren't meant for acoustic guitars. Their lyrics screamed into a mic for a rapacious audience, desperate words acknowledging our collective experience. But the two wealthy-beyond-imagination guys on this beautiful stage with their arrays of custom-built guitars weren't hungry anymore. Not with their West Vancouver mansions and multi-million dollar recording studio built in a former furniture warehouse in the old hood. While I was proud of what they had accomplished, the Muzak they were playing wasn't what I had bought tickets to see.

A beautiful, professionally designed slideshow played on giant screens behind them. Photos of the band from their breakout show forward.

"Isn't that one of yours?" Terry asked as a bold black & white side shot of Kelly singing to a screaming Japanese girl floats across the screen from left to right. A graphic at the bottom of the photo said The Commodore Ballroom, Expo86. I shook my head. The band played one-hundred-and-seven shows in random venues around the city during the five months the fair was on. It was insanity. They introduced themselves to a whole new audience from across the globe. I was working full time with Gina as social workers by then. We went to a few of their Expo shows, but I had stepped back from photography. The lure of a steady pay check beat the pittance bands could pay me. Besides, if I had taken that shot, I would have moved to the right to get the girl in the same focus as Kelly and so the mic didn't cover as much of his face. Once a photographer, always a photographer.

Another song ended with polite applause. The two on stage drank their imported bottled water—no more pint mugs of rye & ginger for them—and changed guitars again.

"You figure they'll play any of their Mayo songs?" Gina asked.

"I don't know. But there's only one way to find out," I said with a grin.

"Huh?"

I yelled out, "Play 'My Girl's Radioactive'!"

The crowd laughed, but I guarantee most have never even heard the song. Kelly and Norm grimaced. Norm leaned up to his mic. "We'll pass on that one, thanks."

Kelly added, "We're staying clear of high school on this tour."

Another laugh from the audience, despite no one knowing why they were laughing.

"Sellouts," Terry said. The rest of us nodded.

We waited as they picked up new instruments—they had averaged a guitar change per song. When Mayo started, they could only afford one guitar each. They had played the same battered, crap, no-name electric guitars for the entire show—unwilling to stop to replace broken strings for fear of losing their momentum. They would barrel on, accidentally creating fresh sounds along the way. Magic every single night they were on a stage.

Then the lights behind Kelly and Norm faded up, revealing a modest string section.

"What the ever-loving fuck?" Neil muttered, receiving yet another glare from baldie. Another raised finger convinced baldie to turn back to his bored trophy wife, who had been skimming Instagram the entire show.

A sickening tightness curled around my stomach. I loved this band and had loved them since that first night in that East Van alley. I had been there with them for their band's growth and was part of their evolution. I was complicit in their disastrous performances and had celebrated their triumphs with them. And now this.

With a glance from Kelly, the strings began. They were beautiful. Haunting, arranged with brilliance. Norm joined in, showing off his secretly acquired Flamenco guitar skills. It took me twenty bars to recognize the song. A rush of conflicting emotions suddenly engulfed me as Kelly sang, soft and delicate, in Spanish. A tidal wave of feelings, but one more than any other—betrayal.

'Standing in Your Shadow' was the ultimate song about being left behind. About having the one you love outshine you. A song about letting someone go so they can be the best they can be, knowing you would be left behind. They were playing that same song but a fancy Flamenco version, with strings, sung in Spanish.

I stood up with a jolt, causing the well-dressed behind me to huff and agitate. Gina looked up at me, confused.

"Colin, are you Ok?"

I shook my head. No words could explain the emotions roiling in me. I pushed past Terry and Neil towards the aisle. Sitting through this was impossible. People stared as I climbed the stairs. With these ticket prices, what kind of idiot left before the encore? But I didn't care. That wasn't my band on that stage. I pushed open the doors out into the lobby, not looking back. I knew my friends were right behind me, each feeling precisely as I did.

7

I stumbled through the empty lobby. The two guys restocking the merchandise table paused from stacking shirts and CDs to watch me shuffle past.

Arriving in the grand foyer, I had to stop since I didn't know where I was going. My head was completely messed up. Sure, a band could grow old and change up their sound. I got that. They didn't have to be angry young men when they're wealthy and middle-aged. But, shit. Angry youth songs played on a fucking ten thousand dollar acoustic twelve-string guitar with a string section borrowed from the Vancouver Symphony Orchestra was wrong. Did everything have to change?

Gina turned me around and took my hands.

"That… that wasn't what I expected," I said.

She nodded because she got it. "Yeah, I understand."

I wanted the energy of my youth, but that wasn't what they were offering. Kelly and Norm had a nostalgia show now. It was a comfortable look back at their career for part-time fans and their tag-along partners. Not too loud, not too quiet, just right. A Goldilocks tour.

"I thought they'd have more edge. I thought they were going to be the same, I guess."

"How can they be the same, Colin? They're in their fifties, like us. The raw unknown of youth got replaced by something far less exciting but much more comforting. Lots of money makes angry young men contented." Gina smiled, then gave me a gentle kiss.

Neil, engrossed by the stunning Asian women in slinky dresses strutting past on stiletto heels, said, "Yeah, yeah, those assholes got old and now suck balls. Let's buy a round of drinks and hit the tables!"

A half-hour later, the casino floor filled with the rest of the audience, a dark river of middle-aged music fans entering the clear lake water of serious gamblers. The actual players resented us being in the room. We didn't belong there, we didn't fit in, and we didn't know how to play. But we had money, so the croupiers and table bosses smiled and welcomed us with open arms. But with one hand dipping into our wallets for their cut.

Neil ordered us four beers and elbowed his way up to a twenty-dollar craps table.

I hated gambling. I'd rather buy a lottery ticket and enjoy a week of daydreams about what I'd do with the winnings. Putting my money down on a craps table for less than a minute before watching it disappear forever into the pockets of the casino owners was ridiculous.

But this was what Neil did. Amongst other things.

We pooled our remaining money after Terry paid for the beers. I handed it to Neil and told him to make us rich.

To begin with, he did well. Our pile of chips increased, much slower than the professional gamblers around us, but building up. To my surprise, Neil refrained from large impulse bets which could wipe us out, showing a calm focus I had never seen before. We milled quietly behind him, apprehensively watching.

"Colin? Yipper?" I turned around and saw an old classmate in front of a row of slot machines.

"Brian," I said. Brian Hagar looked rich. Balding, but rich. He had a Palm Springs tan, a glaringly large expensive watch, and a stylish suit worth more than my stereo—new.

"Shit, look at you four. Still hanging together? Damn, that's a hell of a friendship. Were you at the show?"

We nodded but didn't say anything. None of us had liked Brian in school.

"Wasn't that something and a half? I bumped into Kelly and Norm over Christmas in Palm Springs. You know they have places there, right? Like old school week."

"Must have been a hoot," Neil said, not taking his eyes off the craps table.

Brian made a fan of business cards appear like magic. "You guys in the market? Looking to downsize, upsize, maybe slip into a funky condo?"

"Uh, no, we're not in the market. We didn't buy in when we should have."

Brian kept on rolling out his marketing spiel as a bored young Chinese trophy arrived at his side. She alternated between indifference and outright boredom. He introduced her as his wife and realty corporation partner, Winnie. Put on the spot, she gave us a fast once over. I watched her analyze our shoes, watches and Gina's purse. Then she slipped on a bright fake smile and said to me, *"Hěn gāox"ng jiàn dào wǒ zhàngfū de yīxiē xuéxiào péngyǒu."*

I hated this. Instant assumptions about my upbringing and my heritage. The same shit all my life. I gritted my teeth, smiled and said, "Sorry, I don't speak Mandarin. Well, I can order dim sum, but that's about it."

She double squeezed Brian's arm. Without appearing to notice this subtle move, he handed over cards and wished us well.

"Maybe we'll see you at our next reunion. Who knows, keep buying lottery tickets, and you might be ready to get into the market then!" Brian said.

With one last smile to the four of us, they slipped back into the well-dressed crowd in search of new prey.

"I always hated him," Terry said.

Neil grimaced. "Goddamn social media. Assholes like that are why I'm not on Facebook. As if I need to have his success pushed in my face every day."

"If you were that successful, you'd be on Facebook and Instagram, pushing it in everyone's faces," Terry said. "I know I would."

"You catch when she realized we weren't ever going to buy a house?" Gina asked.

I nodded. Winnie had us pegged the moment we met.

•

Then a new pit boss confiscated our money, and two burly guards escorted us out of the casino. Neil hadn't mentioned his current ban from the River Rock and its sister casino in the Fraser Valley.

"I didn't think it mattered," he tried to explain.

"Obviously, it did."

"Yeah, well…"

We stood outside the casino. Ferrari's and Lamborghini's pulled up and disgorged young rich Asian kids. Then middle-aged white valets drove the cars off to secure and guarded parking.

"This city fucking sucks," Terry said.

"When exactly were you banned from the casino?" I asked Neil.

"A couple of weeks ago. No big deal."

"Uh, it is a big deal. I suppose that explains why you're late with rent?"

"Temporary cash flow problems," he replied.

We rolled our eyes. Neil and his temporary cash flow problems. He was either flush and splurging on everything or tapped out and begging for leftover food.

All of this was piling way too high on my shoulders. Find a new job that paid at least as well as my old one; find a new place to live with rent at least the same as our old one. And my favorite band had sold out.

I tuned out Gina and Terry squabbling with Neil as a stretch Hummer unloaded a party at our feet. We had to step back as a hundred thousand dollars' worth of jewelry and evening wear blew by, totally ignoring us. For we were the past, and they were the future.

There was a brisk wind off the ocean on the other side of the Vancouver International Airport as we joined the crowd waiting for the SkyTrain on the exposed platform, three stories up in the air. Weary casino and hotel employees endured the start of their long transit trip home to distant suburbs. Beside them were excited post-teenagers dressed up for a night out in one of the dance clubs downtown, and a scattering of tourists, exhausted from long flights, guarding their rolling suitcases while attempting to figure out the correct stop for their hotels. Then there were us, middle-aged and waiting for transit to take us home.

I was so tired of giving this city so much and yet feeling as if it was leaving me behind. No. We had already been left behind. And unless we did something dramatic, something bold, we would be buried under and forgotten entirely. We needed to make new choices. And we needed to make them now.

I turned from staring at the rows of new condominium towers in Richmond, most of the windows dark—the majority owned by people who lived overseas. These were their little safety deposit boxes for money stolen from foreign lands, making them unattainable to people like us who were merely born here.

"Remember when I showed you my time machine?"

"Yeah, we laughed and laughed. You showed us a nice box. Good times," Neil said sarcastically.

"Jesus Christ, Neil, could you be serious for one goddamn moment!"

They reacted, stepping back. I don't yell. Ever.

"Whoa, dude, take a pill. The whole time machine thing was a sad joke," Neil muttered.

"Do I look like I'm joking?" I did not look like I was joking, and they knew it.

Gina looked at me, worried, then said, "Colin, why are you being like this?"

"Because I'm fed up with the turns that my life has taken. Because I didn't make the right choices at the right time thirty years ago, I'm going to be homeless and unemployed at fifty-five. Because this city has abandoned us, and we probably won't survive. So, now's the time to do something."

"And your suggestion is?" Gina asked.

"Exactly what I said. Was I speaking in tongues?"

"You showed us a pretty black box," Terry said. "You're telling me it is a—"

"Yes." I looked each of them in the eye before continuing. "I believe that box is an honest-to-god Time Machine. And we can use it to fix our lives."

"On behalf of everyone present, I call bullshit," Neil said, slouching back on the couch. We were in our living room, Damage Done's first album sonically destroying our nightmare-inducing memories of their all-acoustic concert debacle.

My precious collection of concert stubs were scattered on the coffee table. I couldn't fling the robot puke barcode in my phone from tonights show onto the pile. Another tangible piece of my personal history reduced to one's and zeroes.

My grandmother's black box was upside down on my lap. I looked for anything out of the ordinary.

On the bottom. Of my time machine.

Neil was right. This was bullshit. But what choice did I have? What would you have done if you were in my place? Forget that you might have an actual time machine and continue using it to store ticket stubs? Or would you use it?

"Hang on. Isn't that a slot, Colin, right there at the edge?" Gina said beside me. She was using her phone as a magnifying glass.

"I need something really thin."

Neil handed over a guitar pick I'd scored from Richie Sambora at a Bon Jovi concert. I carefully slipped it into the narrow gap. There was the gentlest of clicks. A part of the base eased slightly open.

I removed the guitar pick and tossed it at Neil triumphantly. "Still wanna call bullshit?"

"A hole in a box. Woo."

Gina gently slid the thin piece of wood to the side. There was a narrow, deep compartment running the depth of the left wall of the box. Gently, we turned the box over and gave it a shake. A tightly folded piece of parchment dropped out into her lap.

"This is so cool!" Terry said, moving to sit on the coffee table in front of us.

It was cool. Indiana Jones cool.

Putting the box aside, I carefully unfolded the parchment. It was thick, clearly old, but in surprisingly good shape. A secret note in a hidden compartment in a mysterious time machine! I turned the note over and sighed in frustration. Intricate Chinese writing covered the page.

Terry asked, "Can you read it?"

I shook my head. In addition to not speaking it, Mandarin was a language I couldn't read—except to order Dim Sum.

Gina asked, "Could we ask your grandmother for help?"

"I don't know. I think she'd be angry that I told you about the machine. I'm supposed to keep it a secret. Let's try to figure it out first."

While Neil grabbed another round of beers from his apartment, we considered our dilemma. We couldn't ask anyone to translate the parchment because we didn't know what it said. It looked old enough to be authentic, so anyone translating it would then know our secret.

"Hang on," Gina said, waving her phone. "Google Translate."

I laid the parchment flat on the coffee table. Gina aimed her phone at it, and we watched her screen as the symbols flickered and fluttered before locking in to display a series of words in English. With a gasp, she looked at me. It had worked!

"Huh. 'Single proof, one minute of the past, grip the pin, turn against the sun.' That's all," I said, reading off Gina's screen. Gina screen-grabbed the translation, so we had it.

Terry considered the words. "Test drive? Go back a minute to prove the machine is real?"

"Makes sense, but what's 'turn against the sun'?"

We tossed ideas back and forth until Neil returned with a six-pack of Red Truck Endless Summer Golden Ale. We filled him in on what we had discovered while he handed out beers. He started to twist off the cap of his beer, but stopped and looked down at the bottle.

"Guys," he said, then makes the universal gesture of opening a bottle of beer. We raised our beers in a toast, but Neil shook his head and repeated the gesture. "Righty tighty, lefty loosey. A counter-clockwise turn of the knob."

"Did the ancient Chinese have clocks? I'm pretty sure the concept of clockwise and counter-clockwise didn't exist before the invention of clocks."

Neil shrugged, twisted the cap off his beer, and expertly flicked it across the living room before taking a long drink.

"The sun!" Terry suddenly exclaimed. "The only reason we say clockwise is that the arms of a clock rotate from left to right, mimicking the sun crossing the sky. It's that way all over the Northern Hemisphere, including China."

I opened the box and stared inside at the polished obsidian knob. Turn against the sun would be a turn to the left. I reached for the knob when Terry stopped me.

"Wait! How will we know you've gone back a minute?"

"My watch. It will be a minute slower."

"Like in Back to the Future when Doc Brown tests the DeLorean with his dog!" Neil said helpfully.

We looked at each other and then at the box. Even if this was a joke, there was no way I couldn't try it. How could I not? Also, going back in time for a minute was more incredible than anything I had ever done in my entire life. It was like the moment before you jumped out of an airplane. A sinking in your stomach, a million butterflies. There was a fear that this was all an elaborate joke, but there was also a rising—not fear, nervous anticipation, maybe—that it wasn't a joke. That it was real.

I checked my phone against Gina's watch to ensure they were synchronized. My heart pounded in my chest. I hoped no one knew. Like stepping out of the plane. That would be a better analogy if I had ever skydived.

"Well, here goes nothing," I said, then twisted the knob gently counter-clockwise. It rotated a half turn and stopped with a click.

I looked up at everyone in their seats. They were unchanged.

Slowly, I held out my arm to show everyone my phone. Gina put her watch beside it.

They were the same, to the second.

Everyone exhaled the breaths we didn't know we were holding.

"Shit," I said and stared down at the box in my lap.

"Like I said, bullshit. You owe us beers, Yipper. Many beers," Neil said in disgust.

I turned the knob again. It rotated and clicked, just like before.

I looked at Gina's watch. Still the same.

Terry said, "What does 'grip the pin' mean?"

"Hold the knob, you knob."

"Neil, a knob isn't a pin, you pinhead."

I looked up at Gina. "He's right, that doesn't make sense."

There had to be something else. It made no sense that a time machine wouldn't have some sort of safety switch built in. I probably had turned that knob at some point in the years since I had received it. I slid my index finger around the inside of the box, pushing down into the corners while Terry and Neil continued to throw elementary school barbs back and forth.

Ow!

I yanked my finger out of the far right corner and watched a small drop of blood ooze from my fingertip. I held it up to Gina who gasped.

"The box needs to know I'm the rightful owner by checking my blood."

Terry said, "So, in addition to being a time machine, that box can also do DNA tests?"

I shrugged. "Let's find out."

I put my finger back into the corner and felt for the pin I knew was there, no bigger than the tip of a sewing needle. With the knob in one hand, I pushed my finger onto the pin and turned the knob counterclockwise until it clicked.

Everyone was the same when I looked up. Nothing had happened, again.

Then Gina held her watch out to my phone.

My iPhone was a perfect sixty seconds behind.

8

Twenty-one days later, on September 29, 2017, at exactly midnight, I went back in time.

The four of us, three dressed in black on black, and me in a suit that flattered nothing about me or the decade it came from, stood on the roof of an old four-story commercial building in downtown Vancouver at five minutes to midnight. The structure that used to house the city's best and largest music store—the beloved, copied but never replicated A&B Sound —was now an empty husk. It was a fading memory of better times when the business of selling music to youth required four floors full of LPs, cassettes, stereo, and televisions, and later, CD's, VHS and Betamax tapes, with brief forays into Laserdisc and other bleeding-edge technologies. But that was over, first ruined by Napster and now gone like Napster.

Street sounds floated up from Seymour Street below. The Railway Club was at the end of the block to the left. The northern edge of Gastown, four blocks to the right. Taxis collected businessmen from the high-priced Gotham Steakhouse one street up. Darkened office towers looked down. Ubiquitous apartment towers lurked in the distance, waiting to move closer and consume what businesses remained.

Was I actually going to go back in time? Was I delusional and had dragged my friends along on a futile quest for a better future when I should send out resumes and search for a new apartment? How bad does your life have to be to push aside overwhelming life crises to obsess over the absurd possibility that I could travel back in time to make things better for us? Would Xanax and a forest meditation retreat have been a better choice?

We were about to find out.

•

Three hours ago, I had been packing my old backpack for a trip unlike any other I had ever taken. Unless this was a practical joke my non-practical joke playing grandmother was playing on me. If that was the truth, then my levels of gullibility were so high I shouldn't be allowed out in public. And yet, we had put so much time and effort into this plan on the naïve and most likely flawed idea that my pretty black lacquered box was more than a place to store old ticket stubs, that it was an actual way to travel back through time. What did that say about our mental states? Our lives were so out of whack we were pinning our future, not on the long odds of a lottery ticket but on an idea—a concept—with an even more infinitesimal chance of success. Not six numbered balls picked out of 49 on the weekly lottery, but of the universally recognized theories of space and time being tossed into a blender and set to pulse.

Everything for my trip was laid out on our bed. Gina double-triple checked for anything which could bust me as being from the future. I had already checked, but the second pair of eyes always helped in situations like this. Except, to my knowledge, no one had ever been in a situation like this.

As we searched for any giveaway post-1984 clothing tags, my newly long hair drooped down over my eyes. Ancient body recollection took over, and a couple of head flips got it back out of the way until next time.

"Are these songs old enough?" Gina asked, holding up a handful of custom mix cassette tapes. I nodded, having written the recording dates—in pen—onto the original cassettes. But I wasn't taking my precious originals. I'd made dubs onto old blank cassettes.

I held up the ties we had found in my father's closet. "Which one works best with this suit?"

"The one the color of puke."

I looked down at the suit I wore. Lapels which could set me aloft in a strong wind; a pattern like the explosion of a half-dozen brown felt pens; and, best of all, suede elbow patches. Any fashion defence of my suit was futile. Gina grabbed the wide tie in the shades of Mexican food vomit and folded it.

"You have batteries for your Walkman?"

I nodded. Gina leant against our chest of drawers. She crossed her arms and watched as I loaded a new battery into my mint yellow Sports Walkman, the one with the built-in AM/FM radio. The one which cost me an entire summer's wages in 1984. But once I survived my parents' dismay overspending the entirety of my savings on that 'silly music player,' my life completely changed. My music now came with me, anywhere and at any time.

Anyone born post-iPod does not know. Tell a kid today that they'd need to physically sit in their bedroom to listen to the music they liked, but only if they'd taken a trip to a record store and purchased the album first. Hell, with four thousand songs on my phone, I had room for thousands more. But back then, PW—pre-Walkman—when I left the house, I left with no music. I rode the bus with no music; walked to school with no music. Get the picture? Nearly all waking hours with no music.

But then came the Walkman. I didn't have to stay in my bedroom to listen to my music. My daily life now had a soundtrack customized by me, for me. Of course, not a complete soundtrack. A 90-minute cassette could contain 24 songs. But c'mon, from zero music to 24 songs? And then another 24 songs in my pocket on another tape? Over a hundred if I had my backpack with me. Could you even imagine? Even if I only had one cassette, I had music—music chosen by me—at my fingertips! Although portable was a bit of a stretch since an original Walkman was about the size of a brick and weighed almost the same. You couldn't attach it to your belt because its heft would drag your pants down to your ankles, so it came with a shoulder strap, allowing you to wear it like a high-tech man-purse.

"Are you sure you want to do this?" Gina asked, bringing me back from my Walkman-induced reverie.

I stopped packing, and she joined me on the end of our bed. She fiddled with the brightly colored afghan her grandmother made for her. It had lain across the foot of our bed since we had moved in together. I took her hand in mine. Then I looked up at the two of us in the mirror above the dresser. I stared at the woman I've loved for more than half my life and liked for even longer. The woman I would risk looking stupid for if tonight's adventure failed and ready to go back in time for if it succeeded. My heart fluttered, and my breath stumbled. I wasn't sure which potential outcome was the cause. She looked up, unwound her fingers from the Afghan, and smiled back. That smile was one I'd loved for all these years. Her cute overbite, a slight nibble on her lower lip, the bit of a pout which had always driven me out of my mind. All of a sudden, I realized that her smiling could be something I would never experience again if this went wrong.

"Colin, did you hear me?"

"You mean, do I want to find out if this is all a joke and we've wasted three weeks instead of finding a new place for us and new jobs?"

She laughed. "Yeah, pretty much."

"How about we deal with all that after midnight? Everything in my understanding of the world points towards my grandmother pulling my leg or having dementia. Hell, everything in written history points to one of those two options. Except my grandmother doesn't have a sense of humor."

"And she's sharp as ever. Mind like a steel trap."

Gina leant in and hugged me, putting her head against my chest. Taking a breath, I hugged her back. I smelled her usual shampoo, her Oil of Olay face cream, her Eau de perfume—Lauren by Ralph Lauren, a scent I associated with no one else—her chest expanding and contracting against me. She pulled me tight.

"But Gina, if my grandmother was telling the truth and that innocent box I store ticket stubs in turns out to be the real deal, then I guess I'll be the first person ever to go back in time."

"Yeah, that's what I'm worried about. You back in time. Alone."

"I'll be fine, Gina. I know that time."

She tipped her head up and looked deep into my eyes. "But it won't be the same as you remember it, Colin. It can't be."

At a loss for words, I kissed her instead of saying something stupid or trite. Kissed her as if I wouldn't ever see her again. I needed to absorb her touch, smell, taste one last time. She kissed back with equal passion. Maybe she was thinking the same as me. We forgot about packing until Neil yelled that our taxi was outside.

I grabbed my battered Minolta camera bag, Gina shoved my laid-out supplies into my old backpack, and we left.

"Do we have to do this at midnight because that's only five minutes away?" Terry fidgeted on the roof, unsure what to do with himself. Three hard weeks creating a plan for my trip—if it worked, and I went back in time—and Terry's non-stop brain had been a significant component of our strategy.

"I doubt it matters when I go back exactly. Neil picked midnight because it's more dramatic."

"Totally the coolest time, and check out how quiet it is up here."

"God, Neil, on an abandoned building, of course, the roof will be quiet."

While Gina and Neil bickered, Terry took me over to the edge of the roof. Terry took my hand in his when we stopped at the low parapet, buses, and taxis cruising by four stories below us.

"I'm reserving judgment on whether this is a joke, Colin. But..."

"What?"

"But if this is real," he said, deadly serious. "You can fuck our lives up if you're not careful. Ripples."

"I remember, Terry, any interaction with anyone can cause ripples, which could possibly negatively affect our present lives."

"No." He gives me a light slap on the cheek to reinforce the 'no.' "EVERY interaction with EVERYONE can fuck up our lives."

I looked at him, startled. He had expressed this same concern a thousand times, but not with the slap. Terry sighed. "God help me, I've gone and drunk the Kool-Aid, and actually believe you'll poof out of existence in a couple of minutes. Please be careful, all right? You're only going for three days, right?"

"Rule 5: three days, three hours, three minutes and three seconds," I said.

"Stay out of sight. Impact nothing. And for God's sake, don't go looking for anyone you know. Especially not the four of us."

"I won't. I promise," I said.

Terry eyed me, gave me a nod, then a kiss on the cheek. He slipped an envelope into the inside pocket of my suit. I looked at him, curious, and he said, "Forget about that. A sort of insurance policy." Then Terry patted the pocket and walked back over to the others.

I had drunk the Kool-Aid as well. An amusing distraction from the realities of my sucking life had become real at a visceral core level. If I didn't go back in time, after weeks of not believing but planning as if I would, it would gut me.

"Two minutes to go, Yipper," Neil called out.

I crossed the tar and gravel roof to the others. I took out my camera and placed it on a welded shut roof vent.

"That's your dad's old film camera, right?" Terry called to me.

I nodded, not making eye contact. I hadn't taken an actual photo in years, so why was I taking a camera back in time? Because I was going back in time! I could take a break from our plan to take a few innocent photographs. That way, I would have proof of my trip if no one remembered it when I got back. Terry had grudgingly agreed that there was no way I could alter the timeline and cause a future catastrophe by taking photos. Unless someone noticed me and then stepped into traffic and died before they wrote and published a life-changing motivational book. I promised to be circumspect and not kill anyone. Terry then allowed me to take back my dad's old camera from the '60s. Which I swapped out for an old-looking but state-of-the-art Minolta DSLR I had picked up on eBay two weeks ago without anyone knowing.

I aimed the camera back at Gina, Terry, and Neil. I set a timer then joined them.

"One for the history books," I said, turning towards the camera in a dramatic pose as Gina handed me my grandmother's black lacquer box. With serious faces, we waited ten seconds until the flash went off. A record for posterity.

Gina took the box back, not letting Neil near it while I packed up my camera and grabbed my old backpack. I stood up and took a breath.

Gina said to me, "Rule 4."

"Only take what you carry and wear."

She nodded.

Terry: "Rule 2."

I said, "Arrive back in the same location you left."

Neil: "Rule 1."

"One trip only."

He nodded. Gina pulled me aside.

"I don't want you to go, Colin. I have a bad feeling about this. You—we—haven't thought this all the way through."

"I'm going to be fine, Gina. Terry's rules when I'm in the past. I swear I'll hide in my hotel room and only come out to do our plan."

Her eyes teared up. "You know why I waited for you? Because you're one of the good ones. You're not an asshole, you never changed. You're that sweet lovable kid I sat in my rec room with a million years ago. So I waited for you to get brave and take a chance and kiss me. But it was never a chance, Colin. I was waiting for you. All those years, I was waiting for you. And I don't want to lose you now."

"What choice do I have? I've got to go back and I promise I will come back to you. I promise."

"You can't promise me that, Colin. You don't know what choices you're going to make back then and how they're going to ripple out."

She was right. I didn't know what would happen. And I didn't know what to say to reassure her. So I gave her a deep kiss which Neil, for once, didn't make a rude comment about. Shit was about to get real. Gina broke our kiss, wiped her eyes, then handed me the box. The three stepped back, leaving room around me for the flames, quantum portal, ion winds, or whatever might happen.

I wished I had something witty to say, but I didn't. The thoughts whirling through my head were stupid and lame, so I stayed quiet. No 'one small step for man...', instead I wondered how much time travel would hurt. The earth was light years away from where it was 33 years ago. Besides travelling through time, I would travel through a shit-ton of desolate and empty space. I was pretty sure that it would hurt. I opened the box and took a deep, nervous breath.

"Have a fucking glorious trip, Yipper! Tell the past Neil says hi!" Neil called out, a massive grin on his face.

His exuberance emboldened me. I grinned back. If this is real, what an adventure I was about to go on. If not, I owed everyone a night of heavy drinking with the money I didn't have. No. This was no place for pessimism. Forget failure. This was the moment to be positive. It was time to kick ass, change our past and save the day!

With those final thoughts echoing in my head, I sucked in a deep breath, filling my lungs, preparing for the emptiness of space. I reached into the box, shoving my index finger into the corner until I felt the prick of the needle. The black obsidian knob was strangely cold and heavy to my touch. I clamped my eyes shut and turned it hard clockwise.

9

Blip

10

Whatever experience I had expected—a momentary sensation of my entire body dipped in rubbing alcohol, then evaporated with a hundred hair dryers; yanked through twisting, twirling tunnels of time and space at the speed of light while screaming at the top of my lungs; splitting into a million separate pieces then thrust back together—didn't happen. Nothing had happened. I'd experienced more exciting moments flicking a room light switch only to find the overhead bulb dead.

Shit. It didn't work. I remained jobless and soon to be homeless. And I was broke, having maxed out my credit to finance my portion of a stupid, imaginary trip back in time. I was a fool, and I had dragged my friends along on this stupid time-wasting folly that I wouldn't ever live down. My fate, from this moment onwards, would be irrevocably tied to my pretend time machine. No doubt Neil had my gravestone carved already. 'Here lies Colin Yip - who totally didn't go back in time.'

"Sorry guys," I said. "Looks like I've fucked us up."

I opened my eyes, still glancing down at the box, my hand on the knob. I gave it another complete turn. Maybe I didn't do it right, but nothing happened. Double shit. Taking my hand off the knob, I looked up to find myself alone on the roof. "Guys?"

I snorted, then started to laugh. The whole thing had been an elaborate prank, I realized. Of course. There's no such thing as time travel. Neil had planted the letter in my room. Gina had changed the time on her watch while I turned back the dial. And after three weeks of slow-playing me, they had ditched me here on the roof. But when I stood back up, it hit me.

The surrounding skyline was different. Lower. Older. The lights on the North Shore mountains, blocked behind towers of glass a minute ago, were visible. I spun around to my left. The sky was bright blue in the west, where there should be midnight black.

Which meant…

Tuesday, June 26, 1984, 8:57:57 pm
3 days, 3 hours, 3 minutes, and 3 seconds to go

I stumbled over to the edge of the roof and looked over. An orange and brown 1950s transit bus, round-cornered like a throat lozenge, rumbled down the street, spewing exhaust. Boxy old cars from the '70s filled the street parking spots. A whirling vortex spun in my head, knocking me off balance. I looked down at my hands gripping the rough brick cornice in an attempt to convince myself I was actually here. I took another cautious glance over the edge. This time, there wasn't an accompanying roller coaster drop in my gut. The sidewalk was full of people in the glow of the bright orange A&B Sound neon sign that stretched the width of the open store.

I slipped down to the rough gravel and leaned back against the low wall protecting me from the city below. My heart pounded in my chest, breath shuddering, and panting like I had run the Vancouver Marathon. The whole marathon, not half.

If I wasn't hallucinating, if Neil hadn't spiked my water with acid like an asshole, if I wasn't currently asleep beside Gina in our bed... If, if, if.

How do you prove you weren't asleep? Or amidst a full-body hallucination? How do you prove a negative?

The gravel was rough under me, the edge of the cornice warm with the day's heat against my head. My hands shook against my jeans. Grabbing a stone from the roof, I dragged it along the back of my wrist, causing a sharp pain to jolt up my arm. Hypothesis one disproven. No way to have been asleep and experience that. Blood seeped out and pooled on my wrist. I could discount Neil dosing me as he had been into our plan as much as any of us. It would have been a cruel joke to play on me. I wouldn't have put it past him, but unlikely.

That left hallucination. Something that had never happened to me in my entire life. What were the odds of this occurring for the first time, on this roof, at this exact moment? If some unknown mental condition had caused this vivid hallucination, had I made up my friends joining me on the rooftop mere moments ago? I didn't believe so. Maybe, but, again, unlikely.

Occam's Razor.

Saw them at the Commodore Ballroom, opening for The Replacements.

Bad joke.

Occam's Razor. The simplest solution was most likely the correct one.

I fumbled in my pockets. After a couple of attempts, I got a cigarette lit.

My heart slowed down a bit, no longer beating to break out of my chest; breaths went in and out less raggedly. I smoked. I considered the options. Calmly, like a brain teaser riddle passed around on Facebook.

The simplest solution.

The box worked. I was in the past.

Three weeks ago

"So what are the rules of this time machine, Colin? Is there an online user manual?" Neil said with a smirk.

I held out an old folded piece of paper I had discovered in another hidden compartment in the base of the black box. "Yes. Here's the original, so be careful with it."

Gina took the paper and unfolded it with care. A heavy page covered in faded Chinese script. We all leaned in to see as Celina stepped up to our table with a coffee pot.

"Huh, that's pretty old. You'd better protect it," she said. Neil started whistling for no apparent reason as Terry sorted the sugar and Splenda packets. Gina folded it up in a futile attempt to keep Celina from seeing it. She couldn't have been more obvious in hiding the paper. Spies, we ain't. Celina shook her head and left our table.

"Guys, we need to be careful with this. We can't have anyone knowing about a real-time machine. Can you imagine the catastrophic damage which could occur if it fell into the wrong hands?"

"Jesus, Terry, an evil triad bent on worldwide domination isn't searching for this box."

"There could be," Terry said. "We'd only know after the ninja's attack and kill us."

"Ninjas are Japanese, and triads are Chinese. They don't cooperate, so we're safe."

Ignoring Terry and Neil, I removed a printed page of regular paper from my pocket and handed it to Gina.

"I got the Google to work its magic. Then I cleaned it up as best I could."

Gina skimmed the translated rules.

"Rule #3. Go back exactly 33 years, 3 months, 3 days, 3 minutes and 3 seconds."

"That's a lot of threes."

"Well spotted, Terry."

"Like the Holy Trinity," said Gina, the lapsed Catholic of our group.

"Snap, Crackle and Pop," added Terry.

"The Belmont, Preakness, and Kentucky Derby," said Neil.

Everyone looked at me.

"Uh, Huey, Dewey, and Louie?" I offered.

Lots of threes.

"Colin, you'd be going back to the summer of 1984."

The table went silent as we flashbacked to that summer. We had been twenty-two, arguably the best summer of our lives. Parties, concerts, little-to-no work pressures, summer off from post-secondary schooling, enough money to not worry about working too much, the perfect life.

"Holy shit, Yipper, you're gonna have an epic time!" Neil said, eyes aglow.

Terry came out of his reverie first and spun the paper around to read.

"Rule #6. You get 3 days, 3 hours, 3 minutes and 3 seconds in the past."

He looked up, his brain whirring. "Seventy-five hours is not a lot of time to change our future."

Now

I was in the past. It was almost too much to comprehend. I thought I could process going back in time, but I couldn't. It was like waking up in a Borneo jungle, with a foreign tribe staring down at me. Except that everything looked like my memories of being young. Hell, it smelled like when I was young. I didn't know how I knew that, but I did. I was me but in the past. The machine had worked. What had been theory was now as real as my heart beating in my chest. What if I wasn't up to the task? What if I couldn't pull off our plan? What if everything?

But I didn't have time to dwell on all those 'what if's.'

It was time to take a deep breath, pull up my big boy slacks and get on with it.

Before leaving the roof, I took a dozen shots of the skyline. Ok, I told Terry it was my dad's old Pentax 35mm film camera—which he bought on a trip to Hong Kong before he married my mom. But why not take my old-looking but super HD modern Minolta instead? No one could tell the difference, and the quality of the shots would be so much better. Like a million times better. Where was the harm in that?

Choosing a shot, making multiple conscious and unconscious decisions about the framing, the settings, the act of committing to push the shutter grounded me somewhat. I took a few more, sliding back into the flow of something I once did a lot. I had put serious photography away like my old Hot Wheels cars, packed in a box in my parents' basement. Everyone had a smartphone with a camera now. The art of planning a shot had shifted to impulse and a lot of selfies.

Taking these same photos with the equipment I had owned in the '80s would have required a lot of planning and complex long exposures. Now, my DSLR adapted to the available light, and I fired off a stream of outstanding photographs, including an impressive set looking down on the street life below. If nothing else, I could produce an epic photo book of my time back in the past. 'Lost Photographs of Three Days in 1984 Vancouver'. Although I would have to come up with a better title.

The thought staggered me again: I'm in the past. I might have been the first person ever to do this. Although, I'd guess anyone else who'd traveled to the past and returned wouldn't be going on Letterman to chat about it. Maybe Bill Gates, Elon Musk, or Jeff Bezos had used a box like mine to succeed. How would any of us know they hadn't? Or if they had?

Enough, no more mind games. I had a meticulously plotted out itinerary and only three days to complete it.

I finished my cigarette on the roof, then butted it out in the coffee can in the staff's not-so-secret smoking area. Plastic milk crates with planks that made benches. Taking your break on a hot tarred roof was slightly more appealing than in the disgusting alley behind the building, I guessed. I packed up my camera, grabbed my backpack, and took a deep breath. The tricky stuff began now.

Step One: descend from the roof to the alley, down the internal fire stairs during business hours, without being seen, and then get to my hotel and hide.

Terry had spent three weeks pounding into my head how every little interaction in the past could be the one that ripples out into our future, causing 'catastrophic damage.' I made the mistake of asking for clarification on what he meant by 'catastrophic damage.' I had gotten a twenty-minute lecture with an extensive list of ways messing with time would render the earth inhabitable for centuries to come.

With that foreground in my mind, I stepped through the propped open fire door. I listened to the silence, then started down the stairs. They had covered the walls from floor to ceiling with promotional posters for albums and concerts of the early '80s. Any other time, I would have paused and appreciated them as a nostalgic piece of music art in a museum now long closed. But not now. Halfway to the alley, a door below me slammed open with a blast of Kenny Loggins' 'Footloose.' I froze. I took a peek down the open center of the staircase. Shit, I could see three hands coming up the railing two stories below. Either staff was moving between floors or going up to the roof to take a break. With no way to bluff my way past them, I ran back up a half flight and through an open door onto the third floor.

Stereos and televisions. Lower lighting, stacks of amplifiers, cassette decks, turntables, speakers the size of Smart Cars. They had created compact rooms to give potential customers the complete experience of their new system. It would have been so sweet to look around. But, remembering Terry's admonitions of full-scale nuclear catastrophe, I jumped on the down escalator before any salesperson started chatting with me. Who knows how an interaction like that could ripple out.

Example: the sales guy talked to me. Which meant he didn't speak to someone else, that someone else didn't buy a stereo, headed home earlier because of it, found his wife in bed with his best friend, killed them with a steak knife and went to prison for life instead of having a child with his wife. A child that would have won a Nobel peace prize for stopping the aforementioned nuclear conflagration. Or nothing might happen, but why take the chance, right?

It took two escalator rides to get to the main floor of A&B Sound, and the place was booming. Nine o'clock on a Tuesday night, and the floor was full of staff and customers. Giant, bulky CRT televisions hung from the ceiling, now playing Dire Straits' Money for Nothing' music video. A crowd of teens observed the bleeding edge computer animation with amazement. Rows of the top-selling albums covered the walls—Lionel Richie, Cindy Lauper, Phil Collins, Nena. I slipped into the small hip-hop section to watch the room for a while. No one had noticed me.

Actually, no one had noticed me at all. It was like I was...

Maybe I had come back in time, but was now invisible.

Who knew what happened when you slid thirty-three years through a vortex in the space/time continuum. If I was invisible, then it was a severe problem. We naively predicated our plan on me being visible. I couldn't do meetings as a ghost.

The video for Van Halen's 'Jump' replaced Dire Straits as I considered my situation. If invisible, could I interact with physical matter? Picking up a nearby copy of Run-DMC's first album resolved that question. But did picking up an LP mean I was visible or not?

I wanted to scream at everyone, 'Can you see me? Look at me! I'm from the future! '99 Luftballons' is Nena's only hit!'

An A&B Sound employee in a bold orange t-shirt, struggling with a heavy stack of LPs, bumped into me.

"Sorry, sir," he said, moving on to the end of the aisle.

I was visible! They could interact with me!

"Thanks," I called after him. He threw me a worried look, then disappeared into a storage room.

Admittedly, the whole invisibility worry had been pretty stupid. But considering my current circumstances, it was as plausible as anything else. My fingers slid along the tops of the albums in front of me. They moved, and I sensed them moving. I was a solid, functioning human. I wanted to jump for joy, high five, and fist bump everyone in the store, celebrating the successful start of my most excellent adventure.

But then I froze. How the clerk had looked at me...

Did I look different, out of place, out of time? Was it obvious I was from the future? Did I smell different? Alien? Wrong? My head spun for a moment. I leaned back against the hip-hop stacks. Dude, calm down. No one was going to beat me to death in a record store. I glanced over at the kids again. They'd wandered down the aisle to the B's where they were discussing Black Sabbath, ignoring me altogether. My paranoia subsided. Time to get outside and into the fresh air.

After a calming breath, I wove my way through the stacks. The desire to stop and browse was painful. Top albums for only $4.99! If anything could come back with me, which I couldn't because of Rule #4, I'd grab a pile of sealed albums and sell them in the future. Or keep them for myself.

Three weeks ago

Gina and I stood on Granville Street, outside the Pacific Centre Mall. Tourists and workers wandered and rushed past us. The sidewalk was busy on a beautiful Vancouver summer day. Traffic snarled to a crawl on West Georgia, heading to Stanley Park. Granville was clogged with busses. Seasoned, professional buskers blocked the sidewalks, causing backups onto the streets with their performances.

"Rule #5. Return from where you go back," I said, slipping out of the way of a dirty young guy pushing a grocery cart full of plastic bags stuffed with his mysterious possessions.

"So accessible now and accessible thirty years ago…" Gina muttered, slowly turning around, scanning the buildings.

"Parkades? Like The Hudson's Bay lot? The top floor is pretty empty most of the time."

"But how can you guarantee you won't pop back and find yourself stuck halfway through someone's car?"

I grimaced. That would make a serious mess of my trip.

"So the same goes for parks and alleys."

"Yeah. I don't want to end up in a tree or crushed by a dumpster."

"How come this part isn't easier?" Gina asked, taking my hand. She led me away from the crowds towards Gastown. As we walked in comfortable silence, each attempting to come up with a solution to this seemingly minor problem.

What I needed was somewhere to make my time trip. That place was safe, private and unchanged now and all of those parameters a mere thirty-three years ago. Gina was right. On the surface, this should have been an easy problem to solve. But this was only one of many we had to work through before I would twist the knob in the lacquer box to see what happened.

"God, remember that night when we climbed up the Sun Tower?" Gina asked as we wait for a light to change. A stream of Lycra-clad cyclists ran the yellow in the dedicated bike lane, almost wiping out a group of Japanese exchange students.

Of course, I did. On what was once the edge of downtown, the Sun Tower had been the tallest building in the British Empire when first built. Sadly, it held that distinction for only two years. It had originally housed the Vancouver World—which became the Vancouver Sun—newspaper. It had loomed above the surrounding low industrial buildings. Its octagonal tower rose to a patinaed bronze dome, with a cupola at the top like the nipple on a huge green breast. Behind it once were tidal flats, which became rail yards, and then dirt parking lots. Then Expo '86. The parking lots had become a mall, and the Sun Tower had been lost behind shiny new condo towers.

Back in the day, after a night of dancing, drinking and silly dares, the four of us had climbed up the fire escape to the tiny cupola. We had drunk cheap rye and watched the sunrise, in awe of the sun easing its way up the North Shore mountains, slowly lighting the suburbs to the east bit by bit. Sure, we could have died either climbing up or down, but there was no time to waste considering outcomes in the folly of youth. And the panoramic photos I took from up there were impressive.

The only problem we encountered was climbing back down after the sun had risen and the business day had begun. Somehow we made it without any workers noticing four 20-year-olds trying their best not to giggle descending the fire escape outside their office window.

"The cupola hasn't changed, but there's lots of visibility from those apartments surrounding it. Someone would see me, especially if there's a flash of light or something."

Gina frowned. "Good point. Damn, I figured I solved it."

We kept walking until I stopped in the middle of the block. Foreign language students pushed and shoved me while never taking their eyes off their smartphones. Gina made it a half step further before I pulled her back.

"Gina, you totally solved it."

"No, I didn't. It can't be near apartments."

"Right. A rooftop, but with surrounding offices instead of condos, that would work."

She turned and saw where I was looking.

"Hmm. Colin, you might have the answer."

•

"Nope. No way onto the roof of The Railway Club," Neil said with authority.

"But what about from the smoking deck?"

"Uh, the deck will be full of smokers who might notice the four of us boosting each other up onto the roof. And the deck didn't exist in 1984."

We were back at the Ovaltine, stuck on solving the location for my time travel. Two steps forward, one step back.

"Well, to be perfectly clear, I'm not going back until we figure out a safe place to use the time machine from."

"Time machine?" We turned as Celina looked at us, her arms piled up with our meals. Gina removed the papers from the table. Celina passed us our food, and we thanked her, but she didn't leave.

"Time machine? Is that what you're talking about?"

Terry laughed, too loud. Neil rolled his eyes and looked away. Gina bit her lip. Shit.

"Yes. We were talking about a time machine," I said. Everyone glared at me, but I continued, "We're writing a screenplay. A movie about a guy who goes back in time."

"A time travel movie. *Ay yah*, not another one," Celina said after a moment and went back into the kitchen.

"Pretty smooth, Colin," Gina said, kissing me on the cheek. "Even better, now we have an excuse when we ask people for help."

Having discovered a reasonable cover story implied we had made progress, so we started eating. I wasn't even a quarter done my Clubhouse when Neil dropped his toast and said, "Holy amazing amazingness."

We stopped eating and looked at him. "You all right?"

"I'm a genius. No, a super genius. The king of the geniuses. I know the perfect location, now and then." With a wide grin, he returned to eating, munching on a stuffed mouthful of eggs and sausage, leaving us hanging.

Finally, Terry said, for the rest of us, "And will you be sharing your solution or not?"

Neil finished a slice of toast, chewing far more than necessary to irritate us even further, before he said, "Remember where I worked when I last had a proper job? Well, I still have my keys to the building. They won't work now, but they sure as shit will work then."

And that was how I had ended up on the roof of A&B Sound.

11

Despite my overwhelming desire to hang around the main floor of A&B Sound and soak in the ambiance, I knew better than to linger. So I slipped out the exit onto Seymour Street and took a deep breath.

I was in 1984. We had hoped the time machine would work because there wasn't any other way out of our predicament. But the cynical part of me figured it was a massive cosmic joke. I would end up standing on the roof, holding the box while my friends stared at me—in the present, out of a job, priced out of the city we'd grown up in.

But here I was, back in time. I knew it in an instant because the vast majority of the people walking past were white. In 1984, Vancouver was a white city, way on the far edge of Canada, and at the end of the world in North America. Even today, if you went over those North Shore Mountains, you could walk the entire way to the North Pole and only cross a half dozen roads on your entire trip. But back now—or was it then?—it had felt a lot more isolated. There weren't many reasons for the rest of the world to come to Vancouver—wilderness, fishing, more wilderness, and not much else. Vancouver had once had a nightlife, but if you compared it to any other large city, you had to put 'night' in quotation marks. You couldn't buy alcohol on Sundays, and government-run liquor stores closed at six. An inconsequential town that thought it was more than it was only because of being the second-largest city in Canada.

On the sidewalk, strangers in non-retro clothing moved past me. Either they were talking with whoever they were with or simply strolled along. No earbuds, no hunching over to text/Tweet/Snapchat/Instagram, no distracted walking at all. Nobody yelled out one side of a phone conversation. If someone appeared to be talking to themselves, they were—so step away.

Thirty-three years disappeared, and everything was like I hoped it to be. Like I remembered. Like it actually was.

Adjusting my backpack, I headed down Seymour Street to find my hotel and check-in. I paused for a moment outside the presently closed Collectors RPM, a new and used shop with a Beatles "museum" upstairs. Right turn onto Hastings Street and past shuttered shops, memories returning as I walked. Trying on cowboy hats in the Western apparel store, but discovering how stupid I looked in a cowboy hat and even worse in cowboy boots. Having a cheap lunch in a Chinese-Canadian restaurant that was now a Starbucks. A row of stores selling locally made clothing, but in the future was the home of the Vancouver Film School.

People waited at bus stops. I avoided eye contact despite wanting to grab them by the shoulders to tell them about the future. I grinned and couldn't stop. The vehicles going by, the people walking along, the familiarity of it all washed over me like a perfect temperature shower. I crossed West Hastings at Victory Square, another place that had been the proud center of Vancouver for a while. But that was before downtown moved even farther west to the corner of Granville and Georgia.

Across Cambie Street sat my hotel, The El-Cid. A narrow old building that was a dirty, half-hearted brown-black. The four story facade implied the builder had hopes for an illustrious future, having invested in elaborate cornices and stonework. There was even checkerboard inlay between the floors. It had a dingy restaurant, The Pancho Villa, on the main floor and a cramped lobby behind grimy windows. It looked horrible. Thus perfect. No concern about room availability. Ever. A bell rang as I pushed open the heavy wooden door into the small reception area. A late-middle-aged guy with a comb-over read the paper and smoked behind the lobby counter. He looked like one of the Gringott's elves from Harry Potter. The low-hanging cloud of Players Unfiltered cigarette smoke forced a cough from my lungs.

He glanced up but said nothing.

"Any rooms available?" I asked, knowing the answer. He made a show of folding up the newspaper before checking the battered registration book. He nodded grudgingly. I was dealing with Mr. Conversation here. That was fine, as I didn't come back to find new friends to hang out with and chat about life. And if I did, it wouldn't be with the sad-sack behind this counter.

"A single for three nights, please."

He sighed, dug around for a pen, but found a grimy stub of a pencil instead. He then pushed a registration form across the desk. I filled it in using a fake name and a made-up Calgary address. I doubted there would be any backlash if I had used my real name—there were more than a few Colin Yip's in the world—but why would I have been at the El-Cid when my actual address was less than a half an hour walk away? Hence a Calgary address the old guy didn't acknowledge.

"$19.95 a night, in advance." Whoa, the elf spoke. I pulled out three old twenties from my living money.

Thanks to E-Bay and a few local currency shops, we had tracked down and purchased four hundred dollars in old pre-1984 Canadian cash for me to use while back in time. We hadn't bothered with coinage, but my wallet contained an array of bills—ones, twos, fives, tens and twenties—each with a much younger Queen Elizabeth on them. Old paper money, not the new flashy plastic bills we had now. The paper ones and twos had brought back long-gone memories of youthful allowance, those bills now replaced with loonies and toonies.

As expected, he didn't ask for any identification. Neil remembered using the hotel for a few affairs back in the day and knew it was less than stringent with their check-in procedures, which explained why I was staying here instead of at the Hotel Vancouver or the Hyatt—both far cleaner and more hygienic choices. And, compared to 2017, super affordable.

He passed me a proper old room key with the hefty plastic tag with my room number inscribed on it. Our interaction was complete. The old guy unfolded his newspaper, lit up a new cigarette, and returned to ignoring me. Clearly, no bellhop would come to assist me to my room with my luggage. I checked my room number on the tag, stepped over to the old elevator, and pushed the call button.

"Elevator's broke," he said, not looking up from the sports section.

He continued through a deep inhale of his hand-rolled cigarette, "J.J. Daigneault, who the hell is he?"

I glanced back. He waved the paper. The back page was about the NHL Draft that had just happened.

"I wouldn't know."

He scowled at me. "It's the start of another garbage season for the Canucks. I don't know why I bother."

I shrugged and left him to his life in the lobby.

It took four flights of creaking stairs that smelled of old grease and rotting food and a walk down the filthy hallway to find my room at the back of the building. I had to struggle to push the door open, the jamb warped with age and a dozen layers of lead based paint. I stepped inside, flicking on the light switch to view my room. My first impulse was to turn off the light again. Old, worn carpeting which might have started as burgundy, walls with patterned velvet wallpaper, yellowy-orange bedspread, and curtains. Anything that yellowy-orange color might have once been white, but the invasive stench of old cigarette smoke hinted at nicotine staining. The ceiling, which had once been white, was the same sick color, proof of many years of chain-smoking.

The smell of a long smoked-in room had seeped into every nook and cranny, marinated into each piece of furniture, ever-present in the air, despite any attempts to eradicate it. My god, Neil had brought dates here? How sad was that? Romance with a side of despair, please. Hold back all hope at the door.

Tossing my pack onto the bed, I stepped over to the window and pulled the curtains apart, releasing a cloud of dust. There was a first time for everything, and my touching the grimy curtains was a first for at least a decade. Looking out the dirty window, I discovered why. My view, if you'd like to call it that, opened to a dark, narrow alley and the wall of another dirty old building. A thin slice of the sky was visible through a haphazard array of electrical cables strung up along my side of the alley. After spending a whole ten seconds taking in the panorama, I shut the curtains again, disrupting more dust.

Despite the all-consuming awfulness of my room and the utter indifference of the guy downstairs, now that I stopped moving, the enormity of where I was—when I was—hit me again. I was in the past! I had done it! For the first time since I had gotten laid off and our house got sold out from under us, I felt hope for the future. Unrestrained, I let out a yell, a hoot, and a round of fist-raised jumps like a kid opening a Xmas present expecting socks but finding an X-Box. I was in the past. With that out of my system, I took stock.

This room would be my hideout for the next three days. Terry's warning returned—check in to my hotel and stay there. Avoid any contact with anyone. Limit my interactions with everyone. Especially people I knew. He was right. Any little thing I did could mess something up, which would impact us when I went back to the future. A movie not coming out until next year.

In the room's corner, across from the bed, sat a battered twenty-two-inch Electrohome television with a heavy chain looping through the top handle and running to a thick eye bolt screwed into the wall behind it. I glanced around for a remote, then stopped. No remotes in 1984. This was old-school TV watching. I sat on the bed while the TV fully warmed up, the screen randomly flickering as it settled in. A green hue across the top quarter of the screen, a sign someone had knocked it hard.

CBC. The National nightly newscast was in progress. Knowlton Nash spoke about Pierre Trudeau's legacy and the upcoming federal election between John Turner—the Liberal party candidate and newcomer Brian Mulroney, the Progressive Conservative party candidate. I could make money on that outcome, knowing the PC's would win the election handily despite Turner having a considerable lead at this point. But I knew all of this, so I crossed the room to change the channel.

Halfway there, I was hit with a sudden clear childhood body memory of doing precisely this, enduring programs not worth watching by being too lazy to get up and hike across the rec room to change the channel. Or adjust the volume. The race with my siblings to dibs on the couch, the last one to dib forced to act as the remote control. First dibs got the TV Guide magazine, which arrived in the mail each week. Back in the days when you had to pay for the knowledge of what would be on television.

The challenge came with finding something we could agree on before our father lost it with the incessant channel changing and literally pulled the plug to end our TV watching. Which he frequently did. We tried to work out our evening viewing in advance, with each of us circling in the TV Guide our show preferences in unique colored pencils. Sometimes it worked, sometimes it didn't. So, like the last dibber in years past, I stood at the TV, turning the dial through the few available channels, looking for something to hold my interest.

CBC, BCTV, then KOMO, KING and KIRO from Seattle, PBS. That was it. Six channels. The entire Vancouver TV world in 1984. At least in a hotel room of The El-Cid.

Click. Love Boat rerun on ABC.

Click. Hiss of an empty channel.

Click. The A-Team on NBC.

Click. Nova on PBS.

Click. Hiss of an empty channel.

Click. Hiss of an empty channel.

Click. Hiss of an empty channel.

Click. A 'formatted to fit on television' version of 'Airport 1977' on CBS.

Click. Hiss of an empty channel.

Click. Hiss of an empty channel.

Click. CBC again.

I sighed, turned off the TV, listening to it shut down with a groan and a sizzle, and went back to the bed. Someone in the next room was watching The A-Team, volume at full. Time to unpack. I hung up the suit and dress shirt in the closet and changed into jeans and a plain t-shirt. I placed my shaving kit on the edge of the sink in the tiny, dirty bathroom. The wide orange rust stain in the sink matched the ones in the toilet and the bathtub. There wasn't a room safe, so our nest egg would stay on my person until I sold it. Unpacking complete.

Pulling a battered, late '70s Robert Ludlum paperback out of my pack, I leaned against the headboard. The sound of the TV in the next room vibrated against my entire body. Mr. T was pitying some fool. I shut the book and closed my eyes in frustration. Seventy-two hours of this? Worse than living at home again, my older sister playing her terrible music in the room next to mine. I swore I considered killing myself the summer she bought the 45 of Paper Lace's 'Billy, Don't Be A Hero,' she played it so much. Over and over again. Non-stop. Agony. I went grocery shopping with my mom once to get away from it. That's how much I hated that song and that feeling of being trapped, unable to escape someone else's noise.

Lying clothed on the bed because I wasn't going to bring a case of 80s bedbugs back to the future, I cycled through the steps I would take in the morning, our carefully crafted plan to make us debt-free and wealthy. Every action, every step debated, argued about and resolved, either on our porch or at the Ovaltine. It took us three long weeks to create a cohesive plan. Even with the four of us plus Celina working to break it apart, it had held solid. As perfect as any plan to go back to the past and change the future could be.

The A-Team ended next door. The TV turned off. Grateful for the silence, I returned to my book. Then the sex—or ritual murder—began on the other side of the wall, right behind my head.

Enough.

I grabbed my room key and shoved it into the back pocket of my old school Levi 501 jeans. To hide my belongings, I dragged the bed out from the wall and dropped my pack down into the corner behind the filthy backboard amongst the fifty-year-old dust bunnies. Once the bed was pushed back the room looked the same as before. Pointedly ignoring Terry's warnings of catastrophe, I grabbed my camera bag, and headed out to visit the city of my youth.

"What can I get ya?" the bartender asked. To my surprise, I remembered her. She had been a fixture here for the '80s and well into the '90s. I had come down with my brother-in-law when his first child was born in 1991. She had shouted us our beers and a couple of shots of rye in celebration.

"What's on tap?"

"Canadian and Blue."

"Quite the selection," I said with a smile. I would have sworn they had a fantastic local beer, Shaftesbury Cream Ale, on tap by now, but obviously not. My memory wasn't what I thought it was. I was trapped in pre-craft beer Vancouver. The only choices being the Molson/Labatt's big boys with their lifeless corporate lagers. If you had grown up in the great beer drought, you'd rejoice in every quirky whit-biere, saison, triple-bock, triple-hopped IPA, sea-salt caramel porter, and double macchiato coffee stout. Yes, I was proud to be a beer snob.

"We could have one keg below, and you wouldn't know."

"True enough." I took a quarter out of the tip jar and tossed it. Heads.

"You win?"

"I've lost either way. Canadian, please."

She grinned and took a glass out of the fridge, then pours me a pint. "$2.00."

After handing her three ones, I took my beer to an open table in the back corner. A battered Georgia Straight—Vancouver's free entertainment newspaper—was waiting for me. In his pre-Boomtown Rats / Live-Aid days, Bob Geldof lived here and worked for the paper, wrote articles. One of early Vancouver's few claims to fame.

I started reading the cover article on John Lithgow, who was starring in Footloose, and then had Buckaroo Banzai coming out in the fall. Sipping my beer, I flicked through the paper, checking out the record specials on the ubiquitous full back page ad for A&B Sound until I found the 'what's on' section. Then I started snickering to myself, remembering bands, clubs, and shows as I read about what would happen during my three days in the past. Not that I would do anything but stay in my hotel room, on Terry's orders.

But I could have gone to check out one of the many strip joints that littered downtown. Most of them long gone—their former locations now mostly expensive condo towers. No.5 Orange lived on—I could pop by and see if Jon Bon Jovi and his band were hanging out there, in town to record their 'Slippery When Wet' album. Yeah. Because that was who I had come back in time to hang out with.

I turned the page to the club listings. Whoa. NoMeansNo was playing at the Town Pump tonight? Los Popularos with Art Bergmann at the Savoy tomorrow? How could I stay in my room at that shitty hotel with all these photo opportunities? Terry, if you can hear me through the mists of time, I promise I won't talk to anyone I recognized.

Someone ripped out the rest of the page, so I moved on to the movie listings. If I had spare time, taking in a film couldn't impact anything, right?

Ghostbusters, Gremlins, Indiana Jones and the Temple of Doom were each playing on the big screen.

Sure, I owned them on Blue-ray, and they're all streaming, but it would be amusing to see any of them in the theatre one more time. Maybe if I accomplished everything tomorrow, I could spend my spare hours hidden in a movie theatre.

I left after one terrible industrial beer, eager to walk down to the Town Pump for some live music. Gastown was quiet. Only a few brave tourists milled around the steam clock. I made good time, pausing only once to frame a pic of a group of girls out on a tear. I caught the moment when their back-combed hair, pink and purple eye shadow, and thick, chunky heels wobbled across the cobblestone street past a couple of old guys in faded suits and fedoras.

The Town Pump had a five-dollar cover—explain to me how three bands can survive splitting my five bucks? I grabbed a Lucky Lager in a brown, stubby bottle from the bar and stepped into the fray. The Pump was a couple of low-ceilinged, claustrophobic rooms at the front, one with the bar and tables, the other with tables and a pool table.

But at the back, through a narrow brick archway, the room doubled in height with a second floor of 'deluxe' seating and a private party room. A single row of chairs stared down at the dance floor and the shallow stage crammed against one wall. With the sound and light booth across the stained and scuffed dance floor, the bands looked from the stage at a two-story brick wall running down the center of the building. Anyone wanting to sit and watch was stage right on a raised seating area or up a flight of stairs to the left. I'd been on that stage, taking photos, and the view was bizarre, performing to that imposing brick wall.

The Legions of Doom finished up their set, punk with a light misting of melody, and NoMeansNo crowded the stairs, waiting to go on. The bands were sharing the same drum kit, so the change over would be quick.

On the steep stairs, I pushed past guys I'd known for years but who didn't even see me. I didn't even appear on their radar. A single chair sat empty against the railing. Yes! There was an unobstructed view down at the crowd milling on the dance floor and seated across the room. Young. Everyone was young. Exuberantly youthful. Mostly, the same crowd as was at the Rail. Under thirty, for sure.

I was the odd one here, and the sensation was weird. The four of us went out in the future, but when we did, the shows we attended attracted a broader range of ages than usual. Maybe it was because we enjoyed checking out new young music. Either way, the vibe was a lot different in here, and people eyed me with a mix of confusion and distrust. What the hell was this old guy doing here? That was what was going through their heads. I would have thought the same thing at twenty-two. Old man, this was our music scene, not yours.

I was a million years old to them. Maybe I should have grabbed the mic and let them all know what they're in for—a future of recessions and massive debt. But with Buck Rogers amazing technology to distract from being the first generation not to have a future better than your parents.

While waiting for the band to start, I sipped my industrial lager and did the math. Being fifty-five in 1984 meant, in this reality, I had been born in 1929. When these kids looked at me, they saw someone born before the Great Depression and the Second World War. Who thought Elvis Presley, not Elvis Costello. Frank Sinatra, not Frankie Goes to Hollywood.

Before I could wrap my head around this depressing train of thought, NoMeansNo exploded onto the stage. The crowd surged forward, the first row of dancers in danger of being pushed up onto the stage with the band if only there were room. I took out my camera and, holding it on my knees, started recording HD video through the railing posts, trusting in the camera's autofocus and auto light settings. But I quickly forgot about my age as the music took hold, unwinding time with each riotous four bars until I felt twenty-two again.

•

After the headline band, NoMeansNo, finally left the stage, I slipped out through the last-call crowd and headed back to my hotel. My ears were ringing from the music, and my lungs were thick from breathing in second-hand smoke for an entire night. That was how pervasive the smoke was, especially on the balcony at the Pump. Like going through a carton of cigarettes without ever needing to light one up. But who cared, and, despite the beer being swill, the bands were fantastic, and I was feeling more alive than I'd felt in years. I patted myself on the back. Despite Terry's admonishments, I had set no catastrophic perils rippling forward to destroy the twenty-first-century world. Now I could look forward to a reasonable night's sleep at my cheap hotel because tomorrow morning, I would revise our life.

13

Wednesday 8am, 64 hours to go

A delivery truck ground its gears as it backed out of the narrow alley outside my window, forcing me awake. My lungs ached like I had worked the night shift in a cigarette testing facility. Rubbing my head, I reached over for my phone to figure out the time. But I didn't have my ever-present smartphone on the bedside table because I was back in time, and they didn't exist yet. I focused enough to read 8:00 on the heavy manual alarm clock screwed to the side table through blurred eyes. The '0' flipped over, becoming a '1'. I'd hoped to rest longer, but with the grating sound of the truck backing up and moving forward for no apparent reason, I wasn't getting back to sleep, so I might as well rise and start my day. And a tremendous day it would be, for today, I changed my future.

I pulled a casual dress shirt on over my t-shirt—I had slept fully clothed because who knew what was living or had died in that bed. After lacing up my battered Doc Martin's, I grabbed my camera bag and headed out.

Behind the desk in the foyer was an old lady, the female equivalent of the old guy who had checked me in last night, right down to the ever-present cigarette. She was engrossed in what could have been the same paper. She didn't look up as I left.

Out on the street, up to Hastings, I looked for a coffee shop to start my day. But in pre-Starbucks Vancouver, instead of finding four gourmet coffee shops at each intersection, I found not a single shop willing to sell me coffee. What the hell...

Ah, right, this was the good old days. Want a coffee? Go to a restaurant. Amazing how fast the world changed. Fast forward thirty years, and now coffees-to-go were everywhere, everyone walking around with their massive Starbucks cups or insulated coffee mugs. But not in 1984, not when I needed it most.

I snapped photos of Vancouver coming to life. What I noticed were all the vehicles that didn't exist then. There were no sleek Tesla's, no SUVs or massive tricked-out pickup trucks. Lots of boxy '70s and '80s cars without a hint of design. Lumbering delivery trucks spewed diesel fumes. Everyone walking was dressed well, not flashy but properly. No tight athletic wear to be seen. Big hair everywhere.

I relaxed into photography mode, observing life around me through the lens of my camera. I had forgotten the joys of seeing the world through the camera's eye. The streets had a certain quiet without technology everywhere. Not a smartphone or iPod in sight.

I found an open cafe and spent $1.49 on a six-ounce cup of terrible coffee in a bulky ceramic mug and a couple of pieces of white toast with grape jam on a matching plate. My request for a coffee-to-go had the waitress looking at me like I was from a strange future where people drove electric cars while drinking eight-dollar pumpkin spice lattes made with organic nut milk. I passed on a refill, the single cup already burning a hole through my stomach lining. They must have started the urn sometime last week, and I had gotten the dregs. Besides, it was time to get back to begin the critical part of my day.

During my return to my hotel, I slipped into a narrow grocery store to grab a pack of Player's Light cigarettes for a buck. That included a pack of matches and eleven cents into the charity pot on the counter. The jaunty sailor on the blue and white pack reminded me of when tobacco companies could market and promote their products, or festivals and sporting events. Not so much nowadays. They were busy trying not to be sued into bankruptcy.

While waiting for the light to change at Cambie and Pender, a young guy stepped around me off the curb, looking to jaywalk. But he started crossing without noticing the orange and brown transit bus speeding up to make the light. He stepped off as the bus sped up. I reached out and yanked him back onto the sidewalk, just in time.

"Jesus! That was close! You saved my life there!" he exclaimed before running across the street as soon as traffic allowed. Shaking my head, I watched as he dashed down the road, disappearing around the corner. The signal had changed again, so I had a moment to wait. A guy my age, in a tan velour jogging suit with a matching headband, strutted into Victory Square, pulling hard on a cigarette.

That was a damn close call with the bus. That kid was lucky I had saved him.

Then Terry's voice boomed in my head, 'Every interaction can fuck up our future. Every single one!' Shit, maybe the bus should have hit that specific kid, and because I had saved him, perhaps he had run off to commit a gruesome murder. Damnit, this was complicated. But maybe if I had been at the corner, he would have seen the bus and not died, so maybe I had kept everything in stasis. Perhaps the bus wasn't supposed to make the light and would run someone over in five minutes somewhere else...

Maybe the cup of coffee I had drunk should have been served to someone else, and now they were late for work and would miss meeting the person they destined to marry, have kids with, one of whom grew up to be Canada's first astronaut and helped destroy a rogue meteorite.

Shit.

I lit a cigarette, my hands shaking, having a taste and smell flashback to smoking this brand in my twenties. I needed to relax, stay focused, and stick to the plan. 'What if's' would debilitate me, and I had to be on track now. Terry's voice in my head was making me crazy.

I finished my cigarette before going into my hotel, only realizing that I could smoke anywhere once I was in the foyer. Possibly not in hospitals. But I had better stick to only smoking outside, or else when I returned forward in time in less than three days, I'd light up in a coffee shop without a thought. Then a swarm of Lululemon-clad mothers would beat me to death with their Fendi baby bags to protect their newborn's delicate lungs.

Damn, that had been a strong cup of coffee.

Once in my room, I put on my snazzy new old suit and slapped more gel into my now long hair. I was ready for the biggest role of my life. It was time for me to pretend to be a suave, polished businessman on a mission from the future.

Two and a half weeks ago

We had passed around my photo albums from 1984, images of parties, concerts, and our public life. The four of us were amply represented, along with pages of Mayo in concert. I had picked up a case of Swans/ White Sails Brewing's Oktoberfest Flammenbeer, and the stereo pumped out UBC's student radio station CITR's Parts Unknown with its eclectic array of rock/pop and indie pop for our ears.

Much to my embarrassment, Gina was the most photographed person in each of the albums.

"What were you doing taking so many pics of me?" she asked with a grin. In 1984, we were about six years away from actually going out. She had understood I had a crush on her but chose not to do anything about it. Instead, she waited for me to make the first move, which I finally did, albeit in a tragically slow manner. Once it was official, our friends vacillated between 'I can't believe you two are a couple' and 'I always knew you'd get together in the end.' I wasn't sure which was worse.

"In what reality would I be taking so many pics of Neil?" I countered, and she laughed.

I turned the page, finding a full-length shot I'd taken of myself, using the reflection in a store window. "There," I said, pointing. "That's what I wore then. That's what I'll wear back."

Faded 501 jeans, a black t-shirt under a sixties suit jacket. Doc Martin's on my feet. My hair was long, down to my shoulders, dead straight, parted in the middle. Gina shrugged. "Not too different from what you wear now."

"Exactly, I'll be comfortable and fit in."

Neil pulled up our iCloud TO-DO list on his phone, checked off '1984 clothes'. "There. One more thing done."

I closed the album. "But these are the easy ones to check off. Finding the location for me to go back from was way harder than we thought."

"Yeah," he countered. "But we solved it, right?"

With a nod of agreement, I sipped my wine.

"That means we check it off."

Hard to argue with that.

Gina said, "What's next on the list?"

Neil scrolled down the long list we had come up with so far. He was about to say something when Terry said, "Hang on." Neil sighed and turned off his phone, placing it on the coffee table. Terry had been like this for every step of this process. Each time the three of us had agreed on a part of the plan, Terry would interject with something only he had spotted. More frustrating, his concerns were always valid and worth considering. But it didn't make the interjection any more pleasant. Sure enough, he had another issue with my clothing choices.

"God, what is it this time, Terry?" Neil groaned.

Terry gave him the finger and said, "That's the perfect outfit for you, Colin, perfect—"

"So, what are you complaining about?"

Terry ignored Neil and continued, "If you become twenty-two when you go back. But you're not a twenty-two-year-old when you go back, right? You're not inhabiting your twenty-two-year-old self's body, are you?"

"Like that '17 Again' movie? Or 'Freaky Friday'?"

"No time travel movie explains what we're doing, Neil. How many times do we have to tell you?"

"Then how did people come up with the ideas for time travel in the first place, huh? Maybe people have gone back in time for centuries, making minor or major adjustments to their lives. Maybe Hitler traveled back in time, and that's why he becomes the Fuhrer."

Terry looked at Gina and me, begging for help. I shook my head and drank my beer. Gina became preoccupied with her fingernail. Terry grit his teeth.

"Leave Hitler out of this, Neil. Please."

"You know I'm right."

"I know you're an idiot."

Terry turned to me and asked, "Do you know if you'll be inhabiting your twenty-two-year-old self's body when you're back?"

"I doubt it. The rules say to only take what I want to bring back. I guess that means I'll be wearing what I'm wearing when I arrive there. If

I were swapping bodies or taking control of the mind of my past body, the rule would say that nothing was going back, now wouldn't it?"

Even Neil was quiet as they considered my logic. In the end, everyone agreed with me, and Terry continued. "All right, so we agree when you go back, you'll be fifty-five years old." We nodded. "Therefore, you'll have to dress like a fifty-five-year-old."

"Right, and I dress the same way I do now, adjusted for the time, so my outfit will be fine."

"No, Colin, it won't," Terry said. "You dress that way now because you're a retro-stylish, metrosexual man-about-town, but normal fifty-five-year-old men in 1984 did not dress like that. If you walk around Vancouver with that outfit on, people will assume you're a pimp spending your nights at Richards on Richards doing coke in the toilet, drinking brandy and hitting on teenaged girls from Surrey who've snuck in."

Gina connected Terry's dots and said, "He's right, Colin. You'll have to look like a professional. A 1984 businessman. Try to remember what your dad wore when we were in high school."

I did and cringed. My dad had worked as a manager at the McMillan-Bloedel pulp mill on the Fraser River. He had worn terrible suits with wide lapels and ties the size of lobster bibs. Terry turned his iPad around, and we recoiled. He had found the 1982 Sears catalog online and was flicking through terrifying images of tan business suits with flared slacks. Slacks. Men in slacks.

"No way I'm wearing slacks," I said.

Gina took my hand, looked into my eyes, and said, "Honey, you have to fit in. Be respectable. Like an honest, professional doing his job before heading out to Burnaby for the delightful meal your loving wife cooked for you."

"Then I don't want to go back. Not dressed like my dad."

"Pretend it's Halloween," Neil said.

"You pretend it's Halloween," I countered maturely.

"Come on, Colin," she said, standing up. "Time to go clothes shopping."

Terry shut off the iPad. "Where will you ever find clothes that horrid?"

"You don't worry about the clothes, Terry," Gina said. "But I'll need your connections to arrange something else."

She leant down and whispered in his ear. Terry's eyes widened. He looked at me, then back at her, then nodded. "I can figure that out."

"Good," Gina said with a grin. I became worried.

"What about me?" Neil asked.

"Don't you have more time travel movies in need of watching for research?"

He hopped up and followed us out the front door. "Next on the list, 'Bill and Ted's Bogus Adventure.'"

"Don't forget to take proper notes this time," Terry called as Neil climbed the stairs to his apartment. Then he kissed Gina on the cheek and went down to his suite to solve whatever she had tasked him to work on.

"Where are we going?" I asked Gina as we left the house.

"Time to pay a visit to your parents."

Say what?

Worse than going to my parents' house—where I had grown up—to rummage through the storage area for my father's old suits was what they had planned for my hair.

As bad as wearing a hideous late '70s tan suit with men's slacks would be, Gina had realized my current fashionable haircut—very short back and sides, long and coiffed back over the top—would stand out in '84. Especially on a fifty-five-year-old Chinese professional going about his business of changing time.

"Well, Colin, it is either my idea or a buzz cut," Terry said with frustration. This discussion has taken up too much of his limited time already. And we were almost out of beer.

"What if I slick it down with Brylcreem?" I asked, desperate for another solution.

"Dude, it won't look right, even all gooped up. Trust us."

I finished my Red Arrow Midnight Umber and sighed. Now that I was out of beer, I had to decide.

I was going to regret this. I knew it. "Make the call, Terry." Terry's eyes lit up. He made the call and set up the appointment.

On the morning of my big trip, I walked out of his film-industry friends' salon with a full head of long black hair. It was streaked with gray, feathered back from a central part, covering my ears and weighing heavily on my collar. Extensions. I had hair extensions. Ostensibly for a short film I was to star in. Gina squealed with laughter. Terry gasped and bit his knuckle. Neil was the first to speak. "Damn. You funky pimp! Get down!"

I glared at them. "Not another word."

Stifling their laughter, they all nodded. "Good. I want to go home now and hide."

"We can spend the afternoon watching Saturday Night Fever!" Terry yelled. The dam broke, and they burst out laughing at me and my disco hair.

14

Step Two of our meticulously thought out plan involved Vancouver's Wall Street.

Dennis Fanshawe, the broker I'd tracked down in the future, had his offices on the tenth-floor of a building on Howe Street, near the Vancouver Stock Exchange. In the future, the VSE moved to much tinier surroundings since everything was done electronically instead of by coked-up twats screaming at each other and waving around pieces of paper on the massive trading floor.

As an amusing aside, the stock exchange floor became, for a while, the women's fashion area of Holt Renfrew—Canada's high-end retailer. That was a metaphor for something, but I didn't know what.

I rode the elevator up with a group of very white, uptight businessmen in bland suits and bad haircuts. Much to my dismay, Terry and Gina had been right. Strolling into this building wearing a t-shirt, jeans, and Doc's would have been unacceptable. Not to mention my formerly stylish hair. Sadly, I fit right in with the group in the elevator. I adjusted my tie as the doors opened on the tenth floor, and I pushed through the crowd out into the hallway.

"Chink," someone muttered behind me as the doors closed.

Ah, the good old days of overt racism. Granted, he'd most likely fought in WW2 in the Pacific. Alternatively, if I had lived my whole fifty-five years in Vancouver since being born in 1929, most of my life would have been as a second-class person, not getting citizenship until 1947, not getting the vote until 1949.

I found Dennis' office and stepped inside, full of pretend confidence. It was your basic setup: receptionist's desk, a couple of hard plastic chairs, a coffee table with a large ceramic ashtray, and a closed interior door with a frosted pane. Nobody sat behind the desk.

"Hello?"

After a moment, the frosted door opened, and a youthful Dennis Fanshawe stepped out. Gone was the soft grey skin, the comb-over, the dark bags under watery eyes, of the thirty-three year older version I had met with mere weeks ago. Instead, I saw a healthy tanned face, luxurious feathered hair and sideburns that fat-Elvis would have been proud to have. In front of me was a man on the upswing of his career and his life.

"Sorry, my girl called in sick today, so I'm on my own," he said, striding across the beige industrial carpeting to shake my hand. "Dennis Fanshawe, broker."

"Colin Yip, investor."

"You've come to the right place, Colin," he said, giving my suave business apparel an approving once-over. To my disgust, my father's old Polyester suit was the perfect outfit for this part of the plan.

"Excellent," I said, thoroughly businesslike.

"Come on in," Dennis said, and I followed him into his office, a smile on my face.

So far, so good.

Two weeks ago

Our planning had hit a snag after having procured terrible clothes out of my father's closet and keys to a rooftop. What was I traveling back to accomplish? That is, if the box was a time machine. But for now, we had to assume, possibly incorrectly, I owned a working time machine, and it would take me back to 1984. Then what?

"Leave notes for us," Neil said, pouring more of Gina's father's wine into mismatching wine glasses on our porch.

"Saying what?"

"I don't know, shit we can bet on and make money, lottery results, something like that."

Terry sipped his wine, looking thoughtful while Gina and I considered Neil's idea.

I said, "That certainly would be simple. I know where each of us was living then. We could each write out notes for ourselves. I take them back and drop them off when we're out. Voila! Our past selves come home, find the notes, do what they say, and then we're rich. No more worries."

Neil was looking pretty pleased with himself. "I'll add the names of the guys to talk to for the sporting bets. Lottery numbers would be even more simple, tell our past selves to buy a ticket with the winning numbers written on the note, and they're the winner. Like taking candy from a baby."

"Except..." Terry interjected before we could start congratulating ourselves. "So you go back and give us notes. One: would any of us believe what the note said? Unlikely. My default assumption would be that it's a stupid joke and ignore it."

"Even if you wrote the note to you?"

"You figure twenty-two-year-old me would recognize fifty-five-year-old me's handwriting? Come on."

"Ah," Neil said. "Put in one test outcome to prove we're legit, then the rest for them to bet on."

Terry nodded, allowing Neil that point, but continued. "Two: What about the people who then don't win those bets? What is the cumulative impact of thirty-three years of them not winning when they should have? What would they have done with their winnings, rippling out to the owners of the stores where they bought their new cars and stereos and clothes?"

Gina and I looked at Neil. He took a sip of wine, stalling for time before he put down his glass, stalling for more time. Then he lit a cigarette, being blatant about the stalling now. He took a deep inhale and said, "Fuck 'em."

I sighed. "Terry's right. No depriving someone else of something to give it to us in the past. Too many ripples."

"This ripple talk is bullshit," Neil said in a sulk.

Terry grabbed a pencil off the table and drew a line across a blank page of paper.

"This is our timeline."

He wrote '1962' on the left end of the line, '2017' on the right, and '1984' to the left of center.

"After Colin goes back to 1984, if he changes the timeline, this happens."

He draws a dotted line that goes up from 1984 and then runs parallel to his original line. When the dotted line gets to 2017, he stopped.

"Colin would have created the dotted timeline during his three days in the past. We would be on the solid timeline. When Colin jumps back into the future from 1984, which timeline would he return to?"

We had agreed ripples would occur as soon as I went back. Worse, anything I did or even touched in the past would potentially impact the future. Maybe not our particular fate, but someone's. Terry's diagram made it all real.

"This ripple talk is bullshit," Neil repeated, not impressed by Terry's diagram. But I was. Impressed and terrified.

"Check out the movie 'The Butterfly Effect'," Gina suggested.

"Back to my list of problems. Number three," Terry said. "What would our mini-me's do with these ill-gotten gains in 1984? Buy fast cars and die on the Sea to Sky highway to Whistler instead of staying home because we couldn't afford to go skiing? Maybe, because of becoming rich, Gina doesn't go into social work and doesn't help someone who kills themself instead of starting a world-changing business?"

I juggled Terry's three complications and realized a fourth.

"Four: If I change our lives back then, what happens to my future self when I return in three days? What if the major change I instigate means I return to the smoldering ruins of Vancouver? Or worse, there's a Starbucks on every corner?"

Terry looked chastened. He hadn't considered that. "Exactly. You have to ensure whatever you do then can not be acted upon until after you return to the present. Otherwise, the odds are improbable we'll still be in these present circumstances."

"But that's the frickin' point, Terry. Colin goes back to make sure we don't end up in this 'circumstance.'"

"But we don't want to end up a thousand times worse. Right?"

Neil was about to argue, but realized Terry was right and shut up.

"So the question is this. How, in 1984, can you help us now, with no impact on all the years in between?"

Silence.

Followed by extended silence.

Shit.

•

Our next meal at the Ovaltine was depressing. We had wracked our brains for a week. What could I do thirty-three years ago that would somehow positively influence our present lives? But while having no impact on the thirty-three years prior. We couldn't attain traction with any other idea, so we kept looping around to secret notes about lottery numbers. Our level of frustration was through the roof, and there wasn't enough of Gina's fathers' bad wine to cool us down. And who said the machine even works, right? I mean, how ridiculous was it even to imagine it could. Was I the only person on the planet with a working time machine? Come on…

"Bearer bonds!" Neil exclaimed as Celina cleared our table. Because of my screenplay lie, we no longer had to be quiet around her. If Celina believed anything other than we were trying to write a feature film, she didn't let on. Neil continued, "Go back and buy a shit-ton of bearer bonds. They're good as cash! Bring them back, and we—the character—is rich!"

"You said one rule was you can only return with what you took?" Celina asked. We looked at each other for a moment.

"She's right," Gina said.

"Ah, shit…" Neil said.

"Kids, if the plot won't work with that rule, why don't you make a new rule?" Celina said with a smile.

"We can't," Neil said glumly. Celina looked at him with confusion.

"I don't understand. If you're the writers, why can't you change the rules?"

The four of us looked at each other before I piped up, "Because we wrote the rules of the time machine first. We've committed to working within those rules."

I looked at Celina. Then she shrugged—fair enough. But she continued thinking, her hands holding our dirty plates. Faye came by, grabbed the dishes from her mother, and disappeared into the back.

"Maybe your problem isn't with the details. What kind of story is it? You've got to start there if you want to sell this. Is it a Quest or a Transformation? Maybe it's a Sacrifice story?"

Terry grinned, "Sure, Joseph Campbell, I saw the Power of Myth, great show."

The rest of us stared at each other in confusion.

Gina said, "We don't know what any of those are."

Celina laughed. "Of course you do. If you watch movies, you know them all. There are only twenty main plots in Western fiction."

Silence.

Celina smiled. "Oh, maybe it's a love story! Like 'The Time Traveller's Wife.'"

Neil said, "Yeah, the hero could go back to save the future but falls for someone in the past and stays behind."

Gina gave me a quick side-eye. That was not part of our plan.

"That's an excellent thought, Celina," Gina said, being polite.

I asked, "How do you know all this about stories and plots?"

"Are you surprised I can ask a question other than 'How do you like your eggs?'"

I was embarrassed. "No, Celina. Of course not. What I meant was…"

Celina waved my stuttering apology off as her eyes lit up with a new idea. "Although the hero could hide the bearer bonds in the past, couldn't he? Then retrieve them when he comes back to the present?"

Neil leaned back, smiling. Despite Celina's possible solution, it meant his idea was a winner. Like he had done his entire life, Neil was keeping tabs on who had the most winning ideas.

"A brilliant idea, Celina," Gina said. Celina smiled and asked if we needed anything else. Our coffee cups were full, so she strolled through the restaurant to the front.

Terry turned to Neil and said, "Where'd you find this bearer bonds idea?"

"'Die Hard.' Hans Gruber is stealing the bearer bonds in the safe of the Nakatomi Tower."

A movie, what a surprise.

"So I go back, find a broker, buy the bonds, then hide them."

"Voila," Neil said.

"They go up in value for thirty-three years, and when I time travel back to now, we cash them in, and we're rich."

Neil was about to agree, but paused, and his smug smile fell off his face. "No. They're like cash, face value."

"I go back. Buy a thousand dollars worth of bearer bonds, hide them for thirty-three years, and now they're worth...?"

"A thousand dollars," Neil whispered.

"A brilliant plan, but not a profitable plan," Terry said.

Shit.

15

"What if you took back a bunch of money and opened a savings account in your name? But didn't you tell your past self about it? Thirty-three years of compound interest should be a pretty substantial amount, right?" Gina said as we sat around our living room, Damage Done's explosive second album on the stereo. Contrary to many bands, after their breakout first album, they followed up with an even more powerful and exciting second album. A record best played loud. It was playing loud.

"Could work..."

"The bank will send out a statement every month for a savings account he does not know about," Terry countered.

"A fake address."

"Then it becomes an orphaned account. After ten years, the bank absorbs the money, and we're left with nothing."

I turned over the album, then returned to the couch beside Gina. She curled her feet under my leg while poking away on her iPhone.

"Can we raise enough money to make the compound interest angle work?" I said. Gina found what she was looking for and turned her screen to me. Damn, even investing whatever money we could collect, it would only be a couple of times greater in value now. Nowhere near enough to enter the Vancouver housing market.

"Neil, is that on our list? How to find money Colin can take back?"

"Nope. Also, he can't take back 'now' money, right? He'll need to have old money."

Two more problems for our list.

Exasperated, I downed the rest of my Steamworks Heroica Red Ale and slumped back on the couch.

"This is insane, guys. This isn't ever going to work. Too many variables we haven't figured out, and then there are the ones we haven't even considered."

Terry sighed and said, "Let's keep going, anyway."

"But if it won't work, why bother?"

"Because what else can we do, Colin? This stupid idea, which you brought up, I'll remind you, is the only chance we have to make it in this cursed city."

"In 'Bill and Ted's Excellent Adventure' they—"

"Neil! Watching old movies has no value here!"

"Why not?"

"Because Colin isn't trying to ace his history report, for God's sake," Terry said, exasperated.

"What about '12 Monkeys'?"

"Hmm. Is there currently a plague killing off most of the world's population?"

"Well, of course not."

"Then there's not much value in that movie either."

Before Neil could continue, Gina called out, "Enough!"

We knew to be quiet when Gina yelled like that. It must have been her Italian upbringing, a thread back to her mother and grandmother, corralling unruly children to the dinner table with only a fraction of terror. Gina continued, "Savings account is out. Same with an investment account. Neil, put them on our list and then cross them off, so we don't loop around to them again."

"Sure," Neil said, opening his smartphone. "Hey, I forgot about 'Looper,' that's about time travel."

"Wait," I said. Our convoluted conversation had rolled around in my head while Damage Done sang about 'Noise n Rhythm,' one of their rare out-of-control songs written on a dare to lure dancing couples out onto the dance floor.

"Way back, didn't you receive an actual paper stock certificate when you bought a stock? Like in a movie where old certificates from IBM or AT&T are worth a fortune? Investments might be the way to go if we can figure out how to buy original certificates…"

"But what stock could you buy?"

"And who would you buy it from?"

How should I know? I'd never bought a stock in my life. None of us had.

One step forward, two steps back.

"All right, let the album finish, then we split up and search the web for stocks Colin could go back and buy," Gina said decisively. Fearing a detention, we all nodded in agreement.

"Walmart. Here's what I found. 'If you had bought $10,000 worth of WMT in 1980, today you would own 74,472 shares worth $3.9 million. Your yearly dividend check would be $108,729.' Loser buys dinner?" Gina said, spinning a fork in her linguini at Nick's, the neighborhood Italian restaurant where we had been coming since we were born.

Terry stopped eating his spinach salad and said, "Microsoft. One hundred $21/shares bought in 1986 would be worth $750,000 in 25 years. So a bit more today. $10,000 then would be worth over four million now."

"Those are the figures we should be talking about!" I said, ignoring my veal Scallopini.

With those kinds of numbers, this might work. We could resolve a lot with a few million dollars. Why go back for anything less? One huge win, and then we would be on easy street for the rest of our lives.

Gina said, "Colin, can you beat four million?"

I shook my head. My afternoon had been taken up looking for a new job, but I had poked around at a list of vice stocks, but none returned anything like what Gina or Terry found. I hadn't found a job either. "It looks like Terry is the winner."

Terry grinned and raised his wine glass in celebration.

"Ahem," Neil said, stopping Terry's smug smile cold.

"Why, I didn't know you could use a computer, Neil," Terry said, but Neil ignored the dig.

"Walmart and Microsoft are reasonable options, I guess."

"Please don't be a dick about this," Gina said, gritting her teeth as Neil watched a short-skirted twenty-something wobble past on overly high heel towards the toilets.

"What have you got?" I asked, attempting to drag Neil back on track before Gina gutted him with her butter knife.

"Apple," he said.

"What about Apple?" Terry said, checking his iPhone. "It's currently selling for only a couple of hundred bucks a share."

"Yup, but in '84, it was only twenty-five bucks. Remember, they'd only come out with the first Macintosh."

The Mac Classic. I remembered seeing one for the first time at a friend's house. A little grey box with a tiny screen. Smiling logo on the login page. I thought my friend was a complete idiot for spending $2500 on a tiny little computer. Hell, you could have bought a new car for the same price. Sure, a fine machine, and the all-new graphical interface and the mouse were super fantastic. But the specs? 8MHz, 128k of RAM, 400k disk drive and a 9 inch monochrome display. Bleeding edge. Oh, and no internet to connect to then.

Neil continued, "Hear me out. If we can send Colin back in time with only four thousand dollars—not ten thousand—he can buy 160 shares."

Terry interrupted, "But 160 times a couple of hundred dollars a share now is only like $35,000. So I still win."

Neil smiled across the table, shaking his head like Terry was about to be shunted into remedial math.

"Wrong. Apple shares have split a few times. To be specific, a lot of times."

I glanced at Gina, a tremor of anticipation in my body. Her eyes filled with excitement. Then we looked at Neil.

"How much, Neil? How much would they be worth now?"

He smiled, popped a piece of calamari into his mouth and said, "Over $10 million, US."

That's thirteen million Canadian dollars.

Ladies and gentlemen, we had a winner.

Now

I sat down on an orange vinyl faux-Danish moderne chair with polished teak arms in front of Dennis' matching teak desk. A strange sort of flashback—or was it flash-forward?—to having met with a sixty-five-year-old Dennis Fanshawe as part of our screenplay research. The same furniture in the same office, although his future secretary was only in her mid-thirties, so couldn't have been part of his original office set up unless she had begun working for him when she was two.

"Well, sure, you could come in and buy stock certificates from me back in '84," he had said, scratching his sagging grey jowls. "A common enough practise, that'd be around the time the brokerage business was shifting over to computers, and damn, they were painful to use back then. I get a cold chill up my back remembering. But I sold them then, sure, in this exact office. I can't remember the last time I saw an actual stock certificate. Other than in old movies, right?"

"So, to be clear," I asked, my iPad on my lap for taking notes. "My character could come in with cash, buy the stock, and that would be that?"

He pondered for a while, the gears turning in his head while I sat in silence across from him. I watched him try to remember the step-by-step process for a rare business transaction from thirty-three years ago. You would have had to let the gears turn for a while as well. I waited, subtly checking off 'find a broker who was working in 1984' on our iCloud shared list.

"You'd have to fill out a form, become a client, but, as far as I remember, yes, that would be about it."

I thanked him and escaped before he started telling me more stories about the good old days. He had shared enough of them at our liquid lunch. His stories were now unnecessary because, if I was lucky, I would be on my way back to those same good old days in less than three weeks.

•

"I'm full up with meetings this morning, what with the girl out for the day. Could you cruise back around three? We'll fill out the paperwork to set up your account, you can make your initial deposit, then we can discuss options, and I have a few timely suggestions on how to begin your investments."

"Oh, I already know what I want to invest in," I said with a smile.

"Have you done this before?" Dennis asked, and I shook my head.

"Well, I've been given good and respected advice to purchase Apple stock."

Dennis looked at me with confusion, tapping the ash off his cigarillo into a colossal crystal ashtray. "Apple? Apple Records? The Beatles company? I'm pretty sure it went into receivership."

"No. Apple Computers. AAPL."

He laughed and looked at me. "Computers? Colin, I appreciate that everyone is offered tips on stocks. Sometimes they're good, and you make money, but most of the time, those suggestions will only make you a poorer man. Apple Computers? I'm sorry, and I hate to say it, but you may as well throw your money out the window. Now, have you heard of American Motors? They're coming out with rather interesting automobile products, guaranteed to be long-term winners."

I stopped him before he got going. "I appreciate your advice, Dennis, but I'm set on buying Apple. Bottom line, I have faith the company will go on to greatness. Who knows, maybe after this computer of theirs, they'll branch out into digital music players, or maybe even a telephone you can carry in your pocket." I gave him a grin, and he smiled the indulgent way my father would when naïve teenaged me said I would be a professional photographer when I grew up.

He raised his hands in capitulation, no doubt realizing he would get his commission no matter what, and said, "You want Apple, you got Apple. I need to give you these warnings, and you understand, right?"

I nodded, all cool and businesslike. Then I stood up, reaching across to shake his hand again. "Three o'clock."

"Three o'clock. With a certified check," Dennis said, standing and shaking my hand.

"Pardon?"

"A certified check. Receiving cash from you would be illegal. A certified check will do fine, or a bank draft."

A wrinkle. Old Dennis had mentioned nothing about certified checks. Or maybe he had, but I hadn't been listening. Shit.

One surprise wrinkle was manageable, no problem. I was an intelligent guy and would figure out a solution.

"I'll see you at three," I said confidently and let myself out of his office.

If I had a cigar, I'd chomp on it. I loved it when a plan came together.

16

I headed back down towards my hotel. Alongside me, taxis, trucks and enormous old cars spewed exhaust into the street. Boy, emission standards had increased a lot in thirty years. The future city was a lot cleaner, bike lanes everywhere, e-cars, and a couple of SkyTrain rapid transit lines crossing underneath. Back now, the buildings were mostly under ten stories, primarily original heavy brick and stone edifices, mighty banks built to impress and reassure, interspersed with random '70's brutalist concrete towers. And again, lots and lots of white people headed places while smoking.

At Hastings and Richards, I turned right, past a filled-to-the-rafters—literally—used bookstore I used to frequent, then down the block past future nightclubs to a short staircase descending below street level. I didn't know if the street was once lower or if they had built the building like that out of spite. Two storefronts were at the bottom of the stairs; one was a barbershop with an old-time shoe shine set up which offered two-dollar men's haircuts—another two dollars for a shave with a straight razor. A tiny old white guy, in a starched white shirt and apron, shaved a businessman. His suit jacket hung on the coat rack beside a row of battered wooden chairs. Another businessman waited his turn, reading a

Playboy magazine. Suzanne Somers, formerly of Three's Company, graced the cover. She dazzled with permed hair, sporting a wide-shouldered purple outfit—with matching hat—which she must have stolen from one of the Pointer Sisters. The barber leaned away and tapped his cigar in a battered metal ashtray attached to the back of the barber's chair. They noticed me outside, and all three give me the eye. I stepped back and turned to the other door.

Step Three of our plan began now.

I pushed a buzzer, then waited for the heavy door to unlock before entering. Inside, narrow locked cabinets covered with heavy glass covered two of the walls of the unpretentious shop. In the back wall were a curtain-covered doorway and more cabinets. Behind the counter, a weary white guy about my age, with awful, receding, early seventies hair, a rumpled brown dress shirt, and matching slacks, rose from the stool he was slouching on.

"Help you?" he said, indifferent, with maybe a light misting of curiosity. Or it could be smoke from his cigarette. 9:30 in the morning and the top half of the shop was a fog, putting San Francisco to shame. I stepped to the counter and said, "Yes, I'm sure you can."

Ten days ago

Our next problem was fundamental: how to pay for the Apple stock certificates once I traveled back?

We'd already figured out we could go to coin shops around the city and buy old pre-1984 Canadian bills for me to use for pocket cash. I was only going for three days, and I wouldn't need a lot of money if judicious. But we couldn't find $4,500 in old money for me to take back to buy the stocks. So what to do? What could I bring back thirty-three years, then sell for $4,500?

Neil, of course, had the first idea. "Take back a bunch of Ecstasy, man. I know who'd want to buy it, and then you're golden."

"E didn't exist in '84," Terry said.

"All the more reason they'll pay a lot for it."

"Sure, start a drug trend a good twenty years early. I'm sure that won't screw with our present lives too much," Gina said, in full sarcasm mode.

Neil huffed and climbed in off his roof to find more beer. The sun had dipped behind the enormous chestnut trees lining our street. Lounging here was pleasant, looking west towards the gleaming towers of downtown.

This element of the plan has had us stumped for four agonizing days. I had found a broker in the same offices on Howe Street as when he started in the business forty years ago. Using our story of writing a screenplay, I'd taken him for lunch and picked his brain about his business in the '80s. Coming to the end of his career, he was thrilled to spend a couple of hours and consume most of a bottle of wine, regaling me with stories of the trading floor, the parties he used to go to, the disco scene at Richards on Richards. Dicks on Dicks was the only club the four of us had vowed never to be caught dead in, leaving it for the yuppies and the gold-diggers. After returning Dennis to his office, he meandered around to confirming that the hero of our screenplay could purchase stock certificates.

But that didn't help us with how to take back $4,500.

Neil climbed out onto the roof and handed out Howe Sound's Devil's Elbow IPA cans to everyone. "What if, once you're back, you take out an overdraft on your checking account?"

"Uh, then twenty-two-year-old me would be broke," I said. "Besides, my bank wouldn't even give me a toaster, much less a four thousand dollar overdraft. Come on, Neil."

"Well, what about your parents? You could go back and then borrow from them. They wouldn't miss it. They're loaded."

Gina sighed. "What's he supposed to do, Neil? Knock on his parent's front door, say 'Hi, I'm your son from the future, let me borrow $4,500 to improve my life in thirty-three years.'?"

"Fine, forget it. Sneak in while everyone's asleep and steal your mom's jewelry. Pawn it, and you're flush with cash."

·"I can't believe you just said that," I said, shaking my head in disbelief. "You want me to rob my parents?"

Neil shrugged. "Of course not. Gina's. Her mom has loads of gold jewelry, and she wouldn't miss a few pieces."

"Why doesn't he go rob your parents, Neil?" Gina said, angry at his suggestion.

He laughed. "Good luck finding anything of value in either of their houses."

And back to square one, again.

"It has to be something small and easy to exchange. Those are the only parameters as far as I figure," Terry said over lunch at the Ovaltine a couple of days later.

"Agreed."

"Diamonds?"

"Like 'A Fish Called Wanda'!"

Terry groaned. "Not even a time machine movie, Neil."

"But easy to sell?"

Silence. No one knew. None of us had bought or sold a diamond.

Celina came up to our table. "Stuck again?" We nodded. She gestured for me to slide over, and she sat down with a sigh. Adjusting her grey hair back into her perfect bun, she looked around the table. "What's the problem now?"

"What does the hero bring to turn into cash in the past?"

Terry added, "Tiny enough to carry back then easy to exchange."

"Hmm," Celina said, pondering our latest dilemma. "Couldn't do diamonds. They're hard to sell. What about stamps?"

Gina started poking away on her phone while we considered the idea.

"They are small. You'd have to find old ones, so we'd pay way more now than our hero would sell them for in the past…"

"What if he can't sell them then? How would he even find a buyer? I'm assuming stamps are contingent on the whims of the marketplace," Terry said.

Celina looked at us. "A good point. Three days in the past, right?" We nodded. "Not much time to track down legitimate stamp dealers."

Gina said, "Stamps beat anything we'd come up with, Celina. Thank you."

A bell rang from the kitchen. An order ready for pick up. Celina sighed and went to deliver someone's lunch special.

"I still say he steals your mom's gold jewelry," Neil said after she had gone. "There was a guy who'd buy it, no questions. Crazy Steve." Neil laughed as he remembered.

Terry sighed. "Can you imagine Colin haggling with a fence named Crazy Steve?"

Neil snorted.

I stopped sipping my coffee as synapses fired in my head. "Gold is always easy to sell," I said. Terry nodded in agreement. "Sure, there's always someone who wants to buy it."

Gina hit me on the shoulder. "You're not robbing my mom!"

"Ow! Not your mom's jewelry! Gold. Plain old gold!"

The next day we cabbed downtown to a coin shop I remembered on Richards Street. It was next door to Lola's in the '90s, then Century House in the '00s, fantastic restaurants where we had enjoyed many an excellent meal. We trooped down the six steps to the tiny shop off an alcove. I pushed a buzzer beside the steel mesh-covered front door window.

"Oh, this doesn't look dodgy at all," Neil muttered, still upset we were ignoring his idea of taking back drugs.

The door clunked open, and we stepped inside.

There were glass-covered display cases on three sides, and a young guy behind the counter played a game on his oversized phone. He paused his game, adjusted his glasses and his hipster beard, then said, "Help you?"

Gina stepped forward, smiling. "We're interested in Canadian Maple Leaf Gold coins."

Hipster pointed towards a couple of cases with individual coins displayed in rows on velvet.

"But there's a caveat," Terry said. "Pre-1984 coins."

He looked confused. We had checked online, and there was no earthly reason to want an old gold coin instead of a new one. The only difference was they have a unique image stamped on them and a different date. I understood why he would be confused, and I would be, too.

I said, "Indulge us."

He turned to his laptop and typed away for a minute.

"How many do you need?"

"Twelve," Neil said. Hipster paused, calculating his commission. He typed more, then shut the laptop.

"That's doable. I've four here on the premises, '79 through '82, and I'd be happy to bring in the rest by the end of the week."

The four of us relaxed. Success! Hipster continued, "The current price is $1,645 each. How about we say $20,000 for the dozen?"

The four of us tensed right back up again. Neil said, "Can you give us a moment?"

He nodded, and we followed him outside.

"What the fuck? We're gonna blow $20,000, so Colin can go back and sell the same coins for only $4500? That's a fifteen thousand dollar loss!"

"You have any other suggestion, Neil?" Gina said. She added before Neil could continue, "Excluding drugs."

"Or Crazy Steve."

Neil paced around the cramped foyer, frustrated.

Terry said, "I don't like it. It'll empty my savings, but I can't see another solution. I can't believe I'm saying this, but I think we go for it. Gina?"

Gina did the math. "When you return with the stock certificates, we'll have over thirteen million Canadian. So, I'm in."

I knew I was in, despite it emptying my severance package. Besides, if it didn't work, we could sell the coins back to hipster dude. I turned to Neil. "Three of us say yes, Neil. You in for 5K?"

He turned around and looked at each of us. "Will this even work? Can you be positive this will work?"

I lied and nodded. How could I know if it will work? I don't even know what would happen when I turned that knob in the box. But I nodded anyway. Neil sighed and leaned over to push the buzzer to let us back inside.

Now

"You were recommended as a buyer of gold coins."

The old guy smiled, avarice washing away his indifference. "I could be."

"You'll have to excuse me for a moment. You can't be too careful with coins like these," I said, removing my belt. My slacks were so formfitting the belt was unnecessary. But, for carrying a dozen gold coins, this belt was essential. Even more paranoid as a traveler than he was in day-to-day life, Terry had picked up the belt for a trip down to San Francisco many years ago. The backing slid off, revealing a thin compartment where a paranoid traveler could stash extra funds, diamonds, a joint or two and, with no additional effort, a dozen pre-1984 Canadian Maple Leaf gold coins. One after another, I popped them out and placed them on the counter between the dodgy old guy and myself. His eyes opened wider with each coin set on the pile. Once the belt was empty, I slid it back on and placed my hands on the edge of the counter, businessman-like.

"I checked the current value," I said. "$412 per coin times twelve coins is a bit under $5,000. I'll take $4,800 for the lot."

The old guy sucked in air between his front teeth with a slight whistle. A kid in grade school did the same thing all the time. I had hated it then, hated it now.

"Where'd you get them?" he asked suspiciously. Fair enough, a strange guy comes into your shop with a handful of gold coins. You had a right to be wary.

"An inheritance. My uncle passed."

"Condolences," he said, not believing me. "You're looking for a quick sale." A statement, not a question. I nodded.

"$4,500." A lowball offer. I should have been insulted. I should have haggled, but I wanted this over. Besides, I was a terrible haggler. Useless at it. When Gina and I had jetted to Mexico to celebrate our tenth anniversary, she wouldn't let me talk to anyone selling anything. I could answer 'yes' at our all-inclusive, but outside, only 'no, gracias.'

I put on an unhappy face. "Fine. $4,500."

He smiled, a smile bereft of dental care. "Wonderful. Now, you wouldn't happen to have the Certificates of Authenticity by any chance?"

Authentic gold coins come with a certificate. Otherwise, he would have to send the currency off for testing and to be assayed. I didn't have time to wait. Except for the coins we bought didn't have certificates. They were legit but lacking in documentation. So what to do?

You had your brilliant partners-in-crime fire up Photoshop, duplicate official certificates found on the web, laser-print those documents out onto high-end bonded paper and voila! Certificates that wouldn't pass in the present, but they were miles beyond perfect in the past.

I smiled at the old guy and removed an envelope from inside my suit jacket.

"I believe these will be in order," I said with a confident smile.

17

Stepping out onto the street, I breathed deeply. I asked myself who was a stylish kick-ass businessman, checking my feathered hair in the mirrored window of a touristy trinket shop. Next up, resolve the unexpected additional complication I learned about an hour ago. Mr. Businessman here had to turn the $4,500 cash in my pocket into a certified check for Dennis. When I had met with Dennis in the future, he hadn't mentioned it. He was off in his full recollections of feathered-haired women he'd picked up at a nightclub instead of the minutiae of decades-old stock transactions.

No problem, there were five hours for me to figure this out on my own.

The only place to get a certified check was a bank. And the best bank to go to would be the Royal Bank, where I'd been banking since I opened my first account as a kid. The main downtown branch was only a couple of streets away. But the more I considered it, the better my actual bank branch became. I was a respectable businessman, for goodness' sake. Knowing my exact account number and, despite not having my passbook, I was pretty sure they'd help me. Not positive, but pretty sure.

And it's not like I ever went in there, anyway. I hadn't talked to a teller in my branch since the introduction of ATMs.

For four quarters, I caught the bus back home.

Thirty minutes later, I was stuck in a long, winding line in my bank branch. In front and behind me, the neighborhood nonna's shuffled forward. They clutched their heavy purses, waited their turn to pay bills, transfer money and make deposits with a teller. There was a single ATM in the lobby, but no one was using it. They didn't trust them. Neither did my parents, not for years. You banked in person during the passive-aggressively short banking hours. I also needed to talk to a teller, so I had to wait. How strange it was to see so many people lining up, waiting their turn, doing nothing but waiting.

Standing in a lineup without fidgeting on my iPhone, checking out Facebook, replying to emails, or playing a pointless game was agony. I guess putting on my headphones and listening to music was an option, but I refrained, like being in a church. A few more steps forward, and I was at the shelf for filling out a withdrawal or deposit slip—pens on chains, stacks of different slips. Like everyone under sixty in the future, I barely went to the bank, even to use the ATM. Imagine if I told the people in line what banking was like now. Bills were paid automatically, or you could pay them from your phone. Send money to anyone with an email address. Buy homemade candles at a craft fair with a credit card from anyone with a Square reader. Pay-Pal. Apple Pay. I wouldn't even mention Bitcoin.

Finally, my turn arrived. A middle-aged woman with a 1960s bouffant —a Mad Men extra—smiled at me from behind her teller window.

"Hello. I'm Jean. Welcome to the Royal Bank."

"I'd like to have a certified check made, please."

"Sure thing. For how much?"

I took out the envelope and slid it through to her. "$4,500."

Jean checked the cash, flicking through the bills to ensure there was a total of 45 hundred's in the stack.

"I'll have to type it up, so can you take a seat in our waiting area?"

That was it? No account number? No nothing? I loved our banking system for the first time in my life. With a smile, I strolled over and sat down in a comfortable chair. She slid a board down over her window and shuffled into the back. The nonna's in line threw me daggers for shutting down one of the four open windows. I shrugged my shoulders in apology. Again, I waited with nothing to do. Oh, for a smartphone with the latest addictive game on it.

Instead, there were magazines displayed on a side table. I grabbed the National Geographic and skimmed a story on traveling from Pakistan to Bangladesh by rail. I considered having a cigarette. A bunch of people puffed away around me. Courtesy ashtrays perched on the tops of the rope stanchions making up the waiting aisles.

"Excuse me?"

I closed the magazine and looked to see Jean. "Yes?"

"Who would you like the certified check made out to?"

I blinked at her, my mind working furiously.

Who did I have it made out to? Dennis Fanshawe? Or did he have a business name I should use instead? Maybe the name of his bank. This is something I should have asked before I had left his office. I had even forgotten to grab a card from Dennis. Shit.

"I'm not quite sure."

"We could make it out to cash, which would mean anyone could exchange it," she suggested.

"Is there any chance I could make a quick phone call?" Jean smiled and took me over to the receptionist's desk, pushing a button on the heavy phone to give me an open line. "And a phone book?"

"Yellow or White?"

He must have a business listing, so I flicked through two inches of Yellow Pages, found his listing under brokers, and placed the call. And it rang through to a static-filled voicemail.

Someone called to Jean from the back, and she gestured for them to wait before turning back to me. I closed the phone book, hung up the phone. I was out of time.

"Please make it out to cash," I said. Dennis could deposit it since cash is cash.

She smiled and went back to the office. You should have grabbed a business card when you had the chance. Dumb move, Colin. I returned to my uncomfortable chair and my NatGeo, shaking my head at myself.

Five quiet minutes passed, and then Jean was back with a business envelope.

"Here you go," she said. I stood up and took the envelope from her. I slid out the check and confirmed the amount on it. I felt embarrassed, like I was insulting her personally, but wasn't taking any chances. I smiled before slipping the envelope into the inside pocket of my suit jacket.

"You've been wonderfully helpful, thanks," I said.

"Happy to help," said Jean, adjusting her bouffant. "Now, you be careful. That piece of paper is as good as cash to anyone who has it."

"I'll guard it with my life," I say with a big smile.

Outside my bank, I was flush with success.

Meeting broker arranged: check;

Coins turned into cash: check;

Cash turned into a bank draft: bonus check.

There was nothing left to do except go back to my hotel to wait until my three o'clock appointment. I would pick up the stock certificates, hide them for future me to retrieve, and kill a couple of days in 1984. Then I would live the high life until I died at an advanced age.

With four hours before I needed to be back downtown, I strolled north on Commercial Drive, my camera at the ready. Everywhere were shops and restaurants from my past. Mom and pop stores, family-run businesses, no chains stores anywhere. It was a beautiful day. The sun was bright, the sky was clear, life was better than good, and I enjoyed walking.

Pausing at the busy local video rental store window, I had flash-backs of waiting on hold on a Friday night to reserve a VHS or Betamax video player to play the movies we hoped to rent.

In high school, no one had owned a video player. A&B Sound had sold them for about 2500 dollars, massive electronic beasts you could put out your back lifting if you weren't careful. Instead, we'd rush to one of the local video stores, hoping to score one of the limited supply of new releases, line up to pay for it, then lug a rental player home, hook it up to a TV in a basement rec room and enjoy a film. Back then, you committed when you rented a video. Not like Netflix now, when you could stop watching one of a million shows or movies and choose something else at no cost.

Then, it would have had to be bad—'Battlefield Earth' bad—to not watch it all the way through. You had to get your money's worth. Remembering, of course, to 'be kind and rewind' or else you'd have to pay the penalty.

Glancing into the store, they had the movies for sale locked up behind the counter. Locked up because to buy a new release was about a hundred dollars for a single film. The studios sure didn't have the entire purchase-and-own-forever thing figured out.

I crossed the street to check out Grandview Park. Its playground was full of kids, most of the mothers nowhere to be seen. Most likely off purchasing fresh produce, fresh baking, fresh meat or groceries while the children entertained themselves. Sure as hell was a different world than today. Now there would be a defensive ring of expensive strollers surrounding the playground, parents, nannies, and au pairs hovering around their offspring, ensuring little Tree, or Soleil or Aubergine wasn't harmed in any way. Progress.

Crouching down, I took a couple of action shots of the kids racing around, playing a game with complicated rules which kept changing with each shift in the breeze. The only adult was an old Italian man in a worn suit, dozing on a bench, a lit cigar in his hand. Through the flurry of children, I grabbed a fantastic shot of him asleep, smoke drifting up from the cigar, while the kids raced around him, my camera freezing them in a blur.

I considered stopping in at Joe's Cafe for a proper Italian coffee, but in this neighborhood, I might run into myself—which would be, according to Terry, bad. Better to head back downtown and take photos there. So I caught the Hastings bus using my valid paper transfer and departed my hood with reinvigorated memories and great photographs.

Once on the bus, I put on my bulky headphones and started up my cassette again, tapping my legs in time with one of Mayo's early self-produced tapes. Halfway through the first song, I noticed the old ladies on the bus staring. I reached under my suit jacket and dialled down the volume. Maybe my music was leaking out of my cheap headphones. But they kept staring back at me. I did a quick glance around. Maybe there's someone behind me being weird—not a rare occurrence if you'd taken a bus in any city in the world—but the entire back half of the bus was looking forward at me.

Strange.

Shrugging, I returned to my music. But then I realized I was the only one on the bus with headphones on. I was the only one with my own music. In 1984, this was strange. In the future, everyone had headphones. Mostly ubiquitous white Apple earbuds but also bulky Beats or other brands. No matter what age, everyone was focused on their smartphones while on the bus or waiting for the bus. Back now, people chatted, read the paper. With my headphones on, I was the weird one on this bus. A fifty-five-year-old businessman who was listening to a Walkman on public transit. If they heard my music—a high school punk/new-wave bands indie cassette release—they would consider me even stranger. What middle-aged man listened to a racket like that? Shameful.

By now, the bus was on East Hastings, nearing Main Street. Traffic slowed as we came closer to the eastern edge of downtown. Bored, I glanced out my window into the Ovaltine Cafe. My God, it looked the same as it did in the future. I struggled to pull my camera out, but the bus lurched forward, accelerating towards the green light ahead. Impulsively, I pulled the cord for the next stop. I needed at least one photo of the Ovaltine while I was back. There were lots of great photo opportunities in Chinatown as well. There was certainly time before meeting with Dennis.

The bus rolled across Main and pulled to a stop. I pushed open the narrow doors and hopped out onto the sidewalk. The bus drove away, revealing the original Carnegie Library across the street. But what was missing was the homeless mall. Ratty blankets laid out with random broken and scavenged product, which in the future stretched along the adjacent sidewalks, forcing pedestrians out into the street.

Despite Terry's voice of warning in my head, I crossed over to take evocative photos of the Ovaltine and its iconic neon sign. What harm was there in taking a photo? None of us would have been down this way on a weekday. Gina and I were at college for our social work degrees; Neil would be asleep after clubbing last night away, and Terry was in the kitchen at The Keg and Cleaver in Burnaby, preparing for the lunch rush. So I was fine, and nothing would happen. Even better, my photos looked amazing. My HD camera did an excellent job of catching the sunlight on the neon sign that rose along the front of the building, businessmen strolling past, some with jaunty hats on, all smoking.

With Chinatown only a block away, I looped around a couple of streets, snapping photographs of everything that caught my attention, my music the soundtrack to my wandering. I had forgotten how much fun picture taking was, something I had done throughout my youth. Stroll around a part of the city like I was doing now, with my music blaring, keeping an eye out for exciting compositions or people, had been one of the great joys of my life. To freeze time. Make a split-second decision about what specific part of a scene in front of me to grab was a feeling of absolute power. A different person standing beside me with an identical camera could never create the same photo I could. Each would be unique, like each performance of a song. That was the power I had felt when I photographed. I had possessed a singular focus on observing the world through the lens of my camera, waiting for the perfect alignment of unknowns, and grabbing my 1/1,000th of a second slice.

When did I stop? I didn't remember for sure. Probably while at college, absolutely before graduation and when I started my full-time career in social work. When I time-travelled forward, I'd have to dig out those reams of old photos and negatives to see what was there that had any emotional value. Maybe I could add them to my expanding coffee-table book idea. By the time I finished photographing Chinatown, my old watch said noon, and I was hungry. Luckily, I knew the perfect place for an excellent lunch.

18

May 1981

Gina, Terry, Neil and I huddled outside our high school automotive shop, drinking from a mickey of rye Neil had stolen from his father's garage stash. We had a joint Gina scored from her old brother for being his alibi for a missed curfew the weekend prior. Terry and I had nothing to offer except a pack of Players Light cigarettes, but that counted. We'd pooled our vices. The joint was mostly dried parsley and the rye was terrible, burning like raw gasoline the whole way down.

"You sure this is actually rye, Neil?" I asked, coughing up a lung before accepting the joint coming around the circle.

"Pretty sure."

"So we could be drinking turpentine," Terry said.

"Terps is clear."

"Not if you use it for cleaning brown paintbrushes."

We considered that for a moment. If that was what we're drinking, smoking would be catastrophic. But none of us had gone up in flames yet, so we decided we were golden. It must just have been exceptionally bad rye.

"Na, the top was sealed. We're good."

"As good as we can be," Terry said.

"But not as good as we're gonna get," Neil said with a smile and a gulp and a shudder and a cough.

Van Tech High School had presented a talent contest as part of the end of the academic year celebrations. Every year, the stage in the auditorium saw a parade of either exuberant yet cringe-worthy performances or wretchedly bad performances. The former were students who had performed in front of audiences their whole lives. They would include a cross-section of the immigrant cultures making up our school. That meant enduring multiple Highland Dancers; bad Italian opera singing; a cheerleading routine; an air band made up of jocks lip-syncing Black Sabbath; that one kid who imagined he was a comedian but wasn't, and so much more!

The standard lineup. Year after sad year. But tonight offered us one significant difference.

Tonight was Mayo's first live performance.

After a year and a half of jacking around in their garage, with us as their only audience, Kelly, Duncan, Paul, and Bucky would have their stage debut. After six months of begging and pleading, cajoling and wheedling, outright lying and threatening, we convinced them to do this show. We'd known they were great from that first time we heard them play—rough, inexperienced, but great.

"Just playing for us in your garage doesn't cut it anymore," Gina said to them after the office posted the sign-up sheet for the talent contest at school. "You're depriving the world of your talent. Like you're all selfish

and whatever. Like you don't care about anyone but yourselves."
Nothing like the righteous indignation of a teenaged girl.

"But we're shit," Bucky said, from behind his drums, bundled in his
ski parka. It was a cold March evening, the rain hadn't stopped falling for
two weeks, and our breath was visible in the uninsulated garage. Kelly
couldn't turn on the ancient space heater because it cost too much
electricity to heat the garage. Also, with it and the amps plugged into the
same single outlet, they'd blow the breaker. Then he'd have to sneak into
the house basement to reset it and face the wrath of their dad watching
hockey in the basement.

So we froze, but the guitars were amplified.

I took a pic of the guys, warming up their hands, toques, and scarfs
over heavy coats. My finger was so cold I couldn't feel the shutter.

"Bullshit, Bucky," I said, rubbing my hands together for warmth.
"Bullshit. Either you get up on the Van Tech stage, blow everybody's
minds, and become the school hero's or give up now. What kind of band
doesn't play live?"

Paul said, "The Beatles didn't play live for the last five years of their
career."

"Well, you're sure as shit not the fucking Beatles, so that doesn't
count," Terry countered.

The guys hemmed and hawed, shifting around to warm their feet.

"Besides, The Beatles played like a million shows in Hamburg before
they were famous," Gina added.

The guys didn't react but continued avoiding eye contact.

I couldn't believe it. They were the best band ever to come out of our
school—well, the only band to come out of our school—but hell, they
killed it when they were rolling. Those months of practice had them
sounding like they played the same song simultaneously, and their lyrics
were surprisingly good. It was too raw and angry for a good grade from
our English teachers, but excellent words to be yelled into a microphone

while a buzz saw of guitars and drums exploded around them. But if they didn't ever leave this garage, they'd fade away and stop practicing. Bucky would sell his kit to buy a shitty car, and that would be that. What might have been would be what wasn't.

I packed up my camera, then pulled open the garage door. I had one more play to make, a risky one, but the band needed the push.

"Where are you going?" Kelly asked. It was early.

"I'm done. Sorry, if you don't get the fuck out of this garage and perform, then I'm not coming over anymore. I can't be your only audience. I want to see you on stage, someplace with a packed crowd, someplace warm."

Then I walked out before they had a chance to say anything to stop me.

Standing in the dark alleyway in the driving rain, I wondered if the others would join me or not. Had I made a futile gesture, and couldn't return without losing face? Trudging towards Victoria Drive, I rethought my position—maybe if I went back and said I was joking—when I heard Gina calling from behind me, "Colin, wait for us!"

Kelly signed the band up the following day.

After finishing the joint, the mickey and half the smokes, we headed inside the auditorium for the start of the show. The school rules meant we couldn't arrive after the show has started. That meant everyone there to see Mayo had to sit through everything else—so no cutting out for a cigarette, except trying to steal one in the toilets. We scored good seats in a group of school friends not too close to the front. You know, the people you hung out with at school, at lunch, but wouldn't phone to hang out on the weekend, unless they were at the same house party—then there was a sort of detente for the duration of the party, before returning on Monday to school-only friends.

"What the hell kind of name for a band is Mayo, anyway?" Dave asked from the row in front of us.

We giggled and shrugged. We knew the story but weren't allowed to tell anyone. The band had sworn us to secrecy.

In eighth grade, at lunch one day, Duncan had unknowingly let a large glop of mayonnaise fall from his sandwich onto his crotch. Perfectly onto his crotch. He didn't notice and had spent most of the afternoon walking around with what looked like a massive cum stain on his pants. When an embarrassed teacher finally took him aside two classes later, Duncan freaked out and raced down the packed hallway to the boy's locker room, screaming, "It's just Mayo!"

And that was why they were called Mayo.

We endured the dancers, the jock's lip-syncing 'Iron Man,' the 'comedian,' and a selection of garbage acts until halfway through the evening. After a bagpiper left the stage, the curtains opened, and Kelly and the guys stood on stage fidgeting with their instruments as a member of the A/V club set up Kelly's vocal mic. Mr. Doyle, our strict and mean Irish vice-principal, had lost the draw in the staff room and was the emcee for the night. After the second act, he clearly was done. I would bet there was a mickey of his own in his brown, off-the-rack suit. The guys started tuning up while Mr. Doyle quieted down the audience, who had ratcheted up in energy, either anticipating a colossal train wreck up on stage or an explosion of carnage and madness. I had my camera out and aimed at the podium as our VP spoke.

"All right, next up is," he looked down at his program, then grimaced. "Next up is Mayo. County Mayo? Could we be lucky enough to hear some traditional Irish music?" He glanced over at the four long-haired teens with their electric guitars. Not much chance they would break into a traditional Irish jig. He considered saying more, but didn't bother.

Instead, he stepped into the wings, leaving the guys alone on the stage, still tuning up. And tuning up. And tuning up.

"They better get on with it," Terry whispered. "Or this place is gonna explode."

"Play 'Freebird'!" A jock yelled out, generating a round of laughter. The noise broke Kelly's tune-up concentration, forcing him to step up to the mic.

I muttered to Gina, "I hope he doesn't do a long pointless intro." She nodded, worried.

Kelly opened his mouth, ready to talk and fill the empty air. We could see he was unsure what even to say, having never been in front of an audience, much less in front of an audience of his mercilessly judging classmates. Thankfully, Bucky, not realizing Kelly planned to talk, started drumming. Paul leaped in on bass for four bars of high speed, four-chord aggression. Kelly stepped back, waited for another four bars. Then he and Duncan jumped up in the air, landing together on the one beat, two screaming guitars joining the others. I didn't know that jump was coming, but my fast shutter finger snapped at the peak of their jump. The two of them, hair all over the place, guitar to guitar, legs kicked up behind them. Pete Townshend had nothing on these two.

An epic start. The crowd went wild. The four of us led the surge to our feet. There was no way to sit down for this. The band noticed the audience and ratcheted their energy up even more. This was what I meant about them needing to be in front of a cheering audience. They fed off of us. We amplified that a hundred-fold and sent it back their way. Repeat until critical mass is reached. Playing for the four of us, they were good, but they were a million times better with eight hundred appreciative teenagers. Their exuberance on that stage brought all the school cliques and tribes together for three shining minutes—the stoners and chess club, jocks and fags, keeners and wasters. We were all on our feet as one united group.

Then Kelly lunged at the mic, pushing his guitar around behind him, and started singing. The words spit out of his mouth, rapid-fire, machine-gun lyrics about the Shah in Iran, the CIA, bombs dropping. He was barely comprehensible but riveting for three explosive minutes until they blasted into the final repeating chorus. Duncan joined him at the mic, and the two of them sang/screamed over and over;

'The world is sitting on the edge tonight!

The world is sitting on the edge tonight!

The world is sitting on the edge of the world tonight!'

Quickly, because we resonated with the height-of-the-Cold-War words he was singing, the entire audience joined in, screaming along at the top of our lungs. It was a glorious moment and a spectacular debut for our friends. It was one for the yearbook pages, discussed for years to come, never duplicated.

Beside me, Gina sang as loud as she could. I desperately wanted to take her hand in mine, something I had wanted to do for years but couldn't. We had been friends for so long that the risk of taking that chance, taking that step, was too much. I wanted to, God, how I wanted to. And this was the perfect moment to take hold of her hand, to change our relationship, but I didn't. I couldn't. Then Duncan grinned maniacally, changed the lyrics, and the crowd willingly joined him;

'The world is SHITTING on the edge tonight!

The world is SHITTING on the edge tonight!

The world is SHITTING on the edge of the world tonight!'

I had abandoned taking pictures, so enveloped in the moment, but when Mr. Doyle stormed out from the side of the stage, I grabbed my camera and focused, catching him pulling the extension cord out of an outlet at the back of the stage. The three guitars and the mic suddenly went silent, leaving only Bucky drumming relentlessly, sweat flying off his face. The entire audience continued to scream out the song's new and improved lyrics.

Mr. Doyle tried to stop us, even as the auditorium lights come up. The burly night janitor with the pervy eyes stomped out and dragged Bucky from behind his drum kit. With the loss of a beat, the audience stumbled to a stop, our hands raised high in the air.

"Enough!" Mr. Doyle yelled in his best drill sergeant voice. "The rest of the show is canceled!"

Even those supposed to go on next were thrilled to get out of following Mayo. Imagine having to walk out onto that stage to twirl a baton after that?

The new school heroes raised their guitars to one final roof-raising cheer before running off to rescue Bucky.

"I knew they could do it," I said to Gina, and she grinned back at me, her face flush, eyes gleaming, hair glistening.

On The Edge - Mayo
Self-released cass-single, 1981

```
He lying in the sun and he be rolling in the sand,
on the equator
They want him in the east but now he living in the west,
who gets him later?
A hundred thousand dissidents were tortured
to their deaths
The Shah politely answers that it's all arithmetic
Americans were everywhere so call the CIA
There might have been some torture but they said it was OK


Taking it in stride 'cause someone's gotta be cool,
they're all fanatics
He said he never did a thing,
it's all a lot of noise and bureaucratics
Kick him out of power now they want to kick him more,
Kick him black and blue they gonna kick him 'til he's sore
```

```
Pretty soon we realize it doesn't really matter
It only takes a bomb or two to knock
the whole world flatter

The world is sitting on the edge tonight
The world is sitting on the edge tonight
The world is sitting on the edge of the world tonight
The world is sitting on the edge tonight
The world is sitting on the edge tonight
The world is sitting on the edge of the world tonight
```

The Cold War, Reagan in the White House, and increased nuclear annihilation threats were foreground throughout my high school life. A lot of us hadn't bothered making long-term life plans—we knew it was all going to be destroyed before we could enjoy it. Better to enjoy what was going on in front of you and be in the thick of it instead of sitting on the edge.

•

Other than chickening out and not taking Gina's hand during their performance, I had made one other error that night. When I went into the minuscule darkroom my parents had let me build in our basement to develop the film, the photos were garbage.

The rock-and-roll art I thought I had was blurry, and I had been way too far away from the stage. Worse, the band and my friends expected to see them soon. I knew they would be unhappy. I could have said the roll got exposed, but I printed out the 'best' pictures and took them to the next rehearsal.

I was right. Everyone was unhappy.

"That was our first show…" Bucky said, holding up the best shot I had —the backs of heads with the band far off in the distance, barely recognizable. Even the photo I was sure would turn out—Kelly and Duncan's jump at the song's start—was a blurry mess.

"I know, I'm sorry," I said, feeling horrible. "I thought I had it figured, but it's not like taking photos around the school for the yearbook."

"No shit," Neil muttered, hogging the joint being passed around the garage.

"It's not a big deal," Gina said, patting me on the arm. "You'll do better next time, right?"

That sympathetic pat on the arm was the worst part. I'd let Gina down.

She was right. I had to do better next time.

No more hiding in the audience, taking photographs from afar. I had to stop observing and start being right in the action. If I wanted to get the pictures that I saw in my head, I would have to become part of the show and not hide anymore. A terrifying thought, but those were the chances I would have to take to make myself, my friends and the band happy again.

19

The bell over the door rang as I stepped inside. So much the same, so very little changed. There was even an elderly Chinese lady sitting on the stool behind the till reading the local Chinese language newspaper. She looked up, and I pointed to an empty booth at the back. She nodded and went back to her paper. I walked through the booths and sat down, leaning against the back wall of the Ovaltine Cafe.

Terry said, do nothing that could affect the future, but how would it affect the future to have lunch? I went out last night and had changed nothing. Nothing happened at my bank. I had taken photographs, and nothing had happened. I needed to eat. If not here, then somewhere else. And it wasn't like anyone here knew me. I was a random middle-aged Chinese guy with feathered hair looking for a BLT and a cup of joe. Fifty-five-year-old Colin never came here in 1984. So time and Terry had nothing to worry about.

Someone had abandoned a copy of Discorder, the raw and random free indie newspaper put out by UBC's student radio station CITR, so I flicked it open. I'd rather have checked out the photos I'd taken so far, but since my digital camera came from a high-tech future, I wouldn't, at least, not until I was back in the privacy of my hotel room. It was like the old days of using actual film when your photographs were a complete mystery until you went into a darkroom, developed the roll, and made a contact sheet. Then, even using a magnifying glass, you couldn't know what you'd got until after the complex process of printing full-sized photographs. That was a lot of time, money and stress to go through before discovering if you took the shot you thought or if you had screwed up your F-stop or ISO setting and had a ruined roll of film.

I started reading an article on Grandmaster Flash when someone said, "You know what you want or do you need a menu?"

I looked up, and Celina—a pretty Celina a decade younger than my present age—stood in front of me. Her hair was long and jet black, not pulled back in a tight grey bun. She was standing up straight, not hunched over with age, and despite a few tiny wrinkles around her eyes, she looked fantastic. How did I not notice her when we came here back in the day? She was gorgeous in a calm but take-no-shit kind of way. I guess I had said nothing because she stared at me, a bit confused. Maybe I wasn't 100% there.

"Sorry, brain fart," I said.

She waited for a beat, then repeated her question.

"I'll have a BLT and cup of coffee, please," I said, trying not to stare. She jotted my order down on her pad, not asking what kind of bread I wanted or if I took anything in my coffee. She turned away, but she paused. "Do I know you?"

My heart tripped. Damnit. Terry was right, perhaps being here was screwing with time. As calmly as possible, I said, "Sadly, no, I've never been in here before."

Celina squinted and looked hard at my face. I kept my gaze steady, afraid of projecting massive guilt if I looked away. The old lady at the till yelled out in Chinese, and the spell broke. Celina rolled her eyes. "My mother. She says to return to work."

"You don't want to make your mother mad."

"You certainly do not want to do that," she said with a smile and a flirtatious flick of her luxurious long hair before heading back into the kitchen to deliver my order. What the hell? Celina, the hard-as-nails grandmother who guarded that same till in the future, was this flirty, sexy woman when we began dining here? I had no recollection of her like this, or like that, or whatever tense I should be using. While I pondered my flawed and skewed memory of being twenty-two, Celina returned with my coffee. I thanked her, then watched as she walked away. A tight pair of slacks showed off her fine ass. Then I stopped myself from watching as she leaned over to clear the table. Get it together. She was an eighty-year-old woman, a great-grandmother!

I sipped my coffee and concentrated on the paper, skimming editorials full of opinions about the upcoming federal election of which I already knew the results.

Celina had brought out my lunch, refilled my coffee, and I was enjoying the strange letters to the editor in the Discorder when I heard myself laugh. But what I was reading wasn't that funny, and I wasn't laughing. Then I laughed again, not in my mouth or in my head, but somewhere on the other side of the room. Sitting up, I furtively scanned the cafe. In a booth at the front, there was a twenty-two-year-old me with that long drooping hair—which needed to be cut short years before it was. Beside him was a whippet-thin, young Neil, the backs of Terry and Gina's heads visible across the booth from them. Ducking down out of their view, I rushed to figure out what to do.

Oh shit.

Oh shit, shit, shit.

What the hell was past-me doing here today? I should be in school! This was bad. This was totally bad. Terry's Catastrophic Disasters of Time and Space bad.

Be calm. Breathe. So far, they hadn't seen me. If I could slip out of here without being spotted, it would be a no harm, no foul situation. If past-me hasn't seen present-me, maybe we didn't impact the time continuum. The mere act of being in the same room as my past-self wasn't affecting either of us at the moment. But what if it already had? I didn't remember skipping college to come for lunch, but there we were. Had I already done something which had already altered my past life? Was it that kid I saved from the bus? Shit.

I needed to get out of here. Now. But I couldn't if young-me was looking my way. As soon as he got preoccupied, I could slip down the hallway to the toilets. From there, out into the alley. Once I was on my feet and facing away from him, it didn't matter if past-me saw present-me. I was nothing but a forgettable middle-aged businessman in a lousy suit heading to the toilet, never to return.

I glanced over the backs of the booths. The four were busy with their menus. Ok, excellent. Time to split. As I rose from my seat, keeping a careful eye on past-me, my camera bag strap caught my unused teaspoon, sending it clattering to the floor. I watched, in horrified slow motion, as past-me glanced up from his menu to look me straight in the eye.

The world pivoted. Up-down, left-right, back-forth.

All the air in my lungs went somewhere else for a split second and then returned, but with a distinct and very different smell, one like a plate of old hot pennies.

My stomach double flipped. Then triple flipped. My spine retracted and expanded at the same time as I dragged my eyes away from my younger self. Overcome with vertigo, I braced myself on the edge of the booth. Past-me shuddered, as if a bucket of invisible ice had splashed down the back of his shirt.

The coffee in my stomach surged towards my mouth.

This was precisely what Terry had warned me about.

Catastrophic Peril.

20

With my entire body spinning in every direction and my heart pounding in my chest like I was overdosing on E at a rave, I stumbled down the back hallway of the Ovaltine Cafe, barely holding myself up on the wall. Somehow I pushed open the fire escape and lunged out into the alley, immediately throwing up the contents of my stomach onto the grimy pavement.

The door slammed shut behind me, rattling my world even more. I attempted to catch my breath, realizing I was hyperventilating again. Christ, how messed up was this? Successfully go back in time only to die from a heart attack in a filthy alley. I leaned against the dirty brick wall beside the fire door. I missed and collapsed. Blackness was my friend, and I felt nothing as my back hit the ground.

•

"Hey!" A distorted voice yelled out.

I shuddered back to reality. Darkness slowed, my vision brightened until the alley walls and overhead wires came into focus, with blue sky above. I was flat on my back on the pavement of the alley behind the Ovaltine. My heart pumped, so I wasn't dead unless Heaven looked like a dirty East Vancouver alley. Which it might, which would teach me to skip church.

A blurry young Celina leaned in to stare down into my eyes. "You all right?"

I attempted to shake my head, failed, and returned to lay motionless on the ground. My right arm stretched out at an odd angle, my suit jacket open. I turned to my side, trying to push myself upright, but I was horribly dizzy. At the end of the alley, my eyes focused enough to spy a scruffy looking guy rushing around the corner. Why was I lying down?

I looked back at Celina, staring down, holding a bag of garbage.

"You Ok?" she asked again.

I found my voice and said, shakily, "I don't know, I think so." I sat up, my head pounding like the worst tequila hangover ever. "But I'm gonna stay sitting here for a moment anyway."

Worried, Celina asked, "Could those guys have robbed you? You have your wallet?"

I checked my back slacks pocket. Yes, wallet was there. Front slacks pocket contained my hotel room key.

"What happened? You seemed fine inside."

"I don't know, maybe a panic attack, something like that. I needed some air so came out here and…"

She put down the garbage bag, reached out her hand, and helped me to my feet. Terribly unsteady but upright. She brushed off my jacket as I took a deep stabilizing breath.

"You're lucky I came out when I did," Celina said with concern.

I nodded slowly, cautiously. "Thank you."

A bit more of my bearings returned then I freaked out. "My camera! Shit, he took my camera!" I stumbled towards the entrance of the alley, ready to follow the bum. Celina took my arm and stopped me.

"Let me go. I need to get it back!" What would happen when they opened the bag up and found a super hi-def digital camera from the future inside? If I even made it back, Terry would kill me.

"You left it inside. My mother has it safely behind the counter," she said. I gave up trying to shake off her grip. A couple more deep breaths brought my heart rate down to merely panicking. Thank God they didn't have my camera. Ignoring the time travel catastrophe of leaving future tech in the past, I would have lost all the photos I'd taken so far.

"You sure you're not hurt?" she asked again, and I nodded. Yes, I'm alright. I think. I merely had to stay in this fragrant alley until my past-self leaves. Relieved, she put the garbage into the bin beside the back door.

"I need to go back to work, but you take your time, yeah?"

I nodded again, but she paused, double-checking my status before pulling open the fire door and heading back inside, leaving me alone in the alley. I shakily lit a cigarette and leaned back against the one clean spot on the brick wall.

Jesus, that was the weirdest sensation I'd ever had. And I had travelling back in time for comparison. I had never considered what would happen if I came in contact with my past-self. Something, sure, but not freaking heart attack symptoms, vomiting, and passing out. My past-self looked like he had a sudden, wicked migraine and hopefully would blow it off as that. Maybe a lingering hangover from last night.

Why were the young us even inside at all? Had I done something to cause a sudden change in their plans? Had I somehow affected this time frame enough to alter my past-self and friends already, so they chose to slip out of their responsibilities and go for lunch? I took a deep inhale and exhale, realizing my thoughts were absurd. Ripples had to take longer to expand out far enough to make that level of change. If young-me was inside having lunch now, then he hadn't even woken up until an hour ago. There had been no time for old-me to impact young-me's routine. So, therefore, young-me being inside was simply a fluke. Random lousy luck on my part. Just because I didn't remember skipping school thirty-three years ago doesn't mean I didn't. Obviously, ditching class happened at least once because we were presently inside.

Unfortunate and unexpected, but I couldn't let it impact my trip back. Wait out here in the alley, then go in, grab my camera bag and head downtown to meet with Dennis, pick up the stock certificates, give him the certified—

Oh no.

My cigarette dropped as I shoved my hand into my jacket. The envelope with my certified check was gone! Frantically, I checked my other pockets, then rechecked each of my pockets. No. My pockets were empty.

Maybe I had left it inside with my camera bag. No. I had explicitly folded and buttoned it into my inside jacket pocket at the bank.

I scanned the alley, hoping against hope that the envelope was lying there. But it wasn't.

Then I remembered. That guy who ran out of the alley. He must have my money—a certified check for $4500. A certified check I had moronically chosen to have made out to 'cash.'

I had been stupid, impulsively coming to the Ovaltine when I absolutely knew better. But I was sure we wouldn't be inside. But I'd never been more wrong in my life. I'd surrendered to the siren song of nostalgia, positive I was safe. I had done something I shouldn't have, and had completely, utterly fucked up.

21

Exiting the alley onto Main Street, I frantically scanned the busy streets and sidewalks for the bums. But they were nowhere to be seen. Why would they be? With the kind of windfall they had in their hands, why would they hang around? Fumbling my wallet out of my back pocket, I double-checked that the living money I came back with was there. Celina must have come out of the restaurant and scared them off before they could grab my wallet out from under me, thank God.

The streets, which were so friendly an hour ago, now felt like pure evil. Out to get me, out to stop me. There was a bullseye on my back, the red laser dot of a high-powered rifle moving over my chest. Going back inside the Ovaltine was out of the question until my past-self had left. At a complete loss, I headed to the bus stop across from the entrance to the cafe to wait.

Which gave me time to consider my mammoth predicament.

Ignoring Terry's warnings had screwed our well thought-out plan. Worse, I didn't merely ignore his predictions. I willfully did the complete opposite. Terry wasn't subtle either about potential outcomes. He would have had his chief concern tattooed onto the back of my hand if I'd let him.

"Don't Fuck With Time."

And yet, I figured I knew better. I took chances for the first time in my life. And look what happened.

If Jean-Claude and his TimeCops existed, they'd be arriving to arrest me at any second.

All I had was two hundred and fifty dollars in my wallet and an appointment with a broker who expected me to hand over my now-lost certified check for $4,500. I needed to figure out how to score another considerable chunk of cash as fast as possible. Either that or admit I screwed up, and our future was now one where we would pay back the additional five thousand dollars of credit card debt we each put in to buy the gold coins. Besides being out of a job and out of our house.

My arrogant stupidity had made our future lives a lot worse, and this was my only activation of the time machine. My grandchildren might get the chance to change their lives with the time machine. But it was unlikely I would ever have children—especially being middle-aged, homeless, and unemployed.

So I sat and smoked, gut-wrenchingly sorry for myself. Was there any way out of my predicament? In this wretched moment, I couldn't see a fix to my problem. We had only pieced together one good idea to take money back into the past. It had been hard for four—five, if you counted Celina —of us to figure it out. There hadn't been a second option. No backup idea. Simply me alone in the past with a plan which I'd completely screwed up in mere hours. I hadn't been taking our plan or our situation seriously. Instead I went back to the haunts of my youth, the Railway Club, the Town Pump, the Ovaltine. I'd gone on a fun ride of nostalgia and my friends were now going to pay the price in the future.

An old delivery truck rumbled past, clutch grinding as the driver sped up for a block before the next light changed and he stopped with a squeal of old brakes. An old Jamaican lady with her groceries in a thin wire trolley wearily sat down on the bench beside me. She stared straight ahead, spine straight, head erect, and waited for the bus to take her home. She might not be thrilled with her life, but at least she understood what was happening in it from one day to the next. If she only realized the seething mass of out-of-time turmoil sitting beside her. One last drag of my cigarette before I flicked it into the street. Her eyes watched the butt land, roll, then have an '81 Buick LeSabre crush it flat. An apt metaphor for my current circumstance.

Maybe I could find one of Neil's dealers and borrow the cash from him. Then not pay it back. So a dealer was out a few grand. What would that matter in the big picture? Except I didn't know any of Neil's dealers. When we were young, he was excellent at keeping his side activities far on the side. And why would they give me the money? They don't know me. I'd have to use Neil's name even to arrange a meeting if I could find them. Then, when my 'loan' defaulted, who would they go to for payback? Neil. Neil would be on the hook for the entire 5K, plus penalties. Physically debilitating penalties. Shit.

I considered hopping the bus to rob Gina's parents, but I didn't know how to pull off a successful B&E. Worse, the ripples from stealing her mom's jewelry would impact us all. Especially Gina. Besides, her mom was most likely at home. She didn't return to the workforce until Gina's youngest brother graduated high school and took off to university in Toronto.

Lighting another cigarette as a bus pulled up, I watched as the old lady hoisted her full grocery cart up the three steep, narrow steps to get inside. The driver stared at me, but I waved him on. He manhandled the door lever with a sigh and then drove off in a roar and a belch of exhaust.

An hour later, having smoked every one of my cigarettes while considering and dismissing potential solutions to my unsolvable problem, I was still sitting on the bus bench when the gang bounced out the front door of the Ovaltine. Finally. Time to grab my camera before going back to my hotel room to continue my futile problem-solving.

They said goodbye to each other on the sidewalk. Then past-Terry and past-me strolled west towards downtown as Gina and Neil walked off in the other direction. My past-self glanced back at Gina, full of longing. I cringed in embarrassment. Was it that obvious how much I liked her? Back then, I was positive I was cool as ice, and my memories had validated that recollection. But here I was, watching from across the street as past-me stared like a sad, love-struck puppy as Gina walked away. Sickening nausea engulfed me. No subtlety at all. Blatantly obvious, and everyone had to have known. But no one said anything, so I continued my secret love-struck routine, embarrassing myself and Gina as well.

Even worse, here I was staring at young-Gina with the same lost-puppy look on my fifty-five-year-old face. She was so stunning and beautiful. Tough as nails, cool as a cucumber. All those trite metaphors wrapped up in an amazing bundle. She flicked her hair out of her face, like she always had, and my heart skipped a beat. Young-me stumbled over a ridge in the sidewalk exactly like old-me would if I wasn't sitting down.

Coming back to my best summer should have been the most fantastic adventure of a lifetime, but this was a new level of soul-crushing awful. Not only were our future chances ruined, but seeing how genuinely pathetic I used to be added insult to injury. Maybe part of being young was not knowing how pathetic you actually were: how could any of us make it to adulthood if we discovered what we were really like? We must have a built-in cognitive block, for if we didn't, we'd have killed ourselves in our early teens. It was essential to believe we were cool, exceptional, and not full of shit. As I looked across at my past-self, it was unsettling how pathetic my present-self found that person—almost unbearably so.

As my past-self and Terry turned the corner onto Main Street and disappeared from view, I rose from the hard wooden bench. I was preparing to head across Hastings to the Ovaltine when Neil took Gina's hand at the far end of the block as they walked away.

What the ever-loving—?

Camera and lunch forgotten, I hurried along the opposite side of the street from Gina and Neil. What the hell were they doing holding hands? They hated each other. He always mocked her, and she always pointed out his sexist and Neanderthal ways. So, with all the animosity between them, why the hell were they walking off together? And why the hell were they holding hands?

Confusion turned to bile as Neil turned them onto Princess Avenue, heading north towards one likely destination. Neil's basement suite. I jaywalked, barely avoided getting hit by a Canada Post truck, and raced ahead to the building across from his place. A businessman in a lousy suit jogged raggedly up the sidewalk past me. After turning the corner of the warehouse, I spun around and peered back, my insides clenching, half from the running, but more from what I feared I would witness.

Gina, please say goodbye and continue walking, I begged as they arrived at the rusted gate to the run-down old house where Neil had an illegal basement suite. He said one of his uncles owned the house, but he had a lot of uncles and many non-uncles who were also called uncles, so who knew which one he meant. Neil, being Neil, wasn't forthcoming about his extended family. Gina released Neil's hand, and I let out a deep sigh of relief. Please, Gina, walk away. Now.

But they continued to chat, all smiley and flirty. Then Neil leaned over and kissed her. On the mouth. I staggered back in absolute shock. Never would I have imagined this. They hated each other. They had always only tolerated each other since we started hanging out. Never had they even been alone together, to my knowledge. But apparently, that was a lie, like how I thought I was cool. I wasn't cool, and Gina and Neil were more than non-friends.

A little rational part of my brain knew this shouldn't matter. She and I weren't going out in 1984. I hadn't even made a move until three years later, kissing Gina for the first time while at the top of the Ferris wheel at the PNE, fireworks exploding in the sky and my heart. But it mattered. She said nothing about ever being with Neil. Never. And she should have. I told her about everyone I ever dated, not that there were many. She'd met a fair number of them. And I believed her when she told me about everyone she'd gone out with, but that was a lie.

Unable to peer around the corner for fear they were kissing outside or, worse, they weren't outside, meaning they were inside doing more than kissing, I staggered off, sick to my stomach.

Coming back in time was the absolute worst thing I had ever experienced in my life. Guaranteed.

22

Wednesday 1 pm - 59 hours to go

The tight city block of Oppenheimer Park, surrounded by mature shade trees, appeared before me. A couple of baseball diamonds. A weary playground in need of repair. I gave up wandering and dropped onto a bench. My entire life—past, present, and future—was a complete shambles. The stolen certified check. Neil and Gina.

Gina and I had started hanging out in the summer after tenth grade. 1979. We'd been in a couple of shared classes and bonded over the essential teenaged subjects—teachers we hated and music.

I was already finding and buying local indie band 45's and EP's, and Gina liked them. But when we hung out, after goofing around at the local tennis court, decked out in our Adidas shorts, high white socks, and cheap rackets, we slouched in her basement rec room and listened to her albums. That summer, five new artists filled our ears: Elvis Costello, The Police, XTC, The Buzzcocks, and Joe Jackson—New Wave heaven. This was our music. Songs that got some airplay on FM, but differed from what our older siblings listened to. We'd kill ourselves laughing when Gina's heavy metal-loving older brother called 'Candy-O' by The Cars an ungodly racket like he was sixty. We passed liner notes back and forth, talking for hours about nothing, comfortable in each other's company. During those long summer days, even considering going out with Gina was inconceivable. She was too cool, too unattainable. I couldn't imagine in my wildest dreams actually dating her. If I had, she would have sensed it and then chilling on a ratty old couch, rolling coins from her one-gallon coin jar, drinking Coke and joking around would have become uncomfortable beyond belief for each of us.

What her parents thought, I hadn't a clue. Clearly, they considered me harmless because they would politely invite me to stay for dinner. But they must have wondered what was, or wasn't, going on in the basement for those many private hours the two of us spent together.

That summer, without knowing it, Gina taught me how to be around women, be real, and not treat them as objects. Spending more time with Neil would have taught me a raft of misogynistic skills. What Gina taught me was much more valuable. So, when I finally built up the nerve to first kiss and then ask Gina out, we'd already been friends for over a decade. Then I escaped the friend zone.

But now what was I supposed to think? Neil and Gina kissing on the street outside his house wouldn't leave my head. Maybe it wouldn't ever. What would I do or say when I returned to the future? Confront her about it or let it slide? Again, we weren't going out in '84, so she hadn't actually cheated on me. But still...

In my brain-shocked emotional state, I wanted to never leave that graffitied bench. But sitting in the park watching a flock of pigeons peck at the scuffed ground wouldn't help me. There was no other choice. Maybe by regrouping, it would be possible to pull this plan off, but only if I didn't spend the next two days moping about Gina and that asshole. I mean, she and I had been a couple for almost thirty years! So whatever happened between her and Neil couldn't have counted for much in the greater scheme of our conjoined lives. But the shock of the sudden knowing, the ice pick of doubt in my psyche over unbidden questions, hurt. A lot. Debilitating, freezing, heart-gutting hurt. Worse, I needed to shove that agonizing hurt, that stabbing pain deep down and do what I was here to do. So, how do you go on through this kind of pain? How do you internally regroup enough to keep going forward? Booze? Drugs? Exercise? Psychotherapy?

For me, when I was in a world of emotional pain, there was only one solution.

My headphones went on. Heartbreak songs? Like every musical artist in the history of the planet, Kelly, Duncan and Norm all had their share of relationships gone bad and had channeled their emotions into their music. Songs like Lied To, She's Not Mine, Amnesia. I flipped over the cassette in my Walkman and pressed play. Of course, like how the perfect tarot card for any situation was the one last turned over, the perfect song awaited me:

What Ever Happened to Boy Meets Girl - Mayo
Indie EP, 'A Side of Mayo.' 1982

You're sitting all alone a place to call your own
She said she would, she said she'd come,
She promised she would phone
She was so disgusted with the way you were last night
You should have just gone home and slept alone

But you're wondering
Whatever happened to boy meets girl
Isn't there anyone in the world for me?

You're sitting waiting there, you wish you had a chair
Your hands are tied, your hands are tied no one even sees
Everything's so hazy in the magazines

```
Can't see the details, was it like, was it really like
```

```
Whatever happened to boy meets girl
Isn't there anyone in the world
Isn't there anyone in the world
Isn't there anyone in the world
Isn't there anyone in the world for me?
```

```
Sitting all alone you're waiting by the phone
You hope she'll call, she said she will, I guess she would
You're  so  disgusted  with  the  trick  photography  in
magazines
About that life you know you'll wait alone
```

```
And you're wondering
Whatever happened to boy meets girl
Isn't there anyone in the world
Isn't there anyone in the world
Isn't there anyone in the world
Isn't there anyone in the world for me?
```

```
Whatever happened to boy meets girl?
```

How could knowledge of something that had happened thirty-three years ago have so much impact? It was like finding out that everyone knew the world was round, but no one had told me, and I discovered it by accident. Something in my core had altered, but I didn't know if it needed to be. 'What difference does it make' fought with 'everything has changed.' But nothing had changed. The events I had seen happened whether I knew about them or not. And now I did. Boys met girls all the time, but why did Neil have to meet up with Gina?

By the time the song ended, I was back at Main and Hastings, and the stupid battery in my Walkman was dead. Extras were in my backpack at the hotel. I'd forgotten how essential a pocketful of extra Duracell's was to portable music in the past. And I was hungry. I double-checked through the Ovaltine Cafe's front window for anyone I knew, then entered.

Celina's mother looked up, frowned, then pointed back to the booth where I had been before. I nodded, chastened, and sat down. My coffee was as cold as my BLT. Picking up a half, I took a bite as Celina stepped up, putting my camera case in on the booth seat. "Good grief, don't eat that. I'll order you a new one."

Before I could argue, she took my plate and cup back into the kitchen, returning with a clean cup and a coffee pot. As she filled my fresh cup, she said, "Wasn't sure if you were coming back."

"I guess I needed more air than I realized."

She nodded, then looked around the mostly empty room before sitting down across from me. She leaned over to the adjacent table, grabbed a cup, poured herself a coffee, and stared at me from across the booth.

"You sure you're all right?"

"A bit shook up."

"I guess so."

We sipped our coffee.

"You from around here? I haven't seen you before," she asked.

"I used to live around here," I said disingenuously. Celina nodded. "And now?"

"Just passing through."

"And you came to the Downtown Eastside for lunch?"

I shrugged. What else was there to say? I'd come back in time and came here despite being explicitly told not to by one of the four youngsters who had been in the front booth, and now I'd screwed up my —and everyone else's—future?

"Nice jacket. What do you do?" Celina said with a wink.

What did I know about her? She'd been a side character in my life for around forty years. But we had talked little during those decades because she'd always been a generation older than me. My mother's age, or my grandmother's. But now, sitting over there, she wasn't the matriarch with her inscrutable gaze, watching the goings-on in her restaurant from behind the counter while her daughter took orders and served food. Now, she was a beautiful, younger woman who was apparently interested in me.

"I'm unemp—I'm working on a screenplay, a movie," I said, remembering how future-Celina helped us out with our plan.

"Interesting. Not what I expected you to say. I figured something in finance, maybe banking, except for the hair. Too long for banking. What's your screenplay about?"

So I told her, sticking to the story future-Celina helped us create. Our hero with his one three-day chance to go back in time to 1984. His plan to buy stock and hide them. Then, after returning to the future, cash them in to ensure his family live the good life from then on.

She considered my 'story' then said, "Why not go back from '84 to 1951? That would be more interesting, wouldn't it?"

"I considered going in that direction," I said, lying. 'Back to the Future' was coming out next year. "But everyone does that in time travel stories. I'm trying something different, with the hero coming back to the 'present day.' It's a statement about how what we imagine as modern and progressive looks pretty old-fashioned when he comes back, especially compared to what the future is like in Vancouver."

"Well, it's your story."

A wizened Chinese cook rushed out from the kitchen and delivered my new BLT. We thanked him, she in Chinese and me in English. I picked up half of the sandwich and took a large bite. Before I knew it, the entire piece had disappeared. So good. A perfect BLT on white bread with lots of Miracle Whip.

The stabilizing effect of having food in my stomach grounded me enough to say, "But now I'm stuck with the next section of the story."

"I'm a bit of a writer. What's the problem?" She was a writer? I hadn't known that. Again, not like we ever had a real talk in the 40 years we had known each other, except for her helping us out with our story in 2017.

"Well, he's back in the past, ticking off parts of his scheme. It's going well, but then he's robbed of the money he took back. So now he's broke, unable to complete his now not-so-brilliant plan."

"Of course, you can't have the story go smoothly for him. It would be pretty boring if it did, right?"

I sighed and nodded. She was right. If this were a movie, the hero would have to have setbacks. In reality, I banked on everything going as smoothly as my morning had. I would finish our 'perfect' plan, then hide out in my hotel room until the time to go forward in time and become filthy rich.

"So what does he do? He can't give up."

"Of course not. I'm stuck. Or, he's stuck. We're stuck."

"Hmm. Quite the predicament. Not like the hero can rob someone because his theft would mess with 'capital T' time." Her mother called to her, gesturing towards a couple milling at the front door. Celina rose from the booth, grabbing the coffee pot.

"Leave it with me. Enjoy your sandwich. I'll be back in a sec. Quite an interesting dilemma you've set your hero up in."

"Thanks," I said. Interesting wouldn't be my choice of word. More like catastrophic.

Ideas come and go in my head while I ate the rest of my meal, then wiped the plate clean with the last of my fries. My thoughts were all garbage, looping from robbing Gina's or my parents to taking out a bank loan and defaulting on it. But the loan idea was a dead end because they'd want my real name and ID. But my ID was from 2017, not 1984, and I was fifty-five, not twenty-two. No one would believe I was me. Maybe if I had grabbed my father's old ID, I could work something out. But even then, after I returned to the future on Friday night, whoever had given me the loan would go after my father for the money he didn't know he owed, which would be the same as if I had stolen it from him myself.

Celina finished taking the new table's order, filled their coffee cups, ran meals out to two other tables, then returned to sit across from me.

"Any brilliant ideas to save my hero?" I asked.

"Not a solution but a twist."

I looked at her with interest.

"There should be someone in the past he goes to talk to, someone who could help him out."

"He can't go talk to his past-self because that would mess with Time too much."

"Of course, but if there were someone else he could see, someone who knows him in the future, that would be a pretty exciting scene. And maybe they could help him out."

I considered her suggestion. It would be a brilliant scene in a movie, full of drama, conflict, shock and confusion. But in reality, anyone I explained my situation to would have me committed in a psych ward—like Bruce Willis in '12 Monkeys'. Which I had re-watched the movie with Neil and a growler of Red Arrow's Midnight Umber. Partially as research but mostly because I liked it. Lucky for me, there wasn't time for electroshock and anti-psychotic drugs before Friday at midnight.

"Great idea. Thanks. It would be a real twist to the story that I hadn't considered," I said.

"Setbacks are good. Well, for your character. It allows him to learn and figure out how to solve his problems. To become better through the process."

Great, the perfect way to spend my time while I was back in time. Learn and become better. Forget that, give me the stock certificates, I'd hide in my hotel room, then blip out of here. The past had lost any interest. I wanted to go back home to my friends and family.

I stopped drinking my coffee. Hmm, maybe Celina had given me a solution. If I was lucky, and the timing was right, my making my appointment with Dennis at three was back to being a possibility. As Celina watched me, my brain whirring, I took out my wallet and put a twenty down on the table.

"Oh, that's way too much."

"You've helped me out a lot, so consider it an advance on your co-writing credit," I said with a smile, standing up along with her.

"You come back and let me know how it goes, please? I'll always be here."

"That sounds like a plan," I promised. There wasn't a chance I would be back in the Ovaltine again before 2017, in case my past-self unexpectedly showed up again. Grabbing my camera bag, I turned around. Celina had her hand out to shake.

"I'm Celina," she said.

I took her hand. The heat from where she was holding her coffee cup made her hand warm. Strong and soft. "Colin. Nice to meet you."

23

Leaving the Ovaltine and Celina behind for good, I walked over into Chinatown. A block off Main Street was a mahjong parlor, accessible through a narrow unmarked door hidden beside a busy restaurant. There was a small check-in desk at the top of a rickety flight of stairs, the clatter of tiles filling the low-ceilinged space behind it. Like everywhere, there was a low level of smoke. Fifteen tables arranged in three rows of five, full of elderly Chinese men and women, engrossed in the games in front of them.

My grandmother, May Fong, was in there somewhere. She spent her days here at a table of four. They would rattle the tiles, gather them at the end of each game, flip them upside down and shuffle them before starting the next match. Maybe May and her friends gambled while playing, and I suspected they did. The old men in the room were for sure. What was the point of playing a gambling game without gambling?

My friends and I had played many a game of Rummoli in my basement rec room, the four of us sitting on the oval woven carpet around a battered coffee table, piles of nickels and dimes in front of us. Games would go on for hours, pausing only for toilet breaks or to flip over an album on the family stereo. We would drink bottle after bottle of Pick-a-Pop—the discount soda, burrow our way through bags of Old Dutch chips and play like we were in Vegas at the high roller table. I would lose a couple of bucks in an evening. Neil often won, and the other two would break even. Looking back, this was when and how Neil picked up his taste for gambling. The highs of winning even a minuscule amount—which was rather impressive when stacked in nickels instead of hundred dollar chips—caught him and took hold. After a few years, we stopped playing, Neil pushing for quarters and even dollar bills as part of the game, which turned a fun evening for me—since I generally lost—into an expensive undertaking. With an addiction to record purchasing and photography, I had little to spare for games of chance. So when Neil started avoiding Rummoli Night to go to the Hastings race track with his uncles, the game fell apart, not very missed by the rest of us. We just folded up the game and put it away with the other board games of our youth—like Risk, Life, and Trouble.

I knew better than to stroll around the mahjong parlor looking for my grandmother, so I asked the lady at the counter if she could pass her a message.

With suspicion, she agreed, butted out her cigarette, and took the jotted note I handed her. With a polite smile, expressing gratitude and respect, I climbed back down the stairs. From experience, she wouldn't leave the counter until the outside door shut behind me. Like I was a criminal casing the joint, she'd watch until I'd departed. Only then would she take the note to my grandmother. All the while monitoring the door, in case I tried to sneak back in.

The restaurant's front window below the parlor was full of roast duck hanging from hooks, other meat arranged underneath. A display was full of assorted buns—pork, coconut, bean—next to the till. No one paid any attention as I walked through to the restaurant at the back and took a seat with an unobstructed view of the front door. The menu was trapped under the sheet of glass on the table. The BLT had me sated, so I ordered a pot of tea and two cups when a waitress zipped up to the table. She scowled; to take up a perfectly good table moments before the lunch rush would require more than tea. I ordered two coconut buns, knowing May liked them. Grudgingly, the waitress left, and I waited.

The restaurant walls were pink, as was the industrial drop ceiling. Framed prints on the wall, old travel posters of China. I remembered staring at them during my family meals here as a child. The then-bold graphics of gorges, towering islands, the forbidden city, Peking, Chungking, of places whose names changed while in elementary school from the original British mistranslations to the current more accurate names.

Servers rushed back and forth into the kitchen at the far end of the room. Visible through the pass-through were bursts of steam and flares of flame from the woks. Plates piled high came one way, dirty dishes piled in bus pans going the other. The din of the kitchen and the restaurant filled my head. If there was background music playing, I couldn't hear it.

The tea and the buns arrived at the table as my grandmother came through the front door. She waved to the people behind the counter and received waves back. They chatted for a bit while she glanced around the restaurant, looking for her twenty-two-year-old grandson, who wasn't there. I raised my hand to get her attention. She saw me—a fifty-five-year-old businessman in a tan suit—then looked behind her as if I was drawing someone else's attention. I gestured again for her to join me and, after considering who I might be, she did warily.

"Do I know you? I was told to meet my grandson," she said, healthy and spry at a young fifty-seven years old. My family had their children at young ages, except for my generation, who had held off until my sister had the first great-grandchild in her mid-thirties.

I gestured for her to sit down and poured her a cup of tea. After rechecking the restaurant for any sign of her missing grandson, she sat, gripping her purse in her lap.

I wasn't sure how to convey what I needed to say now that she was here with me. But she was the only one on the planet who knew about the time machine, which meant she was the only one to talk to about my predicament.

"Grandma May," I began, but she stopped me with a frown and a raised hand.

"You are mistaken. I am not your grandmother."

I leaned forward and looked at her, letting her see my face. She looked closely, not understanding why this stranger was behaving like this. Then I said, "Yes, grandma, I am your grandson. I'm Colin."

She sat back, sharpened her gaze for a moment, then jolted in recognition.

"*Ay yah, moh-ah!*" she exclaimed, then clamped her hand over her mouth. "Colin, you used the machine!"

I nodded. She picked up her teacup with shaking hands and took a sip. When she put it down, her shock was replaced with sharp anger. "You can't be here! What horrible tragedy has happened in the future for you to risk everything and come back? I must have told you not to take the machine lightly! You have to leave now. Do what you must but leave me out of it. I cannot help you. Everything will go horribly wrong if I do!"

"But grandma, I need your help!"

She waved her hands in front of me, warding my words off like they're angry wasps. "No! I cannot know, not anything!"

I backed off, taking a sip of my tea. The coconut buns lay ignored between us. I let her cool down a bit before saying anything else. She drank her tea, and I refilled her cup. I didn't push the conversation because she was avoiding looking at me. She was the most potent force in our family, lucky to be born in Canada right after my great-grandparents escaped China in 1928, ahead of a world war and the Chinese revolution.

"Everything was great," I said. "But then I got robbed and now… Now I don't know what to do. If I don't figure this out, May, I will fail. I need to find four and a half thousand dollars, fast."

She leaned forward, her hands shaking in fury. "You are in peril being here with me. I am in peril being here with you. Time does not like that machine. I should have destroyed it! Now you are here where you could destroy the life we have worked so hard to make!"

She stood up from the table, jostling her cup, and spilled tea onto the coconut buns.

"Grandma…"

"No!" she said, loud enough for adjacent tables to look up. Noticing, she dropped her voice. "No. You stay away from me. Do what you have to do, but do it without my help."

With that, she turned and stormed out of the restaurant, leaving me with cold tea and a plate of wet snacks.

My waitress came over and replaced my empty teapot with a full one. I nodded in thanks; she didn't nod back. The staff were judging me for causing a scene with a regular customer. Fair enough, I had upset my grandmother. But what else was I supposed to do? Where else could I turn to for help now that the one person in 1984 who knew about the time machine had bolted? Only one person alive knew what I'd done and how. Other than Celina, who figured I was writing a dumb screenplay with an implausible plot. Except, for me, this was not fiction; this was my reality.

Look at me, stuck in the past with no way forward. Our meticulously thought-out plan was in tatters because of my stupidity. No longer thirsty, I put a ten-dollar bill on the table and left the restaurant. The responsible action now was to return to my horrible hotel room and watch old network TV until the moment I went forward again.

I started up my Walkman and remembered the battery was still dead. I shuffled along the streets, cutting over to Hastings to start my long, final walk back to my hotel. Across the busy street, the neon sign for the Smiling Buddha Cabaret flickered on and off. Despite my depression and my failure, I paused and took a couple of photographs of the iconic sign. Local rock heroes, 54-40, used a similar photo on the cover of their breakout album and when the club closed for good, their lead singer, Neil Osbourne, purchased the sign for posterity.

It would be nice to do something like that instead of knowing that my posterity equaled one of debt and failure without a solution to my catastrophic screw-up.

24

November 1982

Despite the Smiling Buddha Cabaret being one of those places where ID was optional at the best of times and false most of the time, we were of age for our friend's first legitimate show. On Monday nights, new acts took over the stage. Tonight had four bands, with Mayo being the lowest on the bill, meaning first on stage. A couple of bands from across the Georgia Strait in Victoria—Easy Money and Pink Steel—were the headliners. The crowd was mostly our age, from rival high schools but veterans of the same underage and after-hours clubs we'd been at for years. The Oddfellows, the Ukrainian, Japanese and Swedish Halls all hosted indie bands for a good price. Or we'd all see each other at Luxury Bob's or Stalag 13, not to mention random warehouse spaces. There was a community and a genuine camaraderie at these shows. We may not be friends with everyone, but we knew them as a group.

The four of us arrived early, intent on grabbing good seats. But with four unknown bands playing on a cold and rainy night, scoring a table in front of the stage was as easy as walking up and sitting down. Flush from winning at the horse track, Neil flagged down a waitress with a tray full of 12 oz glasses of cheap beer. He bought eight, never knowing when she'd next be by. Arcane liquor rules meant you couldn't buy a beer at the bar and walk back to your table, so tough waitresses prowled the room, trays full of glasses of beer, knowing they'd sell them in short order.

After their explosive debut at our school, the boys had taken their notoriety and meager savings to one of the many extremely low budget recording studios in town and recorded eight songs in three hours. I'd gotten to be there taking photos, in case this was their only time in a 'real' recording studio. They pressed the best four onto a 45 sized EP. They sold it out of their lockers at school and at Zulu Records and a few other local independent music stores. Kelly tried to get the EP into A&B Sound—the biggest game in town, but their purchasing department wasn't interested —A&B was too huge, and the band was too weird. Who named their group after a condiment? The best part, other than listening to them in relative fidelity from the comfort of our rec rooms, was the cover included the photograph I had taken of the band on that first night we'd found them. They paid me $20 and put my name on the album credits. My resume could now contain the words' professional photographer'! Best I didn't tell anyone that photograph was the only good one I took that night.

With an hour to wait until the band started their four-song set, we pondered their future over cheap beers—would they become the next hot thing from Vancouver? The next Payola's, who'd already moved up from raw indie punk rockers to seasoned professionals? Or disappear forever, leaving nothing but their indie EP?

We finished our eight beers, Neil flagged down a waitress to get eight more. Up on stage, our guys set up. They were their own roadies, having borrowed Duncan's brother's van to bring down their equipment, on the threat of death if the van was damaged in any way while the show was going on. Wisely, they'd brought Paul's dog along, a threatening-looking, loud barking but chickenshit Doberman to leave in the empty van as a living car alarm.

With no introduction or warmup, the house lights dimmed—a good thing since the only redeeming feature of the club was the neon sign outside—and the harsh light from a dozen par-cans flooded the stage. The now-slightly more substantial crowd shifted in their seats as the band readied themselves.

"We're Mayo!" Kelly yelled.

"Who gives a fuck?" someone called back from the pool table.

Before Kelly and Duncan could show off their Scottish heritage by dropping their guitars and attacking their heckler, Bucky started drumming, and they had to let the insult go, for now.

My camera was ready as the band blasted into their first song, 'Pretty Modern,' a power-pop tune about dating a girl who was making all the first moves. It was a great song, but the wrong tone for the room. This was a place for angry, sonic assaults, not self-deprecatory wit. I didn't care because I loved the song, but it did not impress the surly bikers and hardcore punks around us. The song ended with a bang, followed by the requisite catcalls of 'You suck!'

We laughed as the band struggled to ignore the insults and avoid the beer glasses thrown in their direction. They regrouped before diving into that first song from the garage years before. 'Young and Overequipped' brought the crowd back to neutral. The crowd threw another round of abuse at the stage, but the band soldiered on. They knew they had to give it their all, understanding this was what they signed up to do. Climb up on any stage and play as if you'd never play again. Leave nothing behind and play like you didn't give a fuck about the audience. Play because you couldn't do anything else but play. What would these four do if not perform? Could you imagine Kelly working in his father's paint store; or Paul working alongside his father in an automotive repair shop? And

Bucky, the only thing Bucky could do was bang as hard as possible on a drum set, which—if you're not in a band—wasn't an employable life skill.

I moved around the front of the stage, taking photographs as the band ground out a solid wall of sound. I was getting pretty good at photographing bands, making a bit of a name for myself off Mayo's EP cover. Indie groups in town would offer free tickets, copies of their cassettes and EP's or homemade merchandise if I fired off a couple of rolls of photographs at some show. I'd then develop and print off the best ones in my darkroom in my parent's basement. I wasn't getting rich by a long shot, but the bands appreciated my pictures, and I digged that. More than that, I felt like I was doing what I should be doing. I was getting a feel of when and where to be to get the best shots—Kelly screaming into a mic, Bucky lunging for that double cymbal crash, Duncan and Paul leaning on each other while laughing their asses off. I was in the zone. Like the guys up on stage and their music, I was 100% focused on my camera. And I was getting good at it like the band was.

Mayo redeemed themselves a bit with their third, one of their early, three-chord songs about a shitty AM station Duncan listened to while stuck for a summer in Victoria at his grandparents. 'All Your Ears Can Hear' shifted the crowd onto their side with the memorable line, 'CKDA has got to be stopped before they fuck this whole town!'.

A few brave souls bashed off each other on the dance floor in front of the stage as they segued into their last song, which had received a bit of airplay on the local University radio stations. Late, late night—more like early morning—airplay, but it didn't matter, they had radio airplay, and that was what counted, right?

With 'My Girl's Radioactive,' the band clicked with their audience. As they finished, everyone in the room was singing along. Then the stage lights went out, and it was over.

They'd done it. They'd survived their first paying gig. And I had the photographs to prove it.

The first step in their long and uneven march to rock n roll domination.

My Girl's Radioactive – Mayo
Indie EP, 'Hold the Mayo' 1982

Walking with my girl, in the peaceful side of town
I forget about the things that they bury in the ground

Now every time I kiss her, I get a buzzing in my head
And the doctors says, 'Hey boy, pretty soon
you're gonna be dead!'

My girl's radioactive, My girl's radioactive,
My girl's radioactive, What about yours?
What about yours? What about yours!

Don't talk to me about safety, I think that that's a lie
Who you gonna see when we're in a crowd,
when we go out in the dark?

My girl's radioactive, My girl's radioactive,
My girl's radioactive, What about yours?
What about yours? What about yours!

They came to get her when they found out what went wrong
They want to fly her over Moscow,
they want to use her as a bomb

My girl's radioactive, My girl's radioactive,
My girl's radioactive, What about yours?
What about yours? What about yours!

Most of the bands' songs brought up specific emotions for me. They linked to places and events and solidified my memories with an epic soundtrack. Collectively, they were the foundation of my youth. Songs still relevant even thirty-plus years later, and the lyrics spoke to me about my life.

Except for this one. My girlfriend wasn't radioactive. But I was.

All because I'd come back in time, gone to the Ovaltine and had seen my past-self.

25

Wednesday 8 pm - 54 hours to go

I found Dennis's phone number again in a battered Yellow Pages book hanging from a wire in a payphone booth. I caught him just as he was leaving the office. He wasn't thrilled, but let me reschedule my appointment until tomorrow afternoon. My hope was that a brilliant $4,500 brainstorm to salvage our plan would appear in my brain, fully formed. But while waiting for it to arrive, I stood in front of the flickering TV in my foul hotel room. I turned the dial back and forth, hoping to find something inspirational—a ready-made solution to my dilemma. But nothing appeared. If the others were back here with me, we would have a higher chance of finding an alternative way to get my needed cash. But by myself, I was stuck. We had spent so long figuring out this one plan with no other options. I couldn't see any way out of my jam. Not a single way.

I wish I'd at least had the brains to stop at a liquor store and buy a bottle of something to help me drown my sorrows. But the government-run liquor stores were long closed, leaving me with nothing to distract with but prime-time reruns in my dingy, depressing hotel room. The idea of spending my remaining time in the past watching new—to everyone but me—episodes of Dynasty made me sick to my stomach. So, in defiance of Terry's screaming voice in my head, I changed out of my miserable suit, grabbed my jacket and camera bag. I left the continuing semi-sexual pounding of my neighbors behind and headed out to find something to drink. A lot of something.

The Cambie Hotel was down on the next corner. What was now a pretty cool place to go was then a pretty shady place to drink. The hotel pub had an enclosed smoking area and a beer garden outside in the future, full windows letting in real natural light. But in '84, letting pedestrians see into a pub from the street was illegal, so the future windows were a solid brick wall. Heaven forbid a passerby observe an adult consuming a beer. I gave it a pass and kept on walking. I should find myself dinner, but didn't bother. Instead, I smoked, sulked, and wandered.

A couple of turns later, I heard music and realized where I'd been wandering, impact on the time continuum or my future be damned.

The Pig and Whistle was in part of a section of Gastown that was as close to Dublin's Temple Bar district without an overseas flight. The Blarney Stone, The Spinning Wheel, and a couple more. Ireland and all things Irish were trendy, so the Blarney Stone and the Pig had live bands. In the future the dingy pub is a taco joint. There was a bit of a lineup, but I made it inside, settling in at the bar while The Martini Brothers, the Pig's epic houseband, warmed up on stage. Giving up on the complete lack of local craft beer, I ordered a Guinness and a shot of Jameson's from the matriarch who owned and ran the place. Daphne gave me a sharp look while putting down my drinks. Understandable since I was double the age of everyone else in the room.

But who cared? I was there to drink and smoke and be depressed. So being around a bunch of kids would help to spur my depression along. But even the sound of the band starting their first set of comfort-food

R&B, or the exuberance of the young crowd filling the dance floor couldn't make a dent in my foul mood.

Maybe another round of Guinness and Jameson's would. So I ordered another. And then another for moral support.

"Hey, excuse me," someone yelled beside me. I dragged my eyes up from where they'd been concentrating on the battered top of the bar. Luckily, Daphne, the bartender/owner, had removed my empties, or there'd be an impressive row of upside-down shot glasses. An inch of ash hovered at the end of my cigarette as I glanced to my left. A couple of twenty-something girls—back-combed hair and crop-topped UBC sweaters. Parachute pants. Bright sneakers. They looked fresh and happy and slightly drunk.

"I think your coat's on fire," the blonde said, pointing down at my jacket.

I looked down to see my pocket emitting a gentle stream of smoke. Flailing around, I pounded on my jacket until the fire was out.

"Thanks," I said, reaching in and pulling out a still smoldering match. In a fit of drunken brilliance, I had put the lit match into my pocket after lighting my latest cigarette. Great, go back in time and burn down the Pig and Whistle.

"How's about I buy you two a drink since you saved me from certain fiery death?"

They smiled—when you were young and broke, any free drink was a good drink. I waved to the bartender, who set me up again, then took the girl's order. Two California Coolers—alcoholic fruit juice in a fancy bottle, the perfect starter drink for most girls I attended school with, except Gina. Maybe because she had older brothers, or because she was tough as nails, Gina avoided the 'girlie' drinks and stuck to rye, with Coke.

Gina. My Gina. Kissing Neil.

The bartender gave the girls their drinks, with beer glasses full of ice on the side. They fill up their glasses and took long sips. I tossed two tens onto the counter, more than enough to pay for this round and the next. The girls grinned at each other.

I downed my shot and turned to them. "I saw my girlfriend kissing my best friend."

"Oh no!" the two leaned in, sympathetic yet eager for gossip. "That's awful!" I nodded slowly. For nodding quickly would be unwise.

"Have you two been dating long?" the brunette asked.

"Yeah. A long time. And Gina could have told me about it. But she didn't. She didn't, so now I don't know if I'll ever trust her again."

The blonde put her hand on my shoulder, caring and supportive. "Maybe she was embarrassed, maybe your friend made a move, and she couldn't stop him?"

Her friend nodded in sympathetic agreement. A flush of warmth filled me for these girls as they attempted to help me, a complete stranger, feel better about Gina's betrayal. Except, and this was the part impossible to explain, how could it be a betrayal since she and I weren't going out when she kissed Neil? Obviously, I don't know about every kiss she's ever had. But I still felt betrayed.

"Same shit happened to me. One drunken kiss. Stupid and it meant nothing."

"Are you with him? Your boyfriend?" I asked, hopeful.

With an embarrassed sigh, she shook her head. "He freaked when I told him, called me a slut and broke up with me."

"Jason was always a jerk, Beth," her friend said.

We're quiet for a bit, sipping our drinks. Then the brunette hopped off her stool and rushed off into the crowd. Beth watched her go.

"She just saw this guy she likes," Beth explained. "Some guy from our Organic Chemistry class. Cute, but like totally a player, you know?"

Like Neil. Exactly like Neil. The guy who could always charm a drunk girl in a bar. Or a sober girl on the street outside his basement apartment. While I stewed, Beth finished her Cooler, but a quick wave to the bartender lined her up with another.

"Thanks," she said with a bright smile.

"No, my pleasure. In a time like this, I'm happy to have any company."

"I understand. It so sucks, right?"

Behind us, the band started up their second set, filling the room with their particular brand of sound. Beth leaned closer, her shoulder up against mine. We drank and talked about betrayal and exes, and love. The lights from the stage bounced off her eyes, making them sparkle, and I couldn't stop staring at them. She told a story of her high school boyfriend who she caught cheating at a school dance. "He said he slipped! He slipped, and his tongue fell into her open mouth!?"

"Men are pigs," I said.

She smiled at me. "Not every one of them."

"No. I guess not all."

She smiled again. Then we finished our drinks, putting the glasses down on the bar at the exact moment. We laughed. On an impulse, I leaned over to her ear, smelling her perfume through the cigarette smoke, and said, "I've got a room around the corner. You want to get out of here?"

She jolted back from me like I'd hit her with a taser. She scrambled off her stool, putting distance between her and me.

"You fucking pervert! Jesus, you're older than my father!"

"I just—"

"I know what you 'just' wanted, slime bag!" Livid, she hit me on the shoulder with her oversized purse. She wound up to hit me again. A hand reached out of the crowd and restrained her. Before she reacted, Celina stood between the two of us.

Beth yanked her arm back from Celina and glared at her. "You his cheating girlfriend? Or you two old fogies do this for kicks?"

"Whoa," Celina said. "I don't know what's going on here, but Colin collapsed earlier and could have a concussion, so let's take it easy on him, yeah?"

Still offended but slightly mollified, Beth lowered her purse and glared at me. "Don't be a pervert because your girlfriend cheated on you."

Then she stormed off to find her friend. Guaranteed, she would tell her about the ancient asshole who tried to pick her up. My dinner of Jameson's and Guinness hit me in a rush, forcing my spinning head down on the bar.

"Colin? What the hell is going on?"

"I forgot how old I am," I murmured into the bar.

"Come on, let me take you out of here," Celina said, pulling me off my stool and out of the bar.

She installed me semi-upright on a bench in front of the statue of Gassy Jack. He had been the unofficial mayor of Gastown in the 1870s when these dozen blocks were the entirety of Vancouver. Passing car lights whirled around in my head as she popped into a late-night pizza place for a couple of slices to soak up the alcohol in my stomach. Then she sat beside me while I ate, not tasting the cheap pizza at all but grateful for something to occupy my hands. And mouth.

I was beyond mortified. I tried to pick up a twenty-two-year-old! What kind of guy does that? What kind of grown man does that, no matter what he was going through? One who was an idiot. One who had gone back in time and screwed up his life. Who was now trying hard to screw up the lives of everyone around him.

Young ones wandered by, popping in and out of the pubs and bars while I chewed my food. As I finished the last bite of the greasy pizza crust, Celina said, "So, Colin, now you've eaten something, I gotta ask. What was that girl talking about? Why was she so upset with you?"

I shrugged with shame. "I drank too much and hit on her, making an utter fool of myself. Too much Jameson's makes Colin an idiot."

"I heard you the first time. But why?"

"I saw my girlfriend kissing my best friend."

"When?"

"After they mugged me in your alley."

"So how can that be a reason to hit on a teenager? There must be another reason. You seem like a good guy, not someone who would do something so out of character. Not without a good reason."

"I was feeling sorry for myself."

"Yeah, I heard you. But why her, here, now?"

She wasn't stopping. I was embarrassed and stupid, and I wanted nothing more than to go home, to the future, to reap what I haven't sown in the past. I wanted to be anywhere but here and now.

"Colin?"

"Stop," I said, exhausted. This shame was more proof of my inability to do anything right. But who cared? Not me. My life was a multiple car crash of epic screw-ups. What had happened was the icing on the rotting cake of my existence. Fuck it. "The entire story about the screenplay is a lie. That hero guy is me, yeah? Me. I'm from the future, all right? I'm from 2017. In that robbery behind your cafe, they stole the money I needed to make my life better thirty-three years from now. And then Gina kissing Neil—something she swore she never did, and then I got drunk and forgot I was old and—"

Celina stared. "What the hell are you talking about? Gina and Neil?" I looked down at my feet, swaying as the pizza attempted to slow the fermentation in my gut. Or explode out my mouth. "Gina and Neil? Terry and Colin? Those kids in the front booth?"

"Forget it, forget everything I said and leave me alone," I muttered.

She stood up. "Forget it? Too late, Colin." I glanced up at her with one eye shut and saw her put two and two together. "You ran out of the Ovaltine today because you saw you? Young-you?"

I nodded.

"Is this a joke?" She stared, recognition dawning as she saw enough of young-me in old-me.

"No. No joke. I'm from the future. A future where Pierre Trudeau's twelve-year-old son is Prime Minister. Where a shitty house in a bad Vancouver neighborhood costs millions of dollars. A Vancouver hosting the Winter Olympics in 2010. Bike lanes everywhere, electric cars. Everyone has a thousand-dollar smartphone in their pocket that connects to every other smartphone using something called the Internet!" I sounded like a lunatic and should shut up, but I didn't. If my grandmother found out I was talking like this, she would disown me, but my drunk mouth continued. "And you. You've got a daughter, Faye, and since it's…uh…1984, she's about thirteen years old. She's learning the viola, and she hates it."

"Are you following me? How the hell do you know about Faye?"

She stepped back, frightened. She watched to see if I was dangerous, but I was close to inert on the bench. Warily, she came back to squat in front of me. Her skirt pulled tight on her thighs. They were beautiful thighs, muscular. She had smooth skin. Lovely knees.

Celina tipped my head up. I lost my already derailed train of thought. She glared right in my face. "Why would you tell me this? What are you trying to do to me? What is going on?"

I stared up at her. "Celina. This is the truth. I come from the future."

She slapped me. Hard.

"You're a sad, old man who's gone off his medications. Why should I believe you or anything you say?"

I rubbed my hand against my face and winced. "Celina, I'm not off my meds, I promise."

She shook her head in absolute amazement.

"Christ, I thought I finally met a nice, funny, smart guy, and he turns out to be insane!"

Then she turned and stalked off, leaving me with my grease-stained paper plate and an ache in my stomach and my heart.

26

Thursday 10 am - 38 hours to go

The morning came with pain. Lots of pain. I was lying on top of the bedcovers, a pack of cigarettes on my chest along with a half-full ashtray, a butt smoldering. Jesus, the hotel could have burned down with me in it! Gingerly sitting up, I felt where my shoulder ached from Beth's purse. Christ, what had I been thinking? What if she had said yes and come back with me? Would I have gone through with having sex with her? And what if I did, and she got pregnant? I would have gone back to the future, and when her half-Chinese twenty-five-year-old kid did a DNA test in 2001, he would discover that his father was me! Worse, I'd be younger than I was when I had knocked his mother up when she was twenty-two. Even worse, Gina would kill me when she found out I had a child from the past.

My face stung from Celina's slap.

Celina. Telling her the truth last night was a huge mistake. If she talked to anyone, then the ripples would only become worse. I needed to find her and make sure she didn't talk about my drunken babbling. Then maybe I could contain the ripples. If I only stopped making idiotic moves between now and tomorrow night.

Walking slowly, I left the hotel. I'd tossed on my tan suit jacket in the hope a solution would come and I could still make my appointment with Dennis to buy the stocks. But there was no way I'd wear those tight slacks for another minute. I still had my dignity. Not much, but still a bit.

A delivery truck barrelled out of the alley right outside the front door and almost mowed me down. Jumping back, I gave the driver the finger as he barged his way into traffic to a round of angry honking.

My head hurt so much. I stopped at the nearest corner store, bought another pack of Player's Lights, a tiny glass bottle of Anacin and an original Coke to wash them down with. The thought of sitting on a bus for the trip up to the Ovaltine was unbearable. Instead, I walked east along Hastings Street. Past the old Woodward's department store which was now redeveloped as condos. Then past Save-on-Meats, Army & Navy, bank branches and cheap clothing stores, cheaper restaurants. Funky Winkerbean's pub. A bus lunged around the corner towards Pigeon Park almost knocking me down. Only because of the quick reflexes of a young punk who pulled me back was I not flattened across three lanes.

"Fuckin' bus drivers..." the kid said, then asked if I wanted to buy some dope.

I shook my head and kept walking. Twice in five blocks, I'd nearly died. Something that hadn't happened in fifty-five years of living in the city. Something ominous was going on. I hoped it was only a hangover, but I wasn't sure of anything anymore.

Outside the Ovaltine, I paused. Through the window, Celina cleared a booth while her mother accepted payment at the till. I didn't want to go in there and try to explain myself, but I had no choice. She couldn't go around talking about the strange guy she met who said he was from the future, especially to past-me and my friends. What if past-me used the one-time-only time machine before I did? Then where would that leave me? If he used the device before 2017, my using it in 2017 would be impossible. So would me in the past cease to exist? Disappear in a puff of smoke? More fucking time enigmas. I needed Terry here to sort this out. He'd set up a whiteboard and drawn it out, multiple loops of time going forward and back. But Terry wasn't here. Instead, he was waiting for me to return and save the day.

Then Celina saw me through the window. Any ideas about leaving without talking to her faded, so I braced myself and went inside.

Her mother pointed me to the same booth at the back. I nodded. I walked through the restaurant and sat down. Celina immediately slid into the booth.

"What the hell are you doing here?" she said.

"I came to apologize. Forget what I said last night. I was drunk."

"Bullshit. You look like that Colin kid. Just like him, only a lot older."

Shit. I leaned forward in the booth and said, "I made a colossal mistake telling you about me. Please, ignore everything I said. If you don't, you could mess up your life and mine. So, please, rewind your memories and forget everything I said. Consider them the ramblings of a sad, drunk guy from out of town."

"Too late," she said.

"What do you mean, 'too late'? You already told someone? Shit, Celina, this is bad!"

She raised her hand to stop me. "I didn't tell anyone, but I can't forget what you said, either. Too late, you already told me and, God help me," she said, shaking her head. "I believe you."

"Oh," I said, unsure what else to do. Celina believed me, but I didn't know what to do with this information. Having her believe me didn't help with the utter disaster this trip had become, yet it was nice to have someone to talk to about all this.

"So, you want breakfast? Your usual? Well, young-you's usual breakfast?"

I nodded. Waffles and a couple of fried eggs—I was nothing if not consistent. Even if it was being consistent with screwing up. Celina turned over my coffee cup, filled it, and left me to consider my hangover and my fate.

"You are in a world of trouble, aren't you?" Celina said. The cafe had slowed down into the post-lunch lull. She sipped her coffee across from me after hearing my recap of the truth of my situation, not the screenplay version, but the actual events. Knowing what she knew now, I was even more surprised she hadn't called the police. Instead, she appeared fascinated by my story.

"I didn't come back to make us multi-millionaires," I said, even though that was exactly the plan. But I didn't think it would help my case with Celina. "I only want enough to buy us a house, so we don't have to move. I like where I live. See? Not much to ask for, is it?"

"A couple of million dollars for a house in East Van… You're insane. How could people who work in the neighborhood afford to live there?"

"They don't. They can't buy, but the average rent for a one-bedroom is over two thousand dollars. A month!"

Celina was aghast. "That's madness."

I agreed.

"Even with the meticulous organization you put into your stock buying plan, why not have a backup option? Oh, in case you ran into your past-self then passed out in an alley and were mugged of a certified check you had made out to 'cash' like an idiot."

I laughed instead of crying. "Yeah, it beggars belief we didn't consider that as a potential outcome." She laughed with me.

"I'm serious. No other plan?" I shook my head and she sighed. "Too bad. And I helped you out with this scheme? I'm sure I would have suggested an alternative in case something went wrong at the last minute."

I was about to make another witty comment when her words penetrated my thoughts. 'At the last minute.'

The last minute.

My time since I arrived back had been so overwhelming it took me a moment to connect her words with a recollection from the past or the future.

Moments before I turned the knob in the box, before coming back to 1984, Terry had handed me a piece of paper at the last minute. Putting down my coffee, I reached into my tan blazer and removed a folded piece of lined paper. As Celina watched, I opened it up and skimmed through what Terry wrote.

"What is it?" Celina asked. After refolding the paper and putting it back in my pocket, I replied, "There's somewhere I need to go. Somewhere that could help me. Right now."

She looked deflated and slid out of the booth.

"I'll go get your check."

I reached for her arm to stop her.

"Wait. Celina, do you want to come with me?"

27

"Twenty dollars on 'Cosmic Eclipse' in the next race, please." I stood at the teller, a row of impatient men behind me, desperate to place their bets.

"Win, place or show?" the weary woman behind the glass asked.

"Uh. Win. To win. Please."

One of my few remaining twenties slid through the slot, and she passed me my betting ticket. I smiled at her and turned away. The guy behind me, stub end of a cigar smoldering in his mouth, a battered fedora on his head, grinned and said, "You sound pretty sure of yourself. You know something I don't?" He gestured to the folded racing sheet in my hand.

What I wanted to say was, Yes, I know thirty-three-year's worth of information you don't. I knew about America's black president, about wars fought for the wrong reasons, about space shuttle explosions, about Taylor Swift, and Bruce Jenner. Instead, I walked away, pausing for a quick glance back, but fedora guy wasn't looking. He was busy at the teller.

After buying a couple of cheap beers, I rejoined Celina in the stands, where she waited.

"So?" she asked as I sat down and handed her a beer.

I shrugged. "We'll see in a couple of minutes."

Where the note said to go, and where Celina drove us, was the Hastings horse race track, nestled behind the Colosseum and the PNE Fairgrounds. For a Thursday afternoon, the crowd was small. We found excellent seats, back from the finish line. There was an expansive view of the harbor and the North Shore mountains in the distance. To our left, jockeys and horses were ushered into the starting gates for the next race.

What Terry gave to me on the roof of the building, before I turned the knob and came back in time, was a list of the winning racehorses for three specific days in the past.

My safety net.

Terry and his latent pessimism suspected Time would be out for blood once I went back and activated our plan. And he was right. Everything was perfect until the instant I made eye contact with my past-self. Since then, there had been one setback after another. So Terry's worries were valid. But now I knew better and promised myself to take it smooth and easy. Spend a couple of hours at the track to build up my winnings slowly. Then whip over to my bank for a certified check made out to 'DF Brokerage.' All with time to spare before my rescheduled appointment with Dennis to pick up the stock certificates.

"Colin, I appreciate you asking me to come along. I know you didn't have to offer," Celina said. "It would have been smarter to stay away from me since I know you in the future. I mean, being with me is pretty much one of those 'what not to do' in time travel. Other than going and talking to yourself. And we saw how well that worked out."

"We don't have to worry about running into young-me here. This is only my third time at the track. The first won't happen for at least five years. I won't be here today, guaranteed. But I suspect we might see asshole Neil here, hanging with his uncles and a group of slightly connected mob toughs."

"If he's such an asshole, why are you still friends with him?" she asked, sipping her beer.

I sighed. I wish I knew. "We've always been friends. But I'm not so sure anymore."

"Because he kissed your girlfriend?"

I nodded, my wound aching.

"But, and I don't want to be a jerk here, you and Gina weren't going out when they kissed, right?"

I shook my head. Neil knew about me liking Gina a lot. Everyone knew. Parents, teachers, cashiers in the local stores, bus drivers…

Celina put her hand on my arm to soften what she was trying to say. "Maybe she didn't tell you because of embarrassment. You've been a couple for thirty years, which is a lot. And one kiss in your twenties can be something you're not proud of, trust me. Some things are better left forgotten."

"But she should have told me."

"She could have told you. But what would you have done if she did? Break up with her? And when should she have told you? Back when you were only friends? Weird. When you started going out? Embarrassing. While you were celebrating your tenth, twentieth, twenty-fifth, thirtieth? When was the best time for you to find out?"

There was no appropriate answer. I wished I never knew and also wished Gina had told me at an appropriate point in our long relationship. When I would have chosen as a proper point for that conversation was up for debate. Luckily, the announcer introduced the horses for the fifth race, and Celina's pointed question remained unanswered.

Despite knowing the race's outcome, I felt a surge of anticipation as the jockeys readied themselves on their horses. 'Cosmic Eclipse,' in the outside lane wearing blue and silver, sat at 10 to 1. Even with Terry's handwritten crib sheet, my first bet erred on the side of caution. Just in case. Maybe I already screwed up time enough to change the outcome of a horse race.

The horn blew, and the horses exploded out of the starting gates. Celina and I stood up, along with the rest of the crowd. A flash of motion towards the finish line caught my eye as the horses entered the first turn. Sure enough, there was Neil, all swagger and charm in a pack of middle-aged neighborhood men. He waved a bunch of tickets at the horses. Asshole.

The horses, now spreading out, came round the second turn and into the home stretch. 'Cosmic Eclipse' was in the middle of the forward pack, one of four horses churning up dirt as they barrelled towards the finish line. Celina grabbed my hand in excitement. We started yelling, cheering for our horse as it suddenly leapt forward three feet and crossed the line, a nose ahead of what was sure to be the winner. As Celina jumped up and down in victory, I glanced along the stands. Upset, Neil tore up his tickets and threw them onto the ground. He must have bet on the losing horse. I grinned. Payback's a bitch.

Two more cautious bets later, I was up a mere thousand dollars and getting impatient. My appointment with Dennis was coming up, and I still needed $3,500 more. And the thrill of winning wasn't thrilling when you're guaranteed to win. It was like playing chess against a two-year-old.

"Who's the winner of the next race?" I asked Celina, and she checked the paper.

"'Arctic Blast' at 20 to 1." I did the math. If I put $200 to win, I'd be ahead $5K. We could leave the track to the other losers.

I agreed. "I'll go for it, one more bet and then we can get out of here."

She nodded, and I headed out of the stands to place my bet.

The cavernous area under the seats was full of milling bettors, jotting on their race forms, smoking, exchanging tips and lies about jockeys and horses. I was lined up for a teller when Neil came out of nowhere to join the line beside me. It didn't look like he was having a particularly great day at the track. In a childish and immature way, I was glad. But I also didn't want to be this close. Especially if he remembered me from the Ovaltine yesterday or because I looked a lot like my father. I stepped out of line, moving to the teller farthest away from Neil. If he noticed me move, he didn't react, so I figured I had avoided creating more ripples.

"How's your day been?" someone asked.

Fedora and cigar stood behind me. I shrugged.

"I took your tip on 'Cosmic Eclipse,' thanks. My only win so far. Who you figure for this race?"

I didn't want to talk to this guy. Let me hand over my money, grab my ticket, and return to the stands, for god's sake.

"C'mon, help a guy out. You look like luck's on your side today." He gave me what could be interpreted as a friendly smile.

It was my turn at the window, but before I stepped up, I said to him, "I gotta tell you, this bet is my friend's, and she's had terrible picks today. I guarantee you don't want part of this one."

Then I moved forward to the till. I leaned in to hide the money passing under the glass and said, as quietly as possible, "'Arctic Blast' to win." I hoped Fedora didn't hear.

The teller slid me my ticket. I went to leave, but Fedora was right in my face when I turned around. "Good luck," I said, pocketing my ticket.

"Yeah. You too," he said without a smile, then took his place at the till.

I shook my head. This was why I didn't enjoy gambling; everyone was so tense.

They called the race as I returned to my seat. Unlike previously, I restrained Celina, and we didn't celebrate our win. The track now unnerved me, like I'd done something wrong. I had won too many times in a row, and it felt like everyone knew it. It might only be the combination of Neil and Fedora, but I wanted out of there. Now.

"I'll cash this in. Then we can get the hell out of here."

Celina held up her half-full beer. "I'll wait here for you."

I climbed down the stairs to retrieve my winnings as quietly as possible.

Like a lousy spy, I hung back in a corner, and watched for Fedora or Neil to appear. But after a couple of minutes, neither did. If either had won, they would have rushed down to cash in right away. I was in the clear. The teller didn't even react to my win. She counted out forty one-hundred-dollar bills, then slid them through the slot to me without a word of congratulations. I added five more hundred to the wad of bills, giving me exactly what I needed for the Dennis' cashier's check. With the wad slipped into the back pocket of my jeans, I entered the men's toilet to give back my beer.

Alone at the urinal, I ran through my next moves. Suddenly I was shoved hard up against the tiles, my hands trapped in the urinal holding my penis. A large, heavy hand held my head hard, covering my eyes, while another hand reached into the back pocket of my jeans. My cash! I struggled to break free but couldn't. The hand against my head increased the pressure as my ear was pressed brutally flat against the cold tiles. My precious winnings were pulled out of my pocket as I tried to yell, but the hands spun me around and launched me into an open stall. Smashing hard into the toilet, I barely raised my hands in time to protect my face from breaking against the porcelain. I crumpled to the floor, the victim of a perfect mugging. Less than two seconds from start to finish, I never had a chance, never even saw who did it.

Climbing up off the filthy floor, I zipped myself up and stumbled out of the toilet. I was right back to where I started the day. Broke, and with the world against me.

28

Celina knew something was wrong the instant I sat down. I explained what happened while rubbing my ear. It ached from being ground against the tiles above the urinal.

"We have to go to the police, Colin! You can't let those bastards get away with robbing you!"

I shook my head, wincing. "Don't you see? If I go to the police, they'll want my ID, which I don't have. New papers weren't part of the plan. I didn't need a new fake ID if I stayed out of trouble."

She looked at me, worried. "So, what do we do?"

"Thank God you had the sheet. I'll place another bet and win the next race."

She took Terry's notes out of her purse and opened it up. "Imagine what would have happened if those muggers had this piece of paper? They could have bankrupted the race track by closing tomorrow! Talk about—what did you call them?—ripples. Massive uncontrollable ripples."

Shit. Celina was right. Terry's innocent piece of paper was a time bomb waiting to explode.

"Do you have any money left?"

I glanced around, but there was no one near us and no one looking our way. With my cash held low and out of sight, I checked. "I've only just over five hundred left. They stole $4,500, the bastards."

Celina looked up from Terry's notes and stared at me.

"Wait, they stole the exact amount you need to buy the stocks?"

I nodded. Her eyes widen as she continued, "And when you passed out in the alley, those guys stole your certified check?"

I saw where she was going in an instant. "Yeah. Written out for $4,500."

The realization of something important, like the slow then sudden exposure of film on paper, something out of nothing, broke through. Two muggings, each for the same amount? In twenty-four hours? That wasn't a coincidence. That was something more—fate, karma, or something worse. The $4,500 I sold the gold coins for had somehow unsettled the time equilibrium. When we came up with the plan, we were sure that it wouldn't. The coins existed in 1984. I had only put them back in circulation. Once I sold them, the cash I received wasn't from the future, so we were sure there wouldn't be a conflict. Harmless, right?

But something must be out of whack, or else why would I get mugged for the same amount twice? My grandmother never mentioned in her note that Time would actively work against me. But then again, how would she have known? She'd never used the time machine.

We looked at each other, worried. Time was unhappy with what I was doing.

"Colin," Celina said after a moment. "What on earth are we going to do?"

"Start again, make more bets, and win the money back. Afterward, we burn the list, so no one ever gets their hands on it. Then we get the hell out of here. At this point, I'd take a police escort if we could find one."

Safety and security to enjoy life was my default. No one had ever mugged me, never had my life threatened, never been in actual danger. But now I had. I never thought I'd get kicked out of my house. I assumed, wrongly, that I would be there forever. Same with my job. I'd do the work, take the paycheck until I retired. With that security pulled out from under me, the other things in my life that I had felt secure about had toppled like dominoes. I was in a whole new world in my past.

After finding a payphone beside the canteen, I phoned an increasingly exasperated Dennis and re-scheduled our appointment yet again. I guaranteed I would be at his office on Friday morning at 11. Before hanging up, I double-confirmed with Dennis that the certified check should be made out to DF Brokerage.

This time, Celina joined me for each trip to place a bet or cash in our winnings. We went to a different teller for each bet. We even bought a couple of losers, in case someone was watching. Over the next six races, I won back the money stolen from me. But my heart was in my throat, and my pulse pounded like a jack hammer every time we left our seats. We trusted no one—the cleaners, the bartender, the tellers, and especially the other gamblers. With Celina watching out, I bought my tickets early, then retrieved my payouts late to avoid the rush. When we were in our seats, we didn't talk. We sat in paranoid silence, observing the surrounding crowd more than the horses flying past. My winnings were dispersed in my socks and all the pockets of my jeans and my jacket. If someone mugged me again, it would take time for them to collect it all.

By four o'clock, I had won back the money. But I was also sure I'd aged ten years in the nerve-wracking two hours it took.

"Now, let's burn that paper and get out of here," I said, patting all my pockets for reassurance the cash was there. After glancing around to ensure no one was watching us, Celina crumpled up Terry's note and dropped it between our feet. Once we lit our cigarettes, I let the still-burning match fall onto the paper. After a beat, it caught. With our legs blocking the view, we watched as it flared and then turned to ash.

"I hope you don't need it again," Celina said.

"Me too. The muggings are getting more violent. The next time, I might not survive," I said, and looked around with worry.

After grinding the ashes of the paper into the concrete, we rushed down the stairs and out the exit doors.

The courtyard outside the track was quiet. The walls blocking it off from the fairgrounds threw shadows across us. I wasn't confident about making it to where we had parked Celina's Datsun. Nothing like walking across an entire parking lot with Time after you to throw the fear of God into someone. But with no police escort available, we had little choice. We stuck to the centre line in the middle of the road. Our eyes flicked left and right, forward and back like a couple of fearful mice, the sky above full of hawks. I breathed a sigh of relief once we could see her car. The spaces were empty on each side, but we still checked along the rows in front and behind for anyone hiding. Nothing and no one. Celina had her keys out at the ready. She popped her lock and climbed in. She locked her door, then reached across to unlock mine. I was inside in a second and spun to lock my door.

"Safe now," she said, starting the car. Yeah, safe. Except for driving across the city along roads full of trucks, pedestrians, and a vast array of opportunities for Time to take back what it believed was rightfully theirs. Even if we had to be killed to do it.

Celina pulled up at the bus stop outside The El-Cid, and I hopped out to a barrage of angry horns. She would park while I hid my winnings in my room. We were hours past when my bank closed—no late hours back now—so the plan was for me to rise early and take a taxi to my branch for the certified check. Then take another cab to Dennis. Even if I were early for my appointment, I'd hang out in his office waiting room until he could see me—no more taking chances. If Time was serious about stopping me, which it sure as hell seemed to be, I'd do everything to stay out of its way.

The old guy was back at his desk with his smokes and newspaper. He didn't look up as I ran up the stairs. I paused at each floor to make sure there wasn't anyone waiting on the flight above. I wouldn't have been surprised to find someone waiting to mug and then throw me down a flight of stairs.

There was nobody in the hallway on my floor. I ran down to my room, my key already out and in my hand. I unlocked the door, slipped inside, relocked it. Safe. For the moment.

I pulled folded wads of money out of my pockets and socks. $4,500 went in one pile and the rest back into my jeans. Forty-five hundred-dollar bills spread out on the disgusting bedspread. Our future. A couple of deep breaths. A hell of a day that began in hungover futility. Then a pretty large sliver of hope with Terry's emergency note, followed by a quick mugging and now a light at the end of the tunnel. Who'd have thought messing with time would be this complex? Silly question, Terry would.

Terry did.

But where to hide the cash? My pack under the bed? May as well leave it spread out on the bed for all the good hiding it in my backpack would do. I didn't know if the hotel had a maid. My room hadn't been touched since I had arrived. But, knowing my luck, she'd come in while I was out and rob me blind. Then it came to me, an idea from a thousand movies, the best short-notice place to hide valuables. Yanking my pack out, I removed a few of the heavy-duty freezer Ziplock bags brought back for the last part of our possibly achievable plan. After double-bagging the cash, I removed the air before sealing it. I hid the bag inside the toilet cistern, pushing it down in the murky water. Replacing the lid, I considered my hiding spot. Unlikely anyone would look in there, I wouldn't, given the lack of other valuables in my room and the filthiness of the toilet in general.

I had a few hundred dollars in random bills to spend before heading back. Some would be taken up with taxi rides tomorrow and I might have to pay Dennis his brokerage fees in cash. Once I took possession of the stock certificates, there was only one final step. I would have to be careful as hell doing it. Then, at shortly after noon tomorrow, our plan would be complete, and the rest of my time in the past could be spent in hiding.

Grabbing my camera bag, I left my miserable room, double-checking the door lock before descending the stairs to join Celina outside.

29

Without our nest egg weighing down my pocket, my stress levels diminished. Our plan was back on track. There would be no more muggings because I didn't have the cash on me, and I was super careful crossing the street, looking both ways—twice—like my mother had been telling me since I started walking.

Celina and I strolled down to Hastings Street, then up a couple of blocks to the downtown Simpson-Sears department store. In the future, the bottom floors house the downtown campus of Simon Fraser University. I mentioned this to Celina as we entered the high 70s modernist foyer. Concrete and glass, the building enveloped a century-old six-story classical building on the corner of the block like a Sumo wrestler hugging a pillow. We waited for the elevator to take us up to the revolving Harbour House Restaurant at the top of the building. In the future, the restaurant was ironically called the Top of Vancouver, but here and now, it was an excellent place for a great dinner, with a fantastic view of the lower buildings of downtown around us and the North Shore mountains across the Harbour.

We scored a window table, a quiet deuce with a view. The waiter headed to the bar for our wine—German as there weren't BC,

Washington, Oregon, Australian, Chilean or California wines worth speaking of at this point—an ice cold bottle of Blue Nun. I set up my camera on the floor at our window, programming it to time-lapse for the next hour while doing a full rotation. Another excellent piece of history recorded in HD.

After ordering salmon on cedar planks and salads, I felt myself relax for the first time since making eye contact with my young-self. But the original plan we came up with wasn't yet complete. I had a couple of steps to go before truly being safe and ready to go home. But away from the track and with my money hidden, pulling this off and saving my— our—future was a distinct possibility. Now it was time to enjoy a bit of harmless normalcy.

"How did you and Gina finally end up together?" Celina asked after our iceberg lettuce salads with thousand island dressing arrived at the table.

"It's a sad story. I was pretty geeky in school, but good at photography. Good at hiding behind my camera. So I joined the yearbook club and wandered around the hallways taking pics for it. I took a fantastic one of Gina in art class. She and all her friends saw it in the yearbook and liked it. But I still hadn't talked to her by this point."

"Then what happened?"

"She came up to me at my locker and scared the shit out of me. She asked for an 8x10 print of the photo for her to give to her parents for their anniversary."

"And you, of course, said yes."

I nodded. "She joined me in the darkroom while I did the print."

"How romantic." Celina smirked.

"How nerve-wracking. I screwed up three prints before I got one right."

I ate some salad, then continued, "But out of that came a friendship. And then, over a decade later, I asked her out."

"A man with a methodical plan."

"Sadly, not much of a plan. I spent a long time in the friend-zone, for sure."

"The what?"

Oops. Too late to backtrack, I explained the concept of the 'friend-zone.' Celina understood immediately, laughing at the phrase. After a decade in the zone, I continued to be amazed I had graduated from there into a real and proper relationship with Gina. Not like she didn't have guys hovering around her. She was gorgeous in a Laura San Giacomo in 'Sex, Lies and Videotapes' way: thick black hair, smoky eyes, and a coy smirk and smile, which shook more than my pulse. Not to mention a bit of an overbite she could use to get anything she wanted from me.

Then I kissed her on the top of the Ferris wheel. That was that. She'd moved into my apartment within two months.

"How about you? You have Faye, but isn't there anyone in your life?"

"Not now. Life's pretty busy with a teenager, especially as a single mom. Not a lot of time to date."

"Well, she turns out great."

Celina waved her wine glass at me, chastising. "*Ay yah*! Don't tell me anything. I don't want to know."

"I'm sorry. But it's true."

We went quiet, comfortable together, and ate our salads. Without wishing it, the vision of Gina kissing Neil floated up to the forefront again. The lightness of our dinner, our success at the track, faded. Celina noticed my mood shift and put down her fork.

"Ok, what can it hurt? Tell me about life in the future."

"I don't know if I should. Maybe a time cop will appear out of nowhere and arrest us, then take us for brain reprogramming."

"Are time cops a real thing?" she asked, and I laughed, my mood lightening a bit more.

"No, unless you're Jean-Claude Van Damme."

"Who?"

"Forget it. An actor. But he played a time cop in a movie filmed here in the '90s."

That did not impress her. I tried again.

"You wouldn't believe how much TV and film work is in Vancouver in the future. It's the second-largest production city in North America."

"No way!"

I nodded. So much about the future to share. The idea of spending our meal enjoying the shocked look on Celina's face as I described bike lanes on the Burrard Street Bridge or a superhighway to Whistler instead of the nightmare-causing Highway 99 as it existed in 1984 would be fantastic. But I didn't. I couldn't.

Our bleeding-edge-haute-cuisine salmon on a cedar plank arrived. I would have preferred sushi, but that wasn't a dinner choice yet in Vancouver. Hard to believe from walking down any street nowadays. We started eating, and I was surprised the meal was as good as it was. I was definitely future biased when it came to food, beer, and coffee. But this was above average. And the company and the view were spectacular.

"If the future is so bad," Celina asked after our bow-tied waiter had refilled our tiny wine glasses. "Why didn't any of you leave town? From what you've said, I can't imagine you'd want to live here while the entire city falls to pieces."

"Growing up, everything was great, so why leave? Where would I go anyway? Toronto? Montreal? I'm not a fan of months in the freezing cold. Vancouver was—is—pretty great, with lots of music which I love. A laid-back atmosphere—you know, businesses basically shutting down for summer, not like Toronto."

"So, what happened?"

"I guess the World Expo in '86 put the city on the world map. All of a sudden, this wasn't a hick town on the far edge of the world. We were a fun, young, hip city. They updated the liquor laws for craft breweries and allowed Sunday shopping! So why go anywhere else? Overnight, Vancouver was cool, and people from around the globe were coming and telling us how cool we were. We were the shy kid suddenly getting asked to sit with the most trendy clique in high school. I visited friends who'd bailed to Toronto and Montreal, even travelled as far as Halifax on one trip. Sure, they're fun cities, but look at that view!" We stopped talking and gazed out at the sunset glistening on the harbor and the mountains, the sky fading from blue-black on our right to oranges and reds on our left. "How can you leave something like this? Ski in the morning, then sail in the afternoon?"

She couldn't argue with that and we ate in comfortable silence for a bit, enjoying our salmon.

"So what will you do when you go back?" she finally asked, after finishing her plate.

"Retrieve the stocks, cash them in, and take it from there."

"No, I meant, what will happen the instant after you go back?"

I paused. Had Gina, Terry, Neil, and I ever discussed my return? Not really.

With no interactions or impact in the past, our best assumption was that I would find my friends waiting on the rooftop at the stroke of midnight tomorrow. But there had been interactions, and if any of my interactions made an impact, there would be ripples. Maybe tomorrow, when I went back, the A&B building would be gone, and I'd reappear halfway through an inside wall of a new condo development. Or perhaps because of stupid time ripples, my friends had moved away from Vancouver at some point in the next thirty-three years, so I'd go back and be alone. Out of time and space.

"I don't know. If there have been ripples, it could be a real mess."

"What do you mean?"

"Have you got a pen?"

On the back of a piece of paper from her purse, I sketched out Terry's branching timelines and pointed to me on the alternate one, parallel to the reality I had left.

Celina studied the paper, then said, "Are you sure you're on this line? I mean, how do you know the ripples have been big enough to create a new timeline? I can't believe every single unique choice creates a split. That would make for an infinite number of new timelines every second. I choose chicken instead of salmon—a new timeline? I go to Luv-A-Fair to dance instead of the Town Pump—another new timeline?"

"Yes. That's what Terry said would happen."

"But how does he know for sure?" she asked.

"It was something about quantum mechanics."

"So he knows no more than you, or me, or our waiter does."

She sipped her wine and watched me.

Maybe Terry was wrong. Maybe things can happen, and they impact nothing. Not everything we do created ripples. Maybe that was why no one could go back and kill Hitler. Because that ripple would be too big and too much future would be impacted. Time wouldn't allow it. But I could put cream in my coffee instead of taking it black and not alter my future.

The trouble with all these conflicting thoughts was that there was no way to know for sure. I couldn't pop down to the Vancouver Public Library and check in the National Geographic Time Travel Reference Guide, 1984 edition.

"I guess you're right. Not everything I've done while back should force a new timeline. But I won't know until I get back what did."

"What are you going to do?"

"I guess I'll go home and find out."

Celina looked at me with sadness. She'd been enjoying herself. If nothing else, I had added a bit of excitement and peril to her pretty routine life.

"I hope this works out how you want it to, Colin."

Me too.

30

"Well, what shall we do now?" Celina asked as we exited the elevator in the foyer of the Sears Tower.

"You let me choose dinner. Where we go now is up to you," I said with a smile.

She considered for a moment and then grinned, her bright white teeth shining over red lips. "I doubt they exist in the future, but any chance you remember a band called Mayo?"

•

The band had made no public announcements of their name change. Without Twitter or Instagram, no one knew what they had done. These two surprise shows were the first exposure of Damage Done to the public. If you were lucky enough to be at one of them, you'd be telling your friends about it forever. These shows slipped my mind in all the madness of time travel.

Damage Done at the Railway! Their first ever show. How was that for funny? If I'd been asked about using my one trip to come back and see this show in our time travel game, I might have said yes. Missing it, despite working tomorrow's show, nagged at me still. Being here to see them now was a dream come true.

Because I'd taken those early photographs of the band for their indie releases and posters, Kelly had asked me to take photographs for their second show the next night. Despite years of performing, the band didn't want the pressure of any recordings on their first night. If I thought it odd that the group didn't want photos taken tonight, I couldn't remember. Past-me had other plans already. I could see the show tonight because I wasn't here. What young-me would photograph tomorrow night, I'd secretly film tonight. Smooth, huh?

The keepsake key around my neck gave us members access to the Railway Club, but when I went to sign Celina in as my guest she sighed and showed me her members card. Of course, she was a member. The place was filling up, but we grabbed a table in front of the soundboard with an excellent view of the stage. Celina went up to the bar for a couple of beers while I set up my camera on its travel tripod on a narrow ledge above my head. Using a long shutter release cable as a prop, I'd videotape the entire show while innocently appearing to take the occasional photograph. Again, I slid into the comfortable, familiar vibe of the room, the excitement of youth anticipating a show. But, unlike 95% of the room, I knew Damage Done was something explosive that would change the terrain of Vancouver music, of Canadian music. A sound that would do for Vancouver what Nirvana did for Seattle.

All the stresses of the past two days faded as Celina returned with our pints of Molson Canadian. She put them down and slid in beside me on the banquette. While we waited, I expanded on her basic historical knowledge of Mayo, regaling her with stories of their start in the garage and the many performances I had seen. My photos on their 45's. The story of their name. She'd only seen them once, opening for Bolero Lava at Club Soda the year before. She hadn't thought they were too bad but had been there for the headliners, so she paid little attention.

"If this is your favorite band, why aren't you—young-you—here tonight?" she asked, the room almost full by this point. Nearly time for the show to begin. I explained the band didn't want me to take photos of their first official show, but she didn't buy it.

"I call bullshit. If this was your favorite band, Colin, how come you didn't simply show up? Leave the camera at home?"

"Because of an embarrassing and then more embarrassing story. I'm not sure I want to tell you. You might judge me."

"Oh, with that sort of lead-up, I'm sure I will," she said with a laugh.

"I won tickets to a different show, from LG-73. You know, the tenth caller wins? I called and won. Four tickets."

"So what? You could have given them away."

"First, we figured this would be the same-old, same-old show tonight. Yes, they were my favorite band, but how many times can you listen to 'My Girlfriend's Radioactive' live, you know? And then I won the tickets, so we figured 'Why not see someone else?'"

"Enough justification. I'm already judging you, so delaying will only make my judgments worse. Confess. Who did you see instead?"

"Don't you want to guess?"

"I've got a kid and a full-time job, Colin. I don't even bother reading the concert listings. They're too depressing."

"Come on. You obviously know who's playing around town. You found me at the Pig and Whistle because you were there to see the Martini Brothers. You knew about this show," I said.

"I was at the Pig because they play the music of my youth and there are a lot of regulars there I know. I overheard some kids at the cafe mention Mayo. Thought they were talking about condiments. But you're delaying."

"I'm curious."

She sighed. "I couldn't go see live music when I was in my twenties. In the '50s, society kept me locked down. I worked in the cafe, got married, the whole drill. It took us years before I got pregnant. I thought I understood my life, but you don't know what it's like to stop your social life to become a mother. My husband died when Faye was a baby. A car crash on that nightmare highway to Whistler."

"Jesus, that must have been horrible," I said.

She sighed and waved my sympathy away. "I learned to live with it. What choice did I have? I had to recreate myself as a single mom. Faye came with a massive set of rules from society and my parents. So I rebelled. But within reason."

"Canadian reasonable youthful rebellion, I know it well."

"Exactly," she smiled. "When I could get a sitter, I'd slip into some club and watch the kids and over time got to appreciate the music. A middle-aged Chinese woman watching punk bands in smoky clubs."

"That's cool. I mean, we go out to see bands all the time, and it isn't a big deal if there are older people there. I don't think society forces people to like only the music of their generation anymore. Something is liberating about that. I may not like the band and their image, but if I like a song, it's on my phone."

"I don't want to know what that means."

"Forget it. What I'm trying to say is that you're ahead of your time, Celina. You're out seeing bands that aren't from your generation. I couldn't imagine my parents—or grandparents—here tonight. And there is no way they'd want to be. But if Elvis were alive and touring, they'd be fighting for tickets. All that to say that you're a pretty cool chick."

"They still call women 'chicks' in the future?"

"No, but I'm trying to fit in here."

She laughed and said, "Terrific. You're impressed with me and my story. Now, what is yours? Where is young-Colin tonight?"

I sighed, anticipating her reaction. "Lionel Richie and Tina Turner are at the Colosseum tonight. 'Dancing On the Ceiling World Tour.'"

She snorted beer out of her nose, unable to contain her laughter. "'Hello, is it me you're looking for?' A tough indie rock guy like you seen in public at a show like that?"

"Hey," I said, defensively. "The tickets were free."

"So you and I can be here tonight because this is one moment you know exactly where past-you is."

I nodded, about to defend my youthful choices, but the stage lights extinguished. Celina squeezed my arm in excitement. I reached up to my camera, starting the video recording.

The throbbing, steady, barely restrained opening chord of 'Getting Lost' began from the darkened stage. One electric guitar, a muted B chord for sixteen bars, inexorably pulled the room out of their conversations. Then another sixteen bars drew in everyone's attention like a musical black hole. My breath caught in my throat. Even the crowd at the far end of the room realized something was happening. The volume of their loud conversations diminished to nothing. Then the lights came up on the band. Kelly leant against the mic, gripping it in his hands, guitar hanging from his shoulder, ignored. Norm Parfitt—who, six months ago, replaced Duncan when he left for Northern Alberta to apprentice as a welder—churned out that one guitar chord at his mic to Kelly's left. Paul and Bucky, in their usual places, unmoving in the dim light, waited to join in.

Then Kelly took a deep breath and began singing. This was the moment of tectonic shift for the band. Gone were the old high-speed, screaming lyrics, replaced with nuanced, on-the-edge confessional words, ripped out and sung from his heart. At the end of the first verse, he took hold of his guitar, joining Norm but an octave higher as the two harmonized on the one-line chorus. The bass and drum joined in for the second verse, creating a perfect blend of everything one would want from a song.

I filled with long-lost joy. Tomorrow was so long ago for me. It has been over three decades since hearing this song and this resurrected band for the first time. And yet, unlike anyone else ever, I was experiencing them again. The music of my youth, implausibly, impossibly, live again. The song was different, the tempo slightly off to the recording I'd had on rotation since its release. Despite my expectations, the lyrics were different in places, the melodies slightly off. Regardless, I tried to soak it in, revel in the all-encompassing power of the song. But I couldn't disappear into the music as in the past before because I wasn't twenty-two years old anymore. I was fifty-five. I'd lived a long life and the awe of hearing a song I had listened to a million times again wasn't enough to break through what I'd experienced in those thirty-three years. The ups and downs, the ins and outs, the good, the bad and the boring—especially my bizarre, strange, exciting and terrifying three days back in time.

The solo, rough and different from what they would record—had I expected the finished album version of a song performed in front of an audience for the absolute first time?—yanked me back from my thoughts. I glanced over at Celina. She had abandoned her beer on the round table, enrapt by the performance on the stage. Here she sat, in her late forties, and we're the only 'old fogies' in the room. A single mom with a teenager who worked in her family cafe and yet, the look on her face. The joy of discovery. The pleasure of new. Obviously, experiencing a song for the first time again was impossible without amnesia or a lobotomy. Not even time travel could change that. But maybe if I let go of my ridiculous expectations and simply enjoyed the music performed on that stage, I could find that magic again. Because that was what was right in front of me. Pure rock magic. Sure, I had understood this for thirty-three years, but halfway through this first song of their first set, this crowd understood they were part of something so much bigger than an inconsequential band on a tiny stage in a smoky club.

They could deny it if they wanted, claim what they're experiencing wasn't impacting them, but that would be a lie—the damage had been done.

Getting Lost - Damage Done
Eponymous first album 1986 A&M Records

Some emotion happened here
I feel it burn me when I hold it near
I'm Getting Lost, getting lost, getting lost

Like a stranger, like a friend
Sometimes you're near me, then you're gone again
I'm Getting Lost, getting lost, getting lost

My reason tells me that I must find you
My will resists me, then I try to
I'm Getting Lost, getting lost, getting lost

I've got my pleasures, we've had our fun
But it's all worthless when it's done
I'm Getting Lost, getting lost, getting lost

The world is one distraction,
Full of glittering attractions,
Got to break away
Can't afford to stay, Getting Lost

Some emotion happened here
I feel it burn me when I hold it near
I'm Getting Lost, getting lost, getting lost

Like a stranger, like a friend

```
Sometimes you're near me, then you're gone again
I'm Getting Lost, getting lost, getting lost
```

Time ebbed and flowed around all of us. I knew where I was in the current, but I couldn't see either bank of the river. I moved forward, inexorably, towards my final destination. Surrounding me were everyone I had ever known and everyone I would never meet. But there were two Colins in this exact section of the river. We had bumped once, and I had almost drowned. What if he drowned if we bumped again? I could only see the surface of this river. A single plane of existence in a deep black ocean of Time. Were the currents taking me towards a future in sync with my past, or was I getting more and more lost?

31

And then the show was over. Like I had never taken a second breath. The magic that had enveloped us for their performance dissipated in the harshness of the house lights. As a group, we gathered our belongings and stumbled down the steep stairs, ears ringing, eyes burning from cigarette smoke, palates deadened from cheap beer.

The two sets of their new show were all brand-new material written by Kelly and Norm in the previous six months. Tonight had been the very first time they were performed for a live audience. Never played for anyone but themselves before this moment.

Celina and I exited the Railway Club. Excited conversation flowed around us, everyone knowing they'd just seen something amazing. If cellphones existed, every single person would have been texting all their friends, filling them in on what they'd missed throughout the show. As it was, telephone lines would burn as soon as everyone woke up tomorrow.

We walked back towards her car and my hotel in awed silence. Me for seeing my favorite band as they played their perfect first show and Celina for expecting a post-punk riot of Mayo and, instead, getting the perfect first show by Damage Done. Dunsmuir was quiet, a typical summer

Thursday night in Vancouver, and we strolled along, deep in our thoughts. Synapses were firing, creating memory pathways, locking down the experience. We turned left on Hamilton towards Victory Square and the El-Cid.

"Colin, that was one of the best performances I've ever seen in my life. I had no expectations of that, despite what you told me. How on earth did Mayo become that? Did you have any idea before the show?" Celina said into the quiet night air.

I told her I didn't know the details.

Something had happened when Duncan left the band and Norm joined. A magical alchemy occurred. Like when Paul met John, Keith met Mick, or Axl met Slash. Amazing things could happen in our lives if we were lucky enough to meet that particular other who could take our creativity to new, unimaginable heights. But that meant being in the right place and the right time in the right state of mind. Otherwise, we would probably piss them off, and they'd leave without speaking to us.

We stood on the sidewalk by the parking lot where she had parked her tan Datsun 510. A late-night bus rumbled by.

"I should get back to my hotel," I said. "I've got a big day tomorrow."

Celina nodded but didn't move.

"Do you want to come back to my apartment for a nightcap? I've got a pull-out couch that has got to be better than the bed at the El Cid."

She smiled at me, hopeful.

She was right. My bed at the hotel was pretty awful, and who knew what would be going on in the next room while I tried to sleep.

"That sounds great. I could use a drink and a good night's sleep."

"Deal."

She took my hand, and we headed to her car.

Celina's tiny balcony at her third-floor East Van apartment faced downtown. The red-lit 'W' above the Woodward's department store slowly rotated in the distance. I sipped my Rusty Nail and slumped further into the Papasan couch Celina had installed on her covered deck. Despite a dry summer, the couch smelled a bit like rain. She sat beside me with her drink, leaning forward. We dragged on our cigarettes. 'Sound Affects' by The Jam played quietly from her stereo. A bulky fake-woodgrain speaker had been dragged out onto the balcony to not bother her sleeping daughter.

On an upside-down milk crate was a rough clay ashtray—obviously a school project made by Faye, most likely for mother's day. Beside it was a well-thumbed copy of 'The Hero with a Thousand Faces' by Joseph Campbell. I gestured to it. "Some light reading?"

She laughed. "Mostly it puts me to sleep. But it's a fascinating book. I love the idea that all our myths have central core elements that cross all cultures and languages."

"That isn't what I expected you to be reading," I admitted.

"You think I'm more of a Danielle Steele fan?"

"I would never say that."

She laughed, a bit tipsy from her drink.

"He talks about following your bliss. Which is an interesting concept."

"Are you following your bliss?"

She paused and topped up our drinks, thinning out the Grand Marnier with more Scotch.

"How would I have time to? I've got a kid and the cafe to take care of. This is my life and I accept that. Whatever bliss I have, I get in tiny moments in-between all of that. Like sneaking out and seeing an indie band of twenty-year-olds play loud music in a smoky club."

"That's a good way to get some bliss. Although that makes it sound like a street drug."

"What about you? Are you following your bliss?"

I shook my head before I knew what to say. I was absolutely not following my bliss, and I knew it.

She leaned over and put her hand on my leg. "So what happened?"

"Like you, life happened." I sighed. "Hard decisions had to be made. So I made them."

"Lazy answer, Colin."

"Well, what do you want me to say?"

"How about the truth?"

I rubbed my hands through my messy long hair. "Maybe I chose the easy way. Not the road less taken."

"People don't understand that poem at all. It's not the road you choose. It's how you interpret the decision to take one road or the other. Every decision you make means other doors are then shut for you."

"Like this trip back."

"Yeah. Like this trip back."

Even not making a choice was a choice. Throughout my life, I found myself at crossroads. We all did. But we have to keep walking, so at some point we end up on one of the roads presented to us. To stop walking meant we died. I just don't remember why I chose the roads I did. Maybe they chose me.

"So you know the choices you made at those points in your life?"

"Of course!" She seemed shocked at my question. "How can you not?"

"I don't know. What if you were distracted or focussed on the wrong thing and made a wrong choice?"

"Colin, that's the point of the poem. That's what Robert Frost was talking about. We make choices constantly. It's better to make them with some awareness instead of just going with the flow. But no matter what, you've got to get to a place of peace with the choice you made—or didn't make."

I took a big gulp of my drink and shuddered.

"That's too overwhelming."

"Life is overwhelming if you let it."

"Yeah, more so if you're living two lives at the same time."

Celina rose, causing me to slip into the middle of the couch. She put out her cigarette in the clay ashtray. She reached out her hand. "Come on, time for sleep. Everything will look better in the morning."

I doubted it, but let her pull me up. She must have poured me a double because before I could stop myself, we stumbled into a hug against her railing, my arms instinctively encircling her, hers surrounding me. Her heart beat against my chest. She looked up into my eyes.

"I don't think Time's done with me," I said, not louder than a whisper. "I'm afraid I'll be here for the rest of my life."

"It's Ok if you are," she whispered back, then kissed me.

32

I jolted awake in an unfamiliar bed, in a strange room, my heart pounding in my chest. A dream about imploding, of the weight of my body becoming heavier and heavier as I became smaller and smaller, struggling to breathe in a vacuum.

It was like the fever dream I used to have as a kid, sliding down an endless slope, reaching for the one branch that could save me from sliding forever—reaching, reaching, but always missing. But in this one, not only was I sliding away forever, I was floating up and down on a never-ending ocean.

Where was I? Who's room was this? I sucked in a deep breath, then another, trying to calm down. I freaked out again. More deep and calming breaths. I kept my eyes hard shut. But I was still rocking on that ocean. How could that be? Once my nerves were under control, I opened my eyes again. Barely enough light leaked through the top windows of the loft bedroom for me to recognize where I was. Under silk sheets, on a waterbed. Someone stirred under the covers to my side. The waves jostled me. I was in Celina's waterbed, with Celina.

Oh no…

Easing myself out of my side of the bed, I discovered I was still wearing all my clothes. What happened after her kiss was a drunken blur, but I was pretty sure I didn't cheat on Gina and then put my clothes back on. I hoped I didn't. On the floor at my feet, was the remains of my last Rusty Nail. The warm, sweet smell of Drambuie was enough to make me gag, but I did it quietly so as not to wake Celina.

I snuck out of the bedroom and down into the living room. The door to Faye's room, covered with felt-penned 'do not enter' warnings, was half open as I slipped past. I prayed she, like all teenagers, could sleep through a world war. My jacket hung on the back of a kitchen chair. I grabbed it and let myself out, knowing her front door would lock behind me. Once I left, there was no going back.

An apt metaphor for my life.

Thirty years too late, I was realizing all the flaws I never reconciled. Good wasn't good enough. I chose to be acceptable at a job that required nothing great of me, ever. Good was fine—even acceptable. But in what I dreamed of doing, photography, good wasn't great. And great was the minimum. There was no place for Fine in professional photography, no gallery shows of All Right, no coffee table books of Ok.

I'd spend my adult life hiding from great. Because with great comes the risk of awful, of terrible, of shit. To put out monumental art into the world risked failure. Instead of failure, I ran to a safe job that required nothing of me other than to sit at my desk and do the very basic requirements as laid out in the job manual I received on my first day. No pushing the limits required.

There wasn't one catastrophic event that turned me down the road I chose. If I could point to a shattering review of my photographs, or one vicious rejection, looking back at my choice would almost have been easier. 'Look, I didn't have a choice but to quit after that,' I could have said. But nothing like that happened. So, it's impossible to stand here and make a definitive statement of when I made that decision. It just happened. Then, in a long slow sunset rather than a blink of an eye, I wasn't taking photographs. I was formatting resumes for the unemployed.

Regret. But more than regret, a sudden dawning of a life not wasted but squandered. As relieved as my parents were of my stable job, with its pension and benefits, I saw now how my lack of children must look like I had squandered that opportunity. Follow your bliss. But I ran away from my bliss into the arms of security and safety.

I used to take chances in life—not a lot—but a few. Offering to take photos for my high school yearbook was huge. And then everyone liked the images I took. Knowing not to make a fool out of myself with Gina when we were still in school was a huge chance. Getting up the nerve to kiss Gina for the first time was the most significant chance I ever took. That was following my bliss. And it worked.

But then I stopped. Maybe because when I finally got Gina, I wouldn't jinx it by taking any other chances. I went into social work to be close to her, then to get the steady paycheck, all the time with the justification that working during the day meant band photography at night. But as I got busier and busier at school and then working at the employment center, I let the photography fade, so calls from the bands I had photographed got fewer and fewer until they stopped altogether. Getting up early for school put a big crimp in staying up till the wee hours shooting a punk band at an after-hours warehouse party for twenty bucks and all the cheap beer I could drink. It appealed even less once I had Gina waiting for me at home.

I had stopped taking chances. I did what my parents wanted—a steady job with a pension and extended medical benefits. Stability and security foremost. But what had that stability and security gotten me?

This line of thought did my head in. So I gave up, lit a cigarette and kept walking. I was now on Clark Street below the Vancouver Community College branch where I had done my schooling with Gina a million years ago—or would finish a year from now. Across Main Street, the first indications of the new and improved Vancouver courtesy of Expo '86 were visible in excavations and construction along the shores of False Creek. The industrial shoreline of the city would become a beloved pedestrian walkway surrounded by expensive condominiums on the former Expo and Olympic 2010 land. A bright and shiny future for a city that I couldn't afford to live in anymore. But now, it was just a working-class town on the edge of nowhere. Closed auto repair shops, massive old factories, warehouses along 2nd Ave, under-used railway tracks slicing across a street.

Where in the future sat Starbucks and doggy daycares, there were photocopier sales, garages and odd storefronts. To cross False Creek, I turned onto the old Connaught Bridge, low and dingy, while the sleek, wide, and unfinished new Cambie Street Bridge rose to my right. BC Place stadium loomed like a marshmallow bound in a ring of concrete in a sea of parking lots on the downtown side of the bridge.

It was a warm summer morning and—

Summer.

It was summer and I was an idiot. When I left the future, it was September and schools were in session. But here and now, Gina and I were on summer break from our classes. We were working part-time jobs and hanging out with our friends. That's why young-us were in the Ovaltine on a Wednesday morning. Not because of any cosmic ripples, but because I didn't think of that in the future or the past. Not that figuring that out helped in any way. Except maybe Time wasn't completely out to get me.

I fired up another cigarette, shook my head in dismay and considered the early morning quiet. I had less than a day to fix my future, maybe it was still possible if I didn't make any more mistakes. What were the odds of that happening? Pretty damn poor.

I stubbed out my smoke. My head was a fog of Rusty Nails, cigarettes and doubt. But anything is better than standing by yourself on a bridge in the darkness, so turned towards downtown and I walked until I was outside my hotel.

•

I awoke from an unsettling dream full of sirens, yelling, to feet pounding in the hallway outside my foul room. Somehow, the room smelled even worse. I was in a sauna, fully dressed, sweating like a pig. My face was sticky. The wall behind my head was an oven, and I was leaning against it. A spectral figure had been chasing me through darkened alleys, its eyes glowing red.

The door exploded open. An apparition covered in heavy clothes and a horrifying face-covering mask charged inside. A billowing cloud of dark smoke followed it into my room. A light flashed around, blinding me. There was a split second of detached observation of an epic photograph. I choked and made the mistake of breathing in. Stars exploded behind my eyes. I gasped for breath, drawing in more toxic air. I tried to stand, but toppled onto the filthy floor.

The apparition yelled, its voice muffled in its mask.

The light lit up the dust bunnies under the bed.

That was the last thing I recognized before I passed out.

33

Beep.

Beep.

Beep.

Was that the Roadrunner? Was I in a cartoon? I felt as if a boulder had dropped on top of me, flattening me like a pancake. Shit. That made me the Coyote, not the Roadrunner.

I opened my eyes slowly.

The ceiling of an ambulance. A mask over my mouth. Steady beeps of a machine beside my head. The hiss of oxygen.

The overpowering smell of smoke.

What the hell happened to me?

I passed out again.

I opened my eyes again. A middle-aged EMT stared down at me, his face dispassionate.

"Don't worry. You're all right."

I tried to speak and realized I still had the oxygen mask over my mouth. Pulling it off, I coughed up half a lung before stabilizing my breath. I could smell nothing but smoke.

"Why am I in an ambulance?"

The EMT checked the machine by my head and jotted something down on the chart in his hands.

"John Doe, welcome back to the land of the living."

I nodded at him but said nothing. Better to keep my mouth shut for as long as possible. He pulled the mask back over my face.

"Don't go anywhere and you should be all right."

The EMT hung up my chart and left. I breathed in cool, fresh oxygen, then pulled the mask off my face. Getting off the gurney, I had to balance against the wall until I was stable enough to stand upright. I felt like I'd been in a mosh pit for a decade. My lungs continued to hack up black filth. The black t-shirt and jeans I'm wearing reek of smoke. I had to get out of there before someone questioned me, so I shuffled across to the door, holding the wall for balance.

Two fire trucks and a row of police car, lights flashing, block the street outside. Police direct traffic on Hastings. A scattering of people watch whatever was going on. The EMT kneels beside a faintly moving body sprawled in the middle of Cambie Street. No one noticed as I slipped out of the ambulance. Keeping my head down, I walk behind a fire truck, under a band of fluttering police tape and around the corner of the Dominion Building and out of sight. What the hell just happened?

Sitting on a stone wall at the edge of Victory Square, surrounded by fire trucks and emergency vehicles, I barely could comprehend the conflagration consuming my hotel. I almost died in there just hours ago. I considered lighting a cigarette, but the smoke from the fire was blowing my way, and who wanted to add insult to injury.

There was a rumble, and part of the facade crumbled to the sidewalk. Firefighters worked to put out the last elements of the blaze as I watched.

With all hope for our scheme washed down a literal storm drain, all that remained were the clothes on my back and a bit of cash in my pocket. Time machine—gone. Backpack with extra clothes, Walkman—gone. Money for Dennis to buy the stock with—gone. My camera and all the photographs I had taken—gone. My future—gone.

What to do? Did I continue to sit on this low stone wall for the rest of the day, facing the smoldering hulk of my hotel, dispassionately observing how the smoke and steam rose into the angled morning sun? Then climb up onto the roof of A&B Sound for my possible trip back to the future? The safest choice by a long shot. Boring but safest.

Spend the day wandering around town, reliving, and re-fortifying memories of my youth before maybe going back? Less dull, a bit less safe. I had options. But I had to choose the one with the least impact on the past and, therefore, my future.

"Colin!"

I was dragged out of my thoughts to see Celina rushing across the blockaded street, my camera bag bouncing on her shoulder.

She hugged me, then sat down and said, "Thank God, you're Ok! I overheard some regulars talking about the fire at the cafe, so I came down to find you. The firefighters said they suspect it began at the back, either the second or third floor. They're pretty sure they've halted it spreading before it catches the neighboring ones."

I didn't react. I didn't care.

She handed me my camera bag. "You left this last night."

I took it from her, holding it in my lap. At least I had my camera and all the photos I had taken. Maybe they would count for something.

More of the building shuddered and fell on the sidewalk. Emergency workers jumped out of the way. I hoped no one died in the fire. That would be too much of a burden to bear right now.

"I've lost everything," I said to nobody.

"You lost things. You've got your life. What else can you count on?"

"At midnight, I may not even have a life."

"Come on, let's go. There's nothing you can do here, Colin."

She was right. Not a single thing to do. I tried, and tried and tried again and yet here I was, right back where I had started. Who was I to believe I could fake out time? Outsmart the inexorable forward motion of life? Turn back the dial and do my life differently? Believing this plan of ours would work while affecting no one else was insanity. The hubris, the arrogance, the stupidity.

"It's my fault. Everything. An entire building and everything in it burned because I came back. There is no other reason."

"You can't know for sure, Colin," she said.

I sat up, angry. "Of course, I know it. The El-Cid Hotel was standing when I left 2017! And now it isn't when it's supposed to be. A mighty huge ripple, don't you think? What else have I gone and done? Simply because I ignored Terry's warnings, stepped off a bus and stupidly came into the Ovaltine."

"And saw yourself."

"Yeah. Now everything's changed. The cash for Dennis is gone. I don't even know if I'll return without my time machine, since it's nothing but cinders now."

Celina looked at me, worried. "What? You mean you might be stuck here?"

"I might. I don't know. And if I am, what about my future-self? I came back at midnight on September 29, 2017. So what happens then because the time machine is destroyed now, and I've relived the next thirty-three years? Will I blip out of existence in September 2017? Meanwhile, there'll be an old me and young me walking around 1984 Vancouver. I'll have to leave town, start a new life somewhere else. But with no ID, money, anything."

"I'm sure it isn't quite that awful."

"Yeah, well, I'm pretty sure it is." I slumped back and exhaled. "I've lost everything. Time has won. I played with fate and fate took me out at the knees."

I couldn't take time for granted anymore. There's no time like the present, so everything I had ever wanted to do, I had to do before it was too late. Coming back hadn't been what I expected, a Disney World 1980s-land version of a time I thought I knew but now realize I only had the biased and blinkered memories of twenty-two-year-old me, which didn't square with my present experience. I thought I remembered accurately, but memory was a trickster.

Despite my state, I took out my camera and snapped off a couple of shots as the top two floors of my hotel collapsed in on the rest. Once and for all extinguishing the faint naïve hope I had of salvaging the rest of my belongings.

What was in my pockets was everything I now owned. I considered my predicament. Or, more accurately, my predicaments. The ripples I had started had become a series of tsunami-sized waves, threatening to destroy me and everyone around me.

None of this was supposed to happen. Go back and buy some stupid stocks, hide in my hotel room, then return. But maybe that fire would occur, anyway. Perhaps the fire was inevitable the moment I rented a room in that specific hotel. Maybe because I took room 212, the firebug was forced to use room 312 and thus lit a fire where he would have failed if they had given him any other room. If I had listened to Terry and hid myself away, I would have been deep asleep when the fire started instead of barely asleep, tormented with guilt over whatever happened between me and Celina.

So it was quite likely I was alive right now because of my inability to follow our plan.

Or not.

"Colin, what on earth happened to your hair? It… it looks like it's melted."

I went to brush my hands through my long, lanky hair. My fingers caught in the now melted extensions. I sighed.

I'd never looked good with long hair. I thought I wore it well during those teenage years when everyone had long hair. It was an essential part of our collective personas, as were the flared jeans with scuffed cuffs, grey hoodies, and tattered jean jackets. But in the few photos of me during the '80s, I looked like a shy, sweet kid with a bad wig. Kind of like I did right now. I might not know how to solve our future financial disaster, but for the rest of my time in the past, there was one thing repairable, here and now.

34

Friday noon - 12 hours to go

The old guy was in the tiny barbershop beside the coin shop. Ready and waiting to cut hair but with no customers. He sat in one of the hardback chairs, cigar lit, staring off into space. In his gnarled hand was a chipped coffee cup older than him. A few more cups were stacked beside an old Bunn drip coffee machine on the side table. A discolored glass coffee pot simmered on the warmer, reducing slowly. Beside it was an array of months-old Playboy and Popular Mechanics magazines.

He immediately began judging us as we stepped in. On his face was the scowl of your bitterest uncle across the dinner table at Thanksgiving after you mentioned liking something he hated. Ford over Chevrolet. Or the Canucks instead of the Leafs.

Without a word, the barber wearily struggled to his feet, grudgingly gestured to a battered red and chrome barber chair. I crossed the room and sat down. Celina slipped into one of the chairs to wait with my camera bag. I leaned back as he whipped the drape over me, adjusting the paper strip around my neck before clipping the cloth behind my neck.

"What'll it be?" he rasped.

"I was in a bit of an accident. Can you cut this crap out of my hair? Then I'd like short back and sides, leave it a lot longer on the top." It was the same request I'd been giving barbers—and then hairstylists—since the late '90s. He grunted. The trimmers turned on. His pocket radio was tuned to CKNW, the local news and talk radio station. I listened attentively, hoping against hope not to hear a breaking report of mysterious deaths or sudden blazes. But they discussed nothing more crucial than the upcoming federal election and a new petition to build a bridge from the Mainland to Vancouver Island. More talk of the Canucks draft picks.

"Why the hell do we need another defenseman?" he muttered.

Vancouver conversation openers were no different, now and in the future.

Under the hypnotic drone of the clippers, my thoughts wandered to my biggest problem.

If I stayed here in 1984, I wouldn't experience anything new for thirty-three years. The moment an upcoming movie was announced, I could list off the spoilers. Same with TV—Ross and Rachel? The ending of Lost? Janet Jackson at the Super Bowl? No surprises for Colin.

I jolted as the barber nicked my ear. He didn't apologize. Instead, he dabbed something foul-smelling on the cut that stung, then continued cutting the melted extensions out my hair.

No surprises. I could bet big on technology, but to what end? I could move my website off myspace before it faded away. But there would be no delight in finding new music until I was eighty-eight years old. Nirvana, Oasis, Britney, Justin, I'd have to live through them all again. The Macarena.

Then he pulled the drape off. In the mirror was the real me, not the pretend me with the flowing hair and the taupe suit. I rubbed a hand over my head in relief. I wasn't an extra in a Chinese version of 'Saturday Night Fever' anymore. But the relief was fleeting. Despite not hearing of any disaster ripples on the radio didn't mean they weren't already in progress.

The barber spun the chair around and used a hand mirror to show me the back of my head in the wall mirror. I nodded like one does when shown the back of their neck after a haircut. I caught Celina's eyes as she looked up from the Playboy she was reading. She smiled in approval.

While he brushed off my neck, I stared out at the vestibule and the coin shop. A sign hung on its door. I squinted to read it, and my blood turned to ice.

"He not opening today?" I gestured towards the shop across the way.

"Nope. He called here. Had to make that damn sign for him."

"Death in the family, is that what it says?"

"All sudden like."

The guy in that store purchased my coins. Now someone connected with him was dead. Coincidence? Another ripple coming to submerge me? We hadn't researched the shop owner's life history. Why would we? Only if he was in business in the future and the past. Maybe this death in his family has nothing to do with me. Perhaps someone succumbed to cancer. But cancer wasn't sudden, so there was no way I'd affected the progress of someone's disease. But the ripples that burnt down the hotel could have caused someone's death…

Was this the way it would be from now on? A vengeful Time tracking me and picking off each personal interaction of my ill-fated trip one by one? Although I never made it back to meet with Dennis, maybe he was in danger too. And my grandmother, possibly even the mahjong parlor and the restaurant underneath where we had met. What other buildings could suddenly go up in flames like The El-Cid?

The Ovaltine—Ground Zero of where everything turned sour. The building where Celina and her mother worked all day long. In Time's crosshairs.

I yanked out a ten and handed it to the barber. He didn't react to the five-dollar tip, slipping it into the pocket of his white jacket as I dashed out the front door and up onto the sidewalk.

"Colin, where are you going?"

Celina joined me in the vestibule. I explained my fear and watched the color fade from her face.

I hung on to the door strap as Celina bulled her way through traffic on Hastings.

"If anything happens to them, I'll—"

"Watch out!"

She whipped out into the opposing lane to get around a delivery truck and pushed hard up the hill towards Main Street. I watched the skyline for smoke or anything as she cleared the intersection, and there was the Ovaltine. Not on fire. But an ambulance, its lights flashing, was parked right outside the cafe. Pedestrians gawked.

Celina screamed as she saw the ambulance. She yanked her car into a tire-screeching u-turn across three lanes of traffic, somehow not getting us killed. She was out of her seat before we even came to a stop behind the ambulance. I yanked on the emergency brake, and the car stalled out with a shudder. I grabbed her keys and pushed my way through the crowd into the restaurant.

There I found her hugging her mother behind the till. The paramedics worked on someone on the floor. Other than them, the only sign of disturbance was a tipped-over coffee cup at a table, the liquid slowly dripping onto the floor.

"Who is it?" I asked.

Celina released her mother and turned to me. "Jimmy. One of the regulars. Another damn heart attack."

•

After her mother reassured Celina that she was fine, we stepped back outside. In the afternoon warmth, we attempted to calm ourselves down. Everything around us seemed normal. Traffic rumbled past. Pedestrians on the sidewalks. Blue sky above. A breeze brought the smells of the harbor a few blocks north.

"What the hell is going on, Colin?" Celina asked, lighting up a cigarette with shaking hands.

I had no idea what to say. Everything had gone downhill since I stepped into the Ovaltine on Wednesday morning for a BLT. Two muggings and a fire had left my plan in tatters.

"I'm over my head in this. I don't know what's going on anymore."

A boxy City of Vancouver police car rolled to a stop behind her car, still parked illegally by the ambulance. It chirped its siren, and the officer in the passenger seat gestured. Celina jumped, startled. I waved her keys and pointed at the ambulance and the cafe.

"Let's get out of here before they want to talk to us. I don't have any ID."

She nodded, took the keys, and we got into her Datsun. After two attempts to get it into gear, she carefully pulled out into traffic. Celina made two quick rights and pulled into her parking spot behind the Ovaltine. We sat in silence, staring at the garbage bins in the alley. Rotting food had taken over from the smell of the harbor.

"What are you going to do now?"

"If everyone was back here, we could try and figure this out. Come up with a new way of looking at our plan, regroup and try again."

"But they're not here. It's just us."

"It's not like I'm an idiot. I should be able to solve this. It's not like our plan was particularly complicated."

"Are you kidding?"

She's right. Our plan was as intricate as a Swiss watch, delicate as a Faberge egg and not built for the real world nor for contact with the violence of Time.

"Do you think we can outsmart Time and get it back on track again?"

"I don't have much choice, do I? Either I keep trying, or I give up. If I keep trying, Time will try to stop me. But if I give up, then my future is guaranteed to be worse than before I came back. I'll still be unemployed, and we still won't have a place to live."

Two bad choices. But it's not like I haven't made bad choices before. Maybe this time, my choice will be the right one, and I'll be able to return tonight triumphant. Or maybe I'll be dead. Or stuck here to plan my death.

I needed help.

"But where do we start? There wasn't a manual with the machine, was there?"

No manual other than the cryptic list of seven rules. No warning labels in multiple languages plastered over the bottom of the box. No 1-800 number to call for advice. No one to talk to about what I was going through, except—

35

Once again, I sat in the Chinese restaurant below the mahjong parlor, waiting for my grandmother. Like last time, a pot of tea and a plate of coconut buns were on the table. But unlike last time, three cups and three buns. Celina sat beside me as we waited.

Thank God Celina was there. Maybe with her help, we could elicit something more from my grandmother than angry denials. If we couldn't, then I was honestly at the end of my rope. I had nothing to do except wait until midnight for one of six events to happen.

I would return to my lame, hopeless future and try to find a new place to live and a new job to pay off our maxed-out credit cards.

Or I had screwed up so staggeringly and had nothing to go back to—no job, no home, no friends.

Or maybe a random ripple killed me in five years, and I returned to be dead.

Or, worse, the now destroyed time machine was essential to returning at midnight, so instead of going back, the rest of my life would roll forward from here and now.

Or worst of all, I simply ceased to exist.

All those ripples, all those potential outcomes. But which one did I want? Which was best for me? And which one was best for everyone else?

"We'll work it out, Colin," Celina said, attempting to reassure. Despite being impossible for either of us to know how my life would work out, I appreciated her efforts. Not until midnight when I would or wouldn't disappear in a blip from the rooftop. I weakly smiled, about to reply when my grandmother, May, came into the restaurant.

Unlike before, she ignored the man behind the counter and made a beeline through the tables. She sat down across from me, purse in her lap, a scowl on her face.

"Thank you for coming, May," I said respectfully.

She huffed instead of acknowledging, then glared pointedly at Celina.

"She knows?"

Celina and I nodded. May rolled her eyes and gestured to her teacup. After I poured her tea, she took a sip, then put it down. She stared, taking in how I looked. Her grandson, fifty-five years of me, currently two years younger than she was.

"You look like your father."

I nodded. I didn't need the reminder.

"You cut your hair."

I nodded again and brushed my hands through my good old familiar haircut. No more flipping my coif out of my face ever again.

"May, this is Celina. Celina Chow. Her family owns the Ovaltine Cafe."

"It is a pleasure to meet you," Celina said in clear Chinese.

If that impressed my grandmother, she didn't show it. "I know your mother. Fa-Lin."

Celina nodded. May observed Celina and me for signs of something—probably romantic interest—all grandmothers want great-grandchildren. Finally, she loosened her grip on her handbag and sighed in exasperation.

"You used the machine and came back." It was a statement of the obvious. I nodded.

"Yes. It worked like it was supposed to."

"Why? Why did you use it? Is life so bad in three decades you had no other choice?"

I explained my future situation and our plan, leaving nothing out. When I finish, Celina poured us more tea. May frowned then said, "I warned you, correct? I told you about the dangers of using the machine?"

I shook my head. I had never talked to her about the machine before I came back. Because I was afraid she would tell me it was a joke, or she would convince me not to use it.

"Only what you said when I tried to talk to you on Wednesday," I said.

She glared at me. I felt like I had as a child when I'd made a mess playing with Play-Doh in her pristine living room, and it took her hours to clean it up.

"I gave you the box at some point in the future." A statement, not a question.

I nodded. "On my 50th birthday."

"Yet you never came to talk to me about my strange present. Especially after you discovered the instructions."

"No. Since you hadn't used the time machine, I didn't know how you could help me. I thought you'd be mad, or talk me out of using it," I said, embarrassed.

"That is exactly what I would have done."

"Then why did you give it to me?"

May stared across the table. "I haven't given it to you! That box is safe in a trunk in your parents' basement!"

I looked imploringly at Celina, but she was wisely staying quiet. "May, I truly needed to use it. But everything has gotten complicated."

"And you don't know what will be when you go back."

"May, I don't know if I'll even go back! Forget my plan. The money to buy the stock is long gone. But even worse, the hotel fire destroyed the box! That's what I need to know from you. If I don't have the box, can I at least go home?"

"How would I know?"

Celina said, "How did you learn about the time machine?"

My grandmother sipped more of her tea. She pulled an end off one bun, nibbling on it before replying.

"My grandfather gave the box to me. He showed me the instructions and warned me of the dangers."

"How? When was this?" I said, confused. "You never met your grandfather. He didn't escape China…"

"Neither did I," she said.

May refused to make eye contact with me. I glanced at Celina, but she's as confused as I am.

"May? I don't understand."

Finally, she looked up at me, worry in her eyes. "I lied to you, Colin, if, in the future, I said I didn't use the time machine."

"What?"

Then she told us her story.

"My first birth was in Chongqing. My father taught history at the university while his young wife cared for me, her first child. We had a beautiful life, well respected in the community. I had everything I ever wanted, including a younger sister, Ailing. And then the war came. Then Chairman Mao. My parents secretly sent us to live with my grandparents, far away from the city. I was nineteen, Ailing just twelve. My outspoken father was picked up in the first round of collections. I never saw him or my mother again. They claimed we had died, so my grandparents in the country raised us as orphans, giving us new names.

"My sister and I suffered under that regime on a collective farm with my grandparents, aunts, uncles, and cousins. My grandfather had been an artisan, well-known in the local area for his ceramics. After the revolution, his style of art was considered decadent so he put away his wheel and kiln, and lived as a simple farmer. We had to work in the fields every day, under a blistering sun, even though the harvest was so small. It was a famine. My younger sister struggled to keep up, but grew weaker with every passing day. In late autumn she collapsed in the fields, and we carried her home and put her to bed before returning to our labor. She tossed in a fevered delirium for two days, and on the morning of the third day, she died. It broke my grandmother's heart. It broke MY heart. Then my grandmother succumbed to one of the many diseases which ravaged our town. Her passing drained the remaining life from my grandfather."

What she said beggared belief. This wasn't the family history I knew. She was telling me a story about someone else. But looking at her eyes as she talked, no matter how strong my disbelief, what she said had to be true. I only knew the second part of her story. May sipped her tea, collected her thoughts and emotions before continuing.

"Only after her funeral did my grandfather tell me about the time machine. On his deathbed, he showed me a beautiful ceramic bowl. It had an elaborate scene painted on it, a map hidden within the delicate lines. The directions to where he had buried the box. At his urging, I snuck out that night, worried he would pass before understanding what he was attempting to tell me. I found the box. He had buried it behind an old abandoned temple outside our town. When I brought it back, he showed me the hidden instructions on how to use the machine. Then, he begged me to use it and change my life. To go back in time and help my family escape China before the war and Mao.

"The next day, my beloved grandfather died. I had no one. Everyone I had ever loved was dead at the hands of the Communists. What reason had I to stay? So I used the machine."

Celina leaned forward and took May's hand, cradling it sympathetically. May wiped her eyes with a tissue before returning it to her sleeve.

She regained her composure. She broke off another bit of bun, delicately ate it before continuing. "If my grandfather was telling the truth, and his entire story wasn't a last moment of life dementia, I had to warn my parents. So I snuck back to Chongqing, where my parents had lived thirty-three years ago. It took me two weeks of travelling, mostly at night, to avoid army patrols and roadblocks until I made it to the university, which was now the party central command for the city. There I found an out of the way storeroom, shut the door and turned the knob. At first, I believed nothing had happened, that I was the victim of my grandfather's fevered thoughts and would soon be caught and arrested. But when I walked out of the storeroom, I realized I had gone back in time because the university was no longer the Communist Party headquarters. In my ragged Mao clothes, I stood out to everyone. I claimed to be part of a theatre group, stole clothes from the locker room to fit in."

A dim sum cart clattered by, one errant wheel chattering against the floor tiles, distracting the three of us. Not wanting to halt my grandmother's confessional, I waved the cart away. I held my breath as May paused, picking at her coconut bun. I hazarded a glance at Celina, but she was engrossed in my grandmother's astounding story. A moment passed, then another.

"What happened next?" I asked gently.

May sighed, wiped her already clean hands and continued, "Walking those halls, not in fear for my life, not avoiding eye contact, not fearing revolutionaries grabbing me and dragging me off was so unsettling. I waited for my father in his office and told him I was family from the country and needed temporary accommodation. He must have recognized something, an echo of our family. He took me back to his house, the house where I had grown up. I met his wife, my mother, now nearly ten years younger than I. Only then did I tell them the truth. I was their daughter from a terrible future, come back to rescue them. I pointed out so much in their house which was impossible for me to have known. The limited hours I had I spent convincing him and my mother of what would happen if they stayed in China. I begged him to take his young pregnant wife and escape.

"After three days, my father took me back to the storeroom, hugged me, thanked me for saving our family, and then I disappeared. You know the rest, my parents escaped China, sailed on the Empress of Hong Kong across to Canada where I was born, for the second time, in Vancouver. I had hoped to save my family, but in my second life, my parents only had one daughter. My sister Ailing was erased from existence, and it is entirely my fault."

Celina and I stared at her. I didn't know what to think. In that moment, trying to process everything I had just heard, I was stunned and in shock.

After a long pause, Celina finally spoke. "That is why you used the machine. Not to make your life better, but to allow your parents to live."

She sighed. "But that didn't work out. As you know, my father died working on The Second Narrows Bridge when it collapsed in 1958. The same year he was killed in China during my first life. Your great-grandmother died of a broken heart shortly afterwards. They left their families and came to a new country. My father wasn't permitted to teach again. They suffered second class lives full of overt racism and then died.

"I thought I was doing the right thing, using the machine. I wouldn't have survived much longer under the regime, and my death would end our family's history forever."

The ripples of time complicated everything. They pulled us forward, yet kept us tethered to the past.

"So why were you able to use the machine to change the future, but I can't?"

May looked up from her now lukewarm tea.

"Colin, I didn't use it to become wealthy."

"But I don't want to be rich, May. I just want to continue to live in this city. That's all. Live a reasonable and good life without having to spend most of my paycheck to rent a terrible apartment. I wanted to make our lives a bit better. I'm not greedy."

"Oh, ten million dollars in stock isn't greedy?" May scowled. "Ha. Remember your Bible, 'The love of money is the root of all evil.' *Ay yah*, no wonder Time fights you."

She was right. If we had wanted a better life, there were better ways to go about it than gaming the stock market. We should have rethought our plan. We could have figured out the absolute, barest minimum of adjustments to give us the life we desired. Not listen to our greed and gone for the mammoth win. The mammoth win that had a mammoth impact on many lives. That was what I was fighting. We tried to change too much.

36

Friday 4 pm - 8 hours to go

English Bay wasn't much different. An ocean and a beach didn't change in only thirty years. The only differences involved the impact of man. There wasn't a separate bike lane full of rollerbladers, cyclists, and skateboarders. The condo towers of the West End were lower and fewer compared to 2017. But looking out at the water, ignoring the container ships waiting to unload, the view was essentially the same as it would have been over two hundred years ago when James Vancouver sailed into this harbour for the first time. We wandered towards Stanley Park, the outer harbor with its cargo ships at rest on our left, discussing Celina's future and my past.

Celina said, "I'll loan you some money. Not the whole $4500, but enough to buy a bit of Apple stock, maybe enough to put a downpayment on a house. You'd have to continue to work so that you wouldn't become a rich, photographer-about-the-town taking pics of the beautiful movie stars at gallery openings." She smiled.

Wow. She was offering money she didn't have to an itinerant time traveller. How amazing was this woman?

"Celina, as much as I'd love to take your money, I absolutely can't. The ripples of what you would have done with the money will affect the future. My future, your future, Faye's future."

"You can pay me back. With interest," Celina offered.

"No payback until 2017, so thirty-three years of compound interest? I'll be broke again."

She laughed, but I continued, dead serious. "These ripples are no joke, Celina. I can't allow anything to happen to you. You've got a wonderful daughter and a good life. You shouldn't even be helping me. It's way too dangerous."

"But I'm still alive, aren't I? Time's after you, not me. It isn't interested in me as your accessory," she said.

"Because maybe you haven't impacted my plan. Yet."

Celina didn't have any comeback to that. Ah yes, my plan. The one that lay in tatters at my feet.

"Shit! I've got to call my broker!" I said.

"Why bother?"

"My appointment's got to be cancelled. If I don't he might spend the next thirty years wondering about me. Another ripple."

We ran across Beach Drive and entered the lobby of the Silvia Hotel, then and now a landmark. I looked up Dennis' number, again, and called.

He was glad to hear from me.

"Colin, I called down to Apple's head office in California. They can have the stock certificates securely couriered to me by next Friday. But we need to set up your account first."

I stared at the phone in my hand. I could hear Dennis talking but couldn't comprehend what he was saying. Only what he said echoed in my head. Our plan was never going to work. Even if I hadn't been mugged on Tuesday, I never would have had the stock certificates by today. But this wasn't Time working against me, this was me not asking enough questions of Dennis when we met in the future. It was one-hundred percent my fault.

Once we were outside, I told Celina what Dennis had said. "It was never going to work. From the beginning, our brilliant plan was guaranteed to fail."

"I'm so sorry, Colin, I know how much this meant to you."

"All these ripples I've created, all for nothing."

"Not nothing, you got to come back and meet me. See Damage Done's first show. Hang out with your grandmother and finally hear her story."

Celina smiled, and I appreciated her attempt to make me feel better. Meeting her had be great, as had the show, and seeing May as a peer who had lived two lives instead of as my old grandmother.

We walked in silence, my grandmother's multiple life stories swirling around in my head until they suddenly coalesced into a single clear thought.

"Maybe I've been looking at this wrong."

"What do you mean?"

"What if the entire idea of travelling back to profit in the future is where we went wrong? May didn't. Maybe that's why she succeeded. You notice she never mentioned Time fighting her when she used the machine? But Time has been fighting me every minute. What's the difference? What did she do that I haven't? Or, what am I doing that she didn't?"

"Hmm. All your grandmother did was go back and pass on some advice."

Advice which her parents chose to take. They didn't have to. They were offered a choice, and maybe that's what was different. The plan we made in the future didn't include a choice. Sure, we had options once I was back in the future. We could choose not to sell the stock, but we would because after everything I've been through, why wouldn't we?

Too complicated, too complex, a plan with more parts than a Space Shuttle. No wonder it didn't work. We were too clever for our own good.

Celina continued, nudging me out of my thoughts, "So instead of your elaborate plan, what would be something simple?"

What would be simple? My grandmother's plan was nothing more than an honest conversation with her parents. Could I do the same and talk to my young self? But what would I say, and would he even believe me? Would I even believe an old-me at twenty-two? Not likely.

That direct communication worked for my grandmother. Could I talk to my parents and convince them to buy me a house? Better to stay in the past and move to Montreal.

"Going near my young-self was out. We were both physically impacted the last time we were in the same room."

"Are you sure? Maybe you had a panic attack, rushed out to the alley and passed out."

I shook my head. "It was when I saw young-Colin."

"But he didn't pass out..."

I didn't want to think about panic attacks anymore, that wasn't getting us anywhere.

I said to her, "How about a note from me to past-me? 'Do not open until 2017' Then I explain that when he uses the time machine in 2017, not to go to the Ovaltine for lunch."

She looked at me with a face full of disbelief. "But you've already used the time machine to come back. What's the point of telling young-Colin what to do when he uses the time machine? You said you could only use it once. You can tell him whatever you want, but the machine won't work for him."

"Unless he uses it before I used it, then he would be the first me to time travel."

"But then you wouldn't have come back to leave the note in the first place. Or is it the second place?"

A tension headache was building in my skull like the fourth hour of an all-day exam. The looping logic of time travel was becoming too much.

"Hang on," Celina continued. "It's all moot. You have no box. The fire destroyed it."

"No, Time destroyed the box I brought back. My past-me hasn't gotten the box yet. It's still at my grandmothers."

"Are you sure about that?"

I was about to say yes but stopped. Maybe the box got destroyed in all timelines. Not like I could phone myself up and ask. Or visit my grandparents house and check.

Celina rubbed her hands against her eyes. "Keeping track of all of this hurts my head."

"No shit. Even Einstein couldn't figure this out."

This was ridiculous. Our original plan turned out to be pretty damn shaky even when we believed it was foolproof.

"Besides, past-me wouldn't simply believe a random note. It's doubtful I would if I received it. Anyways, the stock plan was flawed from the beginning."

"Maybe there's a completely different way, one not involving the stock market?"

Celina's question rumbled around in my head. Was there an entirely different way of looking at this? Ignore the lottery-sized win because it wasn't happening. There would be no returning as a millionaire. To be honest, I never wanted that. Even with millions in the bank, Gina would keep doing what she did. She loved her job. So what was it I wanted, personally, for me and me alone? Not now, but in the future. I wasn't cut out to be a social worker when I started college, nor when I got employed as one. Helping people down on their luck understand the intricacies of the Canadian welfare system had never been my dream growing up. No surprise there.

But what did I want to do? What did I need to do? Way back in the mists of time when I graduated high school, what were my dreams as I stepped out into the great big world?

Do what you love.

When I was 20, I loved music and photography.

I still loved music and photography.

Excellent clarity, Colin. Clarity that won't help me to solve my future. This wasn't a time for indulging in passions, I needed to figure out a solution, and I was running out of time. I sighed and regrouped, noticing Celina staring at me.

"Back to basics. Forget our complex plan with all those minute gears and cogs and the millions of ripples."

"Basics? Like what started it all?" she asked.

Startled, I looked up from staring at the path in front of me. "Yes. Exactly!"

I trimmed away the cruft and detritus from our plan, digging back to the beginning when our running joke became something much more real. Losing my job wasn't the catalyst for this misguided adventure; losing our home was. Losing the security of that safe place shook up our world, convinced me to use the time machine.

"This all started when we got the notice on where we lived. Maybe that's where the fix needs to be."

"I don't understand. Didn't you want the stocks to buy the house? What can you do now to stop your landlord's kids from selling a house in thirty-three years?"

"Well, I can't stop them now. They're in elementary school. Shit. And I loop myself right back to the stock plan," I said, exasperated.

"Worth a try," she said sympathetically. "Too bad you couldn't go and buy the house today."

"No kidding. I'd need less than $100,000."

I laughed, remembering when buying a house that cost a hundred thousand dollars was a clear sign of insanity. Ken, one of my more pragmatic high school friends, bought a fixer-upper in the late '80's worth far less. In the future, he now owned a couple of dozen rental units. He summered at his 5,000 square foot cabin on Saltspring Island, then wintered at his 5,000 square foot cabana in Mexico.

I also remembered other friends in the early 2000s spending a quarter of a million dollars on condos. I was positive then that they were fools, but now they're sitting pretty in their multi-million dollar retirement plans.

"Doesn't matter anyway, the house isn't for sale, and I don't have the money to make an offer if it was."

"Or the identification to be approved for a mortgage."

"Exactly, I'm a fifty-five-year-old born twenty-two years ago."

My wisecrack stopped me cold. If I didn't go back to the future, this was my new predicament in a nutshell. Trapped out of time, I knew about the future but was far less aware of what should be my past. The sinking realization I might not go back at midnight rocked me again. This reality could be my life starting tomorrow. Waiting until I was ninety years old to buy an iPhone, being too senile to Netflix and chill, enduring the goddamn Macarena again.

Hang on…

"What did you say about ID?"

"You need ID for mortgage approval," she says.

Mortgage. Nobody bought a house outright unless they're a drug dealer. My friend Ken didn't. He paid a bare minimum downpayment. Not $100,000, but only 10% of the total cost. A measly ten grand.

Where was a rock so I could bang my head against it. We'd been idiots chasing after millions of dollars. We only needed enough money for a mortgage downpayment, not to buy it outright.

"Listen, a while after we started renting the house, the owner put it on the market. In '96. Their kids had grown up and moved out. But housing sales were in a real slump, so he pulled the listing after a couple of months. From then on, he was happy to keep us as tenants and take our rent."

"How much did he then ask for the house?"

I struggled to remember. "After the post-Expo housing boom, at the tail end of the early '90's recession? 300, 400 thousand? It couldn't have been much more. A lot less than the three million they're asking for it in 2017."

Because of future new banking rules, our future downpayment would be about ten times as much since we'd have to come up with 20% down and then carry the rest in a million-dollar mortgage. The monthly payments would kill us. Well, not affording food after making our monthly mortgage payments would be what actually killed us.

"If young-me has $40,000 in ten years, he could buy the house when it goes on the market. Then our lives would be great. Our rent payments would cover our mortgage payments. And that would solve our greatest problem in the future. What a joke. All the possible outcomes of using a time machine, and I'm considering having a twenty-five year mortgage to be a success."

"A far cry from owning ten million in Apple stock, but it makes sense," she said. "If only we hadn't burned the race track results."

"I'm pretty sure if we tried that again, simply having the winnings would kill me. Or us. A plane would drop out of the sky, or a gas main would rupture under our feet. And I'd still have to figure out how to deliver the cash to me in 1995."

"So we're back to square one."

I looked over at her, "Maybe not. Leaving young-me cash won't work. It isn't possible to track down that much money in a few hours. But writing a note for myself with a sure bet he can use to win the down payment? Anything he can gamble on a few months before the house goes up for sale?"

"If only someone here knew the future…"

I smiled at her, and she smiled back.

•

"Why is this so hard? How come I'm having such a hard time remembering anything specific?"

When posed with the question about what to tell my past-self, which he could then gamble into $40,000, I was honestly stumped. As a working stiff in the '90s, my focus was on work, attending concerts and partying with my friends. Paying attention to events with outcomes best suited for travelling back in time to gamble on wasn't even on that list. Remembering when a concert happened was no way to make a load of cash—Nirvana in 1994 at the Forum? Pink Floyd at BC Place the same year? Great shows, but who would want to make a bet on them? I remembered nothing else with any accuracy. If I were in the future, Google or Wikipedia would find me a thousand events to fit the bill. If we had thought about this alternative plan before I came back, my pockets would be full of notes.

Instead, with Celina staring at me, I struggled to remember anything surprising or unusual or unconventional in the mid-'90s. Try it yourself. What can you remember from twenty years ago, which you could have bet on to win tens of thousands of dollars?

Celina pulled me out of the way as a kid wearing a tattered Vancouver Canucks shirt with that godawful orange and black exploding ice skate logo raced by on a BMX bike.

"Idiot kid," she muttered. She sat down on a bench, looking out at the harbor, the forest-covered mountains on Vancouver Island visible in the distance. A beautiful, peaceful scene, one of the few reasons to stay living in this city. Nature surrounding it. But instead of soaking in the natural beauty, I watched the kid bike off towards Davie Street.

"How did the Canucks do last season?"

She waved a hand at me in disgust, "Finished third in their division, then the Calgary Flames slaughtered them in the first round. Hard to believe they even made it to the finals two years ago."

"Yeah, I'd forgotten..." The first time the Canucks made it to the Stanley Cup Finals was two years prior. The last, in 2011, resulted in riots and looting downtown. But the second time was in 1994. Gina had won tickets to the sixth game of the third round, but the Canucks won their series in five, so the sixth game never happened. But we kept the tickets as souvenirs of what could have been—stored safely in my time travel box with my other ticket stubs.

Like 1984, the 1994 Canucks making it to the finals was unlikely, like every year since they joined the NHL. They might make the playoffs, but going further was rare. Default position for Vancouver fans—they'd lose, then they win; ah, that was a fluke, they'd never win the next round; repeat until they lose. But in '94, they defied the odds and made it to the finals. An intelligent guy could easily make $40,000 betting on those rounds, especially if he already knew the outcomes. I knew the results because the whole city watched and jumped onto the bandwagon with each additional win. Not the details of each series, I wasn't that big a hockey fan, but the results of each round were locked in my head. 7-5-5-7. The last four digits of my parent's home phone number—one of the few phone numbers available for immediate recall without checking the contacts in my iPhone. Three series wins, then they lost the Stanley Cup finals to the Rangers in New York City.

Holy shit. This could work. My past-self could even skip betting on round one as a test to prove my information was correct. Then he could win huge in series two, three, and four. Best of all, Neil, with his 'family' connections, could make the bets. All I needed to do was to write a note that would convince past-me to take the risk and place the bets.

Grabbing Celina's hand, I pulled her up from the bench. "Come on, let's get over to East Vancouver before my future landlord arrives home from work!"

37

Celina rolled to a stop in the alley behind the house I would live in for most of my life. Currently, the Sefanopolous' live there with their young children—the ones who would evict me in three decades. The backyard trees were noticeably thinner, the North Shore mountains visible where they weren't in the future. The backyards were far less shaded. While I finished writing my note to myself, Celina kept an eye out. For what? I wasn't sure—police, raccoons, time cops. I stuffed the message into an extra Ziplock bag I'd been carrying around in my jacket pocket since futilely hiding the cash in my hotel room toilet and zipped it shut.

"You figure you'll believe the note?" Celina asked.

I shrugged. "I'd certainly be curious. Curious enough to gamble my meager savings on what's written on a note? I don't know. I really don't. Hopefully, I will, but at the same time, am I so gullible I'll risk what little cash I've saved on a note in a bag hidden in a wall? But young-me should recognize the writing, and I've added a couple of bits of info only the two of us could know."

"Like what?"

"First girl I kissed, where I hid my Penthouse mags when I lived at home, intensely private secrets like that."

Celina laughed and climbed out of the car. I joined her in the unpaved alley. Unlike the future, most of the lane was open to the houses with only low fences and minuscule single-car garages. Walk down an alley in Vancouver now, and you'd find wall-to-wall heavy-duty garage doors hiding Ferrari's or Range Rovers. High imposing fences, motion-activated security lights and video cameras popping on and off as you walked past. Neighborhoods turned into secure enclaves befitting a third-world country.

We had driven past the house, ensuring their cars weren't parked on the street out front, before parking in the alley. Now, we slipped through the chain mesh gate after checking that no one was in any adjacent yards —ready to call the police on us. We quickly crossed the neatly mowed backyard and past their lush vegetable garden. Down three steps to the basement door, out of sight below the small back deck and entrance to the kitchen.

Celina's eyes were bright with excitement. This was positively not what she imagined her week involving. Turning to her, I took out my house keys and said, "Fingers crossed."

She crossed her fingers with a nervous grin, and I successfully unlocked the door. We hadn't bothered to change this lock when we moved in. The last time might have been after the house stopped getting regular shipments of coal for heating. In the 1930s.

The door creaked as we opened it, and we froze halfway inside. I looked up at the exposed rafters, but there wasn't any noise from upstairs. So far, so good.

After everything which had gone wrong, I was shocked this part of the plan was working so well.

As soon as we had settled on the stock purchase plan, we'd begun solving where to stash the certificates for thirty-three years safely—a place warm, dry, and secure. A location that was accessible in the past and the present once I returned. Terry had liked the idea of getting a safety deposit box at my bank, but, without paying for thirty-plus years in advance, the bank would have inevitably contacted past-me. Then a curious past-me would have found the stocks, sold them for a fraction of their future worth and probably bought a new camera. We agreed that leaving the certificates with anyone we knew to hold for thirty-three years would be a staggeringly risky idea for most of the same reasons. Anyone could sell the stocks because, like bearer bonds, they wouldn't have my name on them.

So what we needed was a safe place—a place only known to future me. Not even the others could know.

That's why we were in the basement of my future house.

The original plan was to hide the stock certificates up in the rafters and then shim in another old piece of wood to seal them in thoroughly. Then, even if someone refinished the low ceilinged, dirt-floored furnace room in an alternate ripple-filled reality, only a thin sheet of drywall would cover my hiding spot.

I found my chosen nook. It was precisely the same as in thirty-three years—I had checked before coming back in time. This reassured me. We got something right. It had been the perfect spot to hide the stocks for future me to retrieve.

But that spot wouldn't work for this new scheme. This note had to be found during a specific window of time, after Gina and I rented the house but before the Canucks 1994 Stanley Cup run. Luckily, there was a grand total of one spot in the basement, known to only me and past me.

Leaving Celina at the open door as our lookout, I pulled the cord on the bare bulb to take in the space. Where Terry's apartment existed in the future was presently an unfinished basement. It was dingy and dark, with a partial workshop and random long-term storage. To my left stood a massive old furnace and water heater. It smelled of musty dirt and old metal. Dusty vents, ducts, and water lines ran off randomly.

One day, shortly after moving in during the summer of '91, I found a loose brick in the wall. It slid out to reveal a dry, secure space. My secret hiding hole. Perfect for keeping my dope safe, and no one, not even Gina, knew about it. The ideal place to leave a note for 28-year-old me. Past-me was guaranteed to find it well before the Canucks started their second run for the Stanley Cup.

I ducked down and slipped around the back of the furnace. My hand slid over the rough bricks, searching for the telltale gap. Three in from the corner, shoulder height.

Instead, I found nothing but a wall without imperfections—a wall without a loose brick.

I checked again, my heart racing. I rubbed my hands across the rough surface. What the hell? If the brick wasn't loose now, when did it become loose? When I found it, it slid easily from the wall. It wasn't like I chiselled it out myself. But there wasn't a loose brick there now. I groped around again, pushing aside cobwebs and dirt. Nothing but an old, perfectly made brick wall.

Shit.

My brain spun around and around. It was impossible that the ripples I had created while in 1984 had affected the construction of this house. That was multiple levels of impossible. But despite there being a hiding spot in the future, there wasn't one now.

Wait, did I make the brick loose? Does future-me now create the secret hiding spot for past-me? Had my trip back directly affected my previous life? How could that make any sense? Too much of a loop, too much of a ripple to even consider.

Without the hiding spot, my new, improved plan was dead in its tracks.

I stumbled backward into the basement, knocking over a low pile of firewood. What did I do now? Was it future-me who created the loose brick? What happened if I did? What happened if I didn't? Leaving a note for my past-self was a brilliant, low-impact plan, but without that perfect hiding spot, where could I now leave it? Above us, there was the sudden sounds of kids running across the floor. The homeowners were home. A dog barked and scratched at the door leading down to the basement. Time to get out of there, unless our new plan was to get arrested for breaking and entering. Someone called out a questioning hello, which ruled out me creating the loose brick right now. I turned around to Celina in alarm.

"Oh shit, oh shit," she whispered, eyes wide in fright.

Time had screwed me again. Forgetting to turn off the basement light, I grabbed Celina's hand and pulled her outside.

"Go! Get the car started!" I whispered while turning to lock the door as quickly as possible. Celina dashed across the yard and was out of sight before I could get the door locked. Then, I took a deep breath and raced across the backyard, jumped over a short hedge, aiming for the open gate.

"You goddamn thieving sons-o-bitches!" a deep, Greek-accented voice yelled behind me. I swung myself out of sight around the corner of the garage as my future landlord thundered down the back stairs.

"Honey! Call the cops! Tell them they're in a tan Datsun 510 heading north in our alley!"

Celina revved her engine two houses down. I dashed to her car, jumped in, and we raced off in a spray of dirt, leaving behind my last plan in tatters.

38

"Take this turn!"

Celina yanked on the steering wheel, and we slid into the alley behind East Hastings, almost sideswiping a row of overflowing garbage cans. Police sirens were getting closer.

"What are we going to do?" she screamed at me.

"Keep going. Get as far away as we can."

Celina shook her head. "No, they've put out the description of my car. We've got to hide!"

"They didn't get the licence plate. We're Ok."

"No, we're not, Colin! It's my car they're looking for!"

She bounced out of the alley and across a narrow street at speed and continued west parallel to the main road.

I tried to figure out where the sirens were coming from, but they echoed off the buildings around us. Were the police ahead or coming up behind us? There was no way I could survive getting stopped by the police.

"Fine! Pull in somewhere and park!"

She stomped on the brakes and slid to a stop.

On one side of the alley were the garages and high graffitied fences of a residential street. The other was the backs of two and three-story apartments with stores underneath. There were a few parking spaces, most filled, all out in the open.

"Shit!" Celina banged on her steering wheel.

I spotted the entrance to an underground car park at the next corner. Hopefully, the building owners didn't secure it with a gate.

"There, at the end of the block!"

She accelerated, spun the car right and down a short ramp into a dark garage for the apartments above. Luckily for us, there was one open parking space way at the back, and she slid into it and turned off her car.

We sat in the semi-darkness, hearts pounding.

I leaned back and watched the entrance through the dusty Chrysler K-Car beside us.

A police cruiser rolled down the alley but didn't stop.

We waited, and watched. An old guy pushed a shopping cart full of cans and bottles past the entrance but didn't come inside.

"I think we're safe," I said, turning to face Celina.

"Jesus, what were we thinking?" Celina said as she stared at her shaking hands.

"The brick wasn't loose. How can that even be? I know it is in the future because I use it a couple of years from now. It was a perfect plan," I said more to myself than her.

She looked over at me, angry. "Which is what you constantly say, but it always turns out to be the complete opposite of 'perfect.'"

I shrugged. Celina's eyes flared in anger.

"A shrug? That's what you've got? Colin, we were nearly arrested back there! He said he was calling the police!"

She slammed her hands down on the steering wheel. "What the hell am I doing? I have a daughter. I'm running around with a fugitive from Time, trying to make his life better. But all the while, I'm risking making mine a whole lot worse! Killed at the track, burned up in the fire at your hotel, shot in the back by an angry man protecting his home, not to mention the constant danger of just driving in traffic with you! This is insane!"

"I'm sorry," I tried to say, but she was only getting started.

"Sorry?! Colin, you shouldn't have come back. You must understand that now. No matter what your grandmother did, no matter how much better she made her life, you shouldn't have come back." I watched in silence as Celina rubbed her hands against her face in exasperation. She fumbled to light a cigarette. I'd like to have one as well, but decided instead to stay silent in the passenger seat.

"Fuck," she muttered into her hands. "Fuck."

This was the moment to say something supportive to help her out, but she was right. Each minute I spent with her increased the risks to her. Every moment spent here increased the risks to me and my future. I only partially existed in this time. I was a semi-nonperson, which would be my next massive issue at a minute past midnight tonight if I didn't return to the future. Without the box, maybe I'd simply cease to exist. No past, no future, no nothing. But now wasn't the time to mention my problems.

Celina removed her hands from her face and turned to me. "Colin, of the many things I don't understand about the past two days, here's the one that's bugging me the most. What gives you personally the right to come back and mess with time? Why you?"

I gestured for her cigarettes. She passed me one with her lighter. I lit up and exhaled, blowing all my frustrations out my open window.

"Celina, I don't know why me. I don't know if I've messed up enough to impact your life. I desperately hope not. So far, you've only taken a bit of time off work. Pretty low impact, right? But listen to me, that was my last chance. The note was my free throw after the final buzzer. I've nothing left. What I'm trying to say is; I've lost. Time has won, so it shouldn't be coming after me anymore. Therefore, it won't be coming after you either."

She turned to me questioningly. "How do you know, Colin? Where in the rules for this stupid time machine experiment does it say, 'At this point, Time won't try to kill you and the people around you?'"

"I don't know."

She sighed and butted her cigarette out in the ashtray. "No. No, you don't."

She was right. I had no idea what Time would do next to me.

"I can't do this anymore, Colin. Being with you is going to get me killed. Or worse, Faye will be hurt in some way. I'd never forgive myself for that."

I didn't say anything. There was nothing to say. There were no reassurances I could make to her because I had no idea what would happen next.

"You're going to have to go. Now. I'll figure out how to get to the cafe and if the police show up, my mother will lie for me. That's what mothers do."

"But Celina..."

But she'd made up her mind. I could see it.

I got out of her car, shut the door and leaned down to the open window.

"Celina. Please..."

She leaned across the car. Maybe I had a chance to make this right.

I said, "I know that I've—"

She wasn't leaning across to listen to anything I had to say. Instead, she rolled up the window without making eye contact. I wasn't getting a chance to explain. I wasn't getting a chance to do anything but leave. I had screwed up, again.

With nothing else to say, I walked out of the garage, checked for police, and left her for good.

39

Back on East Hastings Street once more. Four lanes of traffic chugged by, filling the air with pre-catalytic converter exhaust. I was back to square one. No, I was back to worse than square one. Our plan was absolutely dead in the water. What was waiting if I went back to the future at midnight? I had no idea. Maybe Terry's worse fear had come true and I would return to a desolate post-apocalyptic wasteland. If I did, it would serve me right for messing with Time the way I had.

I realized now that Time was never something to fool around with. We had taken it lightly, self-centeredly focused on improving our lives, but it was more than that. I had never considered the impact of time in my life, especially when I was young. Floating along in the river that was my life, assuming I'd end up where I was meant to be. But I was wrong. I didn't have to simply float along, inert in the stream. I could paddle to adjust where I was in the current, to see different things on the shore, and find new and exciting experiences along the way. Looking back now, I could see that I didn't do that, not nearly enough.

Across the street, a couple of elderly Chinese ladies pushed their grocery carts home. I reached for my camera to take the shot, but I didn't have my bag hanging on my shoulder.

Goddamnit.

It was in the back seat of Celina's car.

I have never forgotten my camera bag more times than I had on this trip. Previously, it had been an appendage permanently attached to my shoulder. Losing it would have been like losing a limb. But here in the past, I'd left it behind twice in a day. Maybe it wouldn't matter, maybe I wasn't going back. But if I did, I couldn't leave it behind. My camera would cause all sorts of trouble if the wrong person got their hands on it.

Shit. I needed to get it back, fast.

The Ovaltine was right where I left it, intact, not on fire or reduced to rubble by some cosmic force. I thought about just walking in the front door but I didn't want to make a scene, so looped the block and entered the alley to find Celina's car.

I hadn't been in the alley since passing out after seeing my past-self. Unsurprisingly, it hadn't changed, still stinking of garbage rotting in the summer heat, the pavement stained with decades of grime, the walls coated with decades of graffiti. A couple of men lingered by the bins outside the Ovaltine. I moved over to the far side of the alley to get a better view of them. They were intent on something out of sight behind a blue BFI garbage bin. Then I saw Celina's Datsun 510, just visible in front of them. Shit, they were trying to break into her car.

"Hey!" I called out.

One turned to eye me. No fear, no hesitation. He had lanky, dirty, long hair, and wore a filthy jean jacket despite the heat. The other, with a ratty white guy afro and a formerly white corduroy shirt with the sleeves torn off, continued to do whatever he was doing behind the bin, out of my view.

"Fuck off, chink," Jean Jacket said.

"No. You fuck off away from that car." I was never good at insults. Must have been my Canadian upbringing. From the edge of the alley, I grabbed a broken-off slat from a pallet and waved it as threateningly as I could.

Corduroy gave me the finger and went back to wrenching the driver's window open.

I yelled, "Get away from that car. Now!"

"Or what?" Jean Jacket said.

Or what? I'd never been in a fight in my life, despite growing up in a moderately tough part of the city. No getting called out after school to fight in some backyard, no rumbles against rival high schools. I'd never thrown a punch in anger, ever. But I couldn't walk away and let them get my camera.

The time for words was over. Every action film I'd seen flashed through my head. Bond, Bourne, John Wick. I was none of them. But I was furious and scared. And I had three feet of broken wood.

I charged, readying the slat like I was about to hit a home run. Jean Jacket stepped back, startled. Before he could raise an arm, I swung the slat as hard as I could and clocked him on the side of his head. He stumbled but didn't go down.

"The fuck?" Corduroy yelled, jumping forward and pushing me hard, the slat well into its backswing and temporarily useless. Off-balance, I stumbled backwards and tripped over an abandoned mattress. He was on me immediately, raining fists down on my head. I curled up on my side, in an attempt to protect myself. Besides never throwing a punch, I'd never been punched. He was strong, and he'd hit people before. It was agonizing, but I had to do something or he would knock me unconscious.

So, instead of protecting myself, I rolled onto my back and kicked out as hard as I could. Corduroy wasn't prepared for that. One foot caught him in the stomach. He curled forward, in shock, the wind knocked out of him. Elbow, I thought through my pain. My hands were still over my face but I swivelled left, my right elbow sything into his descending nose. It burst open, and he toppled to the ground with a groan and a spray of blood.

I rolled away before he bled on me and scrambled to my feet, still running on adrenaline. Jean Jacket grabbed Corduroy and dragged him away down the alley.

"And don't come back!" I yelled after them. I hurt and would hurt a lot more soon, but I had won.

"Colin?"

I swung around to see Celina standing outside the Ovaltine's back door.

"Jesus, Colin. Where did you learn to fight like that?"

"Movies," I said, wincing.

"Movies?"

I nodded. A smile began to form on my face against my will. My first fight. Two on one. And I had won.

"Yeah. Take that James Bond."

As she came out into the alley, I started to laugh. Then I began to shake as I came down from the surge of chemicals that had filled my system. She stared at me.

"You came back."

I nodded, "I think they were here because my camera bag is in the back of your car. If you had come out before I got here—"

She rushed across the alley and pulled me close, hugging me. Then she let go, punched me in the chest, and stepped back, her face filling with anger.

"If you weren't here, that wouldn't have happened."

"If I wasn't here, it would have been worse."

Celina eyed the alley where the two ran off. "So what now? I'm damned if I'm with you, and I'm damned if I'm not?"

"I think we are entwined and will be until I go back at midnight."

"Shit," Celina said. "And what if you don't go back?"

There was a night, a week ago—or thirty three years from now—when, to our surprise, Terry agreed with Neil's latest film research. So we had settled in on our couch with multiple bottles of red and bags of Miss Vickie's potato chips for a double feature of time travel movies.

The Terminator and Terminator 2.

I tried to get Terry to explain why, of all the films Neil had brought up as 'research', we had to watch this one, but he just said, seriously, "Just watch the films. We'll talk afterwards."

So we watched. Emboldened by Terry's interest, Neil took more notes during the two films than he had in all of Grade 11. The first Terminator would come out a few months after I returned from 1984 and it was a fun night of James Cameron's cinematic brilliance. Except that Terry barely drank and didn't even laugh at Arnold's many famous catch phrases.

"So what was the point of us all watching those films?" I asked him. We were out on our front porch, Neil had gone home to tack his notes to his living room wall and link them with coloured yarn like a textbook conspiracy nut. Gina was getting ready for bed since she still had to work in the morning.

Terry had lit a cigarette and was considering the glowing tip. Finally he said, "What caused everything in the second film?"

"What is Skynet going live for two hundred, Alex."

He didn't laugh.

"No. It was because the government found the first Terminators hand and broken chip that Sarah thought they'd destroyed. And that's why Arnold had to be lowered into the molten steel at the end of T2. That's why we watched the films. You have to understand that if 'this' goes wrong and you're trapped in the past, you must destroy everything you took back. Including yourself. It's the only way to not have everything you know and love destroyed."

Then he gave me a hug and left me alone on the porch with that happy thought. Which I then forgot because I was tired and drunk.

"So what do we do now?"

I sighed and winced. I was going to have some impressive bruises tomorrow. "We stick together. That's all we can do. In less than six hours, either I disappear into the future or I stay here and disappear on my own. Either way, I think you'll be finally safe."

"Do you really believe that?"

Did I believe that? I didn't know. I really didn't.

40

Friday 7 pm - 5 hours to go

"I'm sorry I freaked out, Colin."

We were seated at the back of the Old Spaghetti Factory in Gastown. The exposed brick walls were covered with old-fashioned framed photographs of old Vancouver. Families on their big night out contributed to the din. Between us and the front was an old railcar, repurposed for a special dining experience. That was where I had hoped to sit when we came here for a birthday celebration in my youth. I was still waiting to sit in that car. Our table was full of enormous plates of spaghetti, side salads, garlic bread, and our nearly empty second bottle of Chianti.

Torn between being unsafe on her own and being unsafe with me, Celina had agreed to accompany me through to the end of my time in 1984. We'd kill the hours with some food and wine until climbing to the roof of A&B Sound at midnight.

I shook my head. "No. You were right to freak out. You don't need to apologize, especially not to me. I should do the apologies here. I fucked up your life by involving you in my mess."

"But was my being involved destined to happen? I helped you out with the plan in the future. I'm part of this, whether or not I like it."

"You're part of this because I was stupid and came to the Ovaltine!"

She patted my hand on the table, her strong fingers holding mine down. "Please, let me continue, all right? You're the one who's come back in time—Time!—to fix your future. But nothing's worked. You've got a right to keep trying, and here I am worrying about myself. I should help you."

I held up my hands to stop her. "Celina, I appreciate what you're saying, and you have helped me, but I don't want you to be hurt. I couldn't live with myself if you were, especially for something I selfishly want for my future. I didn't come back to mess with your life. That's not who I am. So, to ensure absolutely nothing else goes wrong, I'm done. We'll hang out until I go back to my staggeringly uncertain future, whatever it may hold. I'll be fine, and I'll survive."

"Ok. Safety first for us, no getting killed," Celina said, putting down her wine glass. "Agreed. Let's call that the default option right now."

"What do you mean, 'default option'? There are no other options."

"Of course there are. There's always something else we can try. Look at your grandmother. She snuck across Communist China to find and save her parents! How hard can it be to slip a note to past-Colin?"

"But I don't know where to hide it!"

"You could leave it with me. I'll give it to him in nine years," Celina suggested. But I shook my head, adamant. "No way. Forget it. Leaving a note with you would be the kind of taunt where you get hurt or even killed. So far as I know, Time hasn't touched you. The muggings and the fire were aimed directly at me because I had the cash that was supposed to become our windfall. My camera bag was a problem for you only if I left it behind in your car. If you had a note in your possession with future events written down, then I'm sure—absolutely positive—you'll be in danger. Exactly like I was at the track."

"I'm always in danger, Colin. We all are. Every day, every time we cross the street. Every time we decide to do one thing rather than another. That's life."

"You're taking this all rather well."

"What choice do I have? Cower under the covers in my apartment and never go out?"

She was right. In my own way, I had cowered in my life. I hadn't taken opportunities that were offered or gone after possibilities I desired. I had chosen the safe road and look where it had gotten me.

I gazed across the table. We'd been through so much in a couple of days. My emotions towards her were becoming more and more complicated. Our kiss wrapped all those complications up in a bundle of passionate confusion.

"Did you ever wonder if there were other time machines out there?" she asked.

"No. I don't think we had."

But logic holds if there was a onetime travel machine—there were others. So where were they? Did we know about them? Did they appear in our dreams, our media, our subconscious? And if they did, was that a big deal or not? Was time always fluid and changing around us? Was it only our tiny minds that needed to put walls and rules around time? It wasn't like raccoons or gazelles pondered their place in a forward-moving timescale.

"Maybe our lives are lived within the ripples of other thirty-three-year trips to the past and we have no idea."

"What would you do? If you had the time machine instead of me?"

She pondered as she ate some garlic bread. "I'd only use it as your grandmother did. To save my family. To make their life better than some terrible alternative. I would happily sacrifice my future to know that Faye was going to be safe."

"And I used it to try get a house."

She didn't comment. It was a weak reason to mess with Time. Indefensible, really.

I continued, "And that was the wrong thing to do. Yet here I am. With less than five hours left in the past. And all I've got to show for it is a note in my pocket that could help young-me get a house with a twenty-five-year mortgage. The Vancouver dream."

"But that's better than nothing, isn't it? It's better than what's waiting for all of you."

Our waiter arrived to clear our plates and drop off two bowls of Spumoni ice cream.

"Couldn't you simply give the note to young-Colin?" she asked after he had gone.

"Sure, but I don't know where past-me is. And with only hours left, there's no way to track him down. I'd have to remember this night out of all the nights between now and 2017. And I had enough trouble remembering hockey games from '94, what makes you believe I'll remember—"

I stopped speaking. Celina looked at me, confused. I leaned back in my chair, mouth hanging open like an idiot. Son of a bitch, I knew precisely where I'd be tonight.

41

Friday 9 pm - 3 hours to go

From our seats at the back of The Railway Club, we awaited my past-selves arrival. I still wasn't sure what I'd do when he did arrive. The note burned a hole in my pocket. Of course, my past-self was coming to The Rail tonight, asked by the band to document Damage Done in their second debut show. He'd missed last nights show because he was at the PNE with Gina, Terry, and Neil for Lionel Richie and Tina Turner. But short of knocking young-me out, even my messing with Time wouldn't have made my past-self miss this show tonight.

"You know, you've avoided talking specifics regarding the future," Celina said, sipping her beer.

"I've let enough slip to make you rich," I replied, glancing down the filling room towards the stage, barely visible through the crowd.

"Probably. But I don't know if I'll do anything with those hints you've dropped."

"I hope you don't. But that's up to you."

Celina nodded. What was she thinking? Yeah, I'd certainly spiced up her week, throwing an ice bucket of doubt over her concepts of time and space. But what would Celina do if I actually went back to my future? Would she talk to past-me while he was having lunch at the Ovaltine next week? Would she become fed up with slaving at the restaurant and use my passing comments to make herself wealthy? I certainly wouldn't blame her if she did. But if she did, would her choices affect my future? I didn't see how they could. But then again, I didn't expect Time messing with me to the extent it has, so maybe her new choices would. Suppose Celina sold the Ovaltine Diner to buy rental properties.

Hell, if Celina sold the Ovaltine, she wouldn't have been able to help us create the plan I was supposed to follow. Which would guarantee I wouldn't be in this place with her now.

"Will I remember you being here? The next time I see you?" she asked.

I nodded. "I don't see why not. I'll come in for lunch. We can have a good old chat and a laugh or two."

"Except I'll be, God, eighty years old!"

"But cute. And feisty."

"Oh, terrific, that's such a relief. With a walker and a hearing aid the size of a brick. Sitting in my mother's place in the restaurant."

I didn't mention her joke being factually accurate—except for the walker.

"You want another beer?"

She downed the remains in her glass and slid it across the table. "A fancy dinner and these fine drinks. You're spending money like there's no tomorrow."

My smile froze. Given the destruction of the time machine, it was likely I wouldn't have any more tomorrows, joke or no joke.

I headed up to get us another round. But instead of getting in the lineup, I pushed my way down the bar to the front to check out the crowd. The club was full and excited. The word on Damage Done had exploded after last night's earth-shattering performance.

I might have the note in my pocket, and a faint semblance of a plan, but I had to be sure I wouldn't pass out if I was in the same space as young-me. If I felt anything at all, I would leave immediately, abandoning Celina at the back of the club. I had Neil's work key and could get myself up to the roof to wait, alone.

Through the smoke, young-me and my friends had settled around the table where Celina and I sat last night. Terry slightly out of place, as always. Neil chatted up the girls at the next table, much to their boyfriends' dismay. Gina, so young and so utterly magnetic. Laughing as past-me made an inside joke, probably about Neil being a slut. Her smile and laugh pierced me—we were so young, so idealistic, such bright, young things. So utterly unaware of what this city had in store for us. What life had in store for us. Seeing her, so close yet so unfathomably far, shattered me again.

I left her to come back in time, left her maybe/possibly/likely spending the rest of her life to wonder what had happened to me. I had it so good, and I tried to make it great. Why didn't I stick with good? Why did I throw all that away on this ridiculous 'adventure' in the past? I missed her terribly, my grown-up Gina. My partner for almost thirty years, the love of my life, no matter if she kissed Neil or not. I'd loved her since we first met, sappy as it sounds. She was bold to my wary; explosion to my simmer.

And if I didn't return to the future, I'd never be with her again. Young-me would hopefully follow fate and end up with Gina as destined. But fifty-five-year-old me, stuck growing inexorably older from 1984 forward, wouldn't experience her ever again. I'd have my millions of memories, but never again a new one. A simple guy trapped out of time, vividly remembering what hadn't happened yet.

Being fifteen feet away from my past-self hadn't caused the world to implode or explode. But I backed off and returned along the bar, past the leather-jacketed guys and the leather-skirted girls. I queued up to grab two more pints of Molson Canadian and watched the crowd for people I know. None of which I could hang out with again if I got stuck in the past. If I didn't do what Terry insisted I do and kill myself, I would have to create an entirely new life. New job, new home, new everything. Who wanted to make a whole new group of friends in your fifties? I'd have to pretend to be from somewhere else, new to town. I'd have to start again, from nothing.

And in the far corner sat this amazing woman I'd spent so much emotional time with during the past two and a half days. Had it only been seventy-some-odd hours? More like I'd been racing non stop for weeks without a moment to breathe.

If I stayed behind, never going forward, was there a possibility of a future with Celina? A step-child, a house—since I knew precisely when to buy into the market—and a life. A second life.

She smiled as I sat down and handed her a beer. What happened to Gina in the future if I didn't return? Stuck wondering until she died where I went? Would she remember me being in her life for those many years before an adventure with a time machine? Or would those memories even exist in the future? If I didn't go back, would I cease to exist? Even as a memory? Worse, would my friends and family spend the rest of their days torturing themselves? Forever wondering where I was, or if I was even alive?

"Are you here?" Celina asked.

"Sorry, a pile of convoluted thoughts got me all distracted. I'm here now."

She laughed. "I meant past-Colin."

"Yeah, they're up front. Where we sat last night."

"And the world didn't end because you're in the same room. That's a good sign, I guess."

I nodded, still deep in thought.

"Colin, why didn't you do more with your photography? If you were as good as you say? And don't say 'life got complex', or something trite like that."

"You ever look back at your life and wonder about what it would be if you'd done one thing differently? If you'd made one different choice? Walk down the less path instead of the more travelled one?"

She stared at me. "Why? I chose what I chose. I couldn't go back to try the other one, so why dwell on it?"

"Yeah, I think I used to think that way, but this trip back has really fucked me up. I'm seeing the choices I didn't make right in front of me through much older eyes. And they are so obvious with that hindsight. Blindingly obvious."

The weight of my past decisions laid like a concrete block on my shoulders.

"So tell me about them."

I didn't want to relive my mistakes. I wanted to forget them, but everywhere I went these past three days brought them to the forefront. It was hard enough to ignore them when I had a thirty-three-year buffer, but being in the room where I made decisions that turned out to be wrong was brutal. I sighed. "Riding on the success of these two shows, Damage Done will go out on a budget tour of Canada in a minivan. Starting next month. They'll do three dozen shows from Halifax across to Vancouver in six weeks. Back home before it snows on the Prairies. After I show the band the photos I will take tonight, Kelly will ask me to come with them. To create the official chronicle of the tour."

"That must be amazing."

"Yes, it would be. Except I didn't go."

She stopped mid-sip, confused. "You didn't go. Why on earth not?"

"You gotta understand something. A professional photographer wasn't a career unless you wanted to work at a Sears portrait studio. It wasn't an option I could have talked to my school guidance counsellor about. They would have told me to take pictures as a hobby, but to use my good marks to get a university degree. Become a lawyer or an accountant or one of a hundred other proper jobs. So I did. I did what I was supposed to do."

I pointed to the front of the club, to where past-me sat with his friends.

"I had—have—one year left of my degree. To drop out for six weeks to go on tour with a band would mean missing the entire semester."

"So?"

I didn't want to talk about what I had felt way back then. But she deserved an honest answer after everything we'd been through. But I hated thinking about who I was back then.

"It's so embarrassingly simple, Celina. Tragically, stupidly simple. I was afraid."

"Afraid of what?"

I still didn't want to say. To put the words out into the air. But Celina wouldn't stop looking at me. She wouldn't accept any bullshit answer, not after what we had been through together.

"Losing Gina."

"But you weren't going out yet, right? How could you lose what you didn't have?"

"I was afraid that I'd lose my chance with Gina if I left. If I didn't stay in school with her and then went to work with her, she'd move on and end up with someone else. I needed to be close to Gina so that when my chance with her appeared, I would be ready. Worse, going on tour with a band went against everything my parents had taught me—grow up, go to school, get a degree, get a steady job and then a wife, house and give them grandkids. Retire with a pension. I had gotten my own place and suddenly had to deal with money and the stress of that was a lot. That's why I stuck to the safe job and the schooling instead of following my passion."

I looked at her. "I was scared. I was a kid and the real world really overwhelmed me. I felt safe in school."

"The world overwhelms everyone when they're young. Or not so young. Do you think this life was what I wanted when my husband died, leaving me with our child? That I want my only legacy to be the Ovaltine?"

"No, of course not. But you should be proud of how you're raising your daughter, and looking after your mother."

"Thank you, but what I'm trying to say is life isn't about base survival. It hasn't been for millennia. You're a smart guy, and you're a smart kid." She gestured towards the front of the room. "You don't need to choose survival. Life has to mean something more. I have my daughter."

"Is that enough?"

"Absolutely. But that doesn't mean I shouldn't look for more meaning. What do you have? What does your life mean? Young-you is about to be given the opportunity to soar. It's just that your interpretation of survival is tuned higher than it needs to be.

"And if Gina is the one for you, which she obviously is, then not being in the same class, or the same job, will not make one bit of a difference."

I began to answer, but that glorious opening muted B chord of 'Getting Lost' rippled through the room, and conversation stops. Again.

"Some emotion, happened here

I feel it burn me, when I hold it near

I'm Getting Lost, getting lost, getting lost."

42

Even from the back of the room, with the band not visible, what occurred was a mesmerizing performance. Tables had grown quiet around us as song after song riveted everyone to their seats. The narrow aisle along the bar was full of patrons jockeying for a view of the band on the low front stage. Celina and I sat back, enjoying the sound of my favorite band; she experiencing songs for the second time I'd heard a thousand times over.

I thought about my life and what Celina had said. Safety was a funny thing that was different for everyone. I had grown up in a stable family, in a stable city in the most stable country in the world. And yet here I was, still desperate for stability. Was it left over in my DNA from my grandmother's traumatic first life in Communist China? I had been scared. But I would bet all my friends were scared, if I could have gotten them to admit it. Differing levels, but the same need for security. Neil with his absolutely fucked up home life, Terry with his familial rejection of his sexuality, Gina with generations of Italian conformity. And we all survived. But would any of us say we were following our bliss and thriving?

The first set finished to rapturous applause, and the band disappeared on their break. The audience moved en masse to line up for more drinks, their excited talk filling the air. So many young, cheerful people with their friends. And then there was me. Fifty-five years old, unemployed, homeless. So old and out of place amongst so much youth.

Celina tapped me on the shoulder as past-me pushed his way through the crowd and into the toilet, camera case over his shoulder. I stood up from the table, the nerves in my stomach spasming. I not only had butterflies, they were butterflies with poisonous fire ant stingers. A quick pat of my pocket confirmed the note was there, sealed in its Ziplock bag.

"Good luck. For both of you," Celina said, squeezing my hand. I squeezed back then pushed my way past the table towards the men's room.

Opening the narrow toilet door, my past-self was in front of me in the line for the urinals. The toilet was tiny, two small stalls and three urinals and young, exuberant, drunk guys pissing in all of them. There were none of the sensations from when I first saw myself on Wednesday at the Ovaltine. No nausea, no headache. My past-self wasn't sensing anything odd either. I didn't know how I knew that, but I did. Wiseass graffiti and band stickers covered the walls. The looping towel was torn and hung down, piled on the floor. The staggering excellence of the band was the only conversation. Finally, my turn came, but I couldn't urinate, so I faked it for a bit, then zipped up and retreated to standing at the door. One other guy exited, leaving only me and past-me alone in the room. I knew fate was on my side as the Railway toilet was never this empty during a band's break.

I put my foot against the door, holding it shut while reaching into my pocket for the note.

Past-me finished up at the urinal.

Just take out the note and give it to him. Then our future would be secure. A straightforward move; hand over the note and leave. But I didn't. Past-me washed his hands as someone outside banged on the door. This was my moment. There would never be another one. I only had two hours before I returned to 2017 or started my life again in 1984. Or I ceased to exist.

Give him the note. Affect the future precisely how you want. Hand over the bag and the enclosed piece of paper. But I couldn't. I couldn't alter my past life any more than I should be affecting Celina's.

I started to take my foot away from the door. He turned, seeing me for the first time.

"I've seen you before," past-me said, attempting to dry his hands on the cloth roll hanging on the wall.

"Yeah, I've seen you too. Around town, taking photos at gigs. Seen your photos, too. They're quality." What I was saying or where I was going, I hadn't a clue, but those words, these sentences, felt right.

"… Uh, thanks."

"You weren't here last night. It was an amazing performance," I said, to keep talking.

"Na," he said, embarrassed. "Was at another show."

"You take any photos there?" I knew the answer was no. I remembered.

He shook his head.

"Why not? You're an excellent photographer, Colin. You have a real touch. So even if you're at a shit show or watching an act that you figure is dumb, take photos and sell them! Where do the Georgia Straight, The Sun or The Province get their pics for concert reviews? From guys like you. And you're a damn sight better than anyone else out there. If you seriously want to be a photographer, then be serious! If not, toss your camera in a box with your old hockey cards, get a safe 9-to-5 social work job and burn with regret for the rest of your life."

The pounding on the toilet door was insistent, but I wasn't finished. Everything I wished someone had said to me at twenty-two came to me unbidden.

"And not only photography. Learn how to shoot film! Your eye for motion in a still photo can certainly translate to film. Check out the Vancouver Film School when it opens in a few years, but be ready when it does."

"Damn, what's with the toilet advice, man?"

I took a breath. Stop the hard sell. Future-me hated that. I had to back off.

"Sorry. What I'm trying to say is this. You can do so much more with your talents than a social worker degree and a job you'll hate. You can't wait for the world to come to you. You can't wait for your dream job or your dream girl. You've got to step up, step out, and risk embarrassment or rejection to get what you really want. The desire for safety is an illusion and will fail you every time. That's all." I raised my hands in apology and took my foot away from the door. It bounced open, and six frantic guys piled in, all unzipping as they entered. Holding the door open, I let my past-self leave first. He did, running his hands through his long hair as he passed me.

"Who are you?" he paused and asked.

Who was I? A good question, I thought. I'm you. Yet, despite our identical DNA, I'm also not you. I'm the only one who knows what you want, deep down in your soul. The only one who knows the mistakes you've made and how they've affected you. I want what you want, and I'm afraid of everything you're afraid of. I'm as scared for you as I'm scared for me. And I'm really, really scared right now.

But none of that I said out loud. Instead, I shrugged and said, "I'm a nobody, Colin. But you can be a somebody."

Here comes a wiseass comment, something to change the energy between us. I knew so because that was precisely what I would say in my shoes. But young-me didn't. Instead, he shook his head like there were bees in his ears and stepped out into the bar lineup.

"And say yes to the band," I called to him as he disappeared into the crowd. Did he hear me? I didn't know. I hoped so. I tore the note to shreds, dropping the pieces into the garbage.

As I left the toilet to the sounds of the audience eagerly welcoming Damage Done to the stage for their second set, I wondered if I had made the right choice. Was there more I could have done? More I could have said? We all secretly wanted advice when growing up, but hearing that advice and taking it to heart was a different matter. Maybe I made a difference in the toilet. Maybe I didn't. And I didn't know how I would find out if I did or not.

43

No Stranger To Danger - Damage Done
Eponymous debut album 1986 A&M Records

Everybody wants a little action
People breaking into separate factions
But it's temporary satisfaction

Where will you be when the market crashes
And the modern world is turned to ashes
In a boardroom making love to fascists

If you're living in the first world
You're no stranger to danger
If you remember the cold war
You're no stranger to the danger
of living in the first world

People starving want to trade us places
They're only looking at our well-fed faces

```
Tired of looking at our tied boot laces

But we have weapons to defend our greed
Anything we want we say we need
Expect no mercy when the slaves are freed

If you're living in the first world
You're no stranger to danger
If you remember the cold war
You're no stranger to the danger
of living in the first world
```

"How'd it go?" Celina asked as I sat back down beside her.

What should I say? I'd torn up my note, and with it, our chances of owning a house in the future? I gave my past-self well intentioned career advice? The most important part was that neither of us exploded, imploded, or disintegrated when we were in the toilet together. For whatever reason, Time left us alone. Despite being on the planet for over fifty years, I had been through more personal danger in the past three days than ever before. I wasn't a stranger to danger anymore. I had faced a litany of threats and come out the other side alive and kicking. No matter what awaited me in the future, I knew something had changed in me. I was less afraid, yet at the same time, possibly more afraid. But in a good way. Maybe that was what it meant to be alive.

It was all a bit too much, so I drank some foul-tasting carbonated water claiming to be beer.

Celina repeated her question.

I thought about it, then said, "It went well."

"Will he believe the note?"

Despite not knowing what would happen in the coming years, I felt Ok. Not excellent, not terrible. Ok. A calm in my chest where there was no reason for one to be. Weird.

"You know that game we play, 'Would you go back in time to—?"

Celina laughed, "Of course I do. Neil once considered going back in time to change his lunch order."

I nodded and smiled, feeling calmer than I had felt in days. "All that thinking about what we would change if we could go back."

"No one can change the past. We can't. I'm guessing I've made decisions this week that will ripple out into my—our—future. But, Colin, you've made changes only you will realize when you get back. I truly hope it all works out the way you want it to."

I sighed and said, "You'll be the first to know. I hope."

We drank our beers and revelled in the performance until the band finished their final song. Then the time to leave was upon us. Patrons had to leave the club, and I had to leave 1984.

Arm in arm like two lifelong friends, Celina and I made our way down the steep stairs and out onto Dunsmuir Street. When we stepped out onto the sidewalk, the first thing I saw was past-Gina, sitting on the hood of a big old car. Past-me sat beside her, silently in love. Neil and Terry bickered like a long-married couple in front of the vehicle.

So young, so alive, so full of hope for the future.

I nodded to my past-self, and he nodded back. Celina stopped outside the Shaver Shop and we lit cigarettes, keeping our distance from the clusters of buoyantly young people. There was my youthful self in his element, with his best friends. I was momentarily an insider and an outsider to the same pivotal event of my life. It was like looking into a living time travel mirror at myself for the last time.

"It feels like the kind of night where everything changed for them, you know?" young-Colin said. "They can't go back to what they were, even if they wanted."

"Well duh. Time travel isn't real," Terry said.

"I meant their sound. It's going to make them famous. You watch."

Gina said, "Maybe you'll become famous because of those photos you took, Colin!"

"Or maybe he forgot to put film in the camera."

"Screw you very much, Neil," young-Colin said. "You wait and see, I got a ton of epic shots tonight."

Gina grinned at young-Colin. "Hey, you're cute when you're confident."

I watched as past-Colin winked at her instead of sputtering and almost inhaling his cigarette. Ripples.

I had done what I could in the past. Now it was like looking out the window as your plane took off at the end of your vacation. Whatever else you wanted to do won't happen because you're on your way back to where you started.

Like me.

Time to see if Time would allow me to go home.

A few yards up from the Railway Club entrance, Celina and I entered the alley running behind Seymour Street. We strolled halfway down the urine and warm garbage smelling block to the back loading dock for A&B Sound. According to future Neil, his old key would open the fire escape door. Then, as long as we didn't go onto any of the store's floors, we could get to the roof without setting off any alarms. Of course, this was Neil talking, so we took what he said—the last part of my failed and abandoned plan—with the largest grain of salt possible. A glance back up the alley confirmed no one was watching us before I even tried the key in the lock.

Neil's old key turned, unlocking the door. Then we were inside. So far, so good. I had said that a lot in the past three days, despite events continually turning out the opposite to how they were supposed to. Quietly, we climbed the stairs, past the posters for long-forgotten bands and albums, for store-sponsored concerts, until the door to the roof loomed in the darkness before us.

I gave the crash handle a push, and it swung open silently. Huh, who'd have thought the final part of our plan would be so easy. Maybe only once you gave up on forcing your dreams would Time leave you alone. Grabbing a cinder block right outside the door, I propped it open so Celina could get back out. It wouldn't do to leave her trapped on the roof for the night. That would be a pretty shitty going away present.

"So, how does this work?" she asked as we walked to the middle of the gravel-covered roof.

Looking around, I found the spot where I came back, a place no different from any other place on the roof, and stood on it. I adjusted my camera bag on my shoulder. Pointing down, I said, "I came back right here. So, according to the rules, this is where I return from."

A cool breeze had come up, and Celina shivered. Or maybe what might happen in mere moments made her go suddenly cold.

"I guess I should thank you," she said quietly.

"For what? We could've died several times in the past few days."

"But we didn't, Colin. You altered what you came back to do so I wouldn't be hurt. That takes real courage to let go of your plans and consider someone else. Me."

There wasn't much to say except the truth.

"I couldn't let you be harmed, not in any way."

She stepped forward and hugged me. I hugged her back. My new best friend. A possible, potential, in-another-life someone much more… that was who I embraced. We hugged until she looked at her wristwatch and sighed. "Any time now."

I nodded and let her go. She stepped back to stand by herself. Pretty, confident, caring.

"I'm going to miss you, Celina."

"I'll miss you, too. Except I'll probably see you, young-you, tomorrow."

I smiled. "Then old-me will come and see you tomorrow too."

She smiled at me. "I'm glad you came to the cafe, even if it ruined your plan."

"I'm glad I did too. You serve a great BLT."

She looked at her watch. "Midnight." She took another step back. "Is there an explosion, a spectral storm or something?"

Shaking my head, I said, "When I came back, there was a 'blip.'"

"Not particularly impressive."

"No, not really."

One minute after midnight.

We stood on the roof in silence.

At midnight, I should have gone forward. Maybe Celina's watch was off. Maybe a space-time wormhole was closed when the machine burnt up, meaning I was not going anywhere. Maybe…

"Forgive Gina, Colin. Forgive a single kiss. You've known for forty years she's the only one for you. So does she, or she wouldn't have waited for you to get the guts to ask her out."

She was talking about more than my story about Gina and Neil. She was talking about us last night. Our kiss. Maybe that was the story she needed to tell herself to make it right. And, I guess, I agreed with her.

Two minutes after midnight.

"You might be seeing two Colins for breakfast tomorrow," I said with a weak smile. I watched her smile at me, her face full of caring and hope.

Because I was on the roof in 1984 with her. I wasn't going home. I was spending the rest of my life here with—

44

Blip

45

Celina vanished in front of me. Not faded out gently like Marty McFly's family photograph. Not exploded into a million points of light. Not shrunk down to a single atom. She simply, completely and utterly vanished. Literally there and then not there.

I was alone on the roof. It worked, I had returned. In an instant, my pent-up fears of being stuck in 1984 dissipated like a vape exhale in a winter wind storm. I loved that year, but I had lived so much more of life to want to start again back then. Sure, by staying in the past, I would have been wealthy. Either from being lazy and gambling on what sporting events I remembered or through investing in the stock market. Or my personal favorite, gaining recognition and renown as an astounding editorial writer. Imagine a long string of successful prognostications regarding world events until I quietly retired in 2017, when I would have to start wondering what the future would bring along with everyone else. Then, just as quickly, my relief was overwhelmed with the sadness of leaving Celina behind.

Along the skyline were the towering metal and glass buildings of present-day Vancouver. The North Shore mountains and the lights on the ski hills were barely visible between them. Wandering over to the edge of the roof, I looked down at the quiet street. A Smart car rolled silently past. I was back.

September 30, 2017 00:03:03

I climbed down the rickety outside fire escape, dropping the last ways onto the top of a huge garbage bin and then jumped to the filthy alley.

I walked out of the alley and past The Railway Club entrance to the corner. A digital clock in the 7-11 informed me my entire trip to the past took only a minute. If so, then why wasn't everyone waiting on the roof for me to return? Maybe a cosmic reset occurred, a pause in Time that I… time to stop worrying what might have happened. I was done, finished, spent.

I was in Vancouver. Present day because no one was smoking and everyone was engrossed in their smart phones. Not some dreamlike mythical Vancouver, a magical Disneyland of my youth, a fabled city of light and music. Nope, this was my city, good and bad, sickness and health, and like it or not, it was the only place I wanted to live on the planet. That might have been the only thing I had learned on my trip back in time and I was going to do everything in my power to ensure me and my friends continued to live, and thrive, here.

A passing cab stopped when I stepped out onto Richards Street in front of it. Time to go home. Well, hopefully home. Who knew anymore? Certainly not me. The driver was wary of my old cash, but accepted it.

I waited on the step until he drove off. The last thing I needed was my weary East Indian cabbie watching me fail to open my front door because someone changed the locks at some point in the past three decades. Seriously, what was going through my head? Why hadn't we ever discussed what would happen when I got back from my time travel? The unspoken assumption was I would make my trip, execute our plan and return without having changed a single thing in the past, therefore not changing a single iota of the present. To essentially slip in and out of the metaphorical waters of 1984 without causing a single ripple. What exactly were the odds of me accomplishing that? A million to one, a billion to one? Probably worse. Try throwing a pebble into a calm lake without causing a ripple. Good luck. My trip was more like dropping a bowling ball from the top of the CN Tower, ripples galore.

With those thoughts weighing heavily, I removed my keys. My room key from The El-Cid, probably the only one left in existence, remained in my pocket. I'd put it in the box with my concert ticket stubs. Except that magical Chinese black box had been burned to a crisp for thirty-three years.

With no small amount of trepidation, I slipped my key into the lock and slowly gave it a turn. To my surprise, the deadbolt unlocked with a slight scrape and a click, as it always had. So far, so good, although whoever now owned the house might not have bothered to change the locks. A Terry level of pessimism held me back from hope. Easing the door open, no dog confronted me. The hall was dark but familiar. Of course, even if present-me hadn't lived in this house for thirty years, it would still be home for present-past-present me.

I kicked off my shoes and hung up my jacket, a row of hooks right where they always were. I picked up my camera bag. No matter what occurred in this house, I wasn't letting it out of my sight. Once I knew I was safe—whatever safe meant when you've been gallivanting around tossing massive stones into the waters of time for three days—I'd put it down. Padding down the hallway in sock feet, I glanced into the living room, which looked the same, especially in the dark. The kitchen, ditto. Finally, the closed door to our bedroom. The final test, what was behind door number one? Was it my loving partner or an angry couple with baseball bats? I considered sleeping on the couch for a moment, but why delay whatever was behind the bedroom door by a few hours?

I gave the door a gentle push. It creaked where it always had, eight inches into its opening swing. I stepped through, shutting it quietly behind me. Standing in the darkness at the foot of the bed, I did my best to calm my heart down. Someone was sleeping, achingly familiar inhalations and exhalations. Despite three days of breathing in cigarette smoke, I recognized the smell of Oil of Olay face cream—the brand Gina had used since high school. Evidence piled up in my favor. I slipped off my jeans and socks and moved around to what hopefully continued to be my side of the bed. Despite not wanting to, I reached out and cautiously felt to see if someone was asleep beside her. Gina would find someone else if I were gone/dead/lost in time. She was a catch and not the kind of woman to stay single long, even if grieving. But there was no one on my side of the bed with their head on my pillow. Pausing before easing back the covers, I reached out and checked the bedside table. There was a charging iPhone right where I left my iPhone to charge. Covering the screen with my hand, I woke it up. My relief at seeing my standard background image of my first SLR camera stilled the last of the nervous pounding of my heart.

I was home and lived in this house with Gina. I slid into my instantly familiar bed. My movement caused her to stir beside me and murmur, "You take any good photos?"

My heart skipped a beat and leapt up into my throat. I whispered, "Yeah."

"Great..." she mumbled, asleep before she finished the word.

I laid back, my head instantly comfortable on my pillow. To my amazement, despite everything that I had experienced in the previous seventy-five hours in 1984, I immediately fell asleep.

46

When I awoke, everything was so staggeringly familiar I was sure I'd woken from the most incredibly vivid dream. One of time travel and muggings and concerts in smoky bars. Shitty beer. An amazing woman named Celina.

Reaching over, I found the other side of the bed empty. I laid back, staring at my familiar ceiling, familiar walls, familiar curtains. These were glimmerings of hope for a familiar life. I checked my iPhone: 10:30 am. No messages, no alerts. The house was quiet and the same as it ever was. My first thought was what to tell the others of my trip. I failed to accomplish what we had gambled our futures on. And now, instead of a stack of stock certificates hidden in the basement behind a brick, we collectively had twenty thousand dollars in additional credit card debt. And we needed to find a new place to live. At least the home I'd left was the same one I came home to. But that was the complete list on the plus side right now. Why not stay in bed today? Because what's the point? The last thing I wanted to do was sit down with my friends to tell them about my adventures in the past and my epic failures. But then again, I may as well get it over with. I pulled back the covers and slid out of bed, kicking my camera bag out of the way.

I paused, pulled the bag up onto my lap and took out my camera. My finger hovered over the power button. Would all my photos of the past be there? What about the videos of those bands? Bring back only what you took. That was one of the rules. But did digital images stored as ones and zeros in a solid-state drive count? Only one way to find out. I powered up the camera and clicked through to the camera roll. Oldest picture first—the four of us on the rooftop, me holding the black lacquer box with modern Vancouver behind us. I clicked forward to the next photo. Nothing happened. No images of the past, no videos of the past. Nothing to prove I travelled back. No future best-selling book of 1984 Vancouver photos by Colin Yip. No newly discovered tapes of Damage Done's first-ever show.

Nothing.

Dejected, I pulled on clean clothes—beautiful, clean 2017 clothes—then slipped my wallet and phone into the pockets of my favorite jeans. As I checked myself in the mirror, I noticed my battered old cigar box on the dresser, exactly where my time machine used to sit. The inside was stuffed full of concert ticket stubs—I clearly had never stopped using it or had started using it again at some point in the past thirty years.

The kitchen was empty, no Gina. The room looked the same, but the print on the wall above the kitchen table was different. A framed poster of a Monet painting, instead of a framed poster of a Manet painting. Was that the extent of the ripples from the past? Terry would love this.

There was a note from Gina on the counter in front of the coffee maker.

'Don't forget the party we are hosting this afternoon. Xoxo G'

Party at our house? I checked the calendar on my phone. There it was, '1:00 party at our house'. It didn't say why we're having a party or for whom. When I left, we had no plans for a party or anything else on the day after my trip. And now we did. Two ripples. How many more would there be?

The best plan was to ignore the party until it began. Right now, I needed breakfast, and I promised someone I'd visit.

The Ovaltine Cafe was the same as when I was last here, thirty-three years and a day ago. Same weary bell ringing over the door, same booths, tables, chairs. Precisely the same, except for the missing haze of cigarette smoke. Thank God. I was grateful to be away from that part of history. After my three days in the past, I was finished with smoking. Given the relentless warnings and the exorbitant cost, not to mention being unemployed, now was probably an excellent time to quit. A smiling, middle-aged Chinese woman came out of the kitchen. I gestured towards the empty booth at the back—my booth in the past. She nodded, grabbed a menu and coffee pot. We met as I sat down. I flipped over the coffee cup, and she filled it.

"Thanks. Is Faye around?"

The waitress laughed. "She might be in later. But I'm not sure. She doesn't tell me when she's coming, and I figure she's keeping an eye on me."

"And how's Celina?"

She stopped smiling and looked at me curiously. "Don't you come here all the time?"

"I haven't been here in years," I honestly, if ironically, said.

"I'm sad to say Celina passed away, oh nearly ten years ago," she said, placing the menu on the table.

A tsunami-sized Time ripple crashed against the shore of my life, destroying everything. I was dragged out to sea to drown, wrapped in heavy chains of guilt. My throat locked shut. Breathing was impossible. My brain attempted to reconcile the words spoken against my known experience of seeing Celina alive less than twelve hours ago.

Jesus.

This was my fault. My spending time with Celina caused her to die. A clear and definite line existed from my time travelling to her death—a cause and effect impossible to deny. But why didn't I know of her death?

Shouldn't I possess dual sets of memories, or at least shouldn't my new timeline have overwritten my old timeline?

"I'll give you a few minutes."

As the waitress walked over to the till and settled in on Celina's mother's stool, I desperately needed the person who helped me the most back in time. But Celina was dead because of me, and I was on my own.

I drank my coffee, missing my friend deeply.

The waitress strolled over to take my order, but my appetite was gone.

"Could you tell me exactly how she died?"

The waitress sighed. "Celina? Well, after the film came out, she moved down to California. She lived a good life, then had a heart attack. It was peaceful. She went to sleep one night and didn't wake up. Luckily, Faye was visiting. She had quality time with her mother and step-father in the days before she passed. I miss her."

"I miss her too."

"How did you two know each other?" she asked.

"We liked the same bands back in the day," I said with a faint smile. The memory of watching Damage Done with her like it was—like it was yesterday. She nodded and sighed again. "You know what you want?"

"I'd love a BLT, please."

"Whole, multi, rye, sourdough, twelve grains or gluten-free?"

So much had changed. "White, please. Plain old-fashioned white bread."

I took my time eating my lunch, reading a Georgia Straight someone else had left behind. Justin Trudeau was still PM, Trump still in the White House, Vancouverites were protesting oil tankers and oil pipelines. Articles with more handwringing over the housing affordability crisis. On a macro level, the world was the same as when I left. My trip had changed nothing significantly in world politics, sports, popular culture, or global finance. Was this what my life would be like now? Subtle and not-so-subtle ripples I should remember, but don't? This was worse than remaining in the past. At least then, I knew with absolute confidence what was coming in my future. In this new world, it was like I had been in a partial coma for three decades but had awoken knowing general history, but nothing personal.

I left a massive tip of antique pre-1984 bills for the waitress when I couldn't sit still anymore. I stood on the sidewalk outside and considered my life. My new second life. Thirty-three years of memories of another life that would seem like a dream to anyone I told. A low-grade science fiction story populated with subtle minor inconsistencies. The print on the kitchen wall and my ticket stub box were just the beginning. Celina moved to California and died. What the hell? How did that happen? What else? Who else was dead now? My parents, Terry, Neil? I was clueless because, in my mind and my memories, they were vividly alive. Celina should be sitting behind the counter inside the Ovaltine Cafe, leaving her seat only to help us with our stupid screenplay plan.

I was a man out of time, with no idea how to cope. Feign an accident and long-term memory loss? A mental episode and breakdown resulting in the same long-term memory loss? There wasn't anyone for me to talk to because I'd be locked up. Like in '12 Monkeys.' There were a significant lack of support groups out there for returning time-travellers. I was on my own until I talked to Gina and my friends. But even then, I suspected no one remembered me using the time machine. Gina would have woken up when I crawled into bed. No way she would have gone back to sleep without finding out if my trip was a success. She would have dragged me down to the basement to collect the stocks immediately. Another likely ripple. Standing on the street as traffic crawled by, I realized that Gina, Terry, and Neil would have no recollection of me going back in time.

My pocket pinged. I checked my phone.

Shit. Time for a party that I had no idea about.

47

I walked back home along streets as familiar as the back of my hand. The city was the same. The streets, the homeless, the cars, everything was the same. It even smelled the same as before I went back. But at the same time, differences were starting to pile up. As minuscule as the Manet/Monet print on our kitchen wall, or as massive as Celina being dead for a decade. My hope for a mental reboot where I'd suddenly remember this new version of my life hadn't happened.

How would I live this half-life, continually relearning what I'd experienced since 1984 without letting it slip that I didn't remember anything at all?

Back at our house, I took a deep breath, plastered a smile on my face like I knew what the party was for, and opened the front door.

"God, Colin, where have you been?" Gina exclaimed, rushing out of the living room and kissing me. I hugged her back, overwhelmed with how much I missed her. I didn't want to let go, but forced myself to.

"I'm sorry. I walked over to the Ovaltine for some food."

"And you got your hair cut. It looks good."

"Uh, thanks. It was a long time coming."

"Why didn't you take your car?" she asked, then pulled me after her. The living room was full of people. My parents on the couch. Terry sat on the love seat, casually holding hands with another guy his age. Neil still looked like Neil, but with his arm around a pretty woman ten years younger than him. There were a bunch of people I either recognized, like my ex-boss, or acknowledged, like neighbors and friends of friends. Everyone raised their drinks to me as I entered. I smiled and said hello. Then I slipped back to the kitchen to find myself a stiff drink, leaving Gina to hostess like the pro she was.

My grandmother, May, was at the counter, making a pot of tea. She smiled, and I gave her a gentle hug. Opening the fridge, I revelled in a vast array of local beers to choose from—not a Molson Canadian or Labatt's Blue in sight. Grabbing a Persephone Black Lager, I took a long, satisfying drink then glanced around. We were alone.

"May," I said, one eye on the door to the hallway in case someone interrupted. "You remember back in '84 when I came to visit you? When you told me the story of your 'other' life?"

She stopped making the tea and turned to me. I was hit with a sudden shock at how old she was. Seeing her, only yesterday, as a spry sixty-year-old was amazing.

May nodded slightly. I'd been holding my breath and exhaled in relief. Her nod confirmed I had gone back. I wasn't post-stroke or clinically insane.

"And now you're back?" she asked.

"Last night, at midnight. We had tea in Chinatown only twenty-four hours ago."

"Or a lifetime ago," she said, adding sugar and milk to the tray.

"You remember each of your lives, don't you?" I asked.

"One in China, then one in Canada, yes."

"How?"

She sighed, clearly wishing not to talk about her history with the machine. "When I was thirty-two years old, I collapsed at the cosmetics counter in the Hudson's Bay store downtown. They said I was in a coma for seventy-five hours."

Three days and three hours, precisely the length of our travels to the past.

"When I awoke, I initially thought I had gone mad, but then I realized what must have happened. The time machine. My two lives. I could now recall them both equally."

I started to tear up. "May, I don't remember. Only what was, but now obviously isn't. I recognize differences, but I don't know when they changed or why. Do you remember meeting Celina? Well, she's dead. She shouldn't be. She wasn't when I went back, but she is now."

May took my hands in hers. Her old, thin, delicate hands held mine supportively.

"May, the world's completely screwed up. I don't understand what happened to me. You have memories of the lives you had, but I don't. Will I remember?"

"I do not know, Colin. The time machine burned to ash. I remember you said this. Maybe its destruction caused this."

Before we could continue, Gina popped into the kitchen, took the tray with the tea from my grandmother with a smile, and left again. "Come on, you two, you're missing the party!"

With my grandmother holding my arm for support, or maybe the other way around, we reentered the living room. I helped May sit down beside my mother on our same-old couch. Bright conversation bubbled around me as I sipped my beer. I nervously scanned the room for differences like Sherlock Holmes, hoping for clues to what occurred in this other life of mine. It was surprising enough to see Terry and Neil in what looked like committed relationships, but then a framed print above my stereo caught my eye. A full-size poster for a movie, bright '90s colors and neon lines, dramatic renderings of the beautiful young leads—Ben

Affleck and Winona Ryder—the Space Needle and the Seattle skyline in the background. 'No Time Like The Past.' It looked like a silly movie. Why would I frame and hang it on the wall? Smiling politely, I crossed the room to read the credits printed at the bottom. 'Screenplay by Celina Chow. Original music by Damage Done. Directed by Colin Yip.' My mind reeling, I turned and looked at the people in the room. Had I directed a film? A real movie? Everyone in the room must have known this suddenly relevant—to me—fact. Everyone but me. One more ripple.

My God, Celina turned our research gathering lie of writing a screenplay into an original script! It being made into a feature film explained her moving to California. My first impulse was to take out my phone and look her up on IMDb. She succeeded where I failed. Or because I failed. I was taking another look at the poster when I felt a hand on my shoulder. Neil. "It amazes me, the two of you coming up with such a crazy-ass time travel story, man. Sucks they changed the setting from Vancouver to Seattle. But that's what they always do, right?"

I nodded and thought, please keep talking, and maybe this will all make sense. Neil, being Neil, did. "Not the greatest film, but it got us this house, so who am I to complain?"

He patted me on the shoulder and rejoined the party. Got us this house?

On the other wall above the stereo hung a gold record. Damage Done's second album, the one that broke them to the world. But with a different cover. The cover from my original timeline was simply the band logo of two woven capital D's on black—similar to AC/DC's 'Back in Black'. This cover was an explosive photo of Kelly and Norm singing at one mic, a wall of upraised hands in front of them, a screaming crowd. Kelly's grin and the pure joy on his face drew my eyes in. Something was written on the glass below the image.

'To the best, AND ONLY, photographer of DD. You're one in a million, Colin!'

Four scrawled autographs surrounded it.

My photograph. It didn't matter that I couldn't remember taking it. The proof was in front of me. Even more astounding was the idea that I was their exclusive photographer. How amazing was that? Especially if their promise still held and I was still their only photographer.

The doorbell rang. Gina, busy with a plate of hors d'oeuvres, gestured for me to answer it. Nodding, I put my beer down on the mantle beside an MTV Music Award for best rock video 1994—Damage Done, Controlled Collapse, Colin Yip, director. What the hell?

The doorbell rang again. I had to put my increasing confusion on hold.

Plastering on my best 'I know what's going on' smile, I opened the front door. A young man stood there, a wide grin on his face. He was in his mid-twenties, half-Asian and casually dressed.

"Happy mortgage burning!" the young man said while hugging me. I hugged him back, reeling. Mortgage burning? Mortgage burning! Somehow, we owned this house!

"Thanks," I said as he stepped back. "I hope we have a similar party before we're in our eighties, dad."

My heart flipped in my chest. This man was my son. My son. I had no idea, no recollection, no memory of him. None, nothing. Jesus Christ, we may have succeeded in owning a house, but what about everything else I missed? All I wouldn't ever know? A million singular events excised from my memory. I was barely aware of my son handing over a bottle of Champagne, then descending the steps again, leaving me on the porch, in utter shock, my fake smile stuck on my face. Gina hugged me from behind and took the bottle.

A son.

I had a son. Joy flooded my body. Followed instantly by heart-wrenching despair. I had a son I had never seen before. I didn't remember his birth, his birthdays, his first everything.

"Grandpa!"

I came back from my despair as a three-year-old boy scrambled up the steps towards me. On the walk was my son—I don't even know his name —with a beautiful Nordic woman carrying a diaper bag. The mother of my grandson. The boy—Jesus, I don't know my grandson's name either— ran to me for a hug, and I swung him up, pulling him tight for the first time in this new life of mine.

An explosion in my head. A soundless, sightless, yet blinding and deafening blast. I was in the midst of a stroke or heart attack. All that work, going back in time and returning, that futile grand adventure, all my lost years, I'd die here on my porch without ever—

And then I remembered. I remembered everything.

"Michael! How's my favorite grandson?"

He looked at me, confusion on his beautiful face. "Grandpa, I'm your only grandson!"

"Silly me, I remember now," I said with a smile and hugged him even harder.

Acknowledgements

In creating the band for this story, I dug out my collection of EPs by indie bands from Victoria, BC from the late 70's and early 80's. These were the bands I had discovered and listened to as a teen, blown away with the incredible realization that there were people creating and recording music in this tiny city on the far edge of Canada—a city far better known for its olde English tea shoppes than being a hot bed of post-punk music.

I'm forever grateful to the open-heartedness of Karl Hourigan, Dave Hill, Rob Lifton and Linda McRae of Easy Money; Pete Campbell and John Carter of Pink Steel; and John Mears (who tragically passed in July 2021) of The Keys for their stories, and their music. I was able to create a mix showing the evolution of my imaginary band from their raw beginnings as Mayo to the finished polish of Damage Done. It's a mix I played a lot while writing. I hope you enjoyed it as much as I did.

To the members of Easy Money, Pink Steel and The Keys, thank you again for your music and inspiration. Thank you to Simon Boniface, Chris Watts, Vern Braun, Pam Meneilly, Pauline Youngs, Garner & Derrick Stone, and everyone on Facebook, Twitter and Metafilter who helped with their memories of Vancouver in the '80s. And special thanks to Judy Zhu for her help with Chinese history.

This wouldn't be what it is without you.

Dave Goossen, Victoria, BC January 2022

The author

Dave Goossen hated creative writing in school. Hated writing poems, short stories, hated it. Until he got the chance to write and create a short video with his friends in Grade 10. Since then he has always written – film scripts, short films, plays and novels. He has also continued to produce, direct and act in short films.

He wrote a 1/2 hour television pilot version of his third novel, 'Seniors High' during Covid which is available if you're interested. 'No Time Like The Past' is his fourth novel. Next up is the sequel to '12 Cups of Coffee' which should be available by the end of 2022.

He lives in Victoria, BC with his wife and youngest daughter.

Find out more at davegoossen.com

If you like this novel, could you please take a moment to give it a good rating and/or review at goodreads.com or amazon.com - either place, search for 'Dave Goossen'. Any sharing on social media really helps get the word out for my novels.

Thank you for your support.

Songs lyrics reprinted by permission

Carter, John. Lyrics to MY GIRL'S RADIOACTIVE. Performed by Pink Steel. 1979.

Carter, John. Lyrics to HERE WE GO AGAIN. Performed by Pink Steel. 1979.

Hill, David. Lyrics to YOUNG AND OVEREQUIPPED. Performed by Easy Money. 1979.

Hourigan, Karl. Lyrics to STANDING IN YOUR SHADOW. Performed Easy Money. Real Gone Songs Ltd. 1980.

Hourigan, Karl. Lyrics to GETTING LOST. Performed by Easy Money. Real Gone Songs Ltd. 1980.

Hourigan, Karl. Lyrics to NO STRANGER TO DANGER. Performed by Easy Money. Real Gone Songs Ltd. 1980.

Hourigan, Karl. Lyrics to ON THE EDGE. Performed by Easy Money. Real Gone Songs Ltd. 1979.

Muir, John. Lyrics to WHAT EVER HAPPENED TO BOY MEETS GIRL. Performed by The Keys. 1980.

www.ingramcontent.com/pod-product-compliance
Lightning Source LLC
Chambersburg PA
CBHW022208010726
47493CB00002B/474